MW01518583

THE
FORMER
PRESIDENT

a novel

WILL
STAEGER

© Copyright 2023 William H. Staeger, Jr.

Print ISBN: 979-8-35094-197-5
eBook ISBN: 979-8-35094-198-2

for Tallulah

PART I:

THE NOTE

-1-

K NEES ARE SHOT. CAN'T JOG anymore, so I ride a bike. I pedal along the running trail, out where you get the icy pinpricks of sea spray plucking at your cheeks. The other thing you get is solitude, made possible by this wide berth between me and my Bozo detail. The latest duo rides along the road about a hundred yards inland, staying street legal yet keeping a view of their charge, while I get the Pacific all to myself.

My ride gets suddenly rough, and I look down to discover the front tire has gone flat. Pulling off the trail, I check my shoulder and observe that the Bozos have already spotted my predicament. I offer a lackadaisical wave to keep them at bay and watch as they dismount and hang tight roadside.

Being hyper-organized, I quickly intuit when my stuff is out of order, and as I unzip the spare-tire kit, I sense something is amiss. This is further confirmed when I find, buried beneath the backup inner tube, a folded slip of paper. This seems near impossible — I packed this kit myself at the counter of the bike shop, and the only people who've had access to it since were the Bozos, who know they'd catch hell if they touched my stuff.

Expecting to find nothing more than the words *Made in China* — a country-of-origin tag required by legislation bearing my signature — I unfold the compact white rectangle, which in turn reveals itself to be a full-size sheet of paper.

On it is a message addressed to me. It's typewritten, the inconsistencies of the ink revealing that the text isn't the product of a toner cartridge:

`Dear Mr. President,`

If anyone is watching you now, please hide this letter and read it another time in private. I apologize
for this rude form of introduction, but I have no
choice in the matter.

I turn to check on the Bozos. One of them is munching a banana. They're
watching — they're always watching — but I can see they're satisfied I'm
keeping busy with the tire. I shield the letter with my body and read on.

I am in need of your help. Again, I apologize: it is
not fair that I burden you with such a plea, yet the
gravity of my predicament requires a degree of dis-
cretion held only by a man of your station. You probably won't remember, but while you were in office,
we met. It was only once, but in that one meeting, I
remember sensing that I could trust you.

A thought comes immediately to mind: *You've got the wrong president.* I flip
the bike, remove its front wheel, disengage the flattened tire from the rim
and return to the note:

I recently began a job in Washington. It's a position I've held before. In many ways my post is not
significant, yet I work with powerful people. Mostly
I am made to feel like a young woman working low
on the totem pole of men's power circles. Because
of the access my job affords, I learned something I
wasn't supposed to learn. I was told to keep it to
myself. When I refused, things began to spiral out
of control.

I am contacting you because the people demanding
my silence have attempted to ensure it by taking
my child.

They kidnapped my daughter.

"Christ," I say out loud.

```
Their conditions have been made clear to me: either
I keep quiet and she stays alive, or I speak out,
and she dies. I need your help in getting her back.
And for the third time in this note, I apologize,
this time for getting personal, but I hope you will
understand my plea in the context of the loss of your
own wife. I cannot lose my daughter.

Her name is Rachel Estrella. She is 32 years old.

I will contact you again with instructions. And
please, no matter what - even if you decide not to
help - please, Mr. President, you must never reveal
what I have told you, or even that you have seen
this letter.

Please destroy it immediately.

                              -Yours in distress
```

I hear footsteps on the rocks behind me and realize I've taken too long. I wad the paper, jam it in my mouth, and chew. It tastes faintly of bleach, but after eight or nine chomps and a painful swallow, it's down the hatch. I've resumed work on the tire before the voice of the top man on my detail rumbles from behind me.

"Use a hand, Mr. President?" he says.

I turn and feign surprise. Wondering, as I do, why I'm playing along — the letter's got to be nothing more than an ill-conceived practical joke by one of my friends, with the agents surely in on it.

"Took me a while to find the hole," I say, "but it's small, so I'll be able to patch it. Save a trip to the bike shop."

"Sorry?"

This sort of thing explaining why I refer to them as the Bozo detail.

"No need to buy another inner tube," I explain, "since I'll be able to fix this one. Right here, right now."

Holding up the miniature tube of glue that comes with the patch-kit, I grin with the sort of enthusiasm encountered only in madmen. Considering I'm universally perceived to be exactly that — stark, raving mad — my little diversion isn't exactly a stretch.

"Right," the top man says.

He turns and marches inland, leaving me alone with the rubber cement, a dull pang of curiosity, and rapidly developing indigestion.

-2-

Rachel Estrella went missing in December — just over six months ago. Her husband and three-year-old daughter vanished with her, leading authorities in Temecula, California, where the Estrellas lived, to speculate on a range of causes far less felonious than might otherwise have been suspected. Three months later, portions of a body confirmed by a medical examiner to be Rachel's turned up near Barstow. Cadaver dogs sniffed out the remains in a landfill just over the Nevada state line, one of the places we Californians pawn our mounds of waste. No suspect was identified, no warrant issued, no arrest made. Rachel's husband and daughter are apparently still missing.

I learn this at Billie's Smoothies, whose proprietress, a vegan triathlete, lets me partake of her store's Wi-Fi while I sip specialty smoothies and wheatgrass shots. In addition to the fact that I find Billie herself quite appealing, doing my digital work on an iPad here — rather than in the state of self-isolation found on my guarded property — provides me at least a whiff of socialization. The Bozos wait outside, convincing themselves they're being unobtrusive — the junior agent giving a strawberry smoothie a try; the top man, pacing curbside, actually smoking a cancer stick in front of a vegan health-foods shop.

The discovery of Rachel Estrella's body could have been staged; I've been briefed on hundreds of conspiracies worse than this prior to pouring my morning bowl of Grape Nuts. But who would manufacture her discovery, presuming it was fake, and why? And if her discovery *wasn't* staged, how could it be possible that the letter-writer, evidently a Washington insider, remains unaware that her daughter's remains have been found? None of it adds up.

A number of tries in my search for the identity of Rachel's mother come up dry. She doesn't get any mention in the stories on Rachel's disappearance, and there's little to nothing on Rachel's extended family in the stories I find. At one point a vigil was held outside her home, but even in the coverage of the vigil, no siblings, mother, or father were photographed or mentioned. Rachel's case was a major national story and I now recall the buzz. Described as a former television producer who worked on everything from cable news programs to *Ellen*, she'd taken a career pause to raise her child, and hadn't yet gone back to work at the time of her disappearance.

Billie sees me close the case on my iPad and approaches from her post behind the counter with a smile. I've known her a year or so, going back a few months before she opened this shop. Her arms are lean and freckled from many hours of exposure to the California sunshine. Her breasts are small, and she never seems to wear a bra. I think she looks damn good.

"When's harvest?" she says. "I always forget. Is it next month? I've got my straw hat and plastic bin from last year, ready to roll."

She's referring to the tangled weave of Zinfandel vines I discovered after acquiring my property up the road. For the period that it captured my interest, I studied YouTube videos and abided by the proper viticulture procedures to get the vines back into production, at which point I inaugurated an annual tradition of recruiting local friends, Tom Sawyer style, to help harvest the grapes.

"It's getting close," I say, "but you're still early. Two months out — maybe three."

"And I'm still invited?" she says.

"Wouldn't have it any other way. In fact, I'm looking for a new foreman if you're interested."

Her sun-kissed face scrunches into a pricelessly cute emoji of inquiry. "Aren't you the foreman?"

"Exactly the point," I say.

Her smile overtakes her face, causing a delicate web of creases to stretch from eyes to chin, and I'm not sure whether I imagine or detect a devilish spark in her eyes. This brings a rush up my spine, not for the first time in response to a simple look from the petite triathlete standing over me from behind the counter.

In the wake of what I like to call my long, strange trip – more on that later — it became necessary to choose a place to live, or hide, perhaps more than live, at the time. Over the course of my travels, I deliberately severed my roots, and the case continues to remain that nobody from either party will touch me with a forty-mile pole. Intending to keep things that way, I discovered Carmel-by-the-Sea, a well-heeled town overlooking the Pacific, and decided it would fit the bill. The weather is mild, the scenery is staggering, and enough artists and their hippie brethren remain — despite too much obscene wealth in the mix — for the place to retain at least some of its character.

At the tail end of my swing through town, a realtor pitched me a dilapidated three-bedroom Craftsman on eleven acres of scruff, and for just a million or two more than you'd expect to pay for the White House, I took it off the market. Foraging through my backyard a day after closing, I came across a weed patch so overgrown it resembled a two-acre geodesic dome. Dug a little deeper to discover the weeds were small trees, and finally that the trees were hundred-year-old, head-trained Zinfandel vines. Turns out I'd acquired one of California's oldest vineyards along with my bungalow and its adjoining acreage.

Once the hobby fascination wore off, I contracted with a local vineyard management firm to help crush, ferment, and bottle the bounty, thereby providing enough cases of Zin to keep a good number of my friends awash in pretty decent wine. After a week-long second year of February pruning, I officially concluded I was overextended as a backyard gardener.

Rising from my stool, I push a fifty-dollar bill across the counter.

Billie eyes it skeptically.

"Hope you found what you were googling," she says, "but fifty bucks is too much for a smoothie."

"Not by much with your prices. But cheaper than a broadband subscription."

"Despite your dreadful party affiliation," Billie says, "you remain my favorite former president."

I slip out into the Carmel sunshine, our typical swirl of morning fog diluting its shine.

———

-3-

Next stop, post office. Despite the likelihood of falling victim to a shooting at these joints and the organization's ceaseless teetering on the precipice of bankruptcy, I prefer to personally place my letters in the U.S. Mail. And man do I send letters. It's an old habit, developed long before the current obsession with snaps and Instagram posts. A habit only intensified by the events of my long, strange trip.

Arriving with my weekly stack of letters, I ask Harry, my favorite of the front-desk staff of three, to supply me with sufficient postage for each envelope.

"Morning, chief," I say, as always.

"Morning back," Harry says, as usual, with a wink, "Mr. *Commander*-in-Chief."

I tell him that was a long time ago, and Harry says it feels like yesterday to him. I unwrap the rubber band from my stack and hand him the letters one at a time.

It's between the eleventh and twelfth that I find the postcard.

It's an alien in my native stack — I don't send postcards, preferring at least the illusion of privacy. Yet there one rests. On its glossier side are four images, arranged in a grid: grapevine rows, harvest crews, a winery building, a general store. A caption adorns the bottom edge: *Sonoma Valley, Wine Country USA*.

I turn it over and see five words. There's no accompanying return or destination address. The words are typewritten, just as with the patch-kit note:

I think she is here.

"Forget to finish that one, Mr. President?" Harry asks.

I look up, snapping out of it. Shake my head.

"Guess so. Old age, Harry — it's getting ugly."

"Tell me about it."

I hand him the next letter, destined for Switzerland, and fold and pocket the postcard. He returns the stack of letters to me, now metered. I saunter to the First-Class Mail slot, knock on the wall, and peer through the opening.

"Lovely Rita," I say. "You know nothing will come between us . . . "

Presently a rich brown iris appears on the other side of the slot. Rita's considerable cheeks blot out most of the fluorescent glow emanating from within.

"Anybody tell you you've got trust issues?" she says.

"I trust *you*," I say.

A key clinks, the wall swings open a foot, and Rita thrusts her thick hand out. Rita is a woman who knows how to eat and cook. I know, because she had me over for Thanksgiving dinner last year, and she's been up to my place a few times. Rita is black — one of the woefully low count of people of color you'll encounter in Carmel, something that may yet keep me from settling here. She doesn't even live in town — keeps an apartment in the Salinas Valley, a forty-five-minute commute away, and runs a catering business on the side to make ends meet.

"Hand 'em over," she says.

I fork over my letters, thank her, and am turning to leave when Rita's other hand appears, laden with a Tupperware container.

"Blueberry," she says.

I seize the container of muffins. "You tow my heart away."

"Yeah, yeah," she says. "See you next week."

I stroll out to my bike, folded postcard burning a hole in my pocket.

-4-

EVERY MORNING, UNDER COVER OF darkness, a clandestine exchange happens in full view of the White House. At the prescribed time, typically 4 a.m. sharp, one agent arrives with a locked briefcase. A second is there to take receipt of the materials within, but only if he conveys the assigned code. Once he does, the briefcase's contents are removed, passed to the second agent, and secured again inside a second locked case.

The item subject to this daily exchange is a document that, pound for pound, contains the deepest concentration of intelligence on threats to the national security of the United States. The document comes encased in a brown leather folder, unchanged since its first use in 1961, its cover embossed, in gold, with the words Top Secret. On every page within the folder, another layer of restriction is printed: For the President Only. Midnight briefings with the heads of every major U.S intelligence organization are held as part of the document's creation, and there is no digital version archived.

At 5:01 a.m. on my thirty-seventh day in office, the second, receiving agent, known as the briefer, presented his credentials at the White House staff gate. Under the watchful eyes of Secret Service agents and U.S. Marines, he was admitted to the West Wing and told, as usual, to wait in the Situation Room. At 5:07 my first assistant took possession of the document there. At 5:10 my alarm clock buzzed, and by 5:20 I was working out on the elliptical I'd had installed off the master bedroom. At 5:55, a breakfast of eggs, toast, bacon, and orange juice awaited me as I emerged from the shower. I wolfed it, got suited up like any other executive, kissed Katie as she climbed out of bed, and proceeded with my commute to the office.

People have their favorite routes for getting to work, and in my case I only had a hundred-yard walk, but preferred to take the ostensibly secret tunnel that was one of Reagan's key renovations. Among other benefits, it gave me an extra minute of quiet before the day kicked in. There are only two entrances to the tunnel — a door built into a bookshelf in the Oval Office, and an elevator leading to the West Sitting Hall outside the President's Bedroom. These are probably the two most carefully guarded places in the world. Pretty safe way to go to work.

At 6:15, my assistant opened the doors to the Oval Office, allowing the briefer, my Chief of Staff, National Security Advisor, and Secretary of Defense to enter. Rejecting the notion of pleasantries at this hour, I called the President's Daily Briefing to order and started in silently on the document. By 6:19, I set the folder down in front of me and nodded to the briefer, who distributed the two additional copies.

Six days prior, a Berlin nightclub frequented by U.S. servicemen had been bombed with an explosive detonated under the DJ's turntables. Two of our soldiers were killed, forty seriously wounded. CIA and Pentagon investigators had been working around the clock to find evidence that would prove what we already knew: then-Libyan President Moammar Qaddafi had orchestrated the bombing as retaliation for a fracas between the Libyan and U.S navies. Today's PDB contained the conclusion of the investigation: we had a smoking gun, a celebratory telex sent from Qaddafi's office to the Libyan Embassy in Beirut the morning after the bombing.

I poured myself a fresh cup of coffee from the catered breakfast bar, returned to my seat and planted the coffee mug on my desk.

"Air strikes," I said. "I want air strikes, and I want them within 72 hours. Any delay beyond that and we're perceived as weak on terrorism. Especially to him. That decision is final. Operational logistics?"

The room was silent before the Secretary of Defense, finished with his read, caught the eye of the National Security Advisor and spoke up.

"Understood, Mr. President," he said. "We're recommending various military targets in Tripoli. There are also facilities in Benghazi we can reach on the same sorties."

"Go on."

"We'll use two F-111s — "

"Four," I said. "I want to overwhelm this son of a bitch. He's currently in Tripoli?"

The briefer cleared his throat. "Yes, Mr. President, as of last night, we've got confirmation he's there."

"Four F-111s," I said.

"Yes, sir, Mr. President," the Secretary of Defense said.

"What are the targets?"

"Barracks, headquarters, commando training bases — "

"Hit the airport."

The National Security Advisor piped in. "You're going to have casualties," he said, "collateral damage, even with the military facilities. We add civilian targets like the airport, we'll have much higher civilian loss of life — "

"I want to hit the airport," I said. "He counted on our being passive. He counted wrong. We're sending the message to him and to others that this will not stand. I'm not an idiot; I recognize that there will be deaths. Armed forces and otherwise. A pilot will get hurt. A bomb will go astray and hit a neighborhood full of people. Our immediate aim, our job, is to save American lives by providing a strong disincentive against future terrorist acts. God help us, but given this aim, the sacrifice is acceptable."

The room fell silent, causing me to wonder, not for the first time, why there was so much silence in such meetings. It wasn't until I stepped outside the box tlater hat I grasped something very basic about the U.S. presidency: first, only the strongest lieutenants are brave enough to challenge your decisions; more significantly, no single human being should be entitled or obligated to make decisions like the one I'd just made, where certain human lives are deemed more valuable than others, and — by that one person's subjective judgment – subsequently extinguished.

I know now that those silences were about exactly that: regular people avoiding or reacting to the handing down of incomprehensibly difficult decisions with immediacy and resolve, sometimes correct, sometimes not. I'd recognized well before then that the only way to make such decisions was to do it quickly and without deliberation. Get the facts, look the facts in the eye, decide. Don't delay. If you hesitate, you're sunk.

"Yes, sir, Mr. President," the Chief of Staff said.

"When?" I press.

"We can be ready in 48 hours," the Secretary of Defense said.

"48 hours it is, then," I said. "Have a nice day, ladies and gentlemen."

-5-

THIS WEEK'S OVERNIGHT GUEST IS Luciana Gomez. Gomez, as she prefers to be called, is a few days shy of her thirty-first birthday and has spent the majority of her last ten years in the forests of her native Colombia detecting and dismantling land mines.

The daughter of a former FARC rebel, Gomez is five-foot-one, trilingual, hot-tempered but sweetly emotional, and someone you'd be wise not to cross paths with. I know this from experience, having literally crossed her path two-thirds of the way through my long, strange, trip. Working my way through a mountainside forest to a set of ruins I'd identified on an old map, I nearly toppled over the edge of a looming cliff when Luciana's shrill scream came from beside me. She started in with Spanish, an AK-47 preceding her out from behind a waxy-leaved bush, then switched to English once I declared I wasn't too smooth with the local language. My Secret Service team was still storming up the hill, weapons drawn, when she explained that I'd been about to stroll into an abandoned front from the country's civil war, laden with at least a dozen live mines she was in the process of deactivating.

I spent the next two days learning how she and her team went about this and, much to the chagrin of my security detail, agreed to pitch in as the junior intern on her squad for a few weeks. We deactivated nearly twenty buried mines before descending back to her group's base camp one month later.

More recently, Gomez mentioned she would be in the Bay Area for a conference, and at my insistence, she agreed to visit Carmel as my guest. This is something I do on a monthly basis — invite friends from all corners. My guests partake of my backyard Zin, consume meals prepared by my USPS friend Rita's catering business, and join me in a bicycle tour of the peninsula or a fishing expedition down the coast. The rotating guest list features an eclectic mix of acquaintances I've encountered both during and after my time in office, and I send each of them home with a framed thank-you letter bearing the presidential seal.

Gomez is staying for three nights, and tonight, the last, I've invited Billie to join us for dinner. I told Billie she could bring somebody, and she's come accompanied by a smarmy-looking guy she apparently cycles with. He looks approximately half her age.

The Zin is flowing. Billie is good with people, meaning that she and the wine are prompting opinionated commentary from Gomez the likes of which she typically avoids in social settings. Gomez has become a significant voice in United Nations and Ted Talks circles opposing American neo-colonialism, and Billie's curiosity has Gomez rolling tonight before I've served the appetizer.

"Colombia has hundreds of thousands of acres riddled with homemade mines, improvised explosives, shrapnel munitions," she's saying. "People can't grow crops or wander off documented roads in many newly populous regions."

Her accent is slight, almost imperceptible, her facile way with multiple languages one of the reasons she's become a Ted Talks darling and the target of countless rants by Republican members of Congress levied against her perceived advocacy of socialism.

"There are that many?" Billie asks.

"Thirty thousand or more, by the best estimates," Gomez says. "Some are sophisticated mines from military manufacturers, some are buried pipe bombs, some as crude as Mason jars stuffed with marbles and gunpowder. They've been left behind by both sides in a fifty-year civil war. A war, I would add, that has been funded by the United States."

"Come again?" This, from Billie's fitness-guru friend.

Gomez's piercing eyes hone in on the cyclist. "The Colombian government and its wealthy elite profit from the agriculture work of peasants in the Colombian countryside," she says, "most of whom work either directly or indirectly for the American corporations that own or control the contracts for the land. FARC emerged as a movement to guard the working class from human rights abuses by the government and these corporations. Colombia's counter-insurgency operations against FARC are supported by the American government through foreign aid and training."

Bearing a presidential term's worth of responsibility for continuing the sort of funding Gomez describes, I decide it might be a good time to duck into the kitchen. I return armed with bowls of gazpacho, which I set out for each of my guests.

"Now hold on, though," Billie's pal says, prompting Billie to place a hand on his forearm. "Isn't the primary reason we've provided aid to Colombia the war on drugs?"

Maybe it's the surge of jealousy I feel on seeing Billie's touch, or maybe it's an instinct to rise to the defense of Gomez — who needs no such help — but I manage to extinguish my ill-fated attempt to steer clear of the discussion as quickly as I made the move to fetch the soup.

"We've funded the murder and torture of Colombian agricultural workers for a hundred years," I say, still standing. "Google the Banana Massacre of 1928 and you'll get a sense of the true purpose of our policy before it was countenanced in arcane foreign policy legislation built around things like the 'war on drugs.'"

"The Banana Massacre?" Billie says, trying her best, by my guess, to derail the train wreck about to strike our dinner party.

"Somewhere between one and three thousand farm workers and their families," I say, "gathering in a town square to peacefully protest working conditions, were gunned down by government troops from the surrounding rooftops to enforce productivity."

"And we had what to do with that?" cycling dude asks.

"The workers harvested bananas for the United Fruit Company," Gomez says, now appearing to come to *my* rescue, "an American firm that has historically controlled the banana industry in Central and South America and the Caribbean. Their dominance through government ties across the region is in fact what coined the term 'banana republic.'"

"Be damned," the cyclist says, "never heard of 'em."

"The company later changed its name," Gomez says, "to Chiquita."

Cycling dude goes quiet for a moment, but I don't.

"Might also be worth noting," I say, "that the U.S. Secretary of State threatened just prior to the massacre to send in the U.S. Marines Corps if Colombia didn't act to put down the movement the town-square protests were said to represent, which he called 'subversive communism.' We've maintained a similar stance ever since, with increasingly more direct and blatant funding policies, some of which I was known for enacting. War on communism, war on drugs, war on terror — different terms, same principle as far as Gomez's homeland goes: fund the suppression of cheap labor's resistance in order to protect the profits. It's a business, and the U.S. owns and runs it."

I pause, noting that I'm now staring down at three relatively shocked faces, soup spoons frozen mid-scoop. Gomez appears bemused and almost ready to giggle; Billie seems utterly surprised at this unhinged side she'd yet to witness; and cycling dude, looking more hurt and embarrassed than anything, has yielded in me a guilty, buffoonish feeling I might have felt had I thrown a punch in a jealous rage.

I offer a thin smile and retake my seat at the table.

"Enjoy the soup," I say.

-6-

IF I COULD REACH THE letter-writer, I'd object to her decision to call me in as her knight in shining armor. The last thing I'm suited for at this stage in life is a surveillance assignment, and while there are certainly experts I could call to do it, the letter-writer has already established that she works in government. Meaning that her need for secrecy aside, she is presumably possessed of the resources to summon surveillance experts directly, rather than doing so through a checked-out former politician.

In my reply, I'd make the point succinctly:

```
I'm sorry for your predicament, but you've reached
the wrong president. My contacts in Washington are
no longer current. In fact, I'm so far out of orbit
I can't even see the planet.

Look, just contact the authorities. Your local police
and sheriff's departments are good places to start.
And for the love of common decency, please stop
sending me these notes. I'm busy trying to convince
myself that I'm enjoying my retirement, and your
clandestine missives offer no help in the matter.
```

I think all this while staring at the key-card in my hand.

Since I've got no way of contacting the letter-writer, the problem I'm now facing is that I'm expected to use the card. It's the kind used by hotels — resembling a credit card but with the hotel's name embossed on the plastic.

It arrived inside a glossy pamphlet adorned with shots of a wine-country bed & breakfast establishment.

The brochure somehow made its way into my hiking backpack. As with the tire-repair kit, I pack this gear myself, having stuffed the main pouch with a Clif bar, a bag of gorp, SPF-50 sunscreen, and pocket binoculars. I prepped the backpack in the mudroom last night, where again only the Bozos and I have got access.

And yet as I paused to sit on this rock outcropping to retrieve the binoculars, three-and-a-half miles up the ridge, there the brochure was.

I could challenge my security detail on the appearance of these notes, since clearly, either their safety measures are ludicrously insufficient or they're in on it. Such a confrontation of this sort would risk the confidentiality the letter-writer asked me to honor, though — and it would also ruin my hike. And these hikes have become more necessary in my routine — part of a campaign to clear my head of the malaise and boredom that I'm learning any retired person (apparently former presidents included) comes to suffer.

The key-card, along with the latest of the notes, spilled from the brochure:

> *Please be our guest at the Mango Tree Inn! A client has handled all charges, including spa services, for 4 days and 3 nights beginning Tuesday. Enjoy Sonoma Valley and its surrounding wine country, where the menu of activities is endless and bountiful.*

There's no mention of Rachel Estrella or any expected duties, and this time the note comes in an invitational font matching the inn's logo rather than via the typewritten format. But the hotel's address coincides with the pictures on the postcard in my stack of mail, too niftily for this missive to be interpreted as anything but the latest round of instructions from my government pen pal.

I replace the room key in the folds of the brochure and return the folio to my backpack. Breaking open the Clif bar, I dig out the binoculars and partake of a technology-assisted look at the red-tailed hawk that inspired me to take a seat on this rock in the first place. The hawk holds its head at an angle, examining something on the ground below. Maybe me; maybe the Bozo detail bringing up the rear; maybe a chipmunk.

I like the way hawks appear both gracefully regal and savagely predatory, but soon relent on my observation of the creature, slip the pack around my shoulders, and get back to the uphill hike. It's imperative to keep a healthy lead on the Bozos — I've found that the appearance on the horizon of two G-men will always spoil even the most inspirational vista.

-7-

I'M CHASING A SHOT OF wheatgrass with a Blueberry Infusion Smoothie, surveying a stack of newspapers while I sip, marveling as ever at how inaccurate most press coverage remains. But it's hard to concentrate on the papers.

It's Sunday, another crisp, clear, breezy morning — we get a lot of these here in Carmel, at least when we aren't fogged in — but despite the easy bustle of the upper crust clientele, Billie looks annoyed, or in the very least troubled, while she preps a batch of avocado-and-cucumber sandwiches.

I fold the papers and bring my smoothie to the counter.

"What did that sandwich ever do to you?"

When she looks up, Billie's rage first draws a bead on me, then evaporates.

"Oh, hi. Sorry," she says. "I didn't realize it was you."

She finishes a sandwich, cuts it in two triangles, sets it on a plate, pushes the plate to the cashier who served my smoothie. Cucumbers fly out of the bin as her fingers assemble a new batch of contents for the next sandwich. She reminds me of a sushi chef, cockily slicing the skin off the cucumbers with the blade rather than a peeler.

"I take it you're having a bad day," I say.

"I don't usually bring this stuff to work," she says. "But yeah, I'm having a not-so-good day."

I hold my hands up in surrender. "Think I owe you and your pal an apology for my political rant the other night. If that has anything to do with—"

"No, it's — " she says, then stops and looks up with a smile. "Actually I rather enjoyed witnessing a reformed Republican talk like all my crunchy friends from yoga and Pilates. Further, I thought Gustavo was a little out of line the way he was pushing the issue, which I told him in no uncertain terms afterward, which led to a series of related and unrelated arguments, which in turn resulted in the demise of our short-lived, so-called relationship."

I blink and our eyes lock for a moment. Kind of a long moment. Soon hers drop and her hands resume their sandwich-crafting efforts, and I believe I detect a slight smudge at the edge of her cheekbones. This causes me to wonder what outward signs I've got that may be revealing the rush coursing through my own veins.

Maybe it's this rush, or the cumulative combination of inputs against that retirement malaise, or maybe it's simply because I can't think of anything else to say — but at this point I pull from my pocket the wine-country brochure. I'd intended to do some research on the inn with Billie's WiFi connection, but Billie's mood has pulled me off course. I set the brochure on the counter and find her eyes again.

"What would you say to the idea of spending a few days in wine country?"

Her eyes find the brochure before ping-ponging between the sandwich components, me, and the brochure again. Realizing I may not have been clear, I say, "With me." Then I see how that could be misinterpreted too, so I add, "In different rooms, I mean, if that's preferable."

Even this doesn't seem to fill the hole of silence, so I say: "Seems I was given a free stay at the place in the brochure here, and it looks like a nice spot. While I was giving some consideration to making the trip, I decided not to go — until now. Having heard of the sordid demise of your so-called relationship, I now maintain that maybe it would do us both some good to take a little trip."

I hold up my hands again, say, "No pressure," and I'm now coiled like a spring, fully prepared to eject like a fighter pilot escaping a terminal spin.

"May I see it?" she says.

I push the brochure across the counter. She sets the work aside, dries her hands on her apron, seizes then examines the invitation, room key, and its folder. After a moment she pushes it back and her fingers return to slicing avocado halves.

"What exactly do you mean by a few days?" she says. "The full four days and three nights mentioned in the brochure?"

I feel the rush overtake me again. "Well," I say, "if I'm going to take measures to slip the Bozo detail — "

"The Bozo — ?"

"Those guys outside who just can't get enough of me."

Her eyes find the dynamic duo, seated at one of her outdoor tables.

"I like to duck out of their protective bubble from time to time. Life, liberty, and the pursuit of non-surveilled happiness. When I do it, I try to stretch the freedom out for as long as possible. So, yeah, maybe we go with the full package."

"Isn't it mandatory that you keep the . . . detail with you wherever you go?"

"In the lengthy period since I left office," I say, "not a single person has threatened me with bodily harm. In fact, once, in South America, I succeeded in ditching them for close to a month. That month was probably the most worry-free stretch of my life."

I shrug, but from the look of Billie's glare — approximating the look Helen Thomas, former dean of the White House press corps, routinely leveled on me during some of my less-than-honest press conferences — my response hasn't satisfied her. She hands a stack of sandwiches to the cashier to package up, lifts the brochure, looks it over one last time, then returns it again to its place beside me on the counter.

"Yes," she says.

I look at her, but she's not looking back. She's looking at a receipt the cashier has held up for her to review.

"Meaning, yes?" I ask foolishly, not even sure she can hear me any longer. "If so, the reservation's for this Tuesday. Does that — "

"Yes," she says.

"So I'll pick you up — "

"You don't own a car."

"No," I say. "But I can arrange one."

"And still shake your Secret Service pals? Why don't we take mine."

I blink, nod, and after a moment, take the brochure from the counter, fold my stack of newspapers, and slip the brochure back into the stack.

"Tuesday it is, then," I say.

-8-

I F YOU'RE UNDER THE ILLUSION that Americans do not live in a police state, behold the U.S. Secret Service. In addition to its more publicly documented protection duties, the agency is also charged with policing counterfeiting offenses against any U.S. or foreign currencies; enforcing illegal electronic fund transfers, false IDs, and bank fraud; providing investigative and forensic assistance in support of cases involving missing or exploited children; running security at events of national significance; and conducting "operations of a confidential nature" at the direction of the president or Secretary of Homeland Security.

There is no congressional oversight of the Service, and its agents have the authority to arrest anyone without a warrant. Its agents comprise a tight-knit organization with few bureaucratic blockers, and the Director of the U.S. Secret Service reports to the Secretary of Homeland Security. A single text message from an agent's cell phone can literally call in the National Guard, a capability essentially shared only by governors and the president.

Agents protecting former heads of state such as myself from danger can also protect the government from us, menaces to society as we may be. And I've certainly engaged in my share of menace — at least if you count as menace such things as sheer embarrassment to the nation, experimental drug use, retreat to a hippie existence, and an ever-expanding web of friendships across geopolitical lines. And some do.

But that isn't the kind of menace I'm talking about.

When you're anointed head of state, you're entrusted with a number of state secrets. Most of these involve standard classified factoids, the routine sort of information you'd expect to hear upon taking office: intelligence-gathering, military, nuclear weapon and power-generation issues, security and law enforcement procedures. Others are more unexpected: clandestine exit tunnels beneath national monuments, weird executive-branch appointees nobody knows about (example: Commissioner, Cataclysmic Asteroid Monitoring Unit, Boulder, Colorado). Other state secrets are more significant and severe, but the constant is that the confidential information shared with you is not intended for mainstream consumption on your departure from office.

There is a clause in the United States Code relating to the authority of the Secret Service stating that their protection may be declined, but to my knowledge, no former president has been granted this request. I've attempted to waive my own protection dozens of times, and while I've never asked fellow members of the former presidents' club how often they've done so, I suspect that most of them have asked for temporary relief and that such requests, like mine, were summarily rejected. When you leave office, it is assumed that those state secrets remain safe in your hands, but just in case you should have a change of heart, there is a policy in place, and that policy is to maintain an in-person security presence around the clock, whether or not protection is your preference.

They are always there. Looking out for you, but keeping an eye on you too.

All that said, despite the Secret Service's determination to keep its assigned team on me around the clock, I've found that slipping the Bozo detail when needed isn't too complicated a challenge this many years removed from official duties. The hard part comes in staying slipped, since Secret Service agents are particularly adept at finding you once you've disappeared. In my case this is due largely to my fairly predictable routine, but they also have the entire federal, state, and local government law enforcement ranks to lean on in conducting their search, and they aren't shy about pushing the limits of their clout when needed.

Whenever I feel this need, I leave a note. It calms them — eventually. First, it's more likely to generate an undiluted form of rage: *How could that hippie bastard give us the slip?* I've been carefully consistent with my latter-day flower-child image in front of these people, and that usually works in my favor. There's no doubt they'll be pissed — but once calm settles in, their perception shifts to something like, *No sweat. Where the hell would granola boy go anyway — he'll turn up soon enough.*

I write tonight's note and tape it on the kitchen door:

Dear Frick & Frack — there's leftover lasagna in the fridge. Don't wait up. Enjoy the vacation while you can. I will!

Leaving the lights on and blinds drawn in my study, I slip out its patio door and pedal away on my hidden second bike, one I trust isn't rigged for a flat tire nor carrying a secret plea for help.

An hour later, just shy of midnight, Billie and I are headed north on Highway 101, the windows down in her Prius, the dry summer wind pushing at our cheeks.

-9-

I'S TWO-FIFTEEN A.M. WHEN WE arrive at the Mango Tree Inn. Per my request with the manager, Billie's room key has been left on the bed in my quarters. I try not to make a big deal out of the second-room thing while helping Billie get situated in the adjoining suite. I insist on carrying her luggage; she laughs but lets me. I've got her by twenty-five years and walk around with busted-up knees from my injury-prone two-year stint as a college quarterback, while Billie, whose bags I'm lugging up the stairs, has completed three Ironman triathlons in the past twelve months. Sure, I'm the weaker sex, but chivalrous I shall remain.

We avoid too much awkwardness in saying goodnight from our respective doors, and retreat for the night accordingly.

I'm climbing into bed when I observe the Bible on the bedside table. It's placed there in a perfectly unobtrusive way, but this is exactly what's making it obtrusive. A hotel-room Bible, as a rule, is stowed in the drawer.

By now I'm prepared to find the letter-writer's next missive beneath every stone, so I'm not exactly shaken when a few items fall into my lap as I open the Good Book. Tonight's offering, tucked into the opening verses of *Leviticus*, consists of four wallet-size pictures and a business card. I leaf through the scripture to be sure I've found all there is to find, but there's nothing else.

The photographs depict three men and one woman. The woman is a redhead; the men, brunette. Was it Red Barber with the famous play-by-play call of Jackie Robinson's major league debut? *Jackie is very definitely brunette.* These three definitely aren't as brunette as Jackie — they could have been typical members of Newt Gingrich's campaign staff — but they've all got dark hair.

The Three Brunettes.

It comes to mind that these photos in the Bible rule out the involvement of my Bozo detail on this delivery, unless they somehow determined where I was going and didn't reveal they'd learned it.

The question of exactly what I'm supposed to do with the photographs is less than clear. The business card, otherwise blank, bears a typeset phone number. It's printed in a professional font, different from the outputs from the typewriter and the inn. Area code 202. Washington.

I flip the card over. On the other side, more words from a printer:

`tell me what you see`

I lift the room's phone and dial the number. In two and a half rings, the electronic female voice with an English accent that seems to be a part of the answering service for every company in the world answers with the standard suggestion that I leave a message after the tone. I hang up and flip over the photos too, but find nothing but the printing company's repeating watermark on the back.

I'm a fan of order, organization, and clear direction, and accompanying this personality trait is a hankering for problem-solving. In office, it was a hallmark of my policy execution: put a variable in front of me, give me gray and vague, and I was compelled to bring color and clarity. It gave me peace of mind to provide and execute a solution that solved the problem.

At this point, the cadenced arrival of communiques from the letter-writer has begun to emerge as a substitute for crossword puzzles in this particular AARP member's post-career routine. I'll begrudgingly admit that not only have I come to look forward to the arrival of each new piece in this jigsaw puzzle, but it seems my dormant hankering for problem-solving has yielded the habit of looking under every nook, cranny, and Bible for the next note.

It's also starting to feel like the letter-writer knows more about my routine than she's letting on.

Setting my wallet beside the Bible, I pull a copy of *Foreign Affairs* from my bag to help guide my way to sleep.

-10-

THE BEDSIDE PHONE JANGLES ME awake. A ray of sunlight pierces my eyes as I answer.

"Yes?"

"Aren't heads of state required to be up before everyone else?"

I eye the clock, which boldly asserts that it's 8:38 a.m.

"Don't think that was true for 40," I say.

"Who?"

"Reagan. The 40th American President. Slept in regularly and famously."

"Well some of us non-dignitaries have already been up and had a ride," Billie says. "I'm glad you asked me to come — the scenery is breathtaking. Practically had the road to myself."

"'Endless and bountiful,'" I say. I sit up and, for no particular reason, check the bedside table. The Bible and my wallet are still there. "If you've already done your road work, you must be ready for the 'breakfast' part of the 'B & B.'"

"They're serving in the garden behind the pool."

"Why don't you see if you can find us a table with a little privacy," I say. "Be ready in five." Being on the lam from the Bozo detail and apparently on a clandestine hunt for Redhead and the Three Brunettes, a subtle table choice seems wise for breakfast.

"Privacy won't be a problem," she says.

In a few moments, making our way past the parking lot and pool, Billie's meaning becomes clear.

The Mango Tree Inn has no other guests.

Not one.

I'm guessing there are a dozen rooms. There's a nice pool and hot tub. Lush landscaping. The inn itself sits back from Highway 12, the Sonoma Highway, on the southern edge of Santa Rosa, shielded by a stand of casuarina trees. We're just north of Kenwood, which puts fifty or more of California's most famous wineries within a fifteen-minute drive, and with a year of relative calm in California's natural disaster cycle, you'd figure this B&B to be pretty popular. There are six tables visible in the garden, a full cooking staff working in the kitchen beyond a hedge. But besides Billie's Prius, the parking lot is empty; nobody's eating breakfast; nobody's lounging by the pool.

The waiter, perfectly cordial and unfazed by the apparent ninety-five percent vacancy rate, takes our orders from an earthy menu. He returns with fresh-squeezed OJ, coffee, a variety of milk and milk-like alternatives, and sweeteners. I take a sip of the coffee, black.

"You know, it may be a bad sign about the food," I say, seeking to deflect any in-depth analysis of the awkward lodging situation, "that nobody's staying here."

Billie gives me a sideways look. Her hair is sandy brown right at the roots, but rockets immediately to blond, as though permanently scathed by the sun.

"By day, at home," she says, "a Bohemian retiree, his only mode of transportation a Mongoose mountain bike. By night, and the occasional morning, a lavish, incurable romantic?"

It takes a minute, but then I get it: she thinks I rented out the whole joint just for us. Disingenuous though it may be, it occurs to me the prudent call is to allow her to think this for now, so I shrug.

"Let's just see about the food," I say.

"Oh," she says with a gleam in her eye that sends butterflies through my chest, "I'm sure it will be atrocious."

-11-

BEGINNING ON THE NIGHT WE met, my wife Katie talked relentlessly about traveling the world. In order to fend off her demands, I promised we'd do it the minute I left politics – a dark art I figured I'd never leave. We visited hundreds of foreign states together on official business, so my intent was for her aims to be fulfilled toward the expiration of my political shelf life. But for Katie, official business didn't count. Doing the president-and-first-lady thing meant Air Force One. Cabinet members. A dozen Secret Service personnel and U.S. Marines convoys. And media — journalists coming along to document your every move, cameras memorializing each step.

Katie did a semester in Europe after her junior year of college. With a couple girlfriends along for the ride, she backpacked her way across the continent, burning a hole in her rail pass, working coat-check rooms to pay her way — and that's how she wanted *our* trip to work. My collegiate experience was dominated by football, or, more aptly put, a disappointing lack thereof, since my budding intercollegiate athletic career at the University of Washington was ended abruptly by a 300-lb. lineman's destruction of my left knee on the first play of my sophomore season opener.

I funneled my football ambitions into academics, finishing a year early and heading to Georgetown Law, where I wound up second in my class — second, as it turns out, to the man who would become my White House Counsel.

As an attorney, I made a fortune for clients and for myself, first by suing corporate polluters, and then by changing sides and representing the polluters to collect even higher fees. Over cocktails with a client one night, it was recommended I run for public office, and with the help of that client's well-funded PAC, I won a seat in the Washington state legislature. The Republican brass soon decided to expend significant resources and groom me for bigger things: they got behind my campaign for the U.S. House of Representatives, coaching me in such things as the sale of my 10,000 square-foot house in Madison Park in favor of a modest home in a powerhouse Republican district north of Seattle. After a stint in the House, I ran for and won the junior U.S. Senate seat, after which I was elected Governor — and following half a term in Olympia, I won the Republican presidential primary and never looked back.

Four months following the conclusion of my term in the White House, Katie was diagnosed with stage III breast and lung cancer. She was supposed to last six months, and she barely made it three.

The moment she died, I was holding her hand. She had a chance to say goodbye to me, and I to her, but it wasn't until she'd taken her last breath that I realized how little time we'd spent together. We were married twelve years, but if I added up the quality time spent privately as a couple, it barely stretched to a single year. We married late and never had kids, so with only that cumulative year left to remember, a void opened up in me. I'd seen my wife in photographs more than I'd seen her in life, and now she was gone.

It was in her last moment of life — watching as she inhaled, and then, very slowly, exhaled one last time — that I decided I would fulfill the promise I'd made to her.

It was time to take that trip.

I set out a few days later to much controversy. Four Secret Service agents were dispatched to accompany me around the clock; the media wouldn't leave me alone, and there were protests — lingering anger over the wars I'd gotten us into, my failure to protect the environment, my alienation of virtually every foreign regime on the planet, and so on. But mostly the problem was this: on the first leg of my trip, I was traveling exactly the way Katie despised. The way that didn't count.

I came home, bagged my plans for a presidential library in Seattle — would have been impressive too, an all-glass design overlooking Pike Place Market — and laid low for a few months. When the news cycle finally passed me by, I bought some hiking boots, cargo shorts, and T-shirts emblazoned with various inflammatory statements broadcast networks wouldn't dare show on the evening news. I crammed everything into a backpack with a bunch of camping gear, stuffed three hundred bucks and my passport in a pocket, and stuck out my thumb.

The Bozos assigned to me that year had to call Washington for backup, and they certainly made the hitchhiking process more difficult. But my travel technique, which typically involved the bartering of manual labor — mine — for lodging or food, got me from Seattle to Guadalajara for somewhere just shy of a hundred bucks. I kept a journal, jotting a note to Katie every night before I went to bed. I also kept track of the many people I met along the way, recording each new friend's contact information and a line or two about our time together in a fat little black book I still possess.

I spent a year in Mexico before heading farther south. I sped up, picking out people and places at random, going where the path took me, never staying longer than a week in any one town with occasional exceptions. By the time I left Central America, I'd shaken the media, though not before they got their last bit of revenge.

It came when I'd arrived in a small village in Nicaragua. The town was populated solely by Native Americans, and over the course of the week I'd been given some generous gifts. I took to wearing the carved stone necklace they'd presented me, and on my second-to-last day, I accepted an invitation to join the elders in an annual religious ceremony pegged to the lunar calendar. Suffice to say that the ceremony involved a small herd of naked men, thick clouds of hot steam, thicker clouds of the local peyote equivalent and, unbeknownst to those of us partaking, a freelance photographer and his Nikon peering through a fold in the tent.

He shot me buck-naked (save the necklace). Dripping in sweat, I also happened to be pulling down a lungful of the native weed from a locally crafted pipe. I learned later that the photographer sold the photo to *Us Weekly* for $250,000, which was apparently enough to warrant the cover. A black rectangle was inserted to cover my privates, but otherwise, there I was, in all my glory, once again plastered across every newsstand in America and beyond, this time bereft of suit and tie (or any stitch of clothing). I never did learn who came up with the headline that accompanied the photo, but on the cover, emblazoned over the photographer's full-color shot of my nude, necklaced bod, was a line that stuck:

BOHEMIAN PREZ BARES ALL

Every major media outlet picked it up, and from that point on I was renamed, and shall apparently always be referred to as, the Bohemian.

Other stories followed — walking on red-hot coals in Fiji, a stint as a matador's apprentice in Malaga, driving a Formula 1 race car in Monaco. But the media cycle had sped up by then, so the feeding frenzy soon waned. Left largely to my own devices and the lesser two-person Secret Service detail you get once they decide you're less important, I took that first year of travel and turned it into four, and then I took the four and turned it into seven.

I never did spend the whole three hundred bucks.

-12-

THE THREE HIGHWAY PATROL CRUISERS that have rolled up outside the restaurant where Billie and I are enjoying lunch on our third day would seem to indicate that my wine-country leave from the Secret Service gauntlet is about to expire.

We've visited a number of wineries each day, hiked, and one morning I even attempted to keep up with Billie on a morning cycling trek. This afternoon we're at a window table in a Glen Ellen restaurant called The Fig, where I've just given her a brief history of my long, strange trip. Another earthy menu has yielded cream of carrot soup for me, an olive plate for Billie, and we're waiting on sandwiches.

"Tell me about your wife," she says as I observe through the window behind her a fourth rig, an unmarked Crown Vic, pull into the red zone out front.

"That's an imposing question," I say.

"Yes. But she must have been quite a woman."

"Why do you say so?"

"Because when she died," she says, "I get the sense you turned yourself into the man you think she wanted you to be. I'm not sure what you were like before, but I think the man you've become is quite something."

The sandwiches arrive — turkey, bean sprouts, and avocado on whole-grain sourdough sliced into triangles. I reach for one. After a bite, chew, and swallow, I say, "I'm not sure you'd feel that way if you'd met me before my trip."

Billie consumes one of her triangles. "You were in favor of war."

I nod. "I was known for that," I say, "but it was more about a foreign policy that required us to confront — "

A flash of reflected sunlight temporarily blinds me, the window of a passing car halting my verbal backpedal. The glare vanishes but draws my gaze out the window, where I see a redheaded woman pass from the shadow of an awning into the sun. She's emerging from the restaurant across the street — the Garden Court Café and Bakery, per the awning. She holds a bag stuffed with what I assume to be food, headed for the adjoining parking lot.

I feel a kind of electric jolt and quickly pull out my wallet, digging for the photographs of Redhead and the Three Brunettes. When I find the shot in my stash, the picture confirms the conclusion I've already reached: Redhead is the person currently exiting the Garden Court Café. I watch as the woman approaches, unlocks, and climbs into a black Toyota 4Runner. She's wearing jeans and a plain green T-shirt, but it isn't her wardrobe that strikes me. There's something very familiar in her manner, something I've seen before.

Billie's eyes sharpen at my pause, and on seeing the pictures she turns to follow my gaze out the window.

"Who's that?" Billie says. "And what's going on out there?"

I would answer her, maybe even with a modicum of honesty, but it's at that moment that a fifth Highway Patrol cruiser jerks to a stop outside and, arriving directly behind it, a familiar black-on-black Yukon. Two events then transpire simultaneously: across the street, Redhead pulls from the parking lot in her 4Runner, turns, and departs from view to my left; and on the near side of the street, my two-person Secret Service detail leaps from the Yukon and marches through the front door of The Fig. It takes me a few seconds given that so much is happening before I finally grasp the familiarity of Redhead's gait:

She and the Bozos share it.

I call it the Federal Agent Strut. It's a unique sort of swagger — the I'm-better-than-you-because-I'm-law-enforcement swagger. I've seen it in ninety percent of the Secret Service personnel they assign me, and now I've seen it in this woman — one of the people the letter-writer was hoping I'd encounter on my complimentary wine-country surveillance trip.

"There you are, Mr. President," booms the authoritative voice of the lead man on my protective detail as he arrives at our table. "You know, sir, you really shouldn't do that. With or without a note."

"Do what?" I say playfully, knowing I don't have much time if I intend to learn where Redhead is heading in her 4Runner. But Bozo-teasing is such an irresistible pastime.

He frowns. "We're charged with your protection, sir, and it's difficult to protect you when we don't know your whereabouts."

"I feel positively safe now that you've reacquired my scent," I say, "though I've got the distinct notion you had a pretty good idea where I was headed to begin with."

His mouth opens, then closes, as I drop a hundred-dollar bill on the table and stand, grabbing Billie's hand.

"Let's drive," I tell her. "I'll explain what I can in the car."

She swipes her phone from the table and comes along. I pat my lead agent on his shoulder.

"Back to the Yukon, my man," I say. "We're on the move."

After a beat of hesitation, he turns and jerks his chin at his number two and they follow us out of The Fig.

As I step into the bright Sonoma sunshine, my brain and sensory perception feel suddenly sharper. As I breathe there's the sensation that the air contains more oxygen. It reminds me of the feeling I'd get out on the campaign trail — a like-for-like adrenaline shot of the sort I felt playing football. I suspect this one is striking me so starkly because it's a double: the enticement and partial deception of Billie on the one hand, and the quandary brought forth by the letter-writer on the other.

All told, it's feelings to follow and a problem to solve.

As we reach the Prius, I stop and lock into Billie's powder-blue eyes.

"There's something I've wanted to tell you since you opened the shop," I say. "In fact, I've wanted to tell you since you showed up in Saturday morning yoga."

Billie half-focuses on me in the midst of the otherwise frenetic activity. "And you want to tell me this now?"

"It's something that — any time I've — " Getting caught up in the words, I abandon this approach, say, "Screw it," reach around, set my hand on the small of her back, pull her to me, lean in, and kiss her. For an instant, her lips are immobile. My eyes aren't fully closed yet and I see hers flick briefly and self-consciously to my Bozo detail. But then her eyes close and her lips are suddenly no longer immobile. My eyes involuntarily close and all there is in that moment is the kiss. When we break, our eyes blur in that one-of-a-kind mutual out-of-focus extreme close-up.

"Well," she says.

I smile. Then frown. Time is dwindling.

"We've got to get moving," I say. "You okay if I drive?"

She grabs the back of my neck, pulls me to her and repeats the kiss, this time more intensely and for a few seconds longer. Then she breaks the seal and gives me a sideways look.

"Unless you've been holding out on me," she says, "my guess is you haven't renewed your driver's license since leaving office. And you want get behind the wheel to chase that 4Runner in *my* Prius?"

She points to the passenger-side door. "Get in. I've got this."

Once we climb into the car and buckle up, she turns and lays another look on me.

"You ever see *I Love Lucy*?" she says.

With a pretty good idea of where she's headed, I fail in my attempt to hold her gaze.

"Yes," I say. "Why?"

"Because before we get too far on this little journey," she says, "you've got some esplainin' to do."

-13-

Billie's got Redhead's SUV in sight about a mile ahead as we turn left, which I register as north, on the Sonoma Highway. I can see that catching sight of the 4Runner before reaching this intersection was key. From The Fig to here involved only local roads, but the two-lane Sonoma Highway stretches around long bends in both directions that would have meant taking a fifty-fifty shot had we lost our visual.

Billie rolls through the stop sign at the junction, quickly passing a Ford F-150 laden with landscaping tools. As we accelerate and sweep around the first wide, easy turn, it's hard not to clock the beauty of the rolling hills, farmhouses, and vineyard rows of the valley.

"Keep your distance," I say. "Half-mile gap's probably good."

"No problem," Billie says.

We lose sight around some turns ahead, but the 4Runner stays in view on the stretches, and judging from Redhead's lackadaisical speed, it doesn't appear she's made us. Also didn't hurt that she departed with her take-out before the full Bozos multijurisdictional convoy roll-up in the heart of the Glen Ellen business district.

Speaking of such, the Yukon follows us some distance back, remaining fairly unobtrusive in our mirrors. The GMC is running solo — my detail seems to have ditched their Highway Patrol escort now that they've found me.

We're headed in the direction of the inn, which spikes my problem-solving synapses another notch. How could the letter-writer, sending me out here with a reservation and four photographs in a Bible, know she was dispatching me to exactly the right place? And if so, why send me at all? The directive — *tell me what you see* — must merely have been a demand to confirm something the letter-writer already knew. And with that swagger in Redhead's step, I've got some rising suspicions about the letter-writer and the supposedly unassuming role she claims to hold in Washington. All of which calls the letter-writer's entire story into further question.

I feel a pang of anger, a sort I've felt before: it's the kind that hits most presidents a few weeks after the inauguration, the point at which you've been exposed to the realities hidden from ordinary citizens like popcorn and dust under the living-room rug. In many ways I've been immune to the rage for years, but it's flowing again now, an angry objection to injustice that works similarly to the converse of love: once you know how to feel it, you will always feel it as long as you're paying attention. I just haven't been paying attention — to either — for one hell of a long time.

The knee-jerk conclusion here is that a federal agent is somehow involved in a kidnapping, and if the facts here approximate the way things typically work with government agencies, that's just going to be the tip of the iceberg. And whatever it is that she's up to, Redhead wouldn't be the type to undertake it of her own initiative. Whether this legitimizes or debunks the letter-writer's take on recent history and her call for help remains unclear.

"Is there some point at which you intend to fill me in on what exactly we're doing here?" Billie says.

I blink back to the moment. The alarming implications of the Federal Agent Strut in a woman ostensibly linked to the abduction of a government employee's daughter dictate that Billie shouldn't be told much — I don't want her exposed to these people, and I don't want them exposed to her. The problem with all of this is that Billie is a relentless person who regularly runs marathons at top speed as the third leg of all-day races in hundred-degree heat. She may not know what she's getting into, but if she becomes insistent on staying involved, I'm fairly certain I'm incapable of holding her back, or holding *all* the information back in the meantime. So I can't stay entirely silent.

"Somebody asked me to do her a favor," I say. "It has to do with some unpleasant business. There are people connected with her work in government who've engineered the unpleasantness. What we're doing now is part of the favor, which logic would dictate I shouldn't be granting. But I'm not typically known for following a course based solely on logic."

"Unpleasantness," she says. Then, "The woman in the 4Runner isn't the one you're doing the favor for, though."

"No."

"The favor's the reason we came up here."

She says it flatly, so there's no telling whether another emotional layer lurks behind her question.

"No." We wind around a long bend and the 4Runner reappears ahead of us on another straightaway as I sense the importance of my answer. "The favor gave me the opportunity to ask you to come. My reservation at the inn was arranged by the person who asked me to help her — but I meant what I said, that I'd decided against it. I wasn't going to help, but your dour morning mood that day in your shop pulled me out of my hang-up on both."

"Both?"

"Taking a leap with you that I should have taken six months ago, and agreeing to help with the favor."

Billie works the wheel for a second or two.

"What kind of help were you asked to provide?"

We're at the point of establishing our trust. If I can't be truthful before the third kiss, then she'd certainly be wise to suspect me of the potential for great mendacity later on. But the plain fact is that there are things in government I've seen — and *overseen* — that she hasn't. And wouldn't want to. She'll be safer in the dark, but Billie's trust is something I don't care to lose.

"Somebody went missing," I say. "This person may have been kidnapped, if not killed, and the redhead we're following probably has something to do with it."

"Is the somebody who went missing a woman, or a man?"

I hesitate but increasingly find my stonewalling efforts futile. "A woman."

"Adult, or child?"

"She's an adult."

"And the person who asked you to help? How well do you know her?"

Relentless.

"I don't know her at all," I say, "though she claims that we'd previously met. She wrote me a letter asking for my help. And since when did you attend interrogation school?"

"I've been through a divorce," Billie says. "So along with the rest of the baggage I bring with me on any trip, to wine country or elsewhere, is a trust meter with a precision read-out. Is she related to the one who's missing?"

"The woman who's missing," I say, all but giving up, "is her daughter."

We drive for another mile in silence and I see that we're approaching Kenwood. The valley floor is off to our left, vineyards visible between stands of oak trees. To the right lies a combination of evergreens and oaks, more woods and hills than fields, the steep, rising, forested slopes signaling the base of the foothills.

"I shouldn't have asked you to come," I say.

Come to think of it, I shouldn't have come myself.

But had I not, my long-neglected synapses would not be firing like they are now. Redhead's Federal Agent Strut has stirred dregs of bitterness I thought I'd put aside for good. The shot of adrenaline I'm feeling tells me that pulling my head out of the sand was one of the better decisions I've made in years.

Billie turns and fixes her gaze on me.

"Yes, you should have," she says. "And I'm glad I came too. Among other reasons, you've got a spring in your step, the countryside is breathtaking, and I've just learned you're a really good kisser."

I feel myself smile in spite of the circumstances.

"Thought that was just you," I say.

"That was decidedly mutual."

Billie takes a hand from the wheel and, with it, touches my knee. It transports me back to our night with Gomez. I like the fact that her touch is on me, rather than Gustavo the cycling date.

Ahead, the 4Runner's brake lights flash and the SUV exits the highway to the right. Billie gradually slows as we watch from our rapidly closing half-mile gap.

"Don't follow just yet," I say. "Continue on the highway."

It's only a few seconds before we fly through the intersection. With a quick flash of sunlight on its tailgate, the 4Runner disappears uphill into the woods.

I catch a glimpse of the sign at the intersection on our way by: Nuns Canyon Road. I don't know this specific lane, but I've spent my share of time up here, and I know this sort of road. It won't have an outlet to another highway.

"Don't you want to follow her?" Billie says.

"Those weren't my instructions. I'm just supposed to report the sighting."

"But we already did more than that," she says.

"There's no outlet on these side roads," I say. In the side mirror, I confirm what I saw in my peripheral vision: a crop of mailboxes stand on a wooden T-beam at the foot of Nuns Canyon Road. "Pretty safe bet that road dead-ends a couple miles in. We've done what the letter-writer asked, and I don't want Redhead to see us."

My automatic use of the terms *we* and *us* indicate, somewhat alarmingly, that Billie's relentlessness has already converted my need-to-know approach, which I'm beginning to regret already.

"So," Billie says, "what now?"

Her hand hasn't left my knee, so for lack of a better answer, I rest my hand on hers. A warmth surges from her skin to mine, up my arm, and into my spine, giving me the feeling we've just passed an addictive drug by osmosis through our fingers.

A familiar sign passes on the shoulder, revealing we're about a mile from the inn.

"I can think of a few ideas," I say, doing my best to keep my eyes on the road.

-14-

B ILLIE OPENS THE DOOR TO her room with her passkey and turns to face me. Her eyes find mine, and after a moment of electric silence, I step in, push the door closed, place one hand then another on her hips, then ease my arms around her, and we kiss. In my grasp, she feels tiny, lithe, firm, and delicate.

My mouth glued to hers, I feel one of her hands behind my head and the other at the small of my back. Her hands pull me against her, and our lips are mashed so hard together we're imprinting each other's cheeks, this wiry little creature pulling my bulk against her with the force of an industrial-strength winch.

We topple, but our clasp doesn't give, so we bounce off the edge of the bed to the floor. I feel her hands exploring me and I do the same, nestling a hand in her short, wind-crisped hair, sliding it down her neck, past a shoulder blade. I dig under the base of her tank-top until I find skin, and when I find it, it's hot. My hand makes its way to one of her intoxicating breasts and she sighs as I reach it. Her hand slips beneath the waistband at the small of my back, and then it's at my hip, and she's using both hands to push down my khakis and I'm finding the snap and zipper of her jeans and soon there is more skin and almost all of it is touching. The carpet beneath us is coarse. It singes our hips, knees, and elbows.

We never make it to the bed.

-15-

I OPEN MY EYES AND OBSERVE that Billie, whom I've never even seen fatigued, is fast asleep. She, like me, is nude, and — as I was a moment before — flat on her back on the floor. I must have been dreaming before I awoke, because despite the blissful state of current events, my thoughts are stuck on the business card with its one-line message:

```
tell me what you see
```

I lie silently for a moment, listening to Billie's light snore. It's feminine, dainty, strong, healthy, and precise. A peaceful, tranquil sound, coming in a gentle rhythm that sounds to me like tiny waves reaching up the sand on a tropical beach.

I rise to one rug-burned knee, lean down, and kiss her on the forehead. I notice, with the curtains drawn and the lights off, that her skin is fairer than her tanned cheekbones would otherwise imply. With so many freckles from hours spent in the sun, Billie's skin always seems golden to me — but now, in the filtered daylight, her naked body resembles a narrow stripe of moonlight.

I find my clothes and exit quietly, making sure her door locks behind me. Covering the five steps between our rooms, I see, and am seen, by the Bozo detail, the two of them hunkered with the engine running in the Yukon. I note that the Yukon and the Prius remain the only cars in the parking lot. I slot the passkey into the lock and slip into my room.

On the dresser in my room are six bottles of wine — one from each of my favorite wineries from our tour. I pick one at random and use the room's corkscrew to open it. In wine country you don't just get the standard-issue plastic-wrapped cups in your room, but high-end wine goblets, and I take one of these and pour myself a glass. Observing, as I do, that the bottle I've selected is a 2018 Merlot from Matanzas Creek Winery.

I sit at the table, pull the business card from my wallet, and stare at the phone number while I drink the glass of wine.

I've seen something worth telling. I can call the letter-writer's answering service and tell her the what, who, and where of it. Resulting, presumably, in her summoning the kind of people she *ought* to have recruited from the outset, thereby relieving me of my supposed duties in response to her haphazardly appearing notes. There's something tugging at the back of my brain about the whole of it, but the vague sense of disquiet doesn't crystallize into anything actionable besides making the call and moving on.

I lift the hotel phone and punch in the numbers, finding I've looked at the card so many times that I've got the number memorized. The same electronic voice asks me to leave a message.

"It's — me," I say after the beep. "You asked me to tell you what I see, and I've seen the redhead from the photos. She was leaving the Garden Court Café in Glen Ellen. This afternoon. It's — " — I check my watch, thinking I should have done this before calling — "June 18. 7:15 p.m. Followed her car this afternoon, a Toyota 4Runner, north on the Sonoma Highway, for just over six miles. She turned right — northeast — on Nuns Canyon Road." I leave the Toyota's license number. "She had a bag of food she bought from the café. Its contents looked like more than one person could eat."

My newly alert mind freezes.

I've just realized, too late, what my disquiet is about. In my cantankerous tendency to critique federal agents, I missed one potential scenario.

If Redhead happens to be a good apple dutifully tackling an assignment, one scenario among many make it possible that Rachel isn't a kidnap victim at all, but instead a witness in protective custody. If true, I've just been used like a dumb mule, following my assigned path without conscious thought, serving only to pinpoint the safe-house for the letter-writer — who could be anyone — whom I've now empowered to call in a hit. My problem-solving habit, preyed upon and forced into servitude.

I immediately regret having made the call.

"That's it," I say into the phone. "That's all. I'm afraid I can't do anything more to help you. I wish you luck in finding your daughter, if that's who Rachel actually happens to be."

I set the phone back in its cradle.

Walk through the possible scenarios.

There's no credence whatsoever to the premise of Redhead being a country mom out to fetch a meal for her kids. Her walk told me exactly who she is: a government agent, and a relatively senior one. And yes, it's possible that in my worst case as mule, Redhead is on assignment protecting a witness. But there are other explanations in between, both innocuous and sinister. Within the middle range rests the initial notion, still entirely valid: the case where Rachel, still alive and kicking, has been kidnapped by Redhead and the Three Brunettes with bad intentions on orders from above, and they are currently holding her somewhere up Nuns Canyon Road.

A senator once told me over lunch that wise leadership requires equal parts nobility and prudence: nobility in aiming for hopes and dreams, prudence in planning for the nightmare of the worst case. Unfortunately, my recent thrill-seeking actions — motivated, I'll admit, in part by the need to have something to do beyond my puttering retirement routine — have now empowered the nightmare scenario just as feasibly as any other. The letter-writer will now act on the intel I've delivered, and the actions she takes will hold the answer on Rachel's fate as well as Redhead's. The right or the wrong people could die, or be saved, all served up on a platter by yours truly, with zero control on my side over the outcome.

There's no goddamn nobility in that.

There will now be a lag — a gap between the message I've just left, to the moment the letter-writer listens to it, on to the execution of the logistics required to deploy the intended response. If nothing else, the letter-writer clearly required some form of confirmation. This means she's unlikely to have placed additional resources in Glen Ellen or Kenwood in advance, meaning further that some quantity of minutes — sixty, maybe ninety — will pass before she's able to act. At the conclusion of this gap, the answer will come, and the time for prudence will have passed.

But that gap is not yet over.

I roll the empty wine glass back and forth in my hand, then set it on the table. From my view through the room's half-opened curtains, I can see the crest of the foothills. The sun appears harshly white and low, reaching the final stretch of its march behind the hills. The layout of the valley here is similar to the geography in Carmel, so by my guess there are some sixty minutes of daylight remaining.

Maybe ninety.

I re-cork the bottle, rummage through my travel bag, and come out with the navy-blue sweater I've worn for a couple of our wine-country dinners. I find my jeans, switch them for the khakis, stuff my wallet and a few things I always keep with me into my pockets, and lace up my hiking shoes. I find the pad of hotel stationery beside the Bible and write a note to Billie. I step out of the room and slip the note under her door, feeling a bit like I've just ditched her the way I ditched the Bozos:

Dear Sleeping Beauty;
Went for a bike ride. See you soon.

The sun already looks lower in the sky as I unchain and mount my bike. One of my security team audibly releases the emergency brake on the Yukon and I feel more than see them following as I pedal out the driveway and hang a left.

I shift up through the gears, building speed as I head south on the Sonoma Highway in the direction of Nuns Canyon Road.

-16-

FIFTEEN MINUTES LATER, I TURN up the hill, the Yukon prowling a half-mile behind. I clock the numbers on the mailboxes near the base of the road: escalating, oddly, by threes, they run from 113 to 152. Fourteen properties.

It's a single-lane, pot-holed ride that begins flat, flanked by oaks, then narrows and rises steeply into evergreens and brush — steep enough to require me to get off and walk the bike. I've gone nearly a mile before I see the first driveway, blocked by an aluminum gate. It's impossible to see whatever house lies beyond, if one exists at all. I get back on the bike and ride uphill, seeing property entrances appearing more frequently, if irregularly, in a more compact succession. I start to wonder whether this was such a golden idea. Didn't really plug the slow ride up the hill into my thinking, so I'm not even halfway through the addresses and it's getting hard to see in the declining light. And I'll learn nothing, let alone the truth, if a landscaping truck comes hauling downhill and turns me into roadkill.

Some of the dwellings are visible from the road; some even boast a car or two, mostly pickups. By the time I reach the eleventh property, it's nearly pitch-black and I've seen no sign of Redhead's 4Runner. I'm beginning to yearn for the downhill ride when, well back from an unmarked gate on the twelfth, I catch the reflection of a porch light against the window of a parked car. I pull to the side of the road for a steadier look, but it isn't until I retrieve my binoculars from my pack that I confirm the reflective vehicle to be the black 4Runner.

My spot on the road offers me a good look at the two-story residence. It's got a farmhouse look, but the place is too stiff and modern to be authentic — probably a manufactured home. I peg it at around two thousand square feet.

It occurs to me that if the situation is as dangerous as I've speculated, it isn't exactly the wisest move to hover beside the front gate. I put the binoculars away, ride a quarter-mile up the road, and find a place to hide my bike in the bushes. I check on the Yukon — my team is closer now, no doubt wondering what the hell I'm up to, but I see they're respectful enough of my emerging scheme to douse their headlights and keep their distance. On foot, I climb through the underbrush, pushing ten or fifteen yards into the property.

I crouch in a copse of pine trees and take another magnified look.

Most of the rooms are dark, but light does filter in from other parts of the house. The place has a modern layout — eat-in kitchen overlooking a family room, formal dining room and den downstairs, and what looks like two beds and baths on the second floor. A television flickers in the family room but I can't see anyone watching.

A light bangs on in the kitchen and Redhead appears, wearing the same clothes as before. I watch through my lenses as she opens the fridge, pulls out a plastic bottle of what appears to be soda, untwists its cap, and makes her way back to the television. She leaves the kitchen light on, allowing me to observe the sparse nature of the decorating. This may not mean much in and of itself, but from out here in the woods, my restless brain finds the factors adding up. The house doesn't look lived-in — it looks like a vacation rental.

Or a safe house.

I swing my lenses to the other rooms, finding similar décor: few-to-zero works of art on the walls, only the bare necessities of furniture, shelves and counters with an utter lack of knick-knacks. Outside, there's a second car in the driveway, a midsize Ford pickup. Security company signs protrude from the yard at fifty-meter intervals, short, diamond-shaped warnings to intruders like me that the place is alarmed and patrolled.

The placement the signs causes me to notice the second structure.

Across the side lawn is a former barn, or at least a building built to look like one. The exterior of the structure is dark, though rectangular outlines of light are visible behind a pair of windows. Workshop? In-law suite?

Safe house? Abduction chamber?

The intelligent part of me knows that either of the last two possibilities are enough to justify pedaling away and going home, maybe even reaching out to the authorities. But my problem is this: if the scenario on which I've now empowered the letter-writer to act involves one of the latter two possibilities, then I need to know which one it is. It will answer what I've come here to determine: the truth of Rachel Estrella's fate and the culpability of Redhead and the Three Brunettes in her capture, assuming she has been captured at all.

I move a little closer to the buildings while holding to the cover of the foliage. My new angle puts the family room of the main house squarely in view: the flicker of the room's television casts light on its viewers, the inconsistent flashes revealing the outlines of a man and woman. In the glare of a commercial, I see the faces. One of them is of course Redhead, back from the kitchen with her soda. The other, seated in a separate chair, is a man, and one I recognize. It's one of the Three Brunettes from the photos in my wallet.

A car door opens audibly on the road behind me but I don't hear it close. A glance confirms that my detail has now exited the Yukon and they are approaching my hiding place on foot.

I know that the second structure, the in-law suite, could hold my answer. But I also know there will be closed-circuit cameras, lights likely riding on sensors and, for all I know, snipers ready to ace any would-be intruders foolish enough to approach the barn. On the other hand, I've got covering support from a pair of agents who help even out the odds.

I start across the lawn toward the barn.

Outside of weekly Tai Chi workouts and the binoculars, I'm of course unarmed, so as I walk, crouched, across the grass I feel as naked as when the photographer snapped his shot at the powwow. But I soon reach a gravel path beside of the structure, none the worse for wear.

Peering back, I see the Bozos arrive in my previous encampment at the edge of the bushes. A hoarse whisper from my lead man floats across the lawn.

"Mr. President! What you're doing may not be safe, sir!"

I offer a half-hearted wave of acknowledgment and creep slowly around the corner of the barn until I come to a window on the side facing the woods. I squat and duck under the level of the sill, and can see as I approach that the window is cracked open, with maybe a six-inch gap open to the outside air. The curtains inside have a slight break in the middle, which might give me enough space to see through.

Having come this far, it's time to see what I can see.

I take a breath and slowly lift my head above the sill until I can peer through the opening in the curtains — and what I see, I suppose, is no surprise. Two men are seated on a couch and leather chair in what appears to be a media or living room. They too are watching television. The room leads directly into a kitchen, and between the kitchen and living room is a hallway leading back to another part of the house. These men are as familiar as the couple in the main house: they're the other two Brunettes.

Something catches my eye, and I crane my neck to gain a direct line of sight. Against the near wall just to my right is a side table. It's the kind on which you'd set your keys and wallet — which these men have done — but where you'd also, if you were a kidnapper or protective federal agent, place your firearm.

Which one of the Brunettes has also done.

There's no sign of Rachel Estrella. And the gun, of course, is confirmation of nothing. In the end, I'm not sure what I expected to find. I'm no closer —

Chunk.

I go blind, my brain seeking explanation —

"Hey!"

It's a cop's voice — a *federal agent's* voice — authoritative — deep — and it isn't one of the Bozos.

"*Back away from the house now!*"

Blindness easing, I grasp that a set of floodlights has just lit the property like a football stadium. I'm caught in full view of the main house, and Redhead and her partner have leaped from the porch and are now running toward me across the lawn.

Guns drawn.

From specific experiences too numerous to mention, I know something about federal agents. They are often good people, but the fact is they are not to be trusted. The reason for this is nothing personal or judgmental: it's their role in the hierarchy of government. At the heart of it, they are soldiers. No different from a U.S. Marine or an Air Force fighter jock, they are required to follow orders, and the elected and appointed people giving the orders are, on a four-out-of-ten-times basis, some of the worst human beings in the free world. There is rotten fruit at the top of our trees, and this I know as fact.

Maybe the letter-writer is the rotten apple in this orchard; maybe it's a different superior in the chain who's gone sour. But since I've managed to set myself directly in the line of fire before determining the answer, there's no debate on what to do next, no waiting to see if my two-man detail are fast enough to get to me in time. Not if I want to make it out of here in one piece.

I reach up, push the window open against its stops, and half-climb, half-flop my way over the sill, crashing to the floor inside. I hear ricocheting bullets, chipping wood and plaster. Breaking glass.

They're shooting at me.

It's confusing because there's no sound of gunshots, but I'm ducking instinctively as I hear the shattering housing materials.

They're using silencers.

Out of the line of fire from Redhead and the first Brunette, I turn and stand, hoping this slow-motion break-in won't prove fatally slow, and grab the pistol from the side table. My hip hits the table and the table falls with a clattering crash as I lean back against the wall, but I've got the gun and I hold it up against the two Brunettes in the living room.

Then I *do* hear gunshots — firecracker sounds, familiar and distinctive. Sig Sauer P229 .357 semi-automatics, to be precise. Secret Service-issue. No Bozos they, my agents are firing back.

The first of the Brunettes in the room, caught in the act of darting for cover, stands half-hidden behind a closet door, his own pistol drawn and half-raised. The other man, having leaped up from the leather chair but made it no farther than that, raises both hands. He's unarmed, so I'm assuming it's his gun I've taken.

That's when the usual recognition sets in.

"Jesus," the unarmed one says.

"The fucking Bohemian!" says the other.

"What the hell is *he* doing here?"

A cacophony of firecracker-like gunshots and the *pfft-pfft* of silenced bullets coming from the lawn escalates into a shattering crash before a man — the Brunette from the main house — crashes in backward through the fragile front door that's already been pummeled by projectiles aimed at me. He hits the floor, multiple bullet holes in his flesh already bleeding out. He groans but remains otherwise motionless.

I turn back, too late, as the Brunette who'd been near the leather chair bolts down the hallway and out of sight. By the time my eyes return to the Brunette by the closet, he's got his gun trained on my forehead.

He hesitates — rotten or not, following orders or no, it's safe to assume not every federal agent will shoot a former U.S. president at point-blank range. Unfortunately for the Brunette, it turns out hesitation was not an option for him. Two reports from a Sig Sauer sound out from the other side of the busted door, the gun falls from the Brunette's hand, and he topples.

Then another body falls in through what's left of the door in a fusillade of silenced bullets. As he bangs past the unhinged door and strikes the floor, I can clearly see it's the lead man on my detail, who probably just saved me from a kill shot, but has now paid the price for my insanely conceived ride up this mountain.

Goddammit.

Two more gunshots, Sig Sauer again, and a woman's voice barks out an angry yelp. I peer out through one of the shattered window panes to see Redhead land face-first on the grass some ten yards from my junior agent. My agent is doing no better, though — as I watch, his gun arm drops, the Sig Sauer falls to the turf below, and he too falls, first to his knees, then sideways to the ground. They've taken each other out.

The aftermath of this Wild West shootout is noisily silent. I focus, taking count: both agents on my detail are down. Redhead must have shot the junior man but his vest, or fortitude, kept him going long enough to strike back.

There's only one left. He ran this way, down the ha —

The hard pain of a blunt object impacting the side of my head is mercifully brief. In a merged sequence of sensations, the room tilts on its axis, my vision flips to a strange shade of gray, and all goes dark.

-17-

"Sir? Mr. President!"

It's a woman's voice. Coming to me from the darkness. I think immediately that it must be Redhead, so I tense up, then remember that Redhead was felled, and retreat to my black haze.

"*Mr. President!* Can you hear me?"

It's not Billie; I don't recognize the voice at all. It's a struggle to open my eyes, an act that delivers a flared, smudged band of bright light to my field of vision, causing stabs of searing pain to assault all corners of my skull. The head and shoulders of a woman lean over me in the fog. I'm on my back, I think. I try blinking and the focus improves. The woman's face is familiar, but I can't yet remember where I am or why I should recognize the face.

"That *is* you, isn't it?"

I try for an answer but nothing emerges from my vocal cords. After another blink, the woman and the room around her come more crisply into view, the images still painfully bright against my headache.

Then my mind awakens on its lag with my vision, and finally I understand.

"I'm happy to see you," the woman says. "I'm happy to see anyone. But I've got to ask — what in God's name are you doing here?"

The woman asking me this perfectly reasonable question isn't supposed to be here. She isn't supposed to be alive, let alone wondering aloud why I'm lying half-comatose in her room. I sputter my next words, my sluggish brain attempting to work through the meaning behind the realization.

"Rachel," I say. "You're Rachel Estrella."

-18-

THE ROOM IS 8'x10' TOPS, with a miniature bathroom visible through an open, narrow door. There are no windows. The furnishings are purely functional: full bed, reading chair, slim bookshelf, small table with two folding plastic chairs, 20" TV with a DirecTV box beneath it. The walls are the exception to the otherwise Spartan surroundings: covering nearly every square inch are artworks by a child's hand. All highly colorful, mostly done in crayon, some of them extraordinary. A door to my right resembles one from a bank vault, seen from the inside: made of reinforced steel with no handle or knob, it looks imposingly thick. The room's walls are made of concrete, and it's cold in here, wine-cellar cold. The design is innocuous enough, but I feel the pull of claustrophobia — my body knows I've awakened in an underground bunker.

I lift myself to a sitting position on the floor. Behind Rachel, seated in the reading chair, open book in her hands, is a girl in a flower-pattern dress. She looks no older than three or four. Both mother and daughter, assuming they're that, have neat features behind pale olive skin, the kind that's deceptively light when kept out of the sun, but instantly bronzed when exposed to the rays, and neither of these two has seen any rays in a very long time. Rachel has deep, dark rings under her eyes and angular creases in her brow that look to me like the combined effects of simmering rage and overwhelming fatigue.

"You're alive," I say when the ricocheting pain yields within my skull.

"Yes," Rachel says.

"Media coverage insists otherwise," I say.

"I've seen that media coverage." She motions to the TV, but her eyes haven't left me, her forehead keeping those angular creases as she studies me. "You know, I've never met a president before."

"Well, now you've met a retired one," I say, "who obviously has no future in hostage rescue. I assume you saw who dumped me on your floor?"

She nods. "One of my revolving team of jailers. The big, fast one."

"Dark hair," I say, "silenced gun?"

"Yes. But the silencers weren't working. I heard shots. What do you mean by 'hostage rescue'? Did you come with police? Are you saying this was an attempt to rescue Elena and me? Why are you here?"

I take in some air and try to focus through the haze of headache.

"I'm here because your mother asked me to find you. She told me you'd been abducted and asked me to find the people who were holding you. She's only sent me letters, so we've never met. But she indicated you were being held in this region and set me up in a nearby inn. I saw one of your . . . jailers, and followed her here. I came alone, with the exception of my Secret Service detail. I think your jailers killed my agents. But not before mine took down three of them."

She stares at me for a long while before blinking, almost like she has to click in and out of her thoughts.

"Then there's only the fast one left."

"Afraid the sole survivor got the best of me," I say.

"But why wouldn't you have come with police — "

The sharp sound of a firecracker, distant but clear, interrupts Rachel. It's followed by three more pops. Rachel lifts her head and looks at the ceiling. The sounds have come from somewhere above our room.

"They're shooting again," she says. "No one else came with you?"

I shake my head. "No. Well, not someone who — "

Rachel bangs repeatedly on the big steel door. "Who's there!" she yells. "Down here! Get us out!"

I find a knee, push hard with my other leg, and get myself up against the bed. Staring at the ceiling, I register the horror that we are locked in a cold, isolated dungeon. It is a sinking, terrible feeling that has already broken ranks with the hope that I'll see daylight again. Rachel must know this feeling with far too much intimacy — the fact that she appears sane after months in captivity is surprising to the point of impossibility.

Rachel bangs on the door again but soon relents and moves to Elena's side. She seems emotionless about her actions — like she's tried banging and yelling in vain ten thousand times to no avail but knows never to cease trying.

"You call them your jailers," I say. "Were they the ones who abducted you to begin with? Or are they merely sentries assigned here later? Did you know them previously?"

"They took all three of us. Into a van in the parking lot of the Starbucks we always use. But no, I don't know who they are. Or why they took us. They don't answer my questions."

"You said, 'The three of us.' The news coverage mentioned your husband — "

"Dead."

My eyes flick to her daughter, but Rachel's do not. "Elena knows what happened. Where we are. My husband was shot trying to get us out. They bring food three times a day. He ran down the passage when they came with breakfast and they shot him in the back." She pauses almost imperceptibly. "*He* did. The one who brought you down."

"Is this where they've kept you the entire time?"

A very short nod. "Starting with the second night."

A metal-on-metal scrape comes from somewhere vaguely above us. Still distant, it's definitely closer than the gunshots. Rachel stiffens.

"Someone's coming," she says.

Even after only minutes down here, I find my body tensing too, a surge of hope boosting my blood pressure.

A series of other sounds follow, increasingly louder: a door closing; a metallic *clink* that sounds like a chain; an interminable gap of silence; a distant voice, muffled and difficult to make out, indiscernible as male or female; then another, much louder metallic *clink* —

"Watch out," Rachel says. "That's the lock — they're coming in."

I notice she's taken Elena's hand and is shielding her daughter from the door. The *clink* sounds out again, and then I hear a voice — *female.*

"Shit! Which damn key is it! Hello! Are you in there?"

Billie.

"Christ!" I say. "Yes! Billie!"

Rachel swings her gaze to me then back to the door.

The sound of an unlocking deadbolt precedes the heavy door's inward swing — revealing Billie, dressed exactly as she was before our tryst at the inn. Only she doesn't look the same. Her eyes are frantic. There's a gun, one of my agents' Sig Sauers, in her hand.

"Found you," she says. Then her eyes find Rachel. "Is this — "

Rachel bolts, her daughter bouncing behind her like an inner tube tied to a speedboat. She knocks Billie aside and is out of sight in three steps, down the dank hall and into the darkness. We can hear her words, fading as she runs.

"We're getting you out of here, Elena honey. We're getting out — "

Billie extends an arm in Rachel's direction. "I think she's got the right idea," she says.

I don't need much prodding. The two of us dash up the slope of the hallway, hot on Rachel's heels.

"What happened?" I say on the run. "You followed me?"

"How about I cover the explanation later," she says as I struggle to keep pace. The concrete floor is slippery, coated with moss and a sheen of moisture. Ahead, we see Rachel briefly before she pushes through a wooden door and takes the stairs beyond two at a time. I continue fishing for an answer.

"Rachel called him the big, fast one — "

"I shot him. Okay?"

It occurs to me, not for the first time, that everything athletic comes easy to her. Possibly including the firing of a pistol. But I've been exposed to enough agents and soldiers to know that with killing, even in justifiable acts of self-defense, comes psychological trauma.

"Twice," she adds. "Look — I'm a single woman working late hours and I'm often in the middle of nowhere on a bike. I carry pepper spray and I've spent some Sundays at the firing range. This wasn't exactly what I had in mind when getting in those reps at the range."

As we reach the top of the stairwell, I pull my eyes from Billie to find Rachel and Elena standing frozen under the open garage door. The garage is at the rear of the structure. It's dark — the floodlights have doused, whether coaxed by timer, switch, or bullet. There is a Honda Civic immediately outside of the garage door, dark and inert like the rest of the surroundings. Rachel seems unsure of which direction to flee, or even whether to flee at all. I touch her shoulder, which causes her to all but jump out of her skin.

"This way," I say. "We'll take the Secret Service Yukon."

Her eyes are on mine, piercing, surveying, examining, deciding. Then she nods and the four of us are out in the open air, hustling across the grass. I point out the SUV, just visible out on the road, and say, "There it is — you can get in. They leave it open when they're in sight of it. A place they've told me I can use to hide."

Billie, leading Rachel and Elena through the bushes, pauses and turns when she sees I've fallen behind.

"Why aren't you coming!"

"Just a minute."

I've reached the first of my two intended waypoints — the prone body of the lead man on my detail. I feel for his pulse at the neck, then at the wrist. Nothing. When I listen at his mouth and nose, I sense no breaths. There's no gun in sight — Billie must have taken his.

I move over to my junior man's prone body and find zero signs of life from him too.

"Shit," I say. "I'm sorry. I caused this. Thank you for saving our lives." I set my hand on his shoulder and nod, knowing an instant is all the time I can spare.

It's the junior man who inevitably drives. I search his pockets and come out with the key ring that includes a GMC branded fob, find his cell phone in his jacket, and take it too. Then I reach down and close his eyes. I retreat to the body of my senior man and repeat this act before running to the Yukon and leaping in the passenger side, with Billie already behind the wheel. She accepts the keys, fires up the engine, and we're careening down the road. In the headlights, I spot a bike set against an oak tree, recognizing Billie's triathlon cycle. Rachel and Elena finish buckling into the seats behind us as Billie reaches the bottom of the hill.

"Let's turn right," I say, "back to the inn."

She does so and accelerates.

Not the most technically savvy, I've nonetheless been offered "in case of emergency" instructions from my detail, and I put some of this to use now, selecting the emergency-call feature from the cell phone I fished from my junior man's pocket. I enter the number from memory of the letter-writer's answering service.

"Me again," I say after the beep. "I found the place where the people from the photographs are staying. I found Rachel. I have her. Rachel and Elena. Rachel's husband was killed some time ago. Rachel and Elena are okay, but — the people from the pictures . . . they're dead. So are two Secret

Service agents. I'm not sure what will happen now." I hesitate, then say, "Also, I apologize for not necessarily believing you previously."

I hang up and turn off the phone. It occurs to me my message might be too late. If either the Redhead or one of the Brunettes reported to their superiors that the shit had hit the fan — if word got through to the people from whom Rachel's mother was trying to protect herself — then the letter-writer may be in worse danger than before she made the mistake of recruiting me to help. But there's nothing more I can do about that besides the message I just left, and we've got our own predicament at the moment.

Rachel's voice comes to me from the back seat.

"Thank you," she says. "Thank you, thank you, thank you."

"You okay?" I say, and it sounds ridiculous to me as I say it — she's been in captivity for six months. Behind the lawn-mowing equipment. Under the garage. She's not the least bit okay.

"I'm fine. How could I not be feeling fine? I'm out. I'm out." She breathes heavily, a series of consecutive sighs. "Feels good to be on a road. In a car."

She opens her window. Tilts her head into the wind. With a glance I note that Billie is wisely keeping our speed at 55 mph.

Rachel pulls her head back in.

"I need to ask you something," she says. Her tone sounds oddly firm and serious, coming as it is in mismatched form with her relief. "I've been in that room since New Year's Eve. Am I right that it's June 18th?"

"Yes."

"My daughter and I are in your debt in ways I'll never be able to truly express. But there's something — "

When her extended pause doesn't conclude, I turn.

"What is it?"

"You mentioned my mother," Rachel says. "That she sent you clues. And you just left a message for her. Right?"

"Yes."

"Then I don't understand."

"She started with a note," I say, starting in, "asking for my help. She clearly had an idea about the general vicinity where they were holding you — "

"But you keep saying it was my mother."

"Right," I say. "In the first letters, she — "

"It's not her."

Billie gives me a funny look from behind the wheel.

"It's not — ?" I say. "You're sure? She sent me more than one — "

"Of course I'm sure," Rachel says.

Road noise overtakes the car for the shortest of moments; then Elena's high-pitched, no-nonsense voice pipes in from beside her mother.

"Grandma's in heaven with daddy," she says.

Rachel looks at Elena, smiles thinly at her daughter, then returns her gaze to me. "It wasn't my mother sending you letters," she says. "It wasn't her you were leaving a message for. My mother passed away nearly twenty years ago."

Mostly I am made to feel like a young woman working
low on the totem pole of men's power circles.

CLEARLY I WAS THE ONE who jumped to conclusions — but just as clearly, the letter-writer was playing games, *wanting* me to think he was Rachel's mother. If he is, in fact, a man. Could still be a woman – though clearly not Rachel's biological mother.

"Do you have a stepmother?" I say.

"No."

The letter-writer referred to Rachel as his daughter. Unless that too was a lie, my next question is obvious. "What about your father? Could the messages have come from him?"

"What does it matter where they came from?" Rachel says. "Shouldn't we be calling the police? Or going there?"

"I don't think that's a good idea," I say. "Not that simply, anyway. I'll explain — but let's come back to your father. Do you think he might have reached out to me?"

"I suppose it's possible," she says.

"Who is he?" I say. "Where does he work? How can we reach him?"

"He's never told me."

"Does he work in government? Might he be CIA? State Department? EPA?"

"I've never spoken to him. Never seen him. I don't know who he is." She shakes her head, the creases in her brow beginning to look angry. "He was married, and I don't mean to my mother. When my mother was alive, she got checks from him — or from a numbered account we knew came from him. Once she died, *I* got the checks. I still do. My mother told me he was an influential man, but she never told me who he was. Why not go to the police?"

"The people who were holding you work for the federal government," I say. "Their superiors wanted the man or woman who claimed to be your mother — and who summoned me — to keep quiet. About what, I've no idea, but they wanted control of that person, and you were the leverage." I feel more than see Billie watching me. "These people have connections to the police. They may even have control over them."

"*That's* why I was kidnapped? Why my husband was killed? For *leverage*? Leverage over *what*?"

"I don't know," I say. "But six federal agents are now dead, and with your escape, your jailers' superiors no longer have the leverage your abduction gave them. This creates a predicament. Power brokers facing loss of their power are volatile. Our decision on how to handle this — including how to keep you and Elena safe — will need to allow for the likelihood that whoever engineered your abduction will now be prepared to take more extreme steps."

I find myself wanting blood from whoever ordered Rachel's kidnapping. While I'm feeling responsible thanks to my bike ride up Nuns Canyon Road, the rational part of my brain knows that accountability for the murder of Rachel's husband and half a dozen federal agents lies upon the head of the person or persons who arranged to have Rachel and Elena abducted.

Air strikes — I want air strikes.

It's true I may have needed something to break away from my routine. But clearly, following every step of the letter-writer's Easter-egg hunt and cycling up Nuns Canyon Road weren't exactly the most prudent means of doing so. But in riding up that hill, I got my answer: Redhead and the Three Brunettes weren't keeping a witness in federal custody. I wasn't just a blind mule, and Billie, my late Secret Service agents, and I have just rescued an abducted mother and child.

But good people, government servants, died in this cause. And there will now be hornets stirred to action in the nest we've just taken a flame-thrower to.

It occurs to me now, in this freshly unretired state — foolhardy actions and their consequences notwithstanding — that if I can get Rachel, Elena, and Billie to a secure place, it should be possible to devise a plan that would protect them from the hornets. I can worry about torching the hive later.

We round a bend and the splash of color that is the Mango Tree Inn appears ahead on the right.

"Pull in," I say. "We'll switch the Yukon for your Prius. No matter what we do next, we don't need a Secret Service transmitter broadcasting our location."

Billie brakes and turns us into the lot, which remains empty save her car. I deposit my agent's cell phone in the glove box of the Yukon and help Rachel hustle Elena into the back of the Prius. Billie punches its starter and pulls us out of the inn's lot, turning right. She floors the accelerator, the tiny hybrid engine kicking in over the battery power.

"Where are we going?" Rachel says, anxiety now audible in her tone. I know I'm the one causing the anxiety, and I don't feel good about it. But I need a minute or two, or a thousand, to figure this out. And hiding her away — again — may be a necessity in ensuring her safety. She might just have to remain somewhat anxious.

"Same question from me," Billie says. "Where exactly *are* we headed, Mr. President?"

"I'm going to have to come back to you on that," I say.

Billie catches Rachel's eyes in the rear-view mirror and lifts her shoulders in a sort of shrug. As she does this, something seems to be conveyed between them, and I know that in her way, Billie has just bought me some time.

Putting the time to use, I pull my little black book from my pocket, turn on the interior light, and begin scanning the frayed pages.

PART II:

THE ASSASSINATION

-20-

I N ANDERSON VALLEY, A PICTURESQUE stretch of Mendocino County an hour north of Kenwood, I made one of the labor-for-lodging trades of my long, strange trip. In exchange for fourteen hours a day helping my former NASA Administrator, Bob Hansen, plant an apple orchard and construct stone walls around the perimeter of his land, I got the benefit of a cot, space heater, and an excellent home-cooked dinner each night. In our week of side-by-side agricultural labor, I came to know Bob far better than I'd known him as an executive in my administration. I like the man I got to know.

Verifying Bob and Gloria Hansen's address in my little black book, I direct Billie north on Highway 101 to Cloverdale, then west on Highway 128, up and over the back of the coastal mountain range.

The Hansens have clearly improved their lot in life since our last encounter. As Billie turns off the highway onto their property, we're braced by stone walls, palm trees, and a wooden archway, the whole layout illuminated by upward-facing lights that give the impression of a tropical resort. A cast-iron plate cemented into the wall near the archway says Hansen Orchards. None of these accoutrements was here when I last visited, and from the look of the deer fencing that stretches out of sight in both directions, Bob and Gloria have acquired significantly more land.

Olive trees line the middle portion of the gently curving driveway which dead-ends at a large Victorian house. Within the open garage sits a rusting, vintage Chevy Suburban I remember Bob using during my stay here. No one's in sight. I climb from the car, tugging at the Sponge Bob baseball cap Billie bought for me at a 7-Eleven in hopes it would fend off recognition.

I peer into the garage, around its side to the porch facing the property out back. I'm debating whether to climb the porch and knock on the door when the crunch of boot on gravel comes suddenly from behind.

"Be damned if it isn't my old hired hand — come back to seek his cut."

I turn to see Bob Hansen materialize from the garage. He wears jeans, boots, a thick plaid shirt, and a San Francisco Giants baseball cap. Even in the dim light, I can see that Bob's cheekbones and forehead are tanned almost to ebony, his eyebrows singed to gray. He's as sinewy as a hyena. Bob once aspired to be an astronaut, got disqualified by a vision problem, and spent the next twenty years overseeing various facets of the country's space program to make up for it, ultimately running the entire deal. As a scientist and bureaucrat, he'd developed one of the palest complexions I've ever seen.

No longer.

"There a cut to be had?" I say.

"What's it look like to you?"

Not only has the property ballooned, the driveway and entrance expanded, but the house is particularly superior to the double-wide they inhabited at last visit. "If I do have a cut," I say, "it looks as if I'm rich."

Bob's hands emerge from his gloves and we shake.

"It is as much an honor to see you, Mr. President," he says, "as the first time we met."

"First time around I was hitchhiking on the Pacific Coast Highway and hadn't showered in a week. This time," I say, "well, let's just say that things are a little more complicated. So I'd say you're doubly illusioned, but I appreciate you."

Bob glances at the Prius. Rachel's, Billie's, and Elena's eyes peer back.

"I assume they've got something to do with the complicated part," he says. "You and your friends hungry?"

"Me, not so much," I say, "but I can tell you that at least two of the people in that car are literally starved for a home-cooked meal."

Bob cocks his arm and checks his watch. "Been a couple hours since Gloria cleared the table, but she made enough of that casserole to feed twenty. And I don't need to remind you who it is she believes to have been the greatest president in our country's history."

"She may not feel that way much longer," I say, and wave to Billie and Rachel to come on out of the car.

-21-

BILLIE AND I WALK BETWEEN apple trees in an orchard row that appears to stretch to infinity under the moon. Our forearms brush every three or four steps. My pulse quickens a hair each time this happens.

Rachel and her daughter are asleep in one of the upstairs guest bedrooms. The house is just visible some two hundred yards behind us.

"You followed me up Nuns Canyon Road," I say between arm-brushes. "Which means you followed me from the inn. Which means that you probably weren't asleep in the first place."

She's silent for a few steps, then says, "I had the feeling you were up to no good when you tiptoed out of my room. Once you rode off, I had a pretty good idea where you were headed, and I didn't think you should be doing it alone. I waited until your Secret Service team pulled out, then followed a decent way back. I've rarely ridden so slowly." She smiles.

"Thanks."

We let one of the forearm-brushes linger.

"By the time I climbed the hill," she says, "you were nowhere in sight. The Yukon was empty. I think your agents saw me approach, but I was keeping my distance. Which almost backfired. I was far enough away so that I couldn't tell what was happening at first."

"You were there when the lights came on?"

"Yes. Once they did and the yelling started, I moved closer. But I was fifty yards away, if not more. By the time I got through the trees to the lawn, it was all but over. In fact it *was* over. After the firefight I saw you through the window, and a second later I saw the guy behind you hit the back of your neck with a small bar. He dragged you around to the garage. He came back to the house for the keys, unlocked the garage doors, and without realizing it, showed me the way down to Rachel's room by taking you there. The Honda Civic you saw in the driveway when we emerged was parked in the garage at that point — he backed it out, pulled open a steel plate the car was hiding, and carried you down the stairwell."

We U-turn and start back down a second orchard row.

"Once he took you down," she says, "I knew it was the only chance I'd have. It was either call the authorities, which I hadn't yet decided was the right call given your determination to keep things under wraps — or do something then and there."

"Well you certainly did something then and there," I say.

"I borrowed one of your agents' guns — the one in the doorway of the barn. By the time I came around to the garage, there this guy was, his head and shoulders emerging from the secret stairwell. He saw me in the same moment I saw him. At that point there wasn't a choice. I'm lucky his gun started in its holster, even luckier that two of my shots hit him. I'm pretty sure it was the last four bullets in your agent's clip."

"You'd hold your own as a Secret Service agent," I say. "Unfortunately, I nearly got you killed, and I *did* get my two agents killed. Bringing the three of you along in my blind ambition to solve the letter-writer's predicament — whoever he or she may be."

She gives me a look I can't read in the dim moonlight and we walk silently for a moment, my mind replaying the entire episode, a stark contrast of horror and cacophony against the peaceful, electric sensation of our moonlight stroll.

"And Rachel's," Billie says, "and Elena's. You solved their predicament too."

"We did," I say, "And the true fault lays with whoever ordered Rachel's kidnapping. The rational part of me knows that, but I goddamn well wish there'd have been another way to achieve the same end."

We're silent for another twenty yards, but then I make a decision.

"Nobody will know those shots came from you," I say. "Nobody will know you were there. You saved my life, and for that and a few other reasons, you've got me in your corner for whatever's left of my existence. But this is my affair. It's my fault for pulling you into it in the first place, and these are polluted waters of the sort I've seen and navigated before. I don't want you in them. I'll handle the rest. No argument. No discussion."

I've hit these last points to preempt what I know would be her head-strong standard objection to protection by or from me or, for that matter, probably from anyone. To seal the preemptive strike, I turn and pull her to me. It takes a moment of stiffness — Billie still operating in full objec-tion-mode — but then she relents and wraps her arms around my ribcage. I feel her lithe, narrow strength, a sensation I'd imagine experiencing were I to have cradled a golden eagle in my arms.

"Okay?" I say.

She mumbles something into my shirt, which I'm not able to discern, other than to narrow it down to either, "You're right," or "Bullshit."

No matter — I've made my decision, and I'm sticking to it.

Unmoving, we stand there, holding our embrace in the cool, moon-lit night.

-22-

AFTER A BRIEF HUNT THROUGH a desk in the hallway, I'm able to find the two strategic decision-making implements I've typically used to solve strategy challenges, big and small: a pencil and a pad of paper. Billie's asleep on the bed, or so it seems. Turning off the overhead light, I click on the desk lamp at the bedroom's small table and set myself in the chair.

This was been my preferred means of cutting through the seemingly infinite clutter to focus on the decisions at hand. I heard that 40 did it before his mind went, and I figured if it worked for him, it could work for me. As Reagan did, I begin by jotting down random thoughts on the pad as they come to me, advance to jotting down the key words representing the predicament, break the circumstances into columns, then adapt the columns to however many possible scenarios I'm faced with in making the decision at hand — a technique no different from one your average college applicant might use to decide on her school of choice.

I don't know the identity of the letter-writer. For the moment, reaching him, or her, isn't an option, other than to leave additional voice messages on the number provided in the Bible. But if I were able to determine who he or she is —

I write the words from that first plea for help.

You probably won't remember, but while you were in office, we met. It was only once, but in that one meeting, I remember sensing that I could trust you.

There are thousands, maybe a *hundred* thousand people I met *once* — all possessed of the kind of influence that seems to belong to Rachel's father, assuming the parent-daughter part to be true. Powerful, working in government circles, probably wealthy... could be a congressman, or a governor. I met a lot of *them* once.

I write *politician.*

Once, I think, scrawling this word — which *politician* did I meet *once?* The faces come and go. I write as many names as I can think of — politicians and officials of influence — but I can't settle on any that mean anything special. Next I write some obvious points for momentum's sake: *Shootout, rescue, deaths.* I follow these with *Secret Service,* then get going on a column:

The kidnappers are federal agents.

The federal agents were sent by their superiors.

Top feds.

The top feds did all this to keep the letter-writer quiet.

The top feds have something to hide.

I need to find what the feds are hiding.

I ponder and review this column before moving to the right and starting another one:

Deaths of federal agents.

Hide Billie's involvement.

My involvement = impossible to hide.

I'm going to need help.

My head dips. I blink myself awake, read through my composition, lean back, consider for a while what has been tugging at me, then come back to the page. I look down and see that the last line I wrote is barely legible, trailing off absently as I started dozing off while writing it.

I write it again:

Going to need help.

-23-

I JUMP AT THE KNOCK ON the door.

Per the alarm clock on the bedside table, it's 4:49 a.m. as Bob Hansen leans in through the half-open bedroom door to follow his knock.

"Mr. President?" he says. "Sorry to wake you, but we've got a problem."

"What kind," I say.

Billie's head rises from her pillow, eyes coming awake. Bob nods grimly. "Come downstairs and have a look."

Rachel — likely not the deepest of sleepers for the moment — is already out in the hallway ahead of us and joins our procession downstairs. The family room TV flickers as we gather around it.

"Saw it while making my coffee," Bob says.

The television is tuned to CNN. The ticker across the bottom of the screen declares there is **BREAKING NEWS**.

"You're going to want to watch the whole rotation."

My eyes rivet to the words summarizing the story, seared in block letters across the space below the breaking news slug. As I see the words, I feel immediate clarity.

Immediate, terrifying clarity.

The ticker headline reads:

ASSASSINATION ATTEMPT ON PRESIDENT WALKER

Anderson Cooper's head-and-shoulders close-up holds court in the CNN studio, and, in concert with the breaking-news headline, his words take my midnight musings and offer a single, hard-and-fast answer as to the letter-writer's identity.

"For those of you just joining," Cooper says, "there has been an attempted assassination of the President of the United States in our nation's capital. President Walker's exact condition is not known at this time. We'll now go to video of the incident, where the news media was present covering the president's departure from a Democratic fund-raiser. The event concluded just after one o'clock eastern time early this morning. That is when the president was exiting the building — "

A broad stretch of marble stairs plays host to the president and first lady, flanked by a handful of suited-up cabinet members and Secret Service types as they descend to the sidewalk outside the venue, which I recognize as the Katzen Arts Center, a place I too have held fund-raisers. Andrew Reginald Walker, the President of the United States, is a man with nearly as bad a reputation as mine, though for entirely different reasons. In the news footage, he separates from his wife, descends the last few stairs, and touches down on the sidewalk.

Andrew Reginald Walker is a politician I met only once.

I recall the meeting with intense precision: he was the senior Democratic senator from Alabama; I was the Republican commander-in-chief. Even then Walker was known as a ladies' man, but the press spared him the grief it affixed to 42 like a suction cup. Maybe it's because Walker has never denied his rampant womanizing.

We held that meeting over lunch, negotiating the resolution of a bill, but Katie arrived and cut our dialogue short. There was something about Katie's mother — my help was needed. I asked Senator Walker if he wouldn't object to finishing our discussion another time, and I remember he appeared shocked — maybe even impressed — that I would allow family to come first. This, despite my reputation as a workaholic with virtually no time for family matters. I remember his words, coming in a trademark Alabama drawl he was always busy tweaking toward a Texas twang.

"Hell, sure, partner."

It might have left him feeling the way the letter-writer felt:

`It was only once, but in that one meeting, I remember sensing that I could trust you.`

We finished our business on the phone the following day. And something else occurs to me about one of the letter-writer's lines:

`I recently began a job in Washington. It's a position I've held before.`

True, the role of the President of the United States of America wouldn't normally be referred to as a job. But if you were the one in the role, you might call it that. And Walker just began his second term in January.

A position he's held before.

In the newscast footage, Walker approaches his limo, waving to onlookers, when chaos is suddenly unleashed. It happens all at once, actions and reactions bleeding into one: two gunshots sound out. Walker grasps his left shoulder and topples forward. Secret Service agents seize and usher him into the waiting limo. People duck, run, fall, scream. The camera taping the action bounces, wiggles, then drops lens-first to the sidewalk, slammed there, I'm guessing, by a Secret Service agent. The camera lifts again, the view partially obscured by the damage done to the lens, as the limo speeds off and the remaining Secret Service personnel secure the scene.

The footage re-starts in a B-roll loop as Anderson Cooper continues.

"The White House issued a two-line statement, saying that the president has been taken to an undisclosed location and remains in critical condition under intensive care. The statement also said that while the president is hospitalized, power has been ceded to the vice president, in order to, quote, 'ensure that the proper authority and leadership of the country are maintained during this crisis and the president's pending recovery.' It is not yet apparent whether there are any suspects or whether anyone is in custody related to the shooting. President Andrew Walker, in critical condition at this hour."

"Jesus," Billie says.

I turn to Rachel.

"That's him," I say.

She looks at me with that creased hardness to her forehead. "That's — who?"

"The president," I say. "He's your father."

She eyes me sharply – then starts talking too soon and too fast to have taken it in. "*Walker*?" She's shaking her head. "All due respect to a man who's just been shot, you're telling me that philandering, racist, violence-inciting, autocratic jackass — one of the worst presidents in our history — is my *father*?"

"When we took you and Elena out of that subterranean room, we took away the leverage the kidnapping group held on him," I say. "A leverage he didn't know they'd lost — not until he'd have retrieved my second message on the machine. But *they* knew. I'd guess they had security cameras, or alarm sensors, or got a text from Redhead or one of the Brunettes — something that told them what happened. They shot him at one a.m. Eastern, ten p.m. Pacific, or about an hour after our fracas at the farmhouse. At most. Just enough time for word to get back that the leverage had been lost."

"Hate to put it this way, Mr. President," Bob says, "but you'd better keep watching. You ain't seen nothing yet."

Cooper is wrapping a Q&A with a panel of medical experts on Walker's potential prognosis. The split-screen switches full to the anchor again. "Next, in a bizarre turn of events," he says, "comes significant presidential news of another kind."

Cooper's face then cuts to a waist-cropped version of the infamous photograph of the nation's most embarrassing ex-leader — yours truly, emerging from that smokehouse in nothing but the necklace.

The photo transitions to video of the Mango Tree Inn. Multiple local and federal law-enforcement vehicles and yellow crime tape gaudily garnish the once-tranquil B&B.

"Known as much for his antics following his time in office as for his single term as president, the man the media once tabbed 'The Bohemian' has now been named as the chief suspect in a grisly double-murder in bucolic Sonoma County, California," Cooper says.

The previous headline at the bottom of the screen has now given way to a new one:

BOHEMIAN RAMPAGE

"Oh, boy," Billie says.

"According to the Sonoma County Sheriff's Department, the former president, who is now missing, is a 'person of interest' in the Sheriff's Department's investigation into the murder of a husband and wife residing in Sonoma County," Cooper says. "The victims were residents of Glen Ellen, just north of Sonoma. The woman was apparently staying at the bed & breakfast you're seeing in these pictures. An anonymous member of the sheriff's department tells CNN that there is already evidence linking the former president to the victims' room at the bed & breakfast."

Pleasant-looking pictures of Redhead and Brunette number one are put up alongside each other. They look like a yuppie couple. Not particularly like kidnappers or federal agents.

"Is it possible 'The Bohemian' murdered this couple in a fit of jealous rage? That is what authorities are saying the evidence allegedly implies. The explanation is not clear, but a couple is dead today, possibly by the hand of a former president. On this, a day already marred by the shooting of — "

"Turn it off," I say. "Just turn it off."

Bob complies and the room falls silent.

Upstairs, I knew I'd need some help, but as my eyes were closing I hadn't yet determined from whom that help should come. Standing solemnly in my old friend's family room, there remains no need for pad and pencil to decide who I'll need to move to the top of the list.

Having just been hit with the need felt by every newly charged murder suspect, former president or no, my choice and need are clear.

Time to call my lawyer.

-24-

A COMMON MISPERCEPTION ABOUT THE 747-200Bs that transport the American president is that the planes themselves are called Air Force One. In fact, any aircraft carrying the current President of the United States uses the call sign Air Force One at the time the president is on board. Hang glider, Cessna, Gulfstream, 747 White Houses-in-the-sky — doesn't matter: if the chief executive is on the aircraft, it's Air Force One.

At the moment there are three jets in the primary White House fleet: the pair of modified Boeing 747-200Bs, called VC-25As or SAM (Special Air Mission) 28000 and 29000, based on their tail numbers; and a single C-32, a custom Boeing 757-200, designated primarily for vice presidential travel. The three jets are part of the 89th Airlift Wing and are housed at Andrews Air Force Base in Maryland.

Though Reagan never flew in them as president, the bigger VC-25As were his doing, inclusive of American Southwest-flavored interiors chosen by first lady Nancy. Boeing ran late on delivery, so that 41, George H. W. Bush, was actually the first president to travel in them. Until then a C-137 Stratoliner — a customized, long-range Boeing 707 — did the trick. 35, John F. Kennedy, ordered the first C-137 in 1962 — tail number 26000 — and a newer C-137 — tail number 27000 — which came into service for 37, Richard M. Nixon, and remained the primary aircraft in the fleet until the twin VC-25As arrived at Andrews for duty.

Behemoths with 4,000 square feet of interior space, hardened command-and-control electronics, armaments that include flares, countermeasures, and a few classified offensive weapons of their own, the VC-25As are essentially luxury versions of an airborne aircraft carrier. Inside, the planes are equipped with a complete "residence" for the president, an airborne Oval Office, Situation Room, and secondary office cubicles; quarters for senior staff, a medical annex in which surgery has in fact been performed, a kitchen with enough capacity to serve a hundred; plus additional seating for staff, press, and other guests. A doctor, nurse, chef, Secret Service team, and cockpit and cabin crew always fly with the aircraft.

Further, when the president travels aboard a VC-25A, the plane is never alone: escorted by F-16s as the guardians, the Boeing is often preceded by a convoy of cargo planes delivering today's customized roster of security equipment the president would never leave home without. No Secret Service advance-team leader in his right mind would rely on, say, the Pakistani government to provide limos and Humvees for local transportation. The president travels with his own motorcade.

The jets cost $325 million apiece in Reagan's era — a relative bargain, with the tab for the latest order for a refresh breaking $2 billion per plane.

The front half of the main deck of the VC-25A is considered the mobile White House, with the seating and quarters for staff laid out directly behind the office section, the press and other cabins set farther aft. There is an unwritten rule that applies to all seating assignments aboard Air Force One: you may change seats or move around to hold discussions with other passengers aboard the plane at will, but only backward from your assigned place. Like the rule on commercial flights requiring passengers to use restrooms in only their respective cabins, the Air Force One hierarchy serves both a functional and a security purpose and has been honored religiously for decades.

Which meant, on a VC-25A flight to Europe during my third year in office, when White House Counsel Miles H. Glinn crashed a meeting in the airborne Situation Room, he was met with deadpan looks and vaguely shocked silence from the pair of men seated with me at the conference table. Workaholic that I was, I always brought as many cabinet members as possible along on flights — I had them captive, perfect for banging out meetings and making decisions around the clock. The meeting Miles had just crashed, 36,000 feet above the Atlantic, included my Secretary of Defense and Director of Central Intelligence.

"Heard the three of you were in here," Miles said. Receding hairline disguised by a clean-shaven head, Miles was, as usual, extremely expensively attired in a three-piece, pin-striped suit. A pin supported the knot in his red tie and a handkerchief protruded from his lapel pocket. He'd come equipped with his usual accordioned satchel.

"We need to talk," he said, then settled in at one of the seats at the table as the others' eyes roved to me. Miles was known to regularly insinuate himself, uninvited, into White House meetings — but this was Air Force One. You just didn't do it here.

"Tell you what, Miles," I said. "Why don't you just go ahead and ignore protocol, leave your assigned seat, and barge in on this private meeting."

Ignoring me, he pulled out a short stack of papers and set them on the table. One of the on-board Bozo detail had quietly followed Miles in and eyed me now from the doorway. I rolled my eyes and shrugged and the agent nodded and ducked out. Miles deposited his satchel on the vacant chair to his left, planted his elbows on the table, and eyed us one by one.

"The three of you have done a good job of ducking me these past two weeks," he said, "but the jig is up. In the end, you weren't able to avoid the media." Taking the top sheet of paper from his stack, he turned it face-up and pushed it over to me. "A Lebanese newspaper has just run a story on our, and I quote, 'arms-for-hostages deal.'"

"Well, shit," I said.

"I echo that sentiment," the Secretary of Defense said.

"How *a propos*," Miles said, "since that is about what you've now stepped in."

I glanced over the translation of the article and passed it to the Secretary of Defense, who did the same before passing it to the DCI.

"Do you think we're in danger of this getting out wide?" I said.

"Already happened," Miles said. "AP, UPI, Reuters all picked it up." He withdrew a bound report and flipped it to me. "I do appreciate the way you've kept me out of the loop on this scheme, which you were right to do, and I'm not disparaging said scheme in the slightest. But you'll now need my help paddling out of the creek, lest the American public froth themselves into a fervor that sees you impeached, sir."

"Crap," the DCI said on completing his read of the article.

I picked up Miles's binder and started reading it.

"Though you've kept me out of meetings and, as far as I've been able to determine, been *fairly* effective, though not wholly so, at keeping written documentation to a minimum," Miles said, "by the time this plane lands, you are going to have both houses of Congress, the global news media, and the entire American public up your ass. There's a decent chance your presidency may effectively be over."

The Secretary of Defense was watching Miles as closely as I was, and for good reason.

"Unless, of course," Miles continued, "you're prepared to undertake certain steps, and I mean immediately. May I simplify what you're reading?"

I set down the binder and eyed him. Miles Glinn and I became close in law school; he was my natural choice for the White House Counsel job partly on account of our friendship, but mostly due to the fact that he finished top of our class and had become one of the leading criminal defense lawyers in the nation. He had since emerged as my administration's primary fix-it man. As caustic as his manner was, I suspected that today's solution was fully vetted and as tailor-made as his suit.

"Simplify away," I said.

"Just so we all understand the entirety of the circumstances," he said, "a brief walk-through. The seven American hostages recently seized in Syria are currently being held by either Hezbollah, or a terrorist organization over which Hezbollah is known to have influence. We — the United States — currently have a trade-and-weapons embargo on Syria, enacted by the U.S. Senate and signed by you, Mr. President. Separately, in Central America, we are obsessed with pestering the communist regime in El Salvador through the arming of the counter-revolutionary *junta* that seeks to win a second coup and seize power. However, the Bradley bill, which you also recently signed — against the threat of an override by both Houses had you vetoed — outlaws any provision by the U.S. government of military arms or aid to the Salvadoran opposition."

"Yes, go on," I said.

"The ingenious plan devised by the Secretary here, which you privately lauded and approved, was, and is still, very close to effectively killing both birds with its one stone. Arms have been provided to Hezbollah on negotiated terms to free the hostages. The arms were sent by Saudi Arabia, who is separately buying incremental arms from us, with incremental money we've given them as part of a military aid package. The undeclared surplus dollars with which the Saudis bought the arms were in turn wired three days ago through a set of shell organizations to our Salvadoran allies. We expect the hostages will be released within days, and our friends in El Salvador — not the U.S. Congress's friends, mind you, but the administration's — are duly funded. Great plan, right?"

"Right," I said carefully.

"Wrong. Instead, it is a plan you had absolutely no knowledge of," Miles says. "And unfortunately, the shell organizations funneling the money to El Salvador handle their commerce out of Syria, and not particularly securely, it turns out. Therefore not one but two international agreements of which we are signatory have now been violated, and our involvement in these violations exposed. In view of this plan's diabolical secrecy and illegality, its perpetrators must be unearthed and justice served on behalf of the American people."

The Secretary of Defense was getting nervous. "Now, wait," he said, but Miles interrupted.

"Don't worry, Gene, you'll be safe. But we will need a scapegoat, and I've chosen the appropriate man, as covered in that strategy binder. Lt. Col. Whitford Sealy will be the fall guy here."

My turn. "Now hold on — "

But Miles interrupted me too. "Yes, he conducted a brilliant hostage rescue last year. His promotion to the El Salvador Task Force was well earned. But you will come to find, and announce these findings accordingly, that he went off-rez, doing an end-around against the edict of the American people, in his brokering of this Syria-Salvador affair. Right? All of which, Mr. President," Miles said, more loudly now so as to tamp down the looming objections from the rest of us, "you will state in the second of two press conferences you will hold in the coming three days. Conference one: 'I didn't know this was going on and I'm going to get to the bottom of it.' Conference two: 'I got to the bottom of it, and here are the facts.' The American public will be pissed, briefly distrustful of you and your administration, but your presidency will survive."

Leaning back in my chair, I eyed Miles, pondering this strategy.

"The hostages will still go free," I said, "and the funding already sent to El Salvador will probably remain. The problem being that Whit Sealy, a good man, in getting axed, will probably be indicted too — and likely get stuck doing time."

Miles waved a dismissive hand.

"I'll keep him out of jail," he said, "and you'll pardon him on the last day of your term. Sealy will be famous — he'll write a book in a few years and be rich. Oh, and one other note: all three of you will need to shred and delete a volume of correspondence, which is technically illegal but also nearly impossible to track if done properly. I will give you instructions on how to do so. Are we in agreement?"

With little pause from any in the room, I garnered the glances of assent from the DCI and Secretary of Defense, faced Miles, and nodded.

"Agreed," I said, then reached for a button on the underside of the table that summoned the Secret Service man outside the door. "Now get the hell out of this meeting and back to your seat, Counselor."

"As you wish, Mr. President."

-25-

I REACH MILES GLINN FROM A burner cell phone we've just bought from a general store in Boonville, twenty minutes west of Hansen Orchards. Bob has loaned Billie his Subaru Outback for the chauffeuring duties, and I'm making the call from the back seat, dipped below the window line and fully accessible to some blankets and miscellaneous paraphernalia in the hatchback were I to need to hide from prying eyes. Billie pulls into a gravel service road at the edge of town once she hears I've made the connection.

The offices of Glinn & Willis, the firm Miles started once he resigned from my administration, consume two floors of the Transamerica building in downtown San Francisco, but Miles now works out of his home in Tiburon, in Marin County. There's a number I know to use to reach him — he made me memorize it years ago. It connects to a 24-hour phone service, and is a number that will always get him.

"Frank Potus for Miles," I say when a woman answers, "Service."

My words reflect a longstanding though not too inventive code of ours: Frank for Former, POTUS for the obvious.

"One moment."

Classical music plays on the line before I hear a double-beep, then Miles's voice.

"Well," he says.

"Yes," I say. "I haven't sat in front of a television for a couple hours. It getting uglier?"

"By the minute."

"I'd like to talk," I say, "and I'd like to do it today. But doing so on the phone probably isn't a good idea."

In addition to his former role as Mr. Fix-it, Miles has, ever since, advised me to be more cautious than I've generally chosen to be, and has therefore had frequent occasion on which to gloat. He's never actually said "I told you so," but his tone usually implies he's thinking those very words. Today he sounds a little stiff, leaving the gloating for another time.

"Probably not," he says.

I've given some thought to where we should meet and how to say it.

"Maybe we could take another one of those trips we've enjoyed," I say. "No need for any voyage."

A short silence is eclipsed by his answer.

"I'm glad you stuck to your day job," he says, "passing up the opportunity to work as a secret agent. It probably would not have worked out. That said, I am available at your convenience."

Despite his generally snooty attitude, there has never been any question with Miles: he is always available at my convenience. He is loyal to the bone.

I check my watch, in no mood for jokes.

"I'd rather it be sooner, but my preference is to meet after dark," I say. "Nine-thirty work?"

"See you there."

-26-

Miles owns a large Chris Craft. He uses it mostly to take friends fishing, keeping it moored in a small marina on a canal in the northernmost corner of Tiburon. I imagine the amount he pays in monthly rent for the marina space rivals what most Wall Street bond traders pay toward the mortgage on their home.

Over the years he's taken me out four or five times to troll for salmon, but my cryptic words on the call were meant to suggest we meet on his boat, dockside. Not wanting any surprises at the marina, we've arrived early enough to survey his house before Miles leaves for the meeting. The sun has just set.

Double-checking the address in my journal, I point out an open spot across the street and Billie parallel-parks. According to the clock on the dash, we've got forty minutes — by the time Miles pulls out to head for the boat, we ought to be able to determine whether anyone else is keeping an eye on him.

Thirty minutes pass uneventfully.

It's a narrow street, with parking allowed only on the inland curb. On the side where the homes perch on the hill, short driveways lead to garages and carports. They look mostly like one-story dwellings, but their façades are deceptive. Reaching out and down from the steep hill, most of these places are two or three stories tall, with views to the bay, bridge, and skyline from every floor.

A car passes every five or ten minutes, sometimes slipping into a parking place or vanishing behind a garage door, but mostly driving on down the street and out of sight. We've taken one of the last available spots out on the street.

Ten minutes before we're supposed to meet, I start to worry. Miles always arrives early. He drives a BMW 7-series, and the car has been parked in his carport since our arrival. He could have summoned an Uber or limo and gone early, but Miles loves to drive his own expensive rides. I've been expecting him to open the gate to his courtyard, climb into the Beemer, and speed off down the hill to the boat dock well before now.

Another five minutes tick by with no activity.

"Let's head for the dock," I say.

Billie pulls us out and we find a spot behind the marina six minutes later. We argue briefly about my desire to go alone, with Billie insisting on following a short distance behind.

My latest security detail.

There's a shared walkway between two buildings that takes you out to the marina along the canal. I get out of the car and slip down the path. Nobody intercepts me. The marina is quiet, empty of people, active only in the lapping sound of small waves against numerous hulls and the yellowish wash of overhead safety lights.

I know the code for the gate and enter it on the pad, leaving the gate propped slightly for Billie. It's maybe forty steps to Miles's boat. The cross-hatched dock and its resident boats, including my lawyer's, are as dark and quiet as the path between buildings.

I hop aboard the Chris Craft and poke around. The cabin door is locked and the deck empty — not a soul. I find a place to sit in shadow, out of range of the dock's overhead safety lights, and wait there. Ten, twenty, thirty minutes pass. I can't see Billie in whatever shadowy hiding place she's chosen to keep an eye on me. In fact, I see nothing of note for the entire thirty minutes.

Nobody shows.

At the forty-minute mark, we head back to the car and return to Miles's townhouse. Billie finds a miracle spot maybe two hundred yards uphill from the house and parallel-parks for a second time. The Beemer still occupies the carport.

We were going to meet over an hour ago now.

"I'm going over to the house," I say.

"I don't think that's the best idea," Billie says, but I'm already out of the car and walking. I hear her exit the vehicle, but she doesn't cross the street at my pace, still keeping her distance like she did down at the dock.

Miles's car is empty. His gate is locked.

Unaware of the code for his home, I hit the # sign on the keypad of the intercom. An intermittent buzz sounds repeatedly before Miles's answering machine picks up and his recorded voice asks me to leave a message. I punch the # and * keys in random succession until I succeed in disconnecting the line.

Feeling exposed, I sweep my eyes up and down the road, finding the coast clear outside of a lithe, shadowy figure with a tuft of short blonde hair standing between parked cars across the street.

I reach up, do a kind of pull-up, find a foothold, push myself higher, and swing a leg over the top of the five-foot-high steel gate. I reach for but fail to find any way to support my foot on the other side, rotate my hip, slip, feel myself fall, partially recover, but still manage to tweak my right ankle as I hit the patio on the other side.

I get to the front door with a limp, thinking there's no doubt I've been set up and that this is even more foolhardy of a trespassing act than my invasion up Nuns Canyon Road. The person previously dispatched to shoot President Walker must certainly be waiting behind the door for his chance at me.

But I've got to see Miles.

I need his help. Rachel needs his help. Elena, Billie — we'll all fit neatly into a Miles Glinn fix-it plan once he's able to plug in the circumstances and put his brain to work.

Standing outside his door under a single porch lamp, I can't determine any better strategy than to knock, so I whack the knocker three times against its stop. There's a doorbell, so I ring that too when the knock yields no response.

"Miles!" I say as loud as I dare. When nobody answers, I say it again, louder. "Miles!"

Nothing. I try the doorknob. It turns in my palm, which doesn't sit right with me at all. I push the door open and come in. The lights are on; the nearby refrigerator exudes a muted hum, its ice machine clicking through a cycle as I move into the kitchen.

"Miles?"

The house feels occupied but still; active but vacant. Crossing between rooms, I feel a creeping dread, an icy kind of fear, but since I seem to be caught in this pattern of recurring disaster, the dread soon dampens, and I focus on taking in the surroundings as I move.

Aware of the basic layout of his place, I meander downward. There are three stories, all with the lights of San Francisco twinkling beyond the windows. I repeat Miles's name again to no reply. It's on the bottom floor, in the workout room, that my sense of dread returns with a vengeance.

Miles lies in a heap beside his Peloton exercise bike.

There's no blood on the carpet around him, but he's unconscious at a minimum, and as I rush to him, watching for signs of breathing, I detect no motion from his chest. I reach and seek to find a pulse at wrist and neck — nothing. Then I set my hand on his forehead, hoping for a comforting sign of life —

— and immediately pull back at the clammy, lifeless feel of his face. It doesn't even feel like skin. Miles has become damp rubber.

There are drugs, easily ministered, which cause cardiac arrest before vanishing into the bloodstream, virtually untraceable. I consider then dismiss Miles's chronic problem with his weight, his advancing age, his predilection for deli foods — he was a heart-attack candidate by his own hand, yes. But the timing is untenable.

No damn way.

Miles did *not* have a heart attack between the time I called and the time we were supposed to meet on his boat. Certainly not one resulting from natural causes.

They shot the president — and now they've killed Miles.

My friend is gone.

It occurs to me that Miles's murder is only a preface to mine. That any contract assassin worth his pay would be smart enough to stick around after having injected Miles with his deadly serum so that he might simply and easily plug me full of the same junk. Smoothie-shop proprietress security detail or no.

Get the hell out.

I exit through the workout room's sliding-glass door and take the stairs up along the side of the house. I use the secondary garbage gate to exit to the street, pass Billie's latest spot in the shadows, and hustle with my new limp to the Subaru, Billie now keeping pace alongside me.

"He's dead," I say, huffing up the hill.

"I saw."

"You did?"

"I was watching you through the window."

"Let's get the hell out of here if we even can," I say. "I've got to think."

She gets behind the wheel and starts the engine while I climb into my backseat spot and attempt to detach my brain from my emotions. I will need to deal with the loss of one of my closest friends — probably, I reflect, my closest friend — later.

What are the options now? If not Miles, who can help me construct a fix-it plan?

The first face that comes into my head is my former Chief of Staff, now a prominent mayor in his own right. He would at least be able to help with the authorities —

A sharp rap sounds out on the window beside me.

"Jesus, get down!" Billie says, drawing, in the process, the borrowed Sig Sauer I hadn't known she'd been keeping under her seat. I follow her dictate, but on looking up to check the face of my assassin, I see instead through the passenger-side window a semi-balding man in a sport jacket, hands raised, outstretched palms empty. His face is narrow, almost weasel-like, and he's leaning down cautiously, almost timidly, so that Billie and I can see him most effectively. And while his features are largely lost in the darkness, I can see that he appears to be motioning to me.

I have no idea who he is, how he plans to kill me or, maddeningly, which rotten fruit at the top of the tree decided to send him to ace Miles and me. But as my adrenaline relents, I realize something I do know, at least judging from the gesture he's making.

It appears my assassin is asking me to roll down my window.

-27-

"Go ahead," Billie says with the gun leveled at him through the window. This is looking less and less like a hit, but I find comfort in Billie's athletic grasp on the pistol nonetheless. I flick the tab and lower the window. The man leans forward slightly and I get a clean look at his narrow, nervous features. His hand reaches inside.

"Easy," Billie says.

The man shifts back to palms-out before tentatively extending his hand once more. "Mr. President?" he says. "My name is Skeel. Clem Skeel. I think we should talk."

I see no evident firearm, but I quickly flash to the vision of Miles's body. No bullet was used to kill my oldest friend and he's dead just the same. I ignore the hand.

"Talk about what?" I say.

He tilts his head then flashes his teeth — yellowed, I see, from too many years of cigarette smoke, coffee, or worse. It's a predatory sort of smile.

"About the past ten days," he says.

"Ten days?"

"Yes. In case you were wondering who's been delivering the notes," he says, thrusting a finger into his own chest, "it's me."

The man's words filter through my screen of paranoia.

"As in," I say, "my tire kit?"

"Right, plus the postcard," he says. "And the room key. And the photos in the Bible at the motel." He motions to the empty seat to my left. "May I?"

Failing to understand, I stop trying.

"Fine," I say, sliding over cautiously.

When he settles in the seat next to me and no weapons are readily apparent, I say, "So you're the messenger."

"Yes, sir."

"What did you say your name was?"

"Skeel," he says. "Clem Skeel."

"We haven't met before," I say. "I'd remember your name."

"We haven't," he says, and grins that yellowed grin. "I'd remember meeting you too."

My brain begins to focus, though Miles's fate weighs too heavily for normal synapse function. I feel like I can't see straight.

"I have questions," I say.

"Figured you might."

"How'd you come to be the messenger?"

He nods. As he does, I notice the fine line of a scar in his nearer eyebrow. It ducks into the follicles, forming a narrow naked channel where eyebrow hair has ceased to grow.

"I'm a private investigator," he says. "Work out of Salinas. One morning I hit the ATM and notice the balance line on my receipt has gained four zeroes. I call the bank and learn a wire payment of forty thousand bucks hit my account at midnight, sourced from a numbered account."

"Okay."

"I sit tight on touching the money — figure it for a mistake and somebody's bound to come looking for it. But then I get a call from an old colleague. Says he's confirming my receipt of the 'blind retainer.' I say, 'If that's what it was, I'm confirming it,' and he proceeds to give me instructions on how and where to deliver the first note. Indicated he's be asking me to make as many as five or six deliveries. Each one involving some potential B&E. I didn't have an issue with that, considering the size of the retainer. At least not until I started making the deliveries and found out who I was delivering the notes to."

"Who was the colleague?"

"I worked with him ten years ago in Langley," Skeel says. "I knew not to ask, but I'm assuming he's still there. A company guy, if you know what I mean. The kind that always will be."

Skeel has managed, I note, to answer my question without revealing his colleague's name. I eye Billie, who has lowered the Sig Sauer, but only slightly, as she follows the conversation.

"And you?" I say. "Are you a company guy?"

Skeel grunts. "Not anymore."

I take this as a potentially positive sign about Mr. Skeel.

"Why are you here? Did you kill Miles?"

He turns sharply.

"Who? Oh, hell, no," he says. "It's not — I didn't kill anybody."

"Why, then? That townhouse belongs to Miles Glinn." I point to it. "He's my attorney, my friend, almost a brother. But now he's dead. He was supposed to meet with me on a dock two miles from here. Except that somebody killed him. In his house. And here you are. Lurking outside. Knocking on my window. You think I'm going to believe you don't even know who he is?"

Skeel shakes his head. "This just keeps getting worse," he says, "but no matter what you believe, I don't know who this Miles is. I didn't know why we were here in the first place. Till now."

"We?"

"I've been, well — following you," he says.

I look at Billie and back at Skeel.

107

"For how long?"

He shrugs. "Since the first note."

My mind churns through the meaning of his answer. A lot has happened since he left that note. "That's almost . . . "

"Ten days," he says.

"You've been tailing me for ten days?" I say.

He nods. "Followed you to the — er, to her smoothie shop," he says, gesturing at Billie and her gun. "To the post office, to the bed & breakfast, the tasting rooms, the lunch date, Nuns Canyon Road, the apple farm, the service station. Then here."

"Perhaps we should add you to the roster of my new freelance Secret Service detail. Did your unnamed colleague instruct you to keep tabs on me as well as deliver the notes?"

Another shrug — apparently Mr. Skeel's favorite expression.

"Nope. I'm just a curious guy. Odd set of circumstances, you know — an old CIA buddy dictating secret notes about a missing woman and asking me to hide them in the personal belongings of a former president. Couldn't help myself — just wanted to see if I might find out what the hell was going on. Then — well, I don't need to tell you that things got ugly."

"No," I say, "you don't."

Billie says, "You have a lot of extra time on your hands, Mr. Skeel?"

He holds up his hands in surrender again — apparently his second-favorite gesture. "Hey, I'm no good Samaritan," he says, "but I did get interested in the Rachel Estrella thing. Barstow cops said they found her body — "

"Right," I interrupt.

" — Yeah, so I kept following you. And I might add, that I know, in having followed you, that you didn't do the things the authorities accused you of. Tonight was when I started to think there might be something I could do to help. So I decided to say hello."

I eye him with a withering glare, as though my stare will function like a polygraph and reveal whether he means what he says. When he says nothing in response to the glare, I say, "You didn't exactly offer a helping hand on Nuns Canyon Road."

"I didn't follow you off the highway that night. Not at first. Look, when I saw you ride over to Nuns Canyon with your Secret Service people — and her, behind you," he says, "I knew you weren't leaving dead bodies back at the inn. And obviously I knew what you were in wine country to do. I worked my way up there when I heard the shots, but by the time I could see anything, there were bodies on the ground and you were ripping downhill in that SUV. Bottom line, when I saw the news about the murder at the inn, I knew something was off. Way off. In fact, I'd say it became obvious some major bullshit was going down. You want to know what I first thought, when I saw the story?"

"What," I say.

"Even said it out loud to the TV," he says. "I thought, 'Bohemian rampage, my ass.'"

He looks at me, and the look in his eye — sharp, edgy, a tinge of humor — earns him a temporary passing grade on the polygraph test.

"So I stayed on your tail. I know you've got Rachel and her daughter at the apple farm. My point is that you're doing right by them," he says. "I can't figure out who's doing what, from the kidnapping to the bogus story on the murder at the inn — but I'm confident you aren't good for what's alleged."

Through the windshield, headlights approach then pass. Behind us, I turn and watch as the vehicle's brake lights flash and a garage door opens to swallow the car. While it appears Miles Glinn's real killer might have fled the scene, it occurs to me that we remain in a vulnerable spot.

My brain finds its way forward.

"When's the last time you heard from your CIA buddy?" I say.

Skeel shakes his head. "Few days after he had me drop the pictures and the business card in the hotel."

"Two? Four? How many days?"

"Last time we spoke was two days ago."

I do the math.

"The day before we spotted Redhead," I say.

"Red — oh, sure. That's right."

"How often did you and your CIA buddy speak leading up to that last contact?"

"Every day."

I nod and steer the conversation toward my preferred destination.

"Maybe," I say, "it will help the frequency of contact if he's got a reason to call you back."

"I'm not following you."

"I want you to set up a meeting," I say.

"Between you and my CIA client?"

"Yes. Tomorrow." I think through a place Billie and I drove past in the Prius on our wine country tour. "There's a shopping center southeast of Napa, in Fairfield, I believe the town is called. Have him look up the local Target. There's a sports store beside it. A Big 5, if I remember correctly. We'll meet behind that store. I'm going to need you to be very specific: tell your CIA man you've got somebody he'll want to see, and that you've been told to arrange a meeting at 10 o'clock. After hours, after dark. You are not to tell him that the meeting is with the target of his letter-delivery assignment. Good so far?"

"I've got all that, I'm just not sure — "

"Mr. Skeel," I say, "when this blows over, the first thing I will do on returning home is transfer what I understand to be your recent retainer quote of $40,000. Therefore you will, from this point on, be my client too, provided you accept these terms. As your client, I am asking you to arrange this meeting, in the place, time, and manner I've specified. Can you make it happen?"

After a long moment of consideration, Skeel performs another act in his chronic performance of shrugs.

"Don't see why not," he says.

When a moment passes, Billie lifts the barrel of the Sig Sauer an inch.

"Okay, then," she says. "Why don't you get out of the car — slowly, please — and then we'll all be on our way."

-28-

Y ET ANOTHER HALF-NIGHT'S SLEEP AT Hansen Orchards, already fitful from the start, runs out of steam an hour before dawn. Even in my unconscious depths, the momentum of a pervasive, fatigued sadness overtakes me, and like a hangover headache soon draws me awake.

Miles is gone.

I wasn't a good friend to Miles. Hadn't spoken to him in almost two years. Hadn't seen him in five. But he'd been a force who was always there for me. A force I had assumed would always run with me. His death — his absence — is palpable, and I feel the eclipse of his presence.

In my hunt for the coffee machine, I've somehow beaten Bruce and Gloria downstairs. I find a bag of ground beans and brew a batch. Dreading hearing of further progress in the downward spiral of my current predicament, I nonetheless figure better to know than not, so I click on the TV they've got mounted in a corner of the kitchen. Soon armed with a full cup, I find CNN and dig in on the pain.

Wall Street futures are down 1,300 points, but the rest of the incessant cycle otherwise appears to be recycling itself from yesterday. The coverage doesn't reveal any mention of Billie's involvement in the supposed crime of passion at the inn, and aside from the repeating stories of my alleged atrocities, the national focus seems to have shifted to a more in-depth analysis of the very real attempt on the life of President Walker. He's said to be in critical condition in the ICU at Walter Reed Medical Center, with no additional updates on his status. The vice president offered a fumbling and unremarkable speech in primetime last night, using numerous key words I was always advised to deploy publicly in a time of crisis — *functioning, normal, investigation, progress* — along with the mention of half a dozen executive-branch agencies and the *activity* and *engagement* they're so busy with.

I've felt a nagging sensation around the organizers of Rachel's kidnapping, exacerbated by my realization on the identity of the letter-writer. Taking in the morning news, the nagging sensation becomes more galvanized and tangible. The mystery on who's behind this is less mysterious by the hour, the telltale signs more evident now that I'm thinking — and remembering — more clearly, having pulled the rip-cord and ejected from my retirement routine.

I click off the cable box and spend a few minutes thinking through the statements I intend to make to Skeel's CIA man, forming and adjusting both my wording and the facets of my emerging plan as I ponder the directions I might take depending on the CIA man's reaction.

There's a lick of color visible above the rim of the mountain range beyond the kitchen window. The shape of the mountains is familiar, the comfort of a view seen often, in a prior time, when circumstances lacked the stress and friction of today. Like the sighting of an old friend. My mind downshifts out of prudent mode, and with the view of a slice of my history out the window, another thought of history finds its way into my mind. Of *lost* history. Of Katie, and of being too busy with the predicament of the day, every day, to ever have taken moments with her that I should have.

Maybe it would be a good idea to see about fending off that portion of history from repeating itself.

I pour a second cup along with a refill of my own and head upstairs. Billie's stirs as I sit beside her on the bed, coffee held strategically adjacent to her olfactory sensors. Her eyelids flicker and open.

"Coffee," she says.

"Yes."

"What time is it?"

"Early," I say, "but the sun is about to make its appearance. Why don't you have some of this coffee and put something warm on."

"Warm?" She stirs. "Where are we going?"

"I thought maybe we could take a little ride."

By the time I return to the kitchen, Bob has emerged and is working through his first cup. He inclines his head on my arrival.

"This java is your work, I take it."

"Yessir," I say.

"Setting yourself apart from the masses. Don't think too many of those who followed you in office are capable of making their own coffee without screwing it up. Or crossing the street, or taking a leak for that matter."

He provides an update on Rachel and Elena and we sort through a couple other topics before I ask him whether he's got a Gator or similar ATV I might borrow for the morning.

"Shed across from the garage," he says. "It's unlocked, just lift the door manually. Key's in the ride."

The sun is making its way into view along the ridge crest, piercing helpless dew droplets on trees and shrubs alike as I back out one of Bob's fleet of John Deere vehicles, a six-wheel natural gas-powered machine with fat tires and cushy seats. Billie appears in the driveway, coffee mug in hand, a set of Gloria's jeans and sweater draping her lithe figure in the angled sunrise. When I finish orienting the Gator and push in its parking brake, I see she's already shaking her head.

"No way," she says.

"I want to show you something."

"I don't mean 'no way' on going wherever you're planning on taking me. I mean 'no way' are you driving. Scoot over."

I shrug. "Fine — you steer. I'll navigate."

We ride uphill, Billie bringing us along a trail between orchard sections, the paths not quite the same but close enough to the original layout of the property so that I'm reasonably well oriented.

"I decided there are a couple questions I've got," I say. "Questions I really should have asked by now."

The creases around her eyes harden, if creases can do such a thing. We bounce up the rocky trail.

"Question number one: have you ever been married?"

She looks over at me with only her eyes, defensive at first, then loosening in her posture as she processes where I'm coming from.

"I was married for six years," she says.

"When?"

"In my twenties. After college. He was my big brother in college."

"Big brother?"

"You know, upperclassman fraternity brother keeping an eye on the freshman sorority sister. Which usually means your first college hook-up. Quite a tradition of protection."

"You were in a sorority?"

"You were a Republican," she says.

We crest a ridge and rumble downhill on our trail until a stone wall meets up with us.

"Bear left here along the wall," I say. "And go on."

We parallel the stone wall on our descent, the layout of the orchards and terrain starting to look much more familiar now.

"He, our life together, and my existence as a sorority-girl type seemed a whole lot neater at the beginning than in the middle," she says. "He was a very handsome guy. On the outside. Underneath — different story. Seems to be my usual problem."

"How so?"

"Well, as an example, my friend Gustavo, whose demise and departure I'm certain you were hoping for, was approximately the same type of man."

I decide there's nothing much to add to that.

"And I will confess that for a moment," she says, "after the thing with the pictures in the restaurant, and it becoming obvious you were holding something out on me — even with feelings coming into play . . . "

"You I wondered whether I was rotten on the inside too."

"Yes."

I guide us through an open, rusted, handcrafted gate, at which point I see a portion of the wall that's even more familiar. This is so because I built it. Rougher around the edges than Bob's later, more expert masonry, I see it could use some pointing now, but otherwise my section of hand-hewn wall is holding up fine.

"You wonder no more?" I say.

"No," she says. "I don't think so."

A hundred yards past the gate, we come to a hand-painted sign standing guard over a spread of nine-plus acres of apple trees, planted in much lower density than the other orchard blocks on the property — not in keeping with modern agricultural planning standards.

I nod and ask her to park, which she does.

"Well that's good," I say. "I've had my own concerns. Mine, of course, are of a different sort. The sort where, for example, I'm too old, not as athletic anymore, laden with a corrupt history, washed up and half broken as compared to your fit, youthful vitality and the long, sunny road you've got stretching out ahead of you."

She looks over at me. "And you're concerned no more?"

I look back at her, noting that her eyes seem to be shifting with the sunrise, initially showing a shade of green, but now phasing to blue as the sun moves into view.

"Less so by the day," I say.

"Good. Because your concerns are irrational and ill-founded."

"So you're saying I'm youthful, athletic and pure — essentially flawless?"

"Let's just say you may be overestimating my youthful vitality, and that the long and winding road ahead looks a lot sunnier to me with you along for the ride."

This makes me smile in a way I'm not sure I've smiled since the letter arrived in my patch kit, or for ten years prior for that matter. To avoid any appearance of goofiness resulting from this grin, I climb out of the Gator and gesture ahead on the narrowing path.

"This is what I wanted to show you."

She leaves her coffee in the Gator's cup-holder and follows me fifteen yards around a bend, the wall mirroring the trail's route, until we come to another, smaller, gate spanning an opening in the older section of wall.

The gate is made of a sawed-off piece of old barn door. Painted on a slab of wood affixed to the gate is a send-up of the American presidential seal. Its colors are accurate — blue in the middle, golden rim — and still effusive in their stark, vibrant clarity, as though the paint has been regularly refreshed. There is the usual bald eagle staring out proudly from the center too. On the circle, though, instead of the words SEAL of the President of the United States, the pronouncement has been changed to Orchard of the President of the United States. The eagle's beak is stuffed with a bright-green Granny Smith apple.

Billie arrives beside me and takes in the gate and its moniker. I jerk my chin toward the stone wall stretching in each direction.

"Lot of blisters and heavy lifting went into that wall. And those trees were a lot smaller when we put them in, but they weren't so easy to deal with either."

She nods. "What were you saying about not being athletic?"

"I've told you a few things about my long, strange, trip," I say. "And I know you've caught other stories here and there, like our time at dinner with Gomez. But this was one of my favorite stops. An extended stay — my longest. Bob and I put in all nine acres' worth of trees in this patch. Just the two of us. He hadn't yet figured out how to tap fully into California's migrant labor pool, so I was it at the time. His first migrant hand."

"He and Gloria have had considerable success with what you planted together."

I nod, the past coming back through the haze of the present.

"These are the Granny Smiths," I say. "I've noticed that most of the other trees on the property are Red Delicious. I imagine they learned it worked better to limit the quantity of green apples, which they sold out of the gates as specialty products for a hefty premium. Last I checked, every local store for many miles around carries their cider, pies, and whatever else they make from these original nine acres. Not sure I believe he's being literal, but he told me that they bought the rest of the property off the proceeds of these first nine."

The sun has pushed its full orb over the lip of the mountain range, and now splashes its golden hues across Billie's neck and shoulders. From our vantage we can see down a slope of orchard rows, winding pathways and stone walls, and ultimately the house and road. There are oak trees dotting the property, giving the sloping hills on this side of the road a distinctively California feel. On the other side of the road, the hills rise back up but are populated solely with evergreen trees.

"Bob once told me the original property listing referred to this valley as the place where California meets the Pacific Northwest," I said. "I've always liked it, and I still like it now."

She turns to me, golden in the direct sunlight.

"I like it too."

-29-

W E CROSS A CIRCUITOUS MOUNTAIN road to Highway 29, the main artery running the length of Napa Valley. Going south, the two lanes widen to six, becoming an out-and-out freeway through the city of Napa itself. Considering that news coverage hasn't revealed any mention of Billie's involvement in my predicament, we're growing in confidence on the use of main arterials with Billie at the wheel. To be safe, we've got the radio tuned to a news station, its reporters on repeat of my alleged atrocities and the presidential assassination attempt, but otherwise none of them seem to be issuing anything of substance that would present any escalated danger in Billie's chauffeuring work.

"What are you going to say to him?" she says.

Walls rise up to close in the highway along this section of our drive, protecting the neighborhoods from the road noise of the widened freeway.

"Skeel's CIA man?"

"Yes."

"As is probably obvious," I say, "the people who ordered Rachel's abduction are likely the same people who put out the bogus story about my bed-&-breakfast killing spree. Assuming Walker is still alive, it only makes sense that he and I should organize and collaborate against these people who, in one way or another, are targeting the both of us. I'm planning to propose that we align forces, though I'm stating it in a way Walker should understand when relayed to him, but the CIA man may not."

The part I *don't* say is that I'm starting to believe I know who these people are.

"Got it."

We're silent as she exits just south of Napa and merges eastbound onto Highway 12, which switches to an east-west bearing south of Sonoma, connecting the two wine-country cities and stretching toward Lodi to the east. Darkened vineyards line both sides of the road. A golf course passes on the right, lights illuminating the club's sign as darkness is nearly upon us again.

"When we get there," I say, "drive past the shopping center. Stick to the main drag without turning in. If things look normal after a drive-by or two, we'll pull into the lot. During the meeting, however it plays out, I'd like you stay in the car. With the engine running. Facing the road."

"Copy that."

My stomach knots up as I see the pool of light at the bottom of the hill ahead. The industrial lighting, exposing a handful of stores in a sea of asphalt, drapes across the façade of the Big 5 Sporting Goods and Target beside it.

If Skeel has followed my edict — which I've got no real reason to believe he'll have done — then the CIA man won't know who he's meeting. If Skeel has let the cat out of the bag, I'm okay with proceeding anyway. If my hunch about the CIA man is true, it shouldn't matter: Walker decided to trust this guy, so I probably can too.

I slide lower in the seat, taking some satisfaction from our progress. A mystery man is about to make his appearance and send a coded message — assuming Skeel hasn't already ratted me out.

We crawl across the vacant parking lot in front of the Big 5. No sirens wail. No blue-and-red lights swirl. No commandos leap from behind the row of shopping carts locked up along the front of the store.

"Move in along the side to the back," I say. "Slowly." From the back seat of the Subaru, I mumble my recitation of the three seemingly innocuous sentences I've devised, rehearsing silently so they'll sound smooth when I utter them to Skeel's CIA man.

As Billie turns behind the store, Skeel's car comes into view: a Nissan Maxima, same car in which we watched him leave from Tiburon. He's got it parked beside a trio of dumpsters. The dumpsters are overfilled with flattened cardboard boxes and busted wooden pallets.

Then I see the second vehicle.

Behind one of the dumpsters is a massive SUV. It's a Ford, model unclear, but clearly government-issue. Black-on-black, tinted windows, numerous sophisticated-looking antennae — a customized setup typically reserved for agencies with three letters in their acronyms, its occupants guaranteed to be highly rehearsed practitioners of the Federal Agent Strut.

The door to Skeel's Nissan opens and the sallow-faced private eye rises from the driver's seat with a cautious wave. Our lights are on him; he may be able to tell that this is the same Outback we drove last night, but thanks to our headlight beams, I can see into Skeel's car without his seeing inside ours. No additional heads are visible within the Maxima; a small army of soldiers could be hiding in the government SUV, but I'll discount this possibility for the moment.

"Pull alongside Skeel," I tell my chauffeur. Billie does so, turning around and backing up beside him.

After one last glance into the windows of Skeel's car, I depress the switch and slide my window down. Annoyingly, it doesn't drop all the way, as with most backseat windows in sedans and station wagons.

"Glad you showed," Skeel says. He seems nervous, which I don't like.

"Is your CIA man in that Explorer, or whatever that SUV is?" I say.

Skeel nods. Again, nervously. "Expedition," he says. "But yes."

"What's wrong?"

"Wrong?" he says. "Nothing's wrong. Everybody's just a little on edge. You were a surprise, remember?"

"Wait a minute," I say. "You said *were*. You're saying you revealed the surprise?"

"Only part of it."

I reach forward and set my hand on Billie's shoulder.

"Go," I say.

Skeel reaches toward me with both hands, palms-out, as Billie gets on the gas and the car lurches forward.

"No! Look!" he says. "He's here! There's no cops! No kidnappers! No one to be afraid of! We're cool! You're cool!"

I pat Billie's shoulder in a way meant to convey that she should wait. She stands on the brakes but keeps the transmission in Drive and some juice going on the accelerator.

"If everything's cool," I say out the window, "then what are you so nervous about?"

"I'm nervous about the whole goddamn thing," Skeel says. "Who wouldn't be? Look, you can relax. He's looking forward to meeting with you. He's asked me to wait near the corner of the building. To watch for any cars coming into the parking lot from the street. We're good here. I did as you asked. You're my client, remember?"

I don't buy Skeel's explanation — he's spooked and isn't telling me the whole story. But tonight, in this meeting, so far, no one has been killed or found dead on the floor. It's a step in the right direction and maybe even a good sign. I decide to go with the flow despite the bad vibe I'm picking up from Skeel's nerves; it's too important that I get a message to the president to abandon ship at the first sign of inclement weather.

I jut my chin at Skeel.

"Take your car with you to your lookout post," I say, "and face it our way so we can see your headlights. Flash the high beams if anything out of the ordinary takes place outside our line of sight."

"Will do," he says, appearing far too relieved for my liking as he climbs into his car, backs up, and parks the Nissan where I've asked. He kills the headlights and remains behind the wheel in the dark.

"What do you want me to do?" Billie says.

I turn and refocus.

"Drive over to the Expedition," I say. "In fact, let's back up against the front of it."

"Block them so they can't get out?"

"Not without running us over."

She loops around and backs up, inching closer and closer to the SUV until I feel a bump and we jolt to a stop. I'd enjoy her literal translation of *against the front of it* were I capable of enjoying much of anything right now.

After a moment taken to gather my inner rehearsal and nerves, I get out of the car. Walking self-consciously but without hesitation in my step, I move alongside the SUV. The tinted windows make it impossible to see in, but once again no bullets are flying, so I knock loudly on the driver's side window. In a moment — a *long* moment, standing out here like a sitting duck — the window zips down. As the cool, dry output of the car's air conditioner wafts into the warm night, the man behind the wheel stares back at me with the tired, suspicion-ridden eyes of a spy.

He's late forties, maybe early fifties. His face athletic and angular, hair cut short but not all the way to high-and-tight. He wears a suit and tie. This is not a driver by trade. Whether or not this is Skeel's man, I'd place him as a senior federal officer or other veteran of governmental leadership. Is he driving his own car? Then why a vehicle the length of a hearse?

I can hear the vague sounds of a television news broadcast or radio station playing within the car.

"Greetings, Mr. President," the man says with zero surprise registering in his voice. His expression is neutral and unreadable. "My name is Ed Rudd. I understand you wanted to see me tonight."

So Skeel completely ignored my request for secrecy. Not good — but perhaps irrelevant now that we're here and Rudd has introduced himself.

"That's right." The rest is the part I've rehearsed, and I see no reason not to jump right into it. "Assuming you're the conduit I think you are," I say, "I have a message for you to take back to the man who sent the notes to me. I'll need it delivered word-for-word. With the exact lines I'm about to give – "

I stop. Rudd has raised his index finger in the universal gesture for *hold on a second*. I observe, in the silence, that the CIA man isn't just calm, cool, and collected — he actually seems *bemused*.

He knows something I don't, and looks to be enjoying it.

"Listen," I say, "I don't have time for bullshit. Or private jokes. It's — "

"I appreciate the fact that you reached out to me," the man named Ed Rudd says. "But this could go a lot more smoothly if you went ahead and climbed into the back seat."

That's when I realize that Rudd is not alone.

I feel more than see the presence of the second person in the car — catching only an outline, the edges of a suit jacket, a glimpse of the top of a man's head. Otherwise the passenger is shrouded in darkness, and impossible to see.

"Goddammit," I say, and duck inside Rudd's window, look for and find the appropriate switch on the dashboard, reach over, grasp it, spin it one way, then the other, finally landing on the setting that illuminates the interior of the car. The ceiling lights shower the cabin in white illumination —

And in the seat behind Rudd I see a face I find quite familiar. A face almost everyone would find familiar.

The man with the familiar face lifts his hand and waves.

"Evenin', Mr. President," he says.

I feel my face go slack.

The words the back-seat passenger just used to greet me are precisely the words I'd have chosen to greet *him*.

-30-

I CLIMB INTO THE BACK SEAT beside the President of the United States, who appears perfectly healthy, even unscathed. I'm staring rudely, but I need processing time, so that's what I do. The president's expression is serious — firm — and yet, like Ed Rudd's, partially bemused. His expression doesn't wilt under the heat of my rude stare. A newscast emanates from the small-screen TV mounted on the ceiling between the two front seats. Wolf Blitzer is covering the topic of the precipitous drop in global stock markets and what today's news will mean for tomorrow's NYSE opening bell, all of which of course revolves around the supposed assassination attempt on the man seated now beside me.

"You're supposed to be recovering from a gunshot wound," I finally say.

"Well, yeah, you're right about that," Walker says, his adopted Texas twang now highly developed. "Under intensive care, truth be told. At Walter Reed."

I examine him more fully — no evident splint, bandages, crutches.

"Startling recovery," I say.

In his eyes, I see a counter-examination taking place. I recall his giving me the same look in our first meeting — when Katie had interrupted our discussion and I changed gears. I'm sure I'd changed my manner and posture — Katie had that effect on me — but the usual politicos didn't always pick up on it. Senator Walker had. He'd observed and stored it for later.

"Wusn't any recovery to be made," he says, "a course."

"You weren't shot."

He shakes his head. "Staged. Part a my little scheme from the get-go."

"The scheme involving me, you mean?"

"You and seven others."

"Seven - ?"

"Seven other people I begged to help me," the president says, "just like you. Eight folks, includin' yourself, whom Mr. Rudd here got a message out to. In eight regions, each place a spot where the evidence I'd accumulated pointed to Rachel possibly bein' held there. See, I'd come to believe they never intended to release her."

I keep my eyes on his, working to digest the onslaught of information.

"I teed up the presidential shootin' idea," he says, "to make sure I'd be able to duck out for a minute 'case any of my helpers found her. Freeing me up to go and get Rachel outa harm's way. 'Course now you done that for me."

My processor churns. "To get the chronology here," I say, "you set it up so that a fake assassination attempt would happen the minute you got a positive ID and location on the people you had reason to believe were holding Rachel?"

"Yessir."

"So when I left my first message on your answering machine, it launched your escape plan. *Before* my tussle with Redhead and the Three Brunettes."

He tilts his head. "Redhead — "

"The people in the photographs — the red-headed woman and the three dark-haired men. Who, incidentally, were federal agents. At least by my read. But your escape plan kicked into gear *before* I went back and rescued Rachel. You didn't know I was doing that part."

He considers this, easing back in his seat a hair.

"You familiar with 'extraordinary rendition' teams?" he says. "Technique utilized from time to time in our war on terror?"

"Of course," I say.

"Officially, the program's been set aside. Unofficially, a course, they're still at it. Clandestine squads who're given targets. They currently run on an independent-contractor basis — former feds, now operatin' off the books. We send 'em out to apprehend suspected terrorists. Rendition 'em, AKA interrogate their ass, once we get 'em."

He shifts in his seat.

"Anyway once these sons a bitches told me they had Rachel, I played along but meanwhile immediately recruited a series a different people to help find where they mighta been keepin' her." The way he refers to the people behind Rachel's kidnapping — *these sons a bitches* — causes my shoulders and neck to grow tense. "Tried everythin' I could without givin' myself away," Walker says. "Wusn't till I stopped and thought about the fact her kidnappin' was conducted by feds — as you surmised — that I made some headway. Figgered freelance rendition teams'd be how they'd do it. So I sought out somebody at CIA — Mr. Rudd here — and asked him to look quietly into how many domestic teams we had in operation. Identified eight of 'em. Mr. Rudd dug out the names of the personnel on the teams where he was able to, got their mobile numbers, and tracked the whereabouts a their phones. Indicatin' eight locations where Rachel may a been held."

"All of this under the radar," I say, "of the people making you feel like the 'low woman on the totem pole'?"

A thin smile graces his lips. "Better to keep a lid on who was sendin' the letters," he says. The smile fades as quickly as it came. "Anyhow Rudd and I were able to reach out to the eight civilians I believed I could trust in a pinch, includin' yourself. We hired intermediaries like Skeel for delivery of the communications. Six of you answered or I was able to confirm in one way or another you'd received the missive. Rudd arranged to have photographs of the members of the rendition teams, plus whatever clues we knew, sent to you each."

He shrugs, and I consider how, and through whom, he and Rudd might have confirmed the notes had been received and read by me. I also consider how Walker's accent appears to recede when he's covering something serious or technical.

"Minute one a you found a legit sign of Rachel," he says, "I had my assassination ploy on standby. Plan included an operation like you've never seen to get her out, but you went ahead and done that. Thank you."

"Wasn't just me," I say, "and two good men didn't make it out."

"Yes, I heard," he says. "Now that she's out, I intend to do what I intended from the beginning."

"Which is what?"

"Gonna hold an impromptu press event," he says, "at which I'll announce Rachel's existence and kidnappin'. Makin' it public knowledge that's she's still alive and kickin.'"

"Great minds," I say. "I was considering doing something very similar to ensure that the people behind her abduction would no longer have the ability to kidnap her again without exposure."

Walker nods. "Plus, in my presser, I'll be comin' clean on some skeletons in my own closet. Basically I'll be shovin' just about all that these boys thought they had on me up their south side."

I nod too, now fully convinced of just who *these boys* are.

"Ask you a question?" I say.

"What we're here for."

"What did you hear? Or see? Or learn?"

"Come again?"

"What is it that made these people work so hard to keep you quiet?"

Walker leans his head back, turns, and holds my gaze awhile. I can't read his expression. After a moment of this, he breaks off the look and peers out the front windshield of the SUV.

"I can give you all that in due course," he says, "but tell you what. First I got somethin' more important I'd like to get to."

"What's that?" I say.

"Kinda like to see my daughter. Fact of the matter is, I've never met her. And I thought, dreaded even, there might have been a chance she'd be taken from the world before I ever did get to."

I suppose my laundry list of additional questions can wait — at least for now. I incline my head in the direction of Bob's Outback, where my getaway driver awaits.

"If you care to follow me, it will take about seventy minutes from here," I say.

Walker nods gravely, so much so that I wonder whether it's all an act. Putting on another layer to go along with the manufactured accent.

"Might well be the longest seventy minutes," he says, "of my life."

When Walker says nothing more for another minute, I abandon my useless internal debate on the man's sincerity, climb out, and slip into the rear seat of the Outback. Billie eyes me curiously in the rear-view as I sit quietly for a few seconds.

"You appear strangely calm," she says.

I catch the reflection of her eyes. "Probably in shock. Let's roll."

"Where to?"

"Back to Bob's place. They'll be following. I'll fill you in on the way."

-31-

BOB HANSEN STANDS BEFORE OUR convoy, shielding his eyes against the dual splash of headlight beams. His expression shifts as he recognizes his Subaru. I get out and walk over.

"Made it back in one piece, I see," Bob says as we come together.

"Indeed. How is it here? Any surprise visitors?"

Bob shakes his head. "Not a soul."

"Rachel awake?"

"Think so. TV in her room's on."

"Gloria have anything nice Rachel could wear?"

Bob's eyes flick to the Expedition. "Sure," he says.

"Have anything nice for herself to wear?"

Bob looks at me. I lean down, bend inside the open window of the Subaru, and say to Billie, "Do you maybe want to head inside and prepare Rachel a little."

Billie turns off the ignition and says, "Sure."

Bob eyes me skeptically. "Who the hell you got in that SUV, Mr. President?" he says.

He didn't mean it this way, but there seems no other way to answer.

"Exactly," I say.

-32-

RUDD, THE PRESIDENT'S CIA MAN, hovers a few feet back in the Hansens' kitchen, not unlike a man performing Bozo detail, as introductions are made between President Walker and Bob, Gloria, and Billie. Walker thanks Bob and Gloria for their hospitality and turns to Billie.

"Billie, is it," he says.

"Yes, Mr. President," she says.

"Rare name for a woman. Have we met?"

His eyes linger on hers and it occurs to me he may be hitting on my new person.

"Don't think so, Mr. President. Believe I would have remembered."

Rachel and Elena, hand-in-hand, reach the family room, Rachel looking fresh out of the shower. Walker excuses himself and goes to them. Billie eyes me as she steps back to allow Walker to pass.

Facing each other from two paces apart, Rachel and Walker look like opposing statues, their faces the only animated areas in twin towers of stone.

"Hi, Rachel," Walker says after what I estimate to be four minutes.

"Hi," Rachel says.

"You're all right," he says.

The animated portion of her body nods, though the act is barely perceptible to the human eye.

"My husband isn't," she says.

"No. I'm sorry."

After another little while, Walker turns his head partly toward me, eyes still glued to his daughter.

"Maybe we could find a place," he says, "to do some catching up, Rachel and I."

Gloria delivers an elbow to Bob's ribcage and Bob moves past my shoulder.

"This way. You can use my — "

"Actually," Rachel says, "I'd rather we talk together."

The taut, clipped tone of Rachel's words slows Bob.

"Together?" Walker says.

Rachel inclines her chin in the direction of Bob, Gloria, Billie, and me.

"With them."

Walker turns and examines us as all though he's just noticed our presence. He turns back to Rachel. Waiting, perhaps, for Rachel to back down or explain what she means. Rachel does neither. Still holding her daughter's hand, she turns to Gloria.

"Mrs. Hansen, would you mind giving Elena a bath?"

"Of course," Gloria says.

"Elena, honey," Rachel says, "I'll be right up to read you a book and tuck you in."

Elena starts to go with Gloria, then stops and turns to face Walker. "Are you my Grandpa?"

Walker looks to Rachel, maybe for some kind of permission, but when Rachel's expression doesn't provide any answer, he looks back down at Elena.

"Why, yes," Walker says, "I'd say I am."

"Okay," Elena says.

Rachel takes Elena's face in her hands and kisses her daughter's forehead and Gloria leads her upstairs, leaving us with a noisy silence. Rachel eyes me. Billie eyes me. Walker eyes me. When a long moment passes without my discerning what it is everyone expects me to do, I feel the welcome weight of Bob's hand on my shoulder.

"Tell you what," he says. "Why don't I warm up some of our famous Granny Smith cider and we can settle in by the fire. Ought to have enough seats in there for everyone."

I resist the urge to high-five Bob and, instead, nod my assent.

-33-

"Why?" Rachel asks.

Chances are Bob Hansen never expected to host a summit of U.S. presidents in his family room — but tonight, that's what he's got. We hold hot cider in mugs. The fire crackles, though it's mostly for effect on this mild summer night. Walker and I face the others from our hosts' leather reading chairs. Rudd sits on a stool in the kitchen, apart from the group but still in audio-visual range.

"Why what?" Walker says.

"Why was I kidnapped? My daughter abducted? My husband killed?"

Walker sips from his mug and offers a poker face. "Ain't completely sure."

As he takes a second sip of the cider, adding nothing further, I feel another twinge of anger. One thing I'm determined this hastily called summit will be about is answers, whether or not Walker is comfortable giving them. Plain and simple, outside of our own individual predicaments, things are about to tank. The structural integrity of the world's economy and governance relies largely on the stabile force of the United States government, which in turn allows America's financial markets to exert a similarly stabilizing effect. With one American president presumed incapacitated and one of its former presidents accused of a grisly set of murders, we are an inch away from the complete collapse of global finance if not governance, and this guy is playing games with his recently freed daughter. And with me.

I lost the man who was my best and only friend, and it goddamn well wasn't from a heart attack. Along with two good people, no Bozos they, who accepted as their life mission my protection. Someone's going to answer for taking Miles and my security detail, and we won't get any closer to reaping that answer if Walker keeps on with his folksy bullshit.

"Mr. President," I say, "in your first note, you told me that certain 'powerful people' revealed something to you. That they wanted you to keep it to yourself. Assuming that much is true, it follows that whatever it is they revealed to you is highly significant. Rachel's question mirrors the inquiry I posed in your SUV. What did you hear, see, or learn? What is it that made these people work so hard to keep you quiet? The question is not immaterial to the problems we all currently face."

Walker eyes me noncommittally for a bit before shifting slightly in his chair. Merely from his manner, I remind myself to interpret everything he tells us as merely part of the truth. He has clearly bought into the holier-than-thou statesman approach: he wants to be the one to decide what information is disseminated, when, and to whom. He almost surprises me when he answers.

"Last fall," Walker says, "a memo landed on my desk by mistake. Mistake wasn't in the memo's destination — its author definitely intended for me to see it — but in the fact it made it to my desk at all. Never should've."

He pauses, looking thoughtful, before continuing. "The memo came from down low. Analyst. CIA. Mid-level. Kind of person who doesn't get to send the president a memo. Send one to your boss, sure, and if what you got earns its way up, then, yeah, it makes the PDB. But this one was on its own. Still don't know how she got it to me."

"PDB?" Bob says.

"President's Daily Brief," I say. "The analyst was a woman?"

"Yes."

"What was her name?" I say.

Walker hesitates — but answers.

"Laramie," he says. "That's the only way she ID'd herself in the memo — one word. Laramie. Took a while to determine whether that was her first or last name. Turns out it was her last. Julie Laramie, in full."

"What did it say?" Billie says.

Walker shrugs. "Not much. Just two short paragraphs." He turns to me. "Not much different from the notes I sent you."

"What did it say?" Billie repeats.

Walker looks uncomfortable. He shifts in his seat; then he shifts again, digging into the back pocket of his slacks, coming out with a folded piece of paper. It's folded tightly enough to toss — which is exactly what he does. It lands on Billie's lap.

"Why'n't you see for yourself," he says.

When Billie gives him a funny look, which I take for a duplicate of my own reaction — *You've held onto the actual memo all this time?* — Walker sees the look and smiles without opening his mouth.

"Ain't likely there's any more secure place in the world," he says, "than on the person of the President of the United States."

I'd have to agree: if you've got a single document you need hidden, the pocket of a U.S. president probably comes out safer than a lockbox in the vault of a Swiss bank.

Billie unfolds and reads the memo. It doesn't take her more than a few seconds before she passes it to me, though not before snapping a shot of it with her phone. Between the crumpled crisscross of Walker's folds, the fading text of the memo is as legible as the day it was printed. A combination of laser-printed text and handwritten marks, it appears to be a portion of the cover page of a report of some kind:

```
To:    File POTUS

Fr:    CIA - Laramie, 3rd fl, x3728

Re:    5 July Intel
```

```
Dt:     14 Oct
```

CL: C-9

****

```
Topic: Identification of corroborating intel
re: intended ARD-BW incident set for 7/5 of
next year.
```

Pls contact me.

I pass the memo to Bob, who reads it before handing it to Gloria, who passes it to Rachel. Walker looks mildly stuffy, as though he hadn't intended for everyone in the room to read it or an iPhone snapshot to be taken, but doesn't make a move to snatch the memo back.

"Care to translate?" Rachel says once she's read it.

"Some of it's clear enough," Walker says. He tells the room the obvious meaning of POTUS. "The third-floor mention and numbers that follow represent Laramie's office location and phone extension at CIA headquarters in Langley. Devil's in the details though. 'ARD-BW' – initially we weren't sure what the first portion meant," he says. "But the 'BW' was presumed to stand for either 'biological weapon' or 'biological warfare.'"

Billie leans forward. "So she was alerting you to a possible incident involving a biological weapon. Forecast to take place on July fifth?"

"As in, just over two weeks from now," Gloria says.

"Coming back to the details," Walker says, "she's written the classification level by hand — C-9, for Cryptoclearance-9, highest clearance in the federal government."

When he leaves off with a lengthy pause, I clarify.

"Technically a mid-grade analyst would never see something classified at that level to begin with," I say. "Although I have no knowledge as to Laramie's access within CIA, there is no way a memo, or portion of a memo, from anyone in the regular ranks of CIA should have made it to his desk.

Not without somebody very senior intending for it to land there, or by some stroke of luck or genius."

"What do you mean by that — a 'stroke of luck or genius'?" Rachel says.

"The right decision-maker," I say, "or a hard-charger looking for political points might, in a busy, distracted moment, successfully get it passed it up the chain of command to cover his or her own tail. I don't think it's too far-fetched to imagine a junior staffer in the White House handing it to the National Security Advisor just to be safe. Laramie might have anticipated that. Or she might just have gotten lucky."

"Lucky or good as she mighta started," Walker says, "once that memo got to me, Laramie got unlucky pretty quick."

We all look at him.

"After I read what you just saw," he says, "I had my Chief of Staff call the number she gave us. Asked him to arrange a meetin' for the following day. Got set for three, followin' a late lunch with Slovakia's ambassador. Believe we shared some martinis."

"So you were drunk for the meeting?" Rachel says.

"Mighta been," Walker says slowly, "'cept there wasn't any meeting. Not with anyone named Laramie, anyway. At three-oh-five an assistant deputy director, older, nasty-eyed buzzard been working at CIA for twenty-five years, arrives 'on behalf of Laramie,' he says. I let him in and we chat."

My shoulders and neck tense up again on hearing Walker's relayed wording from the official — *on behalf of Laramie.*

"What about?" Billie says.

"Tells me he apologizes for the inconvenience, but 'Laramie has taken ill.' He goes on to explain that the incident referenced in her memo is currently 'under analysis.' 'Being studied,' he says. Then tells me the memo never shoulda been sent. Not without proper authorization. Says they'll let me know when their study is complete. At which point they'll offer their advice."

The way the CIA man spoke to Walker is precisely the sort of wording used in many a meeting of mine.

"I didn't like the old buzzard's tone," Walker says. "Way he spoke felt like a lecture from a parent or teacher. Kind you'd give to a disobedient child. Me bein' the disobedient child in question, I waited two weeks and had somebody fire him."

"Why wait the two weeks?" Billie says.

Walker smiles. "Technique I learned from an old buddy a mine. Keeps 'em from knowin' what they got fired for."

Unable to fathom the merits of this particular strategy, I focus instead on steering the conversation back on course. The sort of old buzzards Walker encountered were the same sort of buzzards who once harassed me, but there's a more immediate issue at stake.

"What about Laramie and the incident mentioned in her memo?" I say. "You said she got unlucky pretty quick, and the old buzzard said she was taken ill. I assume you followed up with her or had somebody follow up on what she sent you. What did you find?"

He shakes his head.

"That's what I'm tellin' you," he says. "We found nuthin'. Turns out she *was* sick — the flu. Progressed nastily too. Checked herself into the emergency room of her local hospital, where she was diagnosed with H1N1 and pneumonia on top of it. By the next day, she was gone, either on account of her own devices or by somebody else's doing. She hadn't formally checked out of the hospital, never turned up at home, and hasn't been seen since. I had people look into the intel chatter on the topic of July 5, any and everything related to what she wrote in the memo, but came up blank. Incidentally, our infectious disease folks informed me that the 'ARD' was likely an acronym for Aerosolized Respiratory Droplets – dispersal technique for the pathogens in a biological weapon. I had members of the White House staff interview Laramie's superiors and colleagues, but it seems wherever she was diggin', whatever she found, she didn't see fit to tell anyone what she was doin' or findin'. 'Cept me a course. And either she didn't survive her illness, or didn't see fit to tell anyone where she went."

"But it wasn't over," I say.

"No. Day after I fired buzzard number one," he says, "buzzard number two joins in on the PDB meeting. Invited by one of my people, I think — still not sure which one. Anyway, afterward, this old dude requests a private audience with me and my Chief of Staff, which we reluctantly provide. Asks me how much I know about the incident Laramie covered in her memo. Here's what I tell him: 'I know everything, and you goddamn well better check with me before you proceed with any more studies, let alone offer any recommendations.' Buzzard number two's quiet for a while. Then he seems to decide somethin', sits up straight, and tells me it's important I leave this one alone. 'Now and in the future,' how he put it. And added for good measure, 'Whether or not you're here in January.' This was two weeks before the election, and you might remember I was hellaciously down in the polls."

"'Whether or not you're here in January,'" Billie says.

"I tell him the meeting's over and that if I weren't gettin' tired of firin' people, his job'd be history too. Decided to leave it at that and so does he and whoever he was workin' for, probably all of 'em figurin' I was goin' down at the ballot box. But the hell with those old buzzards, because I won."

Bob says, "And now they had to deal with you."

Walker nods absently. "Couple weeks after the election results were certified, it happened — a news story, covered only in regional and local press, breaks on the disappearance of one Rachel Estrella," Walker says. "Nobody knows, to this day, that Rachel's my daughter — excepting the buzzards and Rachel's late mother, a course. Still not sure how they found out about this, but it don't matter now. Rachel and her family disappear. I learn this just before buzzard number two shows up for another meeting on Pennsylvania Ave. This time he's a little more direct."

Walker leans forward an inch or two.

"Son of a bitch tells me, word for word," Walker says, "'Now that you've observed the Estrella matter, we assume you will be more inclined to allow our study to proceed, unobstructed, on the Laramie situation.' And knowin' how to play politics with the best of 'em — as you do too, Mr. President" — here, he eyes me — "I say, 'Yes, I hear you. I am so inclined.' I avoided the temptation of referrin' to the man as 'sir' in the most sarcastic tone I could muster. I learned a long time ago that politics is tellin' 'em what they wanna hear while doin' whatever it is you need to do, and that's precisely what I did."

He smiles blankly at his daughter.

Billie says, "But you still don't know anything more about what prompted them to kidnap Rachel? The thing they think you know all about. The July 5 'ARD-BW.'"

"Other than the fact my re-election didn't sit well with the powers that be?" he says. "Nothin' more than was in that memo, or its cover page, or whatever it was you just had a look at along with me."

"Don't you suspect these people, whoever they are, abducted or killed Laramie?" Rachel says, pulling me back to the moment.

"Safe bet they had somethin' to do with her disappearance."

"So who are they?" Billie asks.

"The old buzzards?" Walker says.

"Yes," Billie says.

Walker looks over to me so deliberately at this point that it probably looks as though we'd arranged some kind of cue, and all eyes in the Hansens' family room turn to me.

The tension I've felt in my neck hasn't abated since the realization has slowly sunk in as to the relation between the 'powers that be' to which Walker refers, and the aspirants to such power I was forced to deal with in my term in office. I tilt my head and crack my neck as Walker yields the floor on the topic.

"Mr. President," he says, "care to take that one?"

-34-

"WHEN YOU TAKE OFFICE," I say, electing to take Walker's cue, "you get to put your own lieutenants in place. Cabinet members, department heads, bureau chiefs, secretaries, administrators. But try as you will to outfit your cabinet with as much clout, reputation, and pull as possible, the fact remains that getting anything accomplished in Washington — and I mean *anything* — works about like steering a battleship through the Panama Canal. There's only so much influence you and your cronies can have over the day-to-day direction of the federal bureaucracy. Not to mention the two chambers of Congress, the courts, state and local governing bodies. You need local pilots to help steer the ship, or you'll run aground, hit the wall, or not change course at all."

"Makes sense," Rachel says.

"Enter certain facilitators," I say. "You or your cabinet members meet them in the regular course of business, or sometimes they meet you. You quickly learn which facilitators to use, and how best to use them. Your appointees gravitate toward them. You do it because they're the ones who get things done. Same way, if you came aboard as the CEO of a corporation, you'd learn to use the best executives at the firm to get your goals accomplished."

"Power brokers," Billie says.

"You could call them that," I say. "Problem being, the people who know how to make the federal bureaucracy work for you don't necessarily share your agenda. And after a while — once they know that *you* know that you need them — some of these facilitators begin asking for favors in return. Never directly, understand — it's always channeled through the chain of command, up the intra-agency hierarchies. But pretty soon, you find that some of the key people you need on your side have developed the habit of asking for favors. More accurately put, they ask that you approve, fund, sign, veto, attend, or ignore something for them in return for their accomplishing your goals. Whatever your goals may be. I'll rephrase that: they *used* to ask. It appears, given President Walker's tale, that they've now lost the question mark.

"Pretty soon," I say, "you start to discern a pattern. The requests, the favors, the suggestions, the proposals — they're the same. They're coming from different agencies, different personnel, but it starts to feel like a hammer to the head. There's a platform being thrown at you and you're supposed to move it along. You try not to think about it — at least I tried not to — but you can't avoid it. Eventually you have to face the fact that these facilitators are working together."

"Isn't that their job?" This, from Gloria. "To try and get you to accomplish what the — I don't know, the EPA recommends, for example?"

"There are the authorized agencies and platforms, yes," I say. "Both sorts of agendas are in motion. At any given moment, hundreds are. But there's another layer to it. Your people are in a meeting, and one of the facilitators is there, and he interjects. The facilitator will say that a study's being conducted. That's how they work: they *study* things. When they've drawn their conclusions, they offer their advice. Recommendations; suggestions. Only now, it doesn't sound like they're suggesting any longer. Ordering and extorting."

"And murdering," Rachel says.

"Yes. Bottom line, is you eventually learn either to follow the suggestions, or your battleship will run aground. They've been referred to as the board, the commission, a few other names — but studying and recommending policy has always been their M.O., so I came to refer to them as the study group."

Walker nods and chuckles, which I find to be an odd reaction considering the circumstances.

Billie looks at Walker. "Coming back to the analyst," she says. "Laramie. You had her disappearance investigated, I assume?"

"Not thoroughly enough to find her," he says, snidely enough that I get the sense he's holding back a wink and a smirk. "Not yet. But now I'll have the time to look into that."

I think about his words and manner and put it together.

"You feel you've got leverage on them now," I say.

"Correct," Walker says.

The room is silent until Billie breaks it.

"Do you have a plan to go along with this newfound leverage?"

"Indeed," Walker says with a purse-lipped smile and very little accent. "Once I reveal that Rachel has survived, and share a portion of the story you've just heard, public sentiment will wash these people out. There will be a call from the media and general public for an investigation into the government's involvement in Rachel's disappearance. I'll hold the cards on these sons a bitches."

Walker marches on. "It's time for me to make amends with the American people and get back to work. I'll hold a press conference proclaimin' my good health. I'll cop to the staged shooting, issue an apology for deceivin' my fellow Americans, and explain I felt it had to be done in order that my illegitimate daughter, whose identity remained a secret till this day, be saved. And save her I did, from kidnappers on the federal payroll, with the help of none other than a fellow, former president of this great country."

He leans back in the leather reading chair, causing it to creak. His eyes find Rachel's.

"By announcing your identity as my daughter and documentin' your survival despite erroneous media coverage to the contrary, I figure to succeed in insulatin' you from any further monkey business."

He turns to me. "By announcin' *your* role in Rachel's rescue, I'll be movin' toward clearin' your name." He grins and holds up a hand, making what appears to be the gesture for *check, please.* "Any problems you encounter with local jurisdictions down the line, pen's ready for a pardon. Needless to say, my impromptu press conference ought to settle financial markets as well."

Walker seems ready for the conversation to be over, but Rachel doesn't appear to share his sentiments.

"What about the July 5 'ARD-BW'?" she says.

"I'm havin' it looked into. And if they're sniffin' around for a national security budget allocation to Halliburton because of this study they've run on cell phone chatter about July 5, so be it."

"So that's it?" Billie says.

"That'll do 'er," Walker says, concluding by laying on his manufactured accent as thick as he can spread it.

Billie glares at me. I shrug, the gesture meant to convey that he *is* the president — once he's made up his mind, there isn't much we can do.

Walker stands, reaches over and shakes my hand, then Billie's, followed by Bob's and Gloria's. "Your hospitality is greatly appreciated," he says.

He regally approaches his daughter, standing tall before her. "Been nice seein' you, Rachel," he says. "I'd like it if we could find some more time soon."

He sets a hand on her shoulder, holds that posture for a moment, then turns and strides out of the room. Rudd follows a few steps behind and closes the door as they walk out onto the porch and into the driveway, our audience with the President of the United States concluded.

Summit complete.

-35-

WALKER IS INVISIBLE, HIDING BEHIND the tinted windows of Ed Rudd's CIA-issue Expedition, where none in the plaza can see him. Meanwhile anyone who looks closely enough would spot *me* in two seconds — Bob Hansen isn't exactly the tinted-window type and it's hard to duck low enough to be out of visual range from a plaza crowd in Bob's back seat.

Ten minutes from now, the letter-writer who pled for my help will give a surprise press conference, which — at least once the surprise is revealed — the whole world will watch. Walker will be covering a lot of material, and most of it will be too much for the average American to digest. But when you're the president, the American people give you the benefit of the doubt — once. They believe in you, or want to believe in you, to a point. Most presidents burn through this ration of faith all too early, or on trivial matters that have no business rising to test the public's patience. Walker's grace period remains intact, so he ought to have the chance to redeem himself today.

I expect he'll also be cagey enough to skip the part about powerful people in Washington conspiring to keep him quiet; he'll leave out much speculation on who might have orchestrated the kidnapping or why. What matters, he believes, is that Rachel is safe, and that he's got the leverage he needs in announcing her existence and rescue to the world to keep the old buzzards at bay. And maybe he's right.

According to the news station we've been playing in the Subaru, the Dow Jones Industrial Average has dropped to its second-level circuit-breaker of a twenty percent loss, resulting in the automatic closure of the exchange for the day. Life goes on in Sonoma despite this precipitous fall — and if

Walker delivers his speech effectively, then perhaps life, and the economy in particular, will continue forth with little more than a dent in its side.

Sonoma Plaza, located midway down the southern end of the valley of the same name, is anchored by the town's original mission building, now functioning as city hall, and surrounded, on the squared streets that trap it, by restaurants, boutiques, and real estate offices. Walker will make his speech with the mission behind him, facing south toward Napa Street and the hoard of television cameras that will eventually gather there.

We're parked diagonally on Napa, in a spot that affords us an unobstructed view of the podium. Rachel's in front with Billie; Elena sits beside me. From my aft accommodations, I've got a good angle on both Rudd's Expedition and, partially hidden behind one of the plaza's abundance of oak trees, another familiar vehicle: Clem Skeel's Nissan. There's another pair of black SUVs parked between these two vehicles — Walker's Secret Service detail, back on the clock.

Walker has just had the White House press secretary tip off the nation's news outlets about a surprise press conference. Two news vans have already arrived from Santa Rosa, their reporter-and-cameraman teams lurking near the playhouse steps. A third van, with the latest version of the NBC peacock painted on its white hull, pulls in and parks near our spot against the curb. Two more, then four more arrive. Word is out. As camera crews and reporters emerge from their vehicles, I see the Expedition's passenger-side door open.

President Walker steps into the street. His appearance causes no immediate stir.

It's just after lunchtime — late enough for everyone's afternoon to be underway, early enough for the event to get feature coverage on the prime-time newscasts back east. People mill around the park with cardboard cups of coffee, bottles of juice, sandwiches in wax-paper wrappers. They're seated on benches or in the grass; a pair of joggers works around the park on what by my count is a sixth loop. Three people walk their dogs.

One of the joggers is the first to do a double-take at the man crossing the eastern lawn. She slows down and points so her fitness partner can see. The partner exclaims something or other, which prompts one of the dog-walkers to turn and look, which in turn leads a coffee-drinker to peer from his place on a bench, following the dog-walker's line of sight to Walker. Cell phones are raised. Pictures and video are taken and transmitted.

There's a crackle in the air; the news crews have picked up on it. An approaching news van, its driver in the midst of seeking a decent parking spot, suddenly speeds up and jerks to the curb near a fire hydrant, side door flying open.

Crews mount cameras on shoulders, lift mics from under arms, hustle across the south-side lawn. They've got Walker surrounded before he reaches his destination, but he calmly gestures toward the podium in front of city hall. Four Secret Service agents are in position now, and as they enforce a small perimeter around the podium, reporters converge like enraged killer bees, their camera teams pulling tripods and cords and canvas bags behind the swarm. By now there's enough chatter to be audible behind the sealed windows of the Outback. People emerge from ice cream shops, clothing stores, galleries, the ubiquitous realty offices. They talk, point, spread the word. Someone speaks animatedly into a cell phone.

Walker reaches the podium. He pulls a folded sheaf of papers from the flap pocket of his suit, smooths the pages, sets them down, stands patiently. Walker fiddles around awhile — scratching a temple, brushing an imaginary fuzz ball from his lapel. While he pulls these stall tactics, another news crew arrives, the cameras get planted on tripods, a pair of reporters record introductory remarks, cords are connected to mixers, and a crowd of civilians swells behind the news teams, fanning out in a wide semicircle stretching almost to our parking spot.

Then something happens that stills the crowd in a kind of outwardly flowing wave. Any reporter still doing her stand-up stops mid-sentence, proclaims the beginning of the press conference, and turns. The president has cleared his throat, or possibly just shifted his posture sufficiently to indicate the festivities are about to get underway. I slide my window down, but we're too far away to pick up more than fragments of his words without some accompanying lip-reading.

"For those of you who might be wonderin'," he says, "the answer is *yes*. It's me, my fellow Americans — Andy Walker. Your President. But the answer's also no — I am not in a hospital bed recovering from gunshot wounds. The third answer is another *no* — nope, there was not, in fact, an assassination attempt on my life."

He pauses, chin inclined.

"Clearly I owe you an explanation. I'm here to give it."

It's quiet — I hear the occasional warble and coot from the park's resident sparrow and pigeon population, but nobody outside of the birds makes a sound. Even I find myself caving in to Walker's folksy, no-nonsense charm. He's laying it all on the line, or at least giving that impression quite effectively.

"I've arranged this impromptu press conference," he says, "because I've got something to tell you, and let me get plainly to it. I staged my own assassination. I faked it. And I used that diversion to remain in hiding until now. And before you jump to any conclusions, which I won't blame you for doin', I wanna tell you that I did this in order to ensure the safety of my daughter."

A conversational rumble rolls through the audience — it's a revelation, of course, that he has a daughter, let alone that she is alive and well. Besides the commotion it's caused, his reference to Rachel is the first of my cues. I touch Billie's shoulder. She climbs out and opens the rear door for Elena.

"Ready, honey?" Billie says.

Elena says, "Sure," and climbs out to join her.

They walk around the front of the car. Rachel gets out, comes over, and grasps Elena's hand in hers. I zip down my window.

"Wish us luck," Rachel says.

"Break a leg," I say.

Nobody pays much attention as the three of them work their way around the back of the crowd toward the podium. The wind has shifted, allowing Walker's voice to ride the breeze through my open window.

"Yes. I've got a grown daughter," the president says. "A granddaughter, too. Neither the American people nor my wife has known about this until today. But I've known who she is. And some in the media may have heard her name before. Her name is Rachel Estrella."

I see Billie break from Rachel and Elena, the escort concluding her services as her charges head for the podium, where Walker will momentarily introduce them before the cameras. Sunshine glints off a passing car's windshield to the right, on East First Street. Walker keeps on with his speech.

"You might recognize her name because seven months ago, Rachel went miss – "

Crack.

Strangely, the sound I've just heard isn't what has interrupted Walker. The sound, resembling the pop of a firecracker, comes only after an odd audio-visual lag. In the way that thunder follows lightning's silent rage, Walker first careens back as though he's been slugged by an invisible fist, then topples, at high speed, like a dead weight, an arc of blood spraying from the upper part of his chest. Next, coming on its lag, was the *crack* of the rifle shot. I know immediately from the sheer savage violence that I've just witnessed Walker's death. He cannot possibly have survived the impact of the shell that just penetrated his rib cage — and no special-effects whiz could have fabricated what I've just seen. This is no staged assassination.

The echo of the gunshot bounces around the plaza. People start screaming – talking — running.

He's been shot — from a distance — by a sniper —

Billie, Rachel, and Elena are exposed. I kick open my door and sprint across the lawn against the grain of sudden bedlam. Billie, who has turned around with the same intentions, reaches Rachel and Elena first as I say, "Get Elena!"

Billie takes Elena's hand while I take Rachel's, and we turn and haul ass back to the car, dashing shoulder-to-shoulder with the fleeing crowd.

Screaming and yelling surrounds us now. Something occurs to me, and I crane my neck to get a look at the parked cars on East First Street. I see what I expect to see — the Expedition in its spot, the twin Secret Service Yukons beside it — but I see something else, something my recollection of the reflective flash has told me to look for. Head turned, barely able to keep my balance while I run, I see the sunlight glint off Clem Skeel's sunglasses as he ducks behind the door of his Maxima.

Was Skeel the shooter? There's no rifle visible — but he'd have put that away by now.

We reach the Outback. I open the door to the back seat, push Rachel inside, leap in behind her, and slam the door. Billie gets Elena in on the other side of Rachel.

"Oh my God," Rachel says, only now reacting to the murder of her father and president, seen first-hand in its full brutality. I can only hope that Elena wasn't watching — maybe she wasn't tall enough to see past the crowd. Rachel seizes Elena in an embrace.

Billie backs out and jams the transmission into Drive with a chirp of the tires. The Outback's all-wheel transmission bites the pavement as Billie yanks the wheel to avoid fleeing pedestrians and vehicles, managing all the while to maintain our acceleration curve. She takes us around the southeast corner of the plaza, up East First Street, and away from the bedlam as I steal one last glimpse out the rear window at the plaza.

Rudd and two of the Secret Service men are stooped over the president's prone, bleeding body. I wonder fleetingly whether Rudd is looking for the memo that Walker always kept on his person — the note from the analyst. If that's what he's looking for, he may well find it — but with the picture taken on Billie's cell phone, we printed a hard copy last night in Bob's home office, so Rudd won't be taking the only copy. From his place in the center of a swirl of Secret Service agents, the CIA man stands — and, unless I'm imagining it — catches my eye. Or at least a glimpse of our car.

Billie accelerates and turns the corner.

A building looms, blocking my view of Rudd, and his view of me. A second turn puts the plaza and its chaos behind us, and a quarter-mile later we're northbound on the Sonoma Highway.

PART III

THE ANALYST

-36-

THE SOURCE OF MY HIGH-SPEED decision-making technique was a book. A fellow student told me about it in law school, and I went out when bookstores still existed and bought a copy. The premise of the book was that every decision you face should be settled in five seconds or less — that every choice, even one taken five years to make, is based on essentially the same criteria as what you've got at your fingertips when you are first faced with the choice. Whole or skim milk in your coffee? How much to offer on that house? To send or not to send American soldiers into war . . . The trick is to avoid consideration of pressure or emotion, and simply make the decision based on the factors presented to you. Quickly, firmly, effectively. Five seconds, tops.

I sometimes think that book, by itself, deserves significant credit in my meteoric climb as both litigator and politician. Taking the advice to heart, I discovered that the five-second rule took the mental fatigue out of decision-making, and I followed its premise, without pause or exception, through every step of my career. It aided me greatly. But toward the end of my presidency, I started to think about the stakes again. Decision-making of any kind began to wear me out.

Eventually I lost faith not only in the five-second rule, but in my ability to choose from even the simplest, least significant alternatives. This happens to most presidents over the course of their time in office. Their hair turns gray, their jowls fatten, they grow increasingly out of touch. They come to avoid big decisions at all costs, leaning only into consensus policies that protect their legacy. When stretched past our capacity, I suppose none of us are capable of making a decent decision, even if the universe depends on it.

You see the wisdom in our two-term limit.

However, I now find, from my seat in the Outback on Highway 12, that the switch has been thrown. My internal machinery begins getting to work much faster than before. Not quite on a five-second arc, but faster just the same.

I never would have thought the old buzzards would go so far as to assassinate a sitting president, but now they have. It follows that the thing they're hiding — the secret they believe they're burying by killing Walker — is an even bigger deal than suspected.

Bigger than the life of an American president.

My synapses flip back to the memo the CIA analyst named Laramie sent to Walker:

```
Identification of corroborating intel re:
intended ARD-BW incident set for 7/5 of
next year.
```

The cryptic note might not have meant much to Walker, and at first glance, it might not mean much to me, or any casual reader who might stumble across it. But to the study group — to the buzzards who showed up in the Oval Office attempting to intimidate and warn off the president — it meant *everything*. When their warnings and intimidation tactics didn't work, they decided to wait and see whether Walker would lose his bid for re-election. He didn't. They then resorted to kidnapping, imprisonment, and now murder — taking out the president they were hell-bent on keeping quiet on the topic of the memo.

An incident involving an ARD-BW biological weapon scheduled for July fifth of next year . . . stated in a memo written eight months ago. I pull my eyes from behind my hands and check the date on my watch. It's June 21. An incident involving a biological weapon, two weeks from today. Location unspecified.

We've reached the city limits of Santa Rosa. My eyes focus on the directional signs for the north and south on-ramps for Highway 101 . . . and then I see the *other* posting beside the directional signs. A *services* sign. It's blue and comprised entirely of logos. *Food, gas, lodging* — and another logo too. Designed for those who've just exited the freeway.

Making the first of my five-second decisions, I point to the sign.

"Turn here," I say. "Turn right."

Billie processes from behind the wheel. "We're not taking the freeway?"

"No."

I return to my hyper-clear thoughts as Billie completes the turn, passes under the freeway, and sets out along a road lined with industrial buildings.

"Why not?" Billie says. "What's this way?"

I may not have the "how" down just yet, but I know where we need to go, and I know what we need to do there.

"Washington," I say.

"Washington, DC?" she says. "And we'll get there going this way how exactly . . . ?"

I'll determine who can best help us when we get there, but what's immediately clear to me is that the only way to get at the old buzzards is to find out what they're determined to hide and use it against them. And the only way to do either of these things is set up shop across the street from our opponent — in the power seat, where every key American agency, analyst, bureaucrat, diplomat, and politician runs their store too.

Washington is where the study group maintains their stranglehold on power — so that is where I'm going to take it from them.

I look up and answer Billie.

"We're going Greyhound," I say.

LONG-HAUL PASSENGER BUS LINES COMPRISE one of the last ways to travel in relative anonymity. It involves no TSA security screeners, no conductor walking the aisles, no state cops pulling you over for weaving in your lane. The FBI rarely chews up any of its resources surveying Greyhound or Trailways depots with dragnets searching for fleeing criminals and terrorists — only airports, train terminals, and rental-car agencies typically turn out productive leads, so the resources aren't expended at the bus depot.

People who ride city transit are busy, with places to go on a timetable, but people who take Trailways or Greyhound are in their own world. If they aren't one of the rare students or military personnel eager to get home for vacation but averse to flying, most of these passengers keep their heads down and concern themselves with their own business. Some may not have watched a CNN telecast in their entire lives, and besides being ideal candidates for jury selection, they are also perfect fellow passengers for a wanted former president and his posse seeking to make their way across the country.

Billie buys our tickets at the window with cash — my supply of which will soon run out — while I try Bob Hansen's number on one of the station's payphones. It rings endlessly on both attempts, never landing a person or voice mail. I'm concerned for his and Gloria's safety, but ill equipped to do anything about the concern.

Our departure is announced over the loudspeaker just under an hour later and we board without incident, taking the two rearmost rows. I sit deep in my seat, baseball cap pulled low. The only other passenger, a stubbled older black man carrying a huge duffel bag, narrows his eyes at me as he boards, but he settles into a seat up front without a second glance.

Rachel speaks for the first time since our getaway from the plaza. She's in the seat in front of me, Elena leaning quietly against her torso.

"I barely knew he existed in the first place," she says flatly, "and now my father's dead."

The driver has fired up the engine and the old diesel power plant masks our voices.

"Yes," I say.

"Any possibility he set it up again?" Billie says from her spot beside me. "Could it have been another fake?"

"No," I say. "I saw what the bullet did. I also think I saw the rifle. And possibly the rifleman."

"Who was it?" Billie says.

"It might have been Skeel," I say. "Could be he was there keeping an eye out for a shooter, or watching for some other reason, but there was never any discussion about that. He was parked at an angle that would have worked for a shot. I saw his car beforehand, saw him getting back into his car after – can't be sure, but he might have been the one."

"I thought Skeel was working for Rudd and Walker," Billie says. "And you."

"He was," I say. "But money talks with that guy."

Rachel's eyes have been following our conversation like a tennis match. She locks her stare on me.

"Why are we going to Washington?" she says.

"Because that's where they are."

"Walker's old buzzards?" Billie says.

"Yes. I've always called them the study group. Though they weren't then what they've become today."

Rachel nods. "What are we going to do when we get there?"

"Remove them from the equation," I say.

Billie watches my face. "Remove them?"

"Yes."

"How?"

I withdraw and hold up the folded copy of the memo. "The study group cares enough about whatever it is Laramie discovered to kidnap Rachel," I say, "frame me for multiple homicides, then shoot the president himself when those strategies failed to keep a lid on the information."

"Okay," Billie says.

"It follows that if we unearth what they're hiding — what Laramie found, what Walker never did discover — it could empower us to control the study group. The leverage Walker mistakenly believed he came to hold. The difference being, I don't plan to play political checkers against, extorters, abductors, and murderers. Diplomacy doesn't work against this sort of enemy. We're going to use the information, and the leverage it provides, to remove them."

Billie's eyeing me like I've lost it — a look I've grown quite familiar with.

"So the three — excuse me, four of us — a former president wanted in a double murder, a smoothie shop owner, recent kidnap victim, and her daughter — are off to the nation's capital to find the facts behind Laramie's memo. Facts which the current president, and all the resources the White House brings to bear, could not?"

"Point taken," I say. "But when you consider other options, you'll see that there are none. The only course is to unravel this secret, preferably by finding Laramie herself for crystal clarity on the intelligence."

Air strikes.

"These people will obviously go to extremes to keep their secret silent," Billie says, "but is there still not a case for us to contact some senior federal law enforcement official or other — in, I don't know the groups, but the FBI, Justice Department, Secret Service — and arrange protection? If they hear our side of the story, they'll help, won't they? And Rachel could finally take Elena to her home in — Temecula, right?"

"Yes," Rachel says.

"Yes, at some point we should and will all go home. But we can't yet. Rachel, you aren't safe yet since you weren't shown on camera, though Walker's words could prove helpful. And contacting the feds won't do us any good: as we learned from Rachel's kidnapping, the study group owns, or at least has deep access across most if not all federal agencies. They have people in the FBI, Homeland Security, the State Department. They probably have someone in the Secret Service. There's no Band-Aid here."

Rachel looks at Billie, then at me. "Why Washington? What will we do there that will make any of us any safer?"

"I haven't determined the plan yet," I say. "But we're going to need help, and despite my years away, Washington is where the majority of my former colleagues remain. At least those who've still got their share of clout. The more clout, the less likely they'll already have taken up residence on the study group's payroll. I need to consider whom we can trust, but Washington is where we start."

Billie's look back into my eyes is stiff, but she doesn't say anything more, and Rachel's typically hardened expression retains its normal state — each of which reaction I will take as begrudging assent for joint participation in at least the remainder of this bus ride.

"I suggest you get some sleep," I say. "We've got considerable work ahead and it's a long ride to the Potomac."

With the bus grinding its way east, the time has come to consider everyone I know in Washington. Who's still of weight, who's still in service; who may yet remain insulated from the influence of the emboldened, expanded study group; and who, most important, might actually consider taking my call.

I hunker a little lower in my seat and open my little black book.

-38-

O N DECEMBER 17, 2004, GEORGE W. Bush signed into law the Intelligence Reform and Terrorism Prevention Act. Following recommendations by the 9/11 Commission, the act established a new position in the country's already-bloated foreign-affairs bureaucracy: Director of National Intelligence. The DNI — along with a deputy and bureau of up to 1,500 staffers — inherited oversight of the U.S. intelligence community from the Director of Central Intelligence, a position that had already been handling the same role for decades.

Both military and civilian appointees have served as DNI since the office's inception in 2004; eighteen months ago, President Walker chose a civilian for the post. The man he appointed has worked his entire life in intelligence circles, including a three-year stint under my administration as DCI.

His name is Lou Ebbers.

Late one night during that stint, Ebbers and I sat in the Situation Room. The television screen, one of the largest of its time, crackled with static but otherwise displayed a dim image of a miner's tunnel — or at least something that looked like one. In point of fact it was a recently-seized smuggler's warren that ran under the U.S.-Mexico border near the El Paso-Juarez City crossing, in that moment dedicated solely to our clandestine mission.

The National Security Advisor, Secretary of Defense, and Chairman of the Joint Chiefs of Staff were gathered with Lou and me around the Situation Room's massive table, clustered at the end nearest the television. Staff in my administration called Lou the Silver Fox — iron-jawed with a full head of silver hair, he looked like a guy out of J. Crew catalog.

The speakerphone, placed between us, emitted an irregular high-pitched beep behind muffled voices and the sound of rustling clothes and wind. The beep indicated the audio signal connecting us to the SEALs carrying out tonight's mission was intact. Each of us had separate individual telephone consoles at our place on the table. Ebbers and two of the others were on their phones, speaking in low voices to their respective offices. While the image on the television remained the same — rough reception of nothing but the vacant tunnel — the audio coming from the speakerphone suddenly shifted dramatically.

"Location confirmed. Positions," came a muffled voice.

After more rustling, the sounds of fabric scraping against microphone, a second voice: "Team in place." The first voice then barked in a scrappy whisper: "Four, three, two, one — *Go-go-go!*"

We heard a *thud* that I assumed to be the SEALs' battering ram smashing through a door, ten or more voices suddenly yelling altogether, items crashing to the floor, and gunshots — though they sounded more like the *rap* of a hammer against a slab of marble over the speakerphone. The gunshots ceased. An onslaught of voices —

"Freeze! *Alto! Todos quietos!* Drop your weapons!"

"Hold it! Turn around! Now!"

After a slight pause, the first man's muffled voice: "Three, five, apprehend subject."

Scraping fabric, footsteps, static, rustling — then relative silence. It felt almost anticlimactic. The first man's voice broke the silence, sounding up close and personal, as though he'd dipped his chin to speak directly into the mic.

"Control, we have subject in custody. Alive and well."

Gene, my Secretary of Defense, looked to Ebbers, who quickly nodded his assent. Gene punched the speakerphone off of mute and spoke. "Roger, Team Leader. Proceed to checkpoint."

"Roger. ETA five minutes." Then, muffled again: "Move it out. *Go-go-go!*"

After a span dominated by the rumpled sound of Navy SEALs running down city streets, the leader of the strike team came into view onscreen. The image remained fuzzy and prone to random glitches, so I found myself doubting the live video feed's effectiveness in the identification I was about to make. A commando approached then stepped to the side of the camera. A hand could be seen wrapping around the lens, and with the flick of a switch, the problem was solved, the spotlight mounted on the camera illuminating the tunnel to the point of hyperclarity.

Another trio of men, made up of two commandos flanking the man I knew to be our captive, appeared on camera. Heavyset, dressed in khaki shorts and a short-sleeve shirt, our captive had his hands secured behind his back and his head down. The commandos brought him front-and-center before the camera. He squinted in the light as one of the SEALs lifted his chin, giving me a full view of his wide, mustached, vaguely Latino face.

"Mr. President?" Gene said, prompting me.

"Sir?" Ebbers echoed.

I paused, determined to take my time and make absolutely sure.

Ilich Ramirez Sanchez, more commonly known as Carlos the Jackal, was the Osama bin Laden of my era. He established his reputation in 1975 in a raid on OPEC headquarters in Austria, killing three victims. This achievement led to multiple and continued attacks on Western targets over the succeeding decade, on which he always operated as a gun-for-hire. Carlos worked not just for the Popular Front for the Liberation of Palestine — his first client — but for Stasi, East Germany's secret police organization; the KGB; and a long roster of radical European terrorist organizations. He rapidly became America's public enemy number one and was, by my time in office, the most wanted man in the world.

The publicly documented 1994 arrest of Carlos in Sudan led to his extradition to France, where he was subsequently convicted of murdering two French counterterrorism agents and is currently serving his third life sentence.

The truth of the matter is that the four of us gathered before the television screen in the Situation Room were there a considerable time prior to the supposed Sudan arrest, and the man I was looking at onscreen was Sanchez. In the prior day's PDB, we learned that CIA had determined Carlos' whereabouts, and Ebbers and I immediately set the plan in motion to seize him.

The key, of course, was to make sure that we had the right man.

"Confirmed," I said. "That's him. Are we all in agreement?"

"Affirmative," Gene said.

"Yessir," Ebbers said.

"Agreed," said the National Security Advisor.

Gene raised his voice. "Team leader, identity confirmed. Proceed to delivery point."

Sanchez was pushed aside by the commandos and another face — the stone-jawed, helmeted visage of the SEAL team leader — appeared in the glare of the camera's spotlight. "Roger," came his voice over the speaker as he mouthed the words on a slight delay onscreen. "Will confirm delivery next." The image onscreen upended and went black, the commandos taking the camera, tripod, and satellite link with them as they fled north.

It was two weeks later, in a session of the debrief task force chaired by Lou and Gene in the Oval Office, that a discussion took place between Ebbers and a man on the National Security Council that sealed the fate of Carlos. I hadn't met the NSC member before that day, but assumed he was a regular member of Ebbers' task force. Top of mind that day was the subject of whether and when to release to the public our capture of Carlos.

"If we put it out there publicly, and loudly, that we just caught him," Ebbers said in his trademark Carolina lilt — a genuine one, unlike the late President Walker's — "we'll put a shot of fear down the spine of every aspiring terrorist. You target Americans? You go down. No matter how long it takes, we find our justice. Be an important statement in our counterterrorism efforts."

Miles was there too, and chimed in. "Makes for a hell of a story for you as well, Mr. President. Your numbers will tap the stratosphere. Go a long way toward fixing the damage from the Syria-Salvador affair."

"Can't argue with either point," I said.

"If I may," the NSC member said.

We all turned to him but he didn't appear the least bit intimidated. Had I heard the term used by Walker in advance of that meeting, I'd have immediately thought of him as an *old buzzard*, though he couldn't have been a day over 35.

"The NSC has conducted a study," he said, "the findings of which I'd like to take the opportunity to share with you, Mr. President." He withdrew from a briefcase enough copies for all of a bound report. We took the copies and I leafed through mine as the NSC man continued. "There are two salient reasons covered in the report that argue for maintaining total secrecy regarding our capture of Carlos," he said. "The first, and most obvious, being the opportunity for further interrogation. Based on the number of organizations for which he's worked, and the silo-like access to the top that he's apparently held in each of these groups, the value of maintaining him as a classified asset is nearly immeasurable. It could help us squelch the cancerous threat of European and Mideast terrorism before it overwhelms us."

"That much is obvious," I said. "In any case we will not release information on his capture until we've squeezed every last drop of useful information out of him. So your study, which, incidentally, I don't recall authorizing, is in line with my views so far. Go on."

The buzzard cleared his throat before answering.

"Yes, Mr. President, I believe the National Security Advisor had signed the authorization for the study." I shot a glare at my advisor, who shrugged. We'd take this up later. The buzzard went on. "Reason number two is the paramount importance of establishing a suitable replacement for Carlos as America's public enemy number one *before* informing the general public that we now have our man."

The room fell silent.

After a moment, I broke the silence. "I get the theoretical value of positioning one or more of our enemies as paramount and toxic to our standing as the world's leading superpower. I may even deserve some credit in having written the book on this kind of positioning in my campaign. But you just said *establishing*. Care to explain?"

The buzzard hemmed and hawed at the time, covering his tail with a lot of long words. In looking back now, it occurs to me he may have let slip that word, *establish*, and it may well have been literal. Is it too far-fetched to consider that an organization now immersed in kidnapping, murder, and assassination to hide its secrets might have taken efforts to establish — AKA create — an enemy of the people to serve strategic purposes? And might that organization also have, more recently, taken efforts to establish an operation to conduct an 'ARD-BW' attack for similar strategic purposes?

Ultimately, though for a different purpose than that old buzzard suggested, Carlos stayed in U.S. possession until the day his public arrest was duly staged. This meant, among other factors, that despite many productive interrogation sessions with the world's most wanted man, I missed out on the great potential for re-election publicity that the announcement of his capture would otherwise have provided.

-39-

THE NUMBER I'VE GOT FOR Lou Ebbers in my little black book is his mobile. On the sixth ring, I'm figuring it's no longer a working number, but on the eighth, he answers.

"Ebbers," he says.

"Lou, it's me."

He doesn't respond right away. I hear birds in the background — distant, as though he may be in a park.

"Quite a surprise," he says.

"You in Washington?" I say.

He doesn't hesitate before answering this one, which I take as a good sign. "Inside the Beltway, at any rate. Don't tell me you are? Wasn't it, ah, Sonoma, where you most recently made the — "

"I'm near enough to the Beltway myself," I say. "Can you see me in three hours?"

This time there's clear hesitation. "Mr. Pres — "

"Ignore the media coverage of my plight. What's actually happening is that I've been brought into a shitstorm in the middle of your world. Brought in, in fact, by none other than the twice-assassinated commander in chief. And at the center of the storm lies intel revealing an apparent plan for the detonation of a biological weapon on July fifth. Location unclear."

There's intent behind my tone and interruption technique and flood of details. I want to quickly re-establish our working relationship — Ebbers working for me.

I hear the distant birds as though they're much closer before Ebbers responds.

"Now hold on," he says. "If you expect me to keep up, you've got to slow down. Are you saying — "

"I have in my possession a copy of a memo sent by a CIA analyst directly to the president making mention of this pending strike. No further intel was found by Walker's inquiries, and the analyst has gone missing. I would like your help in finding her."

Birds, background noise. Then, "You're telling me you — "

"I'll give you further details," I interrupt again, "and outline precisely the help I seek, in person. But I wanted you to know the purpose of the meeting. And when we meet, you'll need to come alone. No analysts, no deputies. I don't trust anybody right now, Lou. Can't. And you shouldn't either. So before we agree to meet, I need you to confirm this condition. We meet alone. That acceptable?"

Another beat before he says, "What about you?"

"Will I be alone?"

"Right."

"I'm traveling with . . . I will have one female companion who will join us for the meeting. She's a friend. From home."

After a pause, Lou says, matter-of-factly, "Carmel-by-the-Sea." Then, "How long shall I expect this meeting to last?"

"Depends on you. Won't take more than fifteen minutes to give you the whole story and lay out what we need."

"'We' being . . .?"

"My travel companion and I."

The sound of birds comes again, and the rough noise of what might be a gentle breeze against the phone. "Why don't we make this simple. You remember my house?"

I think for a moment, recalling my three, possibly four visits there.

"Yes," I say. "Nine o'clock?"

"See you then."

-40-

"**Y**OU CAN PULL OVER HERE."

The rare taxi driver we were able to find in this ride-share age, a small man wearing a strange and very large wool cap, complies.

"Two of us are getting out," I say. "We'll need you to wait with the two who stay. You can keep your meter running. I'll give you fifty bucks now, plus whatever the meter reads when we return and a hundred more."

I'm acutely aware that this will stretch our cash supply to nearly zero, but it's the best way I can think to keep Rachel and Elena sheltered while we sit with Ebbers. And it didn't strike me as even a remote possibility that Billie would accept my excluding her from the meeting, so the taxi seat will have to cost what it costs.

The cabbie catches my eye in the rear-view mirror, holds his look as though I'm subject to his judgment call on whether I'm good for it, then nods. I fork over a fifty, which he snatches and pockets.

I turn to Rachel. "If, while Billie and I are gone, somebody approaches in any way, have the driver take you elsewhere, then return here twenty minutes later."

"How long will you be?"

"Most likely an hour at most."

Rachel's eyes flick involuntarily toward the driver, then back to me. She nods and slips her arm around Elena's shoulders as Billie and I slide out of the cab.

Our starting point is Quincy Street, in Arlington, Virginia, a street laden with restaurants, vocational schools and nail salons just under a mile from Lou Ebbers' house. Billie and I wind circuitously as we walk toward our destination, taking side streets and changing directions the whole way.

"Why so far around?" she asks in an alley. "I get the switchback concept, but four blocks west to get ten blocks north?"

"I placed a modicum of trust in Lou when he worked for me, but that was then. It's anybody's bet whether he'll abide by my request for a solo meeting."

"And how does the ultra-long way around address that?"

"He'll be expecting us to come by Uber," I say. "Plus I'm going to guess that anyone he brings will be watching the front of the house, including the streets leading to his driveway, but again, it's anybody's guess. I want to wrap around and check all sides in decreasing loops."

Billie considers this as we approach the street two blocks behind Ebbers' house. Two-story residences, manicured yards, streetlights every two hundred feet.

"Are you planning on knocking? Or are we sneaking in?" she says.

"The latter, if we can, at least as far as arriving on the property goes. I'd hope we could spot any surveillance that way, and I'd also like to see if he's got anyone with him before we enter the house."

"And if he does?"

"We leave the way we came."

We swing around the neighborhood twice, not seeing any agents in unmarked cars, or white panel vans occupying a street corner, or men in hats pretending to have a smoke against a lamppost. I'm well aware this means nothing. Humans aren't even required, given the sensors and camera coverage possible in today's era.

Finally I see what I'm looking for.

"Here," I say, opening a waist-high gate leading behind the darker of two stately homes at the center of the street on the block behind Ebbers' house. "This should get us into his backyard."

"A trespassing beef to accompany your double-murder charge," Billie whispers as she passes me into the back yard.

Along the side of the house behind Ebbers' property, a freshly mowed lawn rests in darkness. The house doesn't have any uncovered windows along its flank; there's a light on somewhere inside, but we get to the back of the property without incident.

At the rear property line, a tall, ivy-ridden fence divides this home from its neighbors. The divider looks to be at least eight feet high.

"Lou's house is on the other side of this fence," I say.

When I leave it at that, Billie looks up at the fence then stares skeptically at me.

"And you're expecting me to climb up and take a look, aren't you?"

I almost smile. Not quite.

"Yes."

-41-

Having encountered only mild embarrassment at the need for Billie to yank me over the top of the fence, we now stare through the rear French doors of Ebbers' three-story house. The back of Ebbers' head and one of his shoulders is visible around a corner through the sun room. That's the only angle we have on him, but from what we can see, he's alone in the room he occupies.

One of the French doors is opened halfway, with the exterior screen door still in place. You forget sometimes, living in coastal California, about the mosquitoes and mugginess of the east coast. Prepared to attempt to pick or break the lock on the screen door, I try it out and find it isn't secured by anything other than an unlocked latch.

Billie follows me into the sun room, and then into the kitchen.

A number of folders are spread across the black marble counter on the island, where Lou Ebbers sits, studying the contents of one of the folders. A half-drunk pint glass of Guinness or some other dark beer rests before him.

It isn't until we pass the microwave and range that he senses our presence. He turns, raising an eyebrow, but remains otherwise immobile. I immediately conclude he's got video security and saw us coming.

"Hell, why knock?" he says. "Just come right on in."

"Just making sure you're complying with my condition."

I come around the island and take a stool across from my old DCI. Billie sits on the stool beside me. Ebbers surveys us unflinchingly, almost appearing to do so as an afterthought.

"Suppose I should be offended you didn't take me at my word," he says.

"Spies don't get their hackles up about somebody failing to take them at their word," I say, "since they never take anyone else at theirs."

My eyes take in our surroundings.

"True enough," he says. "Trust, yet verify?"

Our eyes lock on his uttering of the saying my Russian counterpart was famously known for using in the pair of summits for which Lou helped me prepare. I nod.

"Yes," I say. "And thank you for seeing me."

He shrugs off my thanks in the manner of a sibling or old friend.

"What can I offer you?" He gestures toward his glass. "Guinness? Something stronger? Cabinet's full. I'm rarely here. One of the reasons I chose it as the place we should meet. Maybe coffee?"

I turn to Billie and she shakes her head.

"No, but thank you," I say. I pull the memo page from my pocket and push it across the island. "This is the correspondence I mentioned. It's written, as you can see, by an analyst named Laramie. First name Julie, it turns out."

I allow him a moment to read it, which he takes the time to do before looking up at me.

"July fifth is twelve days from now," he says. "And this actually made it to Walker?"

I nod. "Yes, but why don't you hold your questions and let me walk you through the series of related incidents, in the chronology Walker described, as we understand them to have taken place."

As I recall to be his habit, Ebbers lifts his hands to his chin, folds them and, arms propped on his elbows, rests his chin on his fingers. I proceed to relay all that Walker told us in Bob and Gloria Hansen's study, plus most of what happened before and after, down to details as specific as Walker referring to the study group minions as *old buzzards*. By design I leave certain pieces out, neglecting to mention, for instance, the current whereabouts of Rachel and Elena.

"Which brings us to my request," I say. "I need you to help us find that analyst."

I lean in as I say this. Lou's beer remains half-finished, untouched since our arrival, and his chin-on-folded-hands posture hasn't shifted.

"I leave it to you on how to go about it," I say, "though I recommend that until we learn what Laramie has actually uncovered, the fewer people you involve, the better. It's only after we talk to her and find out what it is that inspired her memo-delivery feat that we'll be capable of turning the tables on the so-called powers that be."

I lean back slightly, stretching a kink in my back. As I do this, Lou begins shaking his head, chin still set on the pyramid of his steepled hands.

"You can't possibly succeed," he says.

"At what?" This, from Billie.

"Taking them on," he says. "Taking them down." He nods absently. "Walker may have called them old buzzards, but as you know they're mostly not old, and they're not really buzzards in any way. In fact, the majority of them are young, smart as shit, and more powerful than you can imagine in active policy-making. They weren't squat when you and I worked together. It's like they were trying to get there, but hadn't quite. Now it's different. Now they own this town. At least the federal bureaucracy. Which means they own the nation. Hell, they all but own *me*, though not in the way they owned Walker, or — "

The hackles suddenly rise along my spine. A finger of ice probes into my brain. Not just because I've risked Billie's and my lives to share, uselessly, our entire story to a man who may well have succumbed, possibly even sold out, to the *powers that be* — but also because a noise has just come from upstairs.

Above our heads and to the right, it sounds to me like the noise made by a person leaping to the base of a stairwell. One of Lou's agents, listening in on the second floor, deciding he's heard enough? Calculating that it's time to emerge from the surveillance room and apprehend the fugitives in the kitchen?

I turn sharply to my old colleague. "Who's here?" I say. I reach over and grab him by his tie. "Who did you bring!"

Still in my grasp, he shakes his head and cranes his neck in the direction of the sound. "No one. I respected your — "

A second sound comes, this time from behind me: the *tinkle* of broken glass.

A break-in — people are coming inside.

I turn viciously back to Lou, shaking him. "Who did you bring!"

But as I call out, I hear Billie yelp. And then I see why she's made the odd noise: a hole has pierced the center of Lou's forehead and a hot flood of crimson has doused my arm and is flooding the island counter and stools beneath.

"Let go of him!" Billie screams. She kicks away my stool and pulls at me, grabbing my arms. My hands are still locked on Lou's collar as Billie barks her orders: "*Let go!* We have to go!"

I release my grip and Ebbers topples, head lopping savagely against the counter on his fall to the floor. My brain snaps to it in time to remember the memo, now partially wet with Ebbers' blood, but which I grab and push back into one of my pockets. Then Billie's pulling me, and we're running, past the stove, through the dining room, and I feel more than see the presence of a figure, clad in dark clothing, as he, she, *it* appears at the top of the stairwell between kitchen and dining room. The figure holds an assault rifle, and pauses — slightly, perhaps only to survey the surroundings, or maybe it's that hesitation people like this commando seem to get stuck with in realizing that it's me in their sights — and then the figure is leaping down the stairs three at a time.

Tugging me behind her like a barge, Billie breaks through the rear screen door, its shredded remains brushing me on my way by, and then we're nearly at the fence — a fence I know all too well from my tiresome effort of climbing it to get in here will be challenging to traverse.

I hear voices from inside the house. *Shouts.* Voices of authority. Of efficiency. Of the military.

Still at full stride, Billie says, "Don't slow down!" and we don't. Ahead of me, she scales the wood panels like an insect, running vertically, my forearm held in her grasp, and then she's got herself turned around, arms draped and reaching back over as she pulls me up to assist in my own attempt at her track-and-field Spiderman leap. I almost make it, but my left knee gives slightly and my upward momentum halts. I'm aware that it's gravity and my own weight that have done me in, but my realization isn't going to propel my body the remaining three feet to the top of the fence, or do me any good at all.

"Come on!"

She's still got me snagged at the elbow, clawing with all ten fingers, hooking me the way a fisherman takes a gaff to a tuna. I swing my other hand around, slapping and grabbing at the ivy until my fingers grasp solid wood. I pull with one arm and Billie pulls the other, and I feel her strength, and the fence and the branches and flowers and leaves and stickers scrape my arms and thighs as we roll over the top. There's a sense of freedom, of victory — right before I plow head-and-shoulders into the hard lawn below. Billie falls on top of me and I feel the explosion of a stinger in my neck as it fires its shot of pain from the peak of my skull to the depths of my tailbone.

I'm able to stand, and Billie's leading again as we retrace our path past the vacant neighbor's house and onto the street beyond. I step ahead of her and lead us across the street.

"We'll have to do what we just did again," I say. "Use yards. They'll have vehicles. We need to stay off the streets — "

"Yes," she says, and we move through the yard across the street, down another driveway, over a picket fence, and we've cleared another block the hard way. A dog barks in the dark, but we've crossed another street, barreling through another two properties.

It isn't until we hit the next front yard that a pair of headlights, turning sharply into the driveway, capture us in their glare.

"Shit! Turn back!" I say. Billie, ahead of me, pivots, and we're crossing to the neighbor's property when I realize something about the car. A man in shirt-and-tie rises from behind the wheel and speaks in a distinctly non-commando tone — one an ordinary man might use when he's just spotted two maniacs, one half-soaked in blood, dashing out from his driveway.

"Jesus!" he says. "What is the meaning of this!"

I do my own pivot and hold Billie with me as I head directly for the driver. My eyes hone in on what he holds in his hand.

"Sorry, buddy," I say as I grab his keys. I lay my hip and shoulder into his body and he tumbles backward. I'm telling Billie to get in the car but she's already in the driver's seat by the time I get the words out. I toss her the keys, scramble around the front of the car, and climb into the front passenger seat as she fires up the engine and jerks the car into reverse.

The guy's on his feet, halfheartedly pursuing, and then we're down the block in his Mercedes. We realize simultaneously that the interior lights are on, displaying us like pets in a fishbowl; it takes far too many seconds, but after a frantic punching-and-pulling session I get the lights doused.

"Take it slow," I say.

"Just another neighbor on a drive?" she says, taking the first turn gingerly. We find our bearings and she makes another turn, retracing our incoming route in reverse. A black American sedan races past in the opposite direction. In the side-view mirror I see the car's brake lights flare red; it bolts sideways into a turn, but not a U-turn. It vanishes from view.

"This — is this the alley we took?" Billie says.

"I think so."

She makes this next turn, painstakingly drives down its length like a NASCAR driver forced to obey the speed limit on pit row, then turns into traffic casually, activating the Benz's blinker, and we're out on the neighborhood's thoroughfare with a handful of other cars. We drive south for fifteen blocks, head east for another five, then north again for four until we hit Quincy.

"They're still here," I say.

Billie pulls carefully behind the taxi. Rachel's head is visible in the back, peering out at our offending headlights. Billie kills the lights and engine.

"Leave the keys for that poor guy," I say, which she does before following me into the back of the cab. I tell the driver to get us going. Undeterred, he eyes me in the rear-view, motionless.

"What are you waiting for!"

Then I realize the answer, withdraw all but the last of my cash, and watch it disappear into his jacket. He nods, flicks the transmission, and drifts coolly into the traffic flow.

-42-

A DOMESTIC LEG OF MY LONG, strange trip once took me back into the nation's capital, where I sat in on an extension course at American University. The course was called *Advanced Foreign Policy Decision-making in the Post-Soviet Era*. Somebody had dropped a flyer for the class on the floor of a Metro subway car, and I noticed that the two-day weekend seminar included as its climax "a role-playing game of international crisis." I remembered the name of the very liberal instructor, Elliott Woodruff, from a list I'd once been shown. The list was a document put out by the FBI with the intent of outing the most fervent communist sympathizers in the Washington area.

Unable to resist temptation, I visited Professor Woodruff minutes before the beginning of the Saturday session and asked whether I might be a worthy addition to his role-playing game in exchange for his allowing me to audit the class. He agreed, and added an invitation for a night of home cooking to the mix.

I wasn't disappointed on either front. Saturday night, I was hosted by Woodruff and his wife, Zasha, a former Soviet deputy ambassador to Canada. On Monday, after the other students drew straws to determine who would play the roles of House Majority Leader, Secretary of Defense, Prime Minister of Israel, and so on, I got to act out the staging of a Middle East crisis alongside them as a hawkish American president. Let's just say the role felt mildly familiar and his students got their money's worth.

On the night of our dinner, Woodruff, glass of cognac in hand, walked me down to his basement as though to show off his wine cellar. But Woodruff's basement hobby was a different one: featuring a photo booth, darkroom, a set of computers and specialty printers, the good professor was housing a fully functional and treacherously illegal passport creation facility. It's that basement I'm hoping to put to use tonight.

Standing now behind a hedge with Rachel and Elena as Billie goes to knock on the Woodruffs' door, I'm wondering how many former colleagues and friends I'll see killed before this thing is over, presuming it will ever end. One thing I've decided: no more establishment people. The study group's reach is too broad in government circles.

Ebbers' last living point, by my read, was that regardless of how deeply he was awash in old buzzards, he wouldn't have been able to help even if he wanted to. The fact is, most of my former colleagues will face the same challenge, real or perceived, if I come to them for help.

Time to move into the pages of my black book reserved for those in the private sector.

An earlier call from our convenience-store burner phone revealed Woodruff to be home; this time I elected not to say a word when he answered, hanging up and saving the surprise for a live appearance. We switched cabs at a local Metro entrance, putting thirty of my last forty bucks to use in covering our trail to the Alexandria address my book lists as *Woodruff - Residence.*

The door opens to Billie's knock and Woodruff's permanently unfashionable perm — a white man's equivalent of an eighties Afro — appears in the doorway. I watch from the hedge as Billie says the things we planned for her to say.

Woodruff says something back and Billie tosses me a thumbs-up.

-43-

WE'RE SEATED IN A SEMI-CIRCLE in Elliot Woodruff's study.

"How's your better half?" I say.

"Oh, Zasha's gone," Woodruff says.

"Gone?" I say. "There's no way that woman left. You two were inseparable."

Woodruff and I have exchanged letters since my visit, but what he tells me next catches me off guard.

"She's dead," he says.

"Jesus. You never said a word. I'm sorry."

He nods. We're seated in his study, where he's served us Frangelico in snifters. Rachel has declined, but as Billie and I sip the sweet hazelnut liquor, I feel it warming my belly before I've drained an eighth of an inch from the glass.

Billie says, "Was she sick?"

Woodruff shrugs. His eyes brush across Rachel.

"She *got* sick," he says. "Violently. This was three years ago. She was diagnosed with an unidentified form of food poisoning. But to be clear, Zasha's symptoms were nearly the same as those of a man whose name you may be more familiar with. He was called Litvenko."

"Alexander Litvenko?" I say.

Woodruff nods.

"Former KGB spy," he says. "Died in '06." While he speaks, Woodruff's eyes fix again on Rachel. Maybe he recognizes Walker's features in her face; maybe not. "Litvenko's death followed a dinner meeting, or tea at his home, depending on whom you believe, with another Russian spy — one whose affiliation with the Putin regime was more up to date. Litvenko was a vocal opponent of Putin. His death was found to be caused by fatal exposure to polonium-210. His fellow spy slipped him a fatal dose of radioactivity."

Billie says, "Are you saying your wife was poisoned too?"

"Nobody suspected it then. But she enjoyed a breakfast meeting with an old colleague the day she grew ill. The colleague happens to have been the same man who dined with Litvenko prior to his death." He sighs. "Zasha and Litvenko knew many of the same things."

Woodruff shrugs, an angry gesture that appears almost spasmodic.

"These and similar problems are responsible for the collapse of the otherwise utopian Marxist-Leninist form of government to which the Soviets originally aspired," he says. "Barbaric, totalitarian, murderous rule is all that resulted. Had they not fucked it up, we might well be enjoying, today, a harmonious, peaceful world in which equality would know no bounds."

When Billie seems unable to summon a response, I say, "She died in a noble cause."

Woodruff's mouth moves; he is looking down at the carpet. Then he claps his hands and snaps his head upright.

"You're so right," he says. "Now what can this old communist widower do for his friend the formerly right-wing and current fugitive ex-president and his companions — all of whom, I might note, are far more lovely than he?"

Woodruff's eyes are pinned to Rachel's.

"Thank you," Rachel says.

"You're welcome," he says cheerily.

"What we would like from you," I say, "is two new identities — and one additional favor."

Billie looks at me once she's processed the incomplete math. "Why only two?"

I look at Rachel as I answer.

"Since we left the plaza," I say, "I've been trying to think of a way to keep Rachel out of harm's way. There's no reason she should accompany us where we'll be going next." I eye Woodruff. "Elliott, there is very little chance that anyone knows we have come to see you. Few, if any people are even aware of our acquaintance. This means that Rachel and Elena would be safe here, so I'd like to ask you to take them in. It might be for a week — could be more. Rachel, I assure you that the good professor is harmless and trustworthy. Despite the crush he already seems to have developed on you."

Rachel studies me for a moment before turning to Woodruff, who smiles and narrows his eyes at me. "Crush?"

It takes another minute — but then Woodruff grunts, sets his empty glass on his desk, rises, and faces Rachel.

"Of course I will leave the decision to you, Rachel," he says. "But you're welcome to stay here with your daughter for as long as you wish. There are two extra bedrooms I never use in the slightest. I have a housekeeper who comes twice a week, and a catering service that brings a series of meals for me weekly. I don't like to cook, but I do like to eat. We'll have more delivered."

"I enjoy cooking," Rachel says.

"Well, then," he says.

Then another clap. "And you?" he says, rotating his aim to me. "I take it you remember where it is I keep the hidden door?"

"Believe I do," I say.

"Then please feel free to lead the way," he says, "to the chamber of imaginatively disguised yet fully documented people."

-44-

WE'RE ON A BENCH ON the grounds of the Library of Congress, sweltering in the Washington humidity with a view of the James Madison Building from across Independence Avenue. People come and go, looking tiny at the base of the building's tall, rectangular columns. It's almost six p.m., which you wouldn't know from the lingering, oppressive sun.

My Elliott Woodruff-engineered disguise falls somewhere between Osama bin Laden without the turban and Tom Hanks in the movie *Cast Away*: unruly beard, wavy, longish black hair, a set of eyeglasses hiding my face. Billie's blonde-fringed chop-shop haircut is fully covered, given over to a long wavy brown perm. She wears a beret, torn jeans, and a poncho-style pullover, her look something in the order of your average UC Berkeley student *c.* 1970. The prosthetics, wigs, and autumn-weight clothes Woodruff had in his subterranean shop aren't making things any easier in the heat, but the anonymity is worth the suffering.

We've changed benches every twenty minutes or so for the past hour.

"Why didn't you try and leave *me* at Woodruff's too?" Billie says.

"The chances of your allowing me to leave you behind were approximately zero percent," I say. "Also, you're already taken."

Billie allows herself a laugh, which brightens my lens on the world, if only for an instant. "That crush was palpable," she says.

"Seemed almost mutual, even."

"It did."

She adjusts her beret and pullover.

"You know," she says, "I've been thinking about something. Can you explain why that strike team at Lou Ebbers' house didn't take a shot at us?"

I consider this and realize she's verbalized my sense that something wasn't quite right in the melee, but which I'd been unable to pinpoint.

"It may be I didn't overthink it because I'm accustomed to people hesitating when they encounter me," I say. "Kind of a celebrity factor, a deer in the headlights phenomenon that occurs almost every time in some fashion. But maybe that isn't what it was."

"The guy in black, at the top of the stairs," she says. "He had a rifle in his hands. He was twelve feet from us. Fifteen tops. At least two, maybe three seconds to take his shot. It's clear he was a pro. If he had been ordered to kill us, or even if he had that authority in a melee, he had eons of time to do it."

I nod. "Most obvious explanation would be that the assignment was to capture rather than kill us."

"A failed mission, then."

"Yes — thanks in particular to my bodyguard pulling me over an eight-foot, briar-laden fence."

I feel more than see her smile as we slip into silence and continue our monitoring of the stairs of the James Madison Building.

"How do you know the man we're waiting for?" Billie says.

"Rusty?" I say. "Long story."

"It doesn't appear I'll be going anywhere for a while."

I smile.

"Not sure what his job title is, exactly," I say, "but Rusty returns books to their rightful place in the stacks. All day long."

"Think it's called a librarian."

"Yes," I say, "but he's different. Do me a favor?"

She looks at me.

"When we approach him," I say, "why don't you try and calm him with some of your — well, your *way*."

"My way?"

"There's a feeling people get when they talk to you," I say. "That you're empathetic to their plight. That you're invested. That you care. Even in their first moments, meeting you."

"Really," she says.

"I speak from experience. And I think we're going to need you to make him feel that way if we've got any chance of getting anywhere with Rusty."

"Why?"

"Like I said," I say. "Long story."

Mercifully, it's then that a hunched-over figure emerges at the base of the middle columns across the street. He ambles to his right, our left, moving through the wide entrance plaza heading east.

"That's him," I say.

Billie follows my line of sight.

"The older guy?"

"He's not as old as he looks."

As we rise from our bench and follow, we're careful to remain a few yards behind, watching and waiting until it's relatively clear Rusty doesn't have any colleague playing catch-up. Nobody appears interested in him as he strolls. His destination isn't clear from his walk. As we reach him, he's approaching the corner. To the left, across the street and on the property from which we'd been watching, is the Thomas Jefferson Building. Catty corner from here is the John Adams Building, and to the right is the entrance to the parking garage of the building Rusty has just exited.

We pick up our pace and close in on him.

"Rusty," I say from over his shoulder.

Rusty's back is bent near the top of the spine, the way some men's posture deteriorates in their eighties, though I know him to be fifty-five, tops. He slows his pace, turns in a weary, slow movement, and proceeds to work his eyes over me, almost lazily, no apparent shift in his demeanor. But I'm well aware he's seeing everything there is to be seen.

"Help you?" he says, sounding nonchalant but continuing to work me over with the eyes of a cat. He bends his stooped neck to take in Billie too, but his eyes keep coming back to me.

"Yes," I say, "you can. Never thought I'd be asking, but I need your help just the same."

Those cat-eyes blink twice — and then the light falls out of them and a kind of deadness overtakes the light. He turns and resumes his stroll, crossing the intersection toward the John Adams Building.

"I don't fucking believe it," he says as he walks. His voice sounds different from a minute ago — more guttural, almost feral. I was expecting this. I've got a few things to say in hopes of turning him.

Billie and I hustle to keep up.

"We went way overboard," I say. "*I* went way overboard. If there's anything I can do to make it up to you, I'm prepared – "

"Stop talking," he says, then halts again. Like a procession of tailgating cars, we nearly collide. He turns and points to Billie. "Who's she?"

Billie smiles noncommittally. "A good friend," she says.

After a withering stare, Rusty starts walking again. Shaking his head as he maintains his pace. "I can't fucking believe it," he mutters.

"I were in your shoes," I say, "I wouldn't have any interest in talking either. I will say that my former and now late White House Counsel did tell me you had grounds to sue the federal government. You likely still have the r — "

"Mr. President," he says, almost under his breath, "will you *shut up*."

I do, and halt involuntarily. Billie prods me and we jog to catch up again.

When we're back up with his pace, he says, "When I said I didn't believe it, I wasn't referring to you having the nerve to come asking for my help."

Rusty's route has taken us to the service side of the John Adams Building, the smaller, older structure relative to the two gargantuan facilities that flank it.

Rusty stops at the top of an unobtrusive stairwell that doesn't appear to have seen much traffic of late. It resembles a rear service entrance at a zoo or theme park, out of view of the paying customers who ogle the marvels of the facility from its front façade. The stairs descend to a set of double doors secured by a chain and padlock down below ground level.

"Then what is it you don't you believe?" I say.

He turns to face me head-on, a feral glint perceptible in his eyes.

"First of all, you can cease and desist with the patronizing suck-up apology angle," he says. "I know it was you who got me this job. I know further that you did so because, once you became an anarchist, or socialist, or Bohemian, or latter-say saint, or whatever the fuck you see yourself as having become, you realized that you had, in your prior life, utterly destroyed the man I was and, despite my dalliances and general foolishness, you recognized that I deserved far better than the hell you put me through. I know further that you'd come to accept, in your new, enlightened state, that you were a heavyweight prick for four full years of authoritarian rule, and you did more damage while in office than any other six presidents combined. But in the end, Mr. President, *I* ought to be the one hunting *you* down. *I* ought to be thanking *you*. Frankly, I've got a dream life, sir, and it wasn't until you fucked me with your big, fat, authoritarian cock that this paradise became possible."

He straightens a notch, leaning back on his heels. It occurs to me that an advanced form of sarcasm seems the only viable explanation for this behavior; he can't possibly be serious. I look at Billie, whose eyebrows are raised.

"But you still haven't answered the question," she says to him. "You know — what it is that you can't believe."

Rusty's eyes rotate to Billie. Then he grins — a long, wide smile of sharp, tiny yellow teeth suddenly exposed to the world — and laughs.

"What I meant," he says, leaning in with a chuckle until he's an inch or two from Billie's nose, "was that I can't believe the ex-authoritarian here has fallen so far that he would feel the need to contact *me*. I expected if this day ever came it would be satisfying, but strangely, it's somehow . . . anticlimactic." He pulls back an inch and shrugs. "I also meant that I can't believe the garbage you people are wearing. Those are the two shittiest works of theater I've yet to witness."

He withdraws from Billie's personal space and steps into mine.

"Mr. President," he says. "Care to get to the point? What exactly is it that you want?"

I'm absolutely positive that his explanation to Billie is not what he meant by his earlier words, and that he's not to be trusted any more than he ought to have been before. He could just as likely have meant, *I can't believe it, I can finally stab him now.* But it doesn't matter, at least as long as the stabbing doesn't take place immediately. If he's willing to provide the help we need, then it's time to get moving.

"It might be better if we answer that question somewhere more private," I say.

Rusty takes a long, slow look at the both of us. Then he spins nimbly and trots down the stairs. From his pocket he removes a janitorial-grade ring of keys. With one of the keys he unclasps the padlock. He removes the chain and opens the doors, revealing a dark hallway beyond. He steps into the door frame, turns, motions down the hall, and looks back at us.

"The hell are you clowns waiting for?" he says.

-45-

I T TAKES A FOUR-MINUTE WALK through a maze of subterranean hallways and stairwells before Rusty unlocks a door with no evident markings, flicks a switch, and leads us into a room. As a sequence of fluorescent overheads flickers to life, my first supposition is that this low-ceilinged, cavernous space might once have housed an early version of a supercomputer network. Row upon row of hulking metal racks stretch hundreds of feet in each direction, the occasional wire protruding forlornly, empty hinges and bolts dangling from random places on the barren frames.

Rusty disappears behind a column.

"Read much Lewis Carroll recently?" Billie says in my ear.

Coming around the column, we're met with a shimmering curtain of beads, the shimmer our clue that Rusty has just passed through. I enter first.

On the other side, there's a bed, table, and makeshift kitchen. Floor lamps cast pools of light on the main living space. Surrounding this basic layout, stretching in a room as wide and long, though not nearly as tall, as a high school gymnasium, are dry-erase boards, easels, cork boards, calendars, charts, file cabinets, bookshelves, and stacks of newspapers, some reaching nearly to the ceiling. There are haphazardly piled books, magazines, newsletters, Standard & Poor's binders, a few old, clunky-looking desktop computers, an iPad, and a newer laptop.

I have a pretty good idea what Rusty does down here. In fact, it's the reason I had us come see him, but it's still creepy to witness.

Sloppily trimmed photo clippings, taken from newspapers and magazines, are taped, glued, or tacked to every available inch of board space around the rim of the room. The photos are of members of Congress, the leaders of federal agencies, notable lobbyists, Supreme Court justices, White House administration staff, and maybe five hundred of the more significant members of Washington's social elite. The snapshots of the luminaries are accompanied by charts, schedules, notes, newspaper articles, Web addresses, street addresses, photos of associates and family, maps and, in nearly every case, long sequences of numbers that, taken individually, look to me like GPS coordinates.

I'm assuming Billie understands from the visuals that Rusty spends his time tracking the whereabouts of all these people, day by day, hour by hour — even minute by minute — so I don't explain other than to run with her Lewis Carroll comment.

"The Mad Hatter," I whisper to her.

Rusty stands before a waist-high fridge, leaning into it with one hand, loosening his tie with the other.

"Soda? Coffee? Tea? Me?"

He comes again with the yellow grin. When Billie doesn't proffer an order, I say, "Tea would be nice."

"Chamomile do?"

"Sure."

"I can see that your girlfriend is aching to know what in God's name is wrong with me," Rusty says. "Desiring, yet hesitating, to demand an explanation as to why I, or anyone else for that matter, would choose to live in such a way." He fills a teapot from the faucet. "You haven't told her what it is I do, exactly, then, have you? Let alone informed her about that whole ugly business of ours."

"Haven't quite gotten around to that yet," I say.

Rusty winks at Billie and flips on the burner of his Coleman stove.

"Let's allow the Bohemian here to brief you on our sordid history," he says, "while I brew our tea and slip into something more comfortable. Then maybe the two of you can get around to telling me how it is I'm supposed to help you out of that septic tank you've managed to dig your way down into. Quite deeply."

-46-

INHERITING A QUESTIONABLE ECONOMY, I caught the brilliant idea that a boost in defense budgets would result in a trickle-down effect on consumer spending. Working with Pentagon personnel I'd just appointed to help me parse out this spending spree, I drummed up a few doomsday scenarios and began issuing statements about our lack of military readiness — how if we didn't begin improving the speed of our armed forces, freedom itself would soon be in grave danger. All was proceeding swimmingly until the military awarded the two largest contracts in the new spending wave to Boeing and Lockheed rather than the smaller aerospace firm over which Rusty Kincaid reigned as CEO.

Rusty, being a hard-ass, did not appreciate the fact that his firm got slighted out of $28 billion despite the $6 million he'd funneled to the Republican party over the years, with a significant portion of that contributed to my campaign. In fact, he took the whole slight as justification for a personal vendetta. He spent another $6 million to get the right people to dig out the truth behind the bogus internal reports I'd used to kick-start the spending spree, and succeeded in exposing numerous examples of blatant corruption — including, for example, a $70,126.47 line-item for a latrine door charged by one of the winning contractors. Ultimately Rusty successfully sparked a movement in the House of Representatives to repeal all of my defense-budget increases and then some.

Not exactly cheery about Rusty's whistle-blowing efforts, I embarked on my own little exposé. With the assistance of the FBI, CIA, NSA, and DEA, I dug up some serious dirt on the esteemed Mr. Kincaid and invited the media, the SEC, and the DOJ to the party. It seemed Rusty, a married man and father of four, was flying his brood to multiple annual Caribbean vacations aboard the company's private jet. Untaxed improvements to his Westchester County mansion were routinely provided by a subsidiary of his conglomerate's main holding company, and the mansion itself, along with real estate holdings in Florida, the Bahamas, and the Yucatan Peninsula, had been financed by zero-percent loans fronted the company — loans that slipped his mind, and the agenda of the company's board, when it came to repaying them, along with what would have been the massive tax bills for these unconditional grants. When he did take legitimate business trips in the company jet, he would arrange for a harem of underage strippers to join him, whom he paid handsomely for sexual favors and occasionally impregnated.

Thus, for his service to taxpayers in reducing my needless Pentagon spending increases to nil, Rusty, once exposed, was rewarded with divorce, $600 million in shareholder lawsuit payments, and federal and state indictments on charges of tax evasion, racketeering, embezzlement, mail fraud, soliciting live sex shows in an aircraft crossing state lines, and prostitution. He went bankrupt from the divorce and civil settlement and pled out the criminal portion of his docket for a fifteen-year federal prison sentence, six of which he served. Afterward, he bottomed out on cheap vodka and what few drugs he could still afford.

By the conclusion of his time in the pen, I'd come to feel pretty shitty about the fate of Rusty Kincaid. I used what influence I still possessed to arrange, through his parole officer, a temporary position working the stacks at the Library of Congress. He couldn't go full-time because of his record, and even getting him on the payroll at all had required the use of a few threats on helpless bureaucrats.

"But it was something," I tell Billie now, finishing my story as Rusty, well over a decade into that same job, serves us tea in his strange and oddly located apartment, the man now clothed in shimmering, powder-blue silk pajamas.

"Oh, yes," she says, "that was really something you did for him." She takes her first, careful sip of the tea.

"Actually," Rusty says, "he really did. Unwittingly, of course, but it wasn't just something. It was something wonderful."

"Because he broke you free of corporate corruption?" Billie says. "Sounds more like autocratic intimidation to me."

"That it was," Rusty says, obviously enjoying himself. "But I had it coming. I was a piece of shit. So was he — but at least the country *asked* for the fumes *he* was giving off. Not so when guilt overrode his good judgment and he arranged to let a loony ex-con like me loose inside *this* place. My God, it's a fucking playground. There's more salient information in this building than a thousand World Wide Webs could ever hold. Plus there are two other monstrosities a hundred times the size of this one right down the block. Want to know something about anything? *Anyone?* Spend a few hours in the Library of Congress. I do — I spend twenty-four hours a day here. Well, maybe twenty-three. Some days, I eat out."

Rusty grins suddenly again and Billie almost jumps at the ferocious and shocking appearance of the yellowed smile.

"Knowledge is power," he says. "In power, glory. And your boyfriend here showed me the light, guiding me out of the vainglorious abyss and to the power of the shelves that surround us." His smile hardens — then disintegrates as suddenly as it appeared. He turns and stares at me. "To your needs, *sir!*"

The way he's barked the *sir* brings me back to the suspicion that not only does Rusty despise me, but in fact has probably dreamed of the chance to cap me, and here I am, trapped in his lair, where he can toy with me for a few hours before pulling the icepick from the freezer. But I get to it nonetheless.

"We'd like your help," I say, "in finding what a CIA analyst named Julie Laramie might have learned around October of last year. We have certain details, spelled out on the cover page of a memo she sent to President Walker before the start of his second term. She was subsequently checked into a hospital with a severe case of the flu before vanishing altogether."

I withdraw the blood-stained copy of the memo from my pocket and hand it over; after a quick once-over at the blood, Rusty sets upon it the way a sponge would to a puddle of water.

"Sorry about the stain," I say. "The memo doesn't reveal much, and Walker claimed none of his people were able to learn anything further about it. But I figured if we came here, you could at least enlighten us as to her role at the Agency. What her assignments were, maybe the names of some of her colleagues. We've got her phone extension, as you see on the memo. Not much more."

Rusty finishes reading and stands. "A moment."

He scurries off and we wait, finishing our tea in silence. Soon Rusty's voice comes from behind a column, arriving a few seconds before he reappears, open file in hand.

"So, then," he says. "Julie Laramie. Analyst, GS-11, directorate of intelligence, CIA, Langley. Was the instigator of a brief hubbub some years ago — seems her superiors weren't interested in hearing about intel that wasn't pro-China, yet she'd unearthed a Revolutionary Army buildup and intended invasion of Taiwan. She managed to get her findings made public. Also managed to get a number of her superiors fired. One quite senior." His eyebrows rise as he reads. "What she — oh. Well. Yes."

"What is it?" Billie says.

Rusty sets the file on the table.

"Of course you're aware that she disappeared from her hospital bed. But it turns out this wasn't the first time she vanished due to a problem with an illness."

"Come again?" I say.

Rusty holds up his hands. "This time, the public version calls her diagnosis the influenza virus. October 19th of last year, she checked into Inova

Alexandria Hospital, shortly after the time you say she came to Walker with her intel. But this is a common technique utilized by undercover intelligence agents and their agencies to — well, arrange a working vacation, I guess you could say. And according to my notes, Miss Laramie — never married, by the way — has had an extended illness of this sort before. The first time I believe was official. The technique is called the Born Again program, in case you wondered."

Billie jumps in. "Faking a hospitalization so — "

"Yes, the whole mystery-illness thing is the usual favorite," Rusty says, "with complications due to underlying conditions, blah, blah, blah. When you see this it's usually the shadow agency, as I prefer to call it. As an FYI, there's a bureau in town that doesn't fall under any particular cabinet member's purview. Counter-intelligence and anti-terrorism-related matters are its concern. The agency's M.O. is to 'borrow' other agencies' people. Its operatives take deep-cover identities and so on, and one way they accomplish this is by 'killing' recruits off, or, if it's a temporary assignment, 'illing' them off — " Rusty grins, pleased at his joke — "usually for the period of time they anticipate the assignment will last. It's sort of the opposite of the witness-relocation program. Pull people in you want from their regular lives and send them out as born-again invisible soldiers, then put them back when they're through with the assignment. Now recovered from their illness."

"This is a frightening conversation," Billie says.

Rusty looks at me, chuckling. "You tell her about some of *your* programs, *sir*?"

I ignore the question. "So this shadow agency," I say, "or some such agency subscribing to the Born Again program, might have decided to use Laramie for an assignment."

"Keep up. No," Rusty says. "I'm saying they *did*, another time. Point being that Miss Laramie would have been aware of the Born Again technique when finding the need to disappear for her own reasons."

He pauses, offering a more relaxed version of his sharp-toothed smile.

"Say you're right," I say. "It will still be challenging to find her, whether or not we know that she vanished for her own protection. And while it would be helpful to find her, doing so isn't the crux of the matter. What we need to find is what she uncovered. What she knew. How do you think we might we go about digging into that?"

Rusty's cat-like eyes flick about, then hover on mine.

"I could be persuaded to offer some advice," he says. "As long, that is, as you're willing to pay the toll."

Billie turns and looks at me. I eye Rusty while answering. "You want us to tell you," I say, "don't you."

"Tell him what?" Billie says.

"Everything. Everything we've been through. Every piece of the puzzle the media got right or wrong. Every meeting, fact, or discussion nobody else knows about — in this case, everything involving Rachel, Elena, Walker, Skeel, Rudd, the study group — everyone. All of it."

I look at Rusty.

"I have that about right?"

"Ooh," he says. "Names! We like names. And the *study group* . . . "

He holds out a hand, palm facing upward.

"Spill it!"

-47-

THE PERMANENT RESIDENT OF THE John Adams Building scratches
his ear with a forefinger, nods, and stands. He hasn't bothered taking
a single note during my lengthy monologue describing the events of our
immediate past.

"I'll need a while," he says.

Two hours and forty minutes later — during which time Billie has
fallen asleep on Rusty's bed and I've tried and failed to become comfortable
enough to allow myself a short rest in the vicinity of Rusty Kincaid — Rusty
re-appears from behind a row of empty shelves. Billie, on edge, is already
sitting up by the time he crosses the room.

"Your friend Laramie is something of a long-distance runner,"
Rusty says.

He's got a manila folder in his hands, but the folder's closed.

"Meaning she knows how to outlast her enemies?" I say.

"No," Rusty says, "meaning, she's a long-distance runner. In the last
four years, she was an official entrant in two marathons, six half-marathons,
and seventeen 10K races. Twelve different cities altogether. There are some
other interesting facets to Laramie's history — raised as a foster child from
the age of seven, a brief romantic sojourn with an operations colleague, and
so on — but it's the running you'll want to focus on."

"Why?" I say.

"In thirteen of her last twenty races, Miss Laramie's registration coincided with another entrant's. In races where finish times were tracked, she

finished within 35 seconds of the other racer in all of these events. First name Victoria — registered occasionally as Tori — last name Fleming." He hands me the folder. "She lives but a short trip away from here aboard our capital's excellent light-rail system."

When Rusty says nothing more, Billie looks from him, to me, then back to Rusty again.

"That's it?" she says. "That's the sum total of your help in finding out what Laramie knew? That she jogs with a friend?"

Rusty steeples his hands together on the table. Eminently patient.

"I've found that females like to have female friends," he says. "And females who exercise, when they exercise with others, prefer to exercise with close friends, more so than with casual acquaintances or romantic partners. Further, busy females with things like CIA careers, or smoothie shops to worry about operating" — Rusty eyes Billie here — "also tend to root their friendship time in productive activities, such as, in Miss Laramie's case, running or, in yours, cycling and triathlons. Killing two birds helps one keep the schedule efficient, eh?"

Billie raises an eyebrow only slightly.

"Therefore if you are looking to unearth what Miss Laramie learned," Rusty says, "and considering that she has vanished, possibly died or been killed, and, further, if you presume, as I do, that she anticipated this trouble, and may not actually be deceased — well, I would figure her to have left, at the very least, some means of contacting her, and at the most, information or evidence of what she knew, with a close friend, likely female. Miss Laramie has no family to speak of. No husband. No children. No living biological parents or foster parents there is any record of her remaining in touch with. There is a man from her past, and another man who figured in more recently — the aforementioned operations colleague — but both are conveniently outside the circles of her regular routine. Tori Fleming appears to have been her best and nearest friend. Therefore if you are looking for clues as to what

Miss Laramie knew," Rusty says through exposed yellow teeth, "it's Tori Fleming on whom you should call."

"What about colleagues at CIA?" I say. "Her supervisor there?"

Rusty yawns.

"It's late," he says. "I'd like some dinner, and a few hours' sleep. You're welcome to stay — there are dozens of cots the library keeps in an adjoining room in case of emergency. For whom and what sort of emergency I have no idea, but they're yours for the night if you like. And if you must know, I dismissed the possibility of Laramie's colleagues and supervisors because you told me Walker had already checked them out."

He jabs his finger into the manila folder, smudging its otherwise neat surface.

"Tori Fleming."

He stares at us — first at Billie for a while, then at me. Fully satisfied with whatever conclusion he's drawn, Rusty nods, pulls a cell phone from a pocket in his shirt, and punches in a number.

"How's Chinese sound?" he says.

-48-

For a city with an urban district so economically troubled, Washington boasts one of the cleanest rail systems in the world. Billie and I, still in our sweltering disguises, disembark from a thirty-minute ride on the Blue Line as daylight begins to filter through the Braddock Road station in Alexandria. During our stroll down Mount Vernon Avenue, we see the occasional jogger, but as we approach the address Rusty gave us for Tori Fleming, we're alone on the sidewalk. It's just shy of six-thirty on this Saturday morning.

The numbers matching the address adorn a small, updated bungalow, three-and-two at the largest, cheery and quaint.

We climb the three steps to the front door and Billie knocks.

Rusty's file contained a series of recent photos, so when the appealing, disheveled woman answers with a grumpy look wearing a sweatshirt, black ASICS leggings, and Brooks running shoes, we know it's the woman we've come to see. The file puts Tori at 33, and the woman in front of us looks about that age. She appears vaguely Filipina.

"Can I help you people?"

I nod but we've decided Billie will do the talking.

"Tori, we're friends of Julie's," she says. "We're looking into something she told us before she disappeared. We think she may have discovered something very important and we'd like to talk to you about it if you have a minute."

In our disguises, we resemble a pair of winos that time forgot, which appears to present a bigger problem than we anticipated. Tori's grumped-up look has already morphed to granite, and if her body language is any indication, our lifeline to Laramie's findings has just fizzled. Improvising, I pluck the copy of *The Washington Post* from her porch and fork it over, hoping the friendly gesture will buy us a few more seconds. I freeze as I notice a photo of myself below the fold on the front page. It's the usual shot — a head-and-shoulders cropping of the famous peyote-toking ceremony. The choice of shots is no surprise, but the front-and-center placement would indicate my most-wanted status isn't waning. In fact, it probably means something new has surfaced.

"Your paper," I say, fighting the urge to open it and check the story. Tori's eyes, now sharpened like a samurai's blade, go the paper. Her hand does not. I forge on. "Julie may have left something with you, or told you something. You might not have realized it. But she almost certainly anticipated she could fall victim to foul play. She might have left something with a friend — with you."

"Who *are* you people?"

Billie and I scramble to dig out then show our fake driver's licenses, provided by Woodruff along with virtually everything else on our persons. She waves them off.

"It's a rhetorical fucking question. I don't care who you are — you're no friends of hers. I know every one of her friends. Furthermore, were you even *acquaintances*, you'd know she never uses her first name. Ever. Period. She's *Laramie*. Got it? And I have no idea where she is, in fact I miss her terribly, and this, whatever *this* is, isn't goddamn helping. Get out."

The door is on its way to the frame when I blurt out my real name and former job, and when she doesn't seem to hesitate, I add, "Of course, these days it seems I'm only referred to as the Bohemian — "

The door creams the doorjamb, the locking deadbolt whacks into place, and we're officially alone on the porch. For a moment, we stand there doing nothing, hoping something will happen, like the door unlocking itself and swinging open on its own. It doesn't.

"That didn't go well," I say.

"No," Billie says. "Now what?"

"This is the 'now.' This is the 'what.' We have to talk to her."

"Come on," Billie says. She starts down the stairs. "We'll wait until she leaves for a run, or goes to get breakfast. Then we'll try again. Tell her something el — "

"Turn around," Tori's voice says from behind me. It catches us by surprise — the deadbolt pulling back hadn't risen over the road noise.

She's directed this order at me, and so I comply, allowing Tori to examine me from head to toe. There's no recognition on her face. Nor does she appear impressed.

"I'd rip off the fake beard to show you it's me," I say, "but I can't risk removing the disguise since I don't know how I'd get it back on. I'll keep talking and maybe you'll recognize my voice. Or manner. But I should probably say, first, that the media has exaggerated my involvement in the events of recent days."

"It's not just the media," she says. "According to the article on the front page of the paper you just handed me, it's the Sonoma County Sheriff, the FBI, the Secret Service, and the U.S. Marshals. They're all after you."

"Marshals," I say. "Not good."

"In addition to your crimes of passion in Sonoma, it's believed you were associating with the man who shot President Walker."

She holds up the newspaper, revealing the story with my picture, and Clem Skeel's picture beside mine, which I hadn't noticed around the crease in the paper.

"Skeel," I say.

"So you *were* associating with him. And you expect me to allow you into my home?"

I stare her in the eye. She's got some tough eyes.

"Doesn't matter whether you do or not," I say. "We can speak out here if you're more comfortable with that. Laramie found something she wanted President Walker to know about. She sent him a memo mentioning it. The memo never should have made it to his desk, but it did, because she was inventive enough to figure out a way to get it to him. In the end, Walker was killed in an effort by someone, or a number of someones, determined to keep Laramie's findings quiet. For all we know she too may have been captured or killed. What Laramie found is important. We believe she will have left a clue, or further detail into what she found, and that it's likely she would have left it with you. In terms of my involvement with President Walker's supposed assassin — the reality is the converse of what you're saying the article implies. Walker came to me for help, which I was obviously not sufficiently capable of providing."

Those eyes stare back at mine. Hard and cold — but not mean. I'm glad not to have faced her in a courtroom. Her look flicks to Billie before returning to me.

"Those are terrible disguises," she says.

The hand that slammed the door reaches back and eases it open, and Tori Fleming walks into her house and down the hall, door intentionally left ajar.

We follow without hesitation.

-49-

TORI OFFERS US THE COUCH and takes the love seat in her living room. Her spot is across the coffee table from us, essentially as far away as possible given the confines of the room. One leg is crossed over the other at the knee, and as we take our seats, she begins rocking her top leg impatiently, almost feverishly.

"Why don't you start by telling me what you know," she says.

I nod and show her my copy of Laramie's memo.

"Sorry about the stain," I say, repeating my refrain. "This is what she sent to the president. It refers to intelligence she discovered relating to an intended incident involving a biological weapon. Walker set a meeting with her, but she didn't show for the meeting. A supervisor of hers came instead, told Walker that Laramie had taken ill, and warned the president off the trail of the issues raised in the memo. As you might imagine, Walker didn't like that. A great deal happened in the wake of this. But most important, by the time Walker was able to dig into things, Laramie had vanished and Walker's people weren't able to learn anything further about her or the concern raised in the memo."

Tori's leg pauses a moment before resuming its energy-burn.

"Laramie and I ran a race three weeks before she was hospitalized," she says. "One week after the race she came to see me. She was perfectly healthy both times. I later read in the paper that she disappeared from the hospital after checking herself in for a severe case of the flu. I tried to see her doctors, but they refused to discuss her situation with me since I wasn't family. I'm the closest thing she's got, but it didn't matter. They weren't letting me in. They asked for my name and I didn't like the way they asked, so I left."

She lays her tough glare on me.

"May I ask an admittedly broad question on a separate topic?" she says.

I nod. "You're the one running this meeting — go right ahead."

"What is it like being the most powerful human being in the world? As a child, I fantasized about being the first female president. I still do sometimes. Actually, often."

"You're a lawyer, correct?" I say, going off of information from Rusty's file.

"Yes. Civil litigation. I won't ask how you know that."

"I'm also a former lawyer. Same area of practice, though with a different specialization. But to answer your question: sitting in that seat is the most exhilarating, demanding, overwhelming, intense, frightening, evil, benevolent, exhausting, energizing and debilitating experience I can imagine a human being withstanding."

"Is it true that former presidents retain access to the President's Daily Brief?"

"It's your prerogative, yes," I say. "I canceled my subscription a year after losing re-election. Enjoyed every day I didn't read it. Too much to know, in its way."

Tori's eyebrows rise. "I'm not sure I'd ever tire of that kind of access."

"I suspect you would. But judging from first impressions, I suggest you keep your fantasy alive. If you can stomach politics, I suspect you'd be highly productive as an elected representative."

Those intense and highly intelligent eyes lock on mine.

"I'll do that. Thank you."

She drops her gaze. After a moment, the leg starts its rocking motion again. "That last time she visited was a Sunday," she says. "Early, the way you've just come. Without calling. But that's typical. She doesn't do phone calls all that much. Anyway she said she'd like to leave something with me for safekeeping and asked if that would be alright."

Billie's eyes rotate to me as a trickle of adrenaline creeps up my spine.

"She had three boxes in the trunk of her car," Tori says. "Said she'd be moving out of the country soon. 'Company assignment,' is how she put it. Made some noise about keeping some clothes and running shoes in my garage for when she came back into town. We both knew there weren't running shoes in those boxes. I didn't say anything — I figured she'd get around to telling me when the time was right. Nobody but you has come and inquired about her, let alone ask about what she left. I am therefore going to assume that nobody knows the boxes are here. Obviously I believe she expects me not to mention this to anyone, let alone show the boxes to random visitors. However, I will also make the assumption she would approve an exception for a former president following up on the issue she raised before her disappearance to the then-current president."

"How did you know the boxes didn't contain running shoes?" Billie asks.

"I never opened them, but I was here when she carried them in, and I had to move them once. There are papers in there, maybe books. They're file boxes, the sort I use to move legal files, with cardboard lids and handles punched out on the ends. Anyway I could tell from the weight. It isn't clothes or shoes."

"May we see them?" I say.

Tori eyes me, waiting as though she's holding onto something for as long as possible before acquiescing. Then she nods.

"I'll take you out there."

-50-

THE INTERROGATOR'S VOICE IS GRAVELLY. Deep. Full of bass, ridden with the grit of a chain-smoker's lungs. He's invisible, only a voice, moving from one side of his captive to the other. Knowing the borders of the frame. Remaining hidden.

"*Where!*" the interrogator says.

The man he's addressing is a dental patient experiencing a macabre nightmare — seated in a reclining chair, outfitted with various instruments in ill repair, he's strapped down by chest, arm, leg, wrist, and ankle restraints so that only his head and neck can move. And where a dentist's office is white and antiseptic, this room is brown, soiled, muddy, rusting, dim, dank. The interrogator's captive sits, restrained, in a lone cone of light emanating from somewhere above the camera lens. There are no markings on the captive's face. No bruises, no cuts, no fat lip or black eye.

The captive raises his head sharply.

"Up your ass-*hole*," the captive says, accent an odd combination of Venezuelan Spanish and Slavic. "Up America's ass-*hole*. Fuck you. Ass-*hole*."

The shadowy torso of the interrogator blots out the image for an instant. The video cuts forward in time, the interrogator backing off when the time-jump completes — re-starting the camera some time later.

The captive, still in the same seat, is now laid flat on his back. There are fresh bruises on his face. His back to the camera, the interrogator brings a narrow blue box over to the chair, opens it, pulls a roll of saran wrap from the box, then suddenly and violently wraps the back of the chair and the captive's face with multiple whipping loops from the roll.

Since his hands and feet are bound, the captive is powerless against the plastic. He struggles but it doesn't do him any good. He's soon convulsing, until the interrogator, wielding a carving knife, stabs a hole in the plastic precisely over the man's mouth. He twists the blade, opening a passage in the plastic wide enough for the man to breathe through. A sucking sound is heard as the captive's chest expands, oxygen-deprived lungs desperately pulling at the air through the tiny, insufficient puncture in the plastic.

The interrogator, face still unseen, strolls calmly out of frame. Ten seconds pass. The captive can be heard wheezing during the interrogator's absence. The interrogator returns with a hose. Water runs from the hose. It lacks a nozzle, so the water flows in a limp, thick stream that makes a sloppy, obscene sound as it splashes on the floor.

The interrogator maneuvers the hose so it dumps its torrent of water on the captive's plasticized forehead. The man's body tenses as the shock of the water blasts into his field of vision.

Then the interrogator aims the stream of water directly at the hole.

The captive's mouth fills immediately. His chest flexes, he attempts to writhe his head back and forth, hips lifting from the chair, but yet again his actions have no impact. In one fluid motion, the interrogator drops the hose, slices one side of the saran wrap, rips it from the man's face, and flips a lever on the dentist's chair. The back of the seat whips its occupant upright.

The captive sputters spasmodically, retches, dry-heaves, sucks at every available molecule of wind. Frantic, crazed, he is no longer a man. He has become a dying beast struggling for survival.

The interrogator says calmly, "Answers, please. Otherwise we go again. Only longer. Starting — well, now."

The interrogator grasps the lever on the chair and lifts the roll of plastic, readying it to wrap the man's head a second time.

"No! Give me question again! *Question!*"

"Where?" the interrogator repeats. "Where will you use it?"

"Washington!" the man in the seat says.

"Washington." Humor is evident in the interrogator's voice. "I see. Where in Washington? Perhaps the White House?"

The plastic wrap is off the roll again. With a kick of the lever the back of the chair slams flat —

"Bridge! Five together!" the captive blurts.

The interrogator halts in mid-smother. Cocks his head a notch. The outline of his hair and ears evident on camera.

"The 14th Street Bridges," he says. He reaches down for the hose, comes back up, blasts its stream into his captive's face without the added feature of the saran wrap. "Which one?"

"No! Stop! I tell! Fuck! *Fuck!*" The captive sputters and gags and coughs until he realizes the hose is off him. "Mason! George Mason!"

"When?" the interrogator says. His voice gravelly and deep again.

The man in the seat coughs and spits. "5 July!"

"In . . . ten months."

"Don't know date today. Yes! Five July! In celebration. Independence Day!"

"You're off by a day."

"Not off!"

The interrogator is silent for a moment. Then he says, "Venezuelan Independence Day."

"Yes!"

"How are you getting it there?"

"By ship," the man in the seat says. "On ocean."

"Ship," the interrogator says, sounding as though he's enjoying a hilarious joke. He reaches down, seizes the hose, and douses his captive's face with the sloppy stream of water. "Give me the name of the fucking boat!"

"Fuck! *Fuck!*" The man in the seat sputters and gags. "Is not sure, but trying for *Maria Sandoval*, the *Maria Sandoval!*"

"What kind of ship?"

"Boxes!"

"Container ship. Leaving from where?"

"Here!"

"Puerto Cabello. Going where?"

"Big — Big Easy."

"New Orleans?"

"Yes. New Orleans!"

"What container?"

"What? What is question — "

"Identifying marks! Number. Brand. You've got the container already. Maybe not the ship, but the container you've got."

For an instant, there's no answer — and the interrogator gets the plastic wrapped around his captive's head again in seconds. He slices an opening over the man's lips, steps back, then squeezes his thumb against the stream of water to create a crisp blast, firing the hose into the face of his plasticized captive like a gun.

When the hose is turned away, the captive sputters, chokes, coughs, then speaks frantically through the hole in the plastic.

"Hanjin! Hanjin 11705! *Fuck!*"

The interrogator replies with something that sounds like "stupid fucking asshole," but his voice is obscured by the sound of the arcing spray as he re-trains it on his captive's face. Choking, gagging objections follow.

The interrogator pauses, perhaps remembering the camera. He releases his thumb from the hose, steps backward to avoid showing his face, reaches over, and the image on the tape turns to snow.

-51-

THERE ARE FOUR INTERROGATIONS ON two discs. Billie and I watch each, multiple times, on Tori's living-room DVD console.

Stowed in the three file boxes, stacked behind a pair of ten-speeds in Tori Fleming's garage, were photocopied pages of handwritten notes, printed copies of articles and Internet research, two DVDs, and, contrary to Tori's suspicion, three brand-new pairs of New Balance running shoes still in their boxes. The shoeboxes may have been meant to deflect any interested party's first probe, as they were covering the documentation beneath.

Orange Post-Its were affixed to the DVD sleeves. Scrawled in the handwriting we've come to recognize as Laramie's, one of the notes says *destroyed 9/27*, the other *destroyed 10/6*. We pored through the papers first, Billie peering over my shoulder as I leafed through them cross-legged on the concrete slab of Tori's garage. The handwritten notes seemed to be Laramie's. The notes, articles, and other documentation were related to Venezuelan port cities, shipping companies, and biological weapons research, including an exhaustive file on the media coverage of a deadly rupture and toxic leak of a substance at a research facility in the Temeron area of Venezuela. We initially failed to grasp the meaning of Laramie's annotations of the various articles relating to the spill, including the words *pest* or *Y. pestis* and references to what appeared to be years — *1740* and *1880* — along with the numbers *30,000* and *2,100,000*.

Then we migrated to Tori's living room to watch the last of the interrogations and the picture became more distinct.

There were three other men being interrogated on the discs. One was a Spanish-speaking employee of the shipping firm that owns the *Maria Sandoval* container ship, admitting on camera to having taken a twenty-thousand-dollar payment in exchange for advance scheduling of the transportation of a container to New Orleans that would circumvent security protocols. The next subject was an official at a Venezuelan bank, who denied in fluent English that he provided banking services for the people involved, but who, after receiving a round of controlled drowning, promptly switched to Spanish and revealed the source, various destinations, and specific account information on an illicit distribution of nearly half a million U.S. dollars in bribes and payments.

The fourth interrogation subject was sixtyish and American, a man appearing shocked at the fact he'd have been taken to the interrogator's grungy little room. The subject was wearing a white lab coat, button-down Oxford shirt beneath. As the camera flicked to life, he sat without restraints in the same macabre dentist's chair assumed by the interrogator's prior three captives.

"'Dees work you do," the same interrogator said to the American scientist in the lab coat, this time deploying a different verbal approach, speaking in a vaguely sourced Spanish accent landing somewhere between Venezuelan and Colombian.

"Yes?" the man in the seat said.

"Is for the government, no? The American government."

"No. Oh, no," the scientist said, shaking his head. "Our lab is independent. Private."

"Unof*feesh*ally, though?" the interrogator said in his trumped-up accent. The flash of the blade of the knife he used in the first recording was seen as he cleaned it on his jeans.

The scientist's eyes roamed to the blade.

"Um, even, ah, unofficially there are no ties," he said, but then started speaking faster, "which is not to say that an American agency or two doesn't have access to our findings through certain clients."

He attempted a chummy smile, which came across as sadness and fear.

"*Si*," the interrogator said. "And the *espeel*. The 'breach,' eh . . ."

The scientist waited for clarification, but, getting none, shrugged and tossed out another feeble attempt at a smile.

"What of it?" he said.

"It was intentional, *si?* A test."

"What? No. God, no. A terrible mistake. With horrible results. I wasn't there at the time. Thank God. I'm told a lab technician accidentally set off a — well, a *can*. In the vacuum zone. The expulsion chamber." He waved a hand as though these terms were beyond the interrogator's brain capacity, no point in explaining them. "The . . . can wasn't permitted where he had it. The specimen organisms were released into the atmosphere via the expulsion fan. None of this was intended."

"Of what use, then," the interrogator said, his accent fading a notch, "is the fan? It exists to expel *clean* air?"

"It's complicated," the scientist said. "Look, there's just no point in explaining the design of the facility. The incident was accidental. The technician was not a suicide bomber or whatever you're implying."

"But he did die."

"My understanding is that he suffered the same symptoms as the others and perished, well, in the same manner."

"This 'can,'" the interrogator said, "when you say *can*, you mean *aerosol* can. And one of these went missing, *si?*"

"I'm not permitted — "

The interrogator stood. Knife in hand. It was big, serrated, and dirty.

"There was one that wasn't found," the scientist said quickly. "Unaccounted for."

The interrogator began a slow pacing routine, pointing his face, as ever, away from the camera.

"And the 'specimen organisms'?" he said.

The scientist eyed his captor, attempting to appear patient, casual. But beads of sweat were now sprouting on his upper lip and forehead, particularly as the interrogator's accent continued to fade.

"What of them?"

The interrogator stopped and leaned down so that he came face-to-face with the scientist. "How much of *that* went missing?"

The scientist blinked.

"The quantity that went unaccounted for on that day, sir, would not present a danger to more than a roomful of people. Not unless more were bred from the missing sample and many more cans were . . . "

The interrogator caressed the scientist's cheek with his empty hand. Ran his fingers through the older man's thinning hair.

"Tell me what you call it," the interrogator said, switching abruptly to accent-free English. "I hear you have a nickname for the organism."

The scientist's sweat now coated his upper lip in a glossy sheen.

"The, er, the Pest," he said. "We call it the Pest."

"'Pest' being short for . . . "

"*Y. pestis*," the scientist said. "*Yersinia pestis*. More commonly known as bubonic or pneumonic plague bacteria."

There was a pause as the interrogator remained silent and motionless for an awkward length of time. Then he said, entirely accent-free, "Let's say I had plenty of the Pest. And enough cans to go with it. In technical terms, enough properly engineered equipment to spread large quantities of aerosolized respiratory droplets of 'the Pest.' What could I do then? Could you stop me? Could anyone?"

"Fire," the scientist said. "High enough temperatures will kill her, but only if it's early enough in the distribution cycle — before she becomes airborne over a wide area, in other words. And for the treatment of infected subjects, certain antibiotics, except the strain developed is resistant to most—"

"She?"

"The Pest," the scientist said, embarrassed.

The interrogator paused again, then said, "And if there's no fire, or you don't burn *her* fast enough? Presuming she is rigged with enough cans to disperse the ARDs? What then?"

The scientist shrugged.

"What then?" the interrogator asked.

"Nothing."

"Sorry?"

"There's basically nothing to be done to stop the initial, exponential spread of the outbreak."

The interrogator stood up straight and patted the scientist on the head.

"*Gracias, amigo.*"

His body blotted out the lens and again the image turned to snow.

-52-

O N OUR SECOND READ-THROUGH, LARAMIE's papers — including the memo – contain deeper meaning. The notes are mostly stapled in two- or three-page groupings. I go first on our re-read, but since Billie reads at twice my speed, the system isn't working.

"Done yet?" she says for maybe the twentieth time.

"Hold on."

Bent over the coffee table in Tori's living room, I finish a set of pages and pass them on. When we've both reviewed the last of the papers, Billie turns the last sheets upside-down and looks at me.

"I think I've got most of it," she says, "but since you're the one with *former president* on his Instagram profile, you mind walking me through the rest?"

"I don't keep an Instagram profile," I say.

"I know," Billie says. "Go on."

"Last fall, Laramie comes across these videos. Makes some phone calls, digs around, confirms some of the things we just watched the interrogator pull out of these people. Based on her Post-Its, the original copies of the videos were destroyed."

"Clearly she made her own copies," Billie says, "and assuming her notes and the interrogations are accurate, she succeeded in confirming that a biological weapons lab in Venezuela was conducting research for the U.S. government."

"Yes, and sometime early last year," I say, "an accident took place at the lab. Hundreds of local residents, living downwind, died. A theft of both a small quantity of the biological agent and an aerosol dispersal device, also known as a can, coincided with the accident. Incidentally, we used to call them 'spinners.'"

"During biological weapons water-cooler talks?"

"They function like fireworks," I say, ignoring her joke. "With a bio-dirty-bomb, the initial, low-temperature explosion releases the spinners, each of which disperses a dose of whatever it holds once airborne. Nerve gas, sarin, mustard gas — "

"The Pest — "

"Or the Pest. We know the years Laramie annotated were the times the bubonic plague broke out, with the number of casualties written beside the year."

Billie nods. "So the theory is that somebody stole a sample of Y. pestis and a spinner capable of dispersing the ARD droplets Laramie referenced in her memo. Then what? Built a biological dirty bomb using these trade secrets and the stolen specimen?"

"Possibly. A genetically engineered version of bubonic plague — not pretty."

"And that same somebody is apparently shipping this device to Washington, DC, by way of New Orleans," Billie says, "to detonate on July fifth."

"Venezuelan Independence Day. Which is an odd date for a mass killing attack, since Venezuela, while far left and despotic, isn't known for terrorism tendencies nor any particular bent on harboring terrorists or their training grounds. Particularly in its recent regimes."

"But whether it's a homegrown Venezuelan group, an import, or an impostor, it's still, at least according to Laramie, a 'corroborated threat,'" Billie says. "Why would the study group, or anybody in government for that matter, want to quash her findings?"

"It is occasionally stunning," I say, "how byzantine and secretive the federal government can be, and often for the strangest or most pointless reasons. But on this one, I think we're forced to conclude that the members of the study group are in on it, or in the very least would prefer for some reason that the attack proceed as planned."

We fall into silence for a moment.

Billie breaks it. "So now what?"

"Time to make another call," I say.

-53-

Rusty Kincaid snorts into the phone.

"*Why?*" he says. "You're asking *why*? Why do you even need to ask? The answer is easy. Next time bring me a more challenging query."

Tori's landline phone, stretched from its plug in the wall, has its speaker activated on the coffee table between Billie and me. We just filled in Rusty on most of what we learned from Laramie's stash.

He doesn't exactly seem bent on continuing, so I prompt him.

"Then why?"

"War," he says. "That's why."

"War," I say.

"Of all people," he says, "you ought to grasp this the fastest. You *do* recall the source of our little *tête-a-tête*?"

"Of course."

"You were trying to keep the economy chugging along by way of untold, unjustified tax dollars flowing into our great military-industrial complex. Eh? Thereby raising corporate profits, employing people, and so on."

"Obviously," I say.

"Your Keynesian strategy, however, was flawed, sir," he says.

"Because you didn't get a contract, you mean," I say.

"Well, yes, of course, but no. That's not what I mean. The big flaw in your strategy was peace. Your angle, while good, was all about theory — readiness in *case* of war. With my help, the media was able to punch holes in your bullshit theory. Bullshit, we didn't have readiness. Bullshit, there was a legitimate threat. However, in a time of actual war — "

I interrupt him as my mind churns quickly through current events. "You're saying the study group actually *wants* the bio-dirty-bomb to go off in Washington so they can start a war and reap whatever benefits the war sows?"

"Now you're getting somewhere."

"And they killed President Walker because he was going to stop it?" I say. "The problem with this theory is that the target of such a counterattack would face puny opposition at best. Why would Venezuela be considered a viable enemy?"

"Come on, you Bohemian twirp," Rusty says. "Think bigger. It's not about *Venezuela*. Who gives a shit about Venezuela? Even Venezuelans don't give a shit about Venezuela. It's about the rising tide of socialism. It's about the Americas. The resources of South America. Venezuelan oil, to be sure — but that's just the tip of it. Brazil's gypsum. Argentinian gold. All that cheapy-deepy labor . . . Be good to all but annex that motherfucker, eh?"

I digest as he continues. "Banana republics," I say.

"Er, well, yes," Rusty says. "Your bottom line, sir, is that your pals in the study group are looking for any excuse to justify, even initiate, a nice, tidy, containable regional conflict. You must ask yourself — or maybe you mustn't — did they hatch this dirty-bomb plan? Or did they just manage to dig it up with some good old-fashioned intelligence-gathering? Doesn't matter. Whether they invented or discovered the scheme makes no difference. Point is, they like it. It fits their agenda. Let the bomb kill ten, twenty, two hundred thousand Americans, affix the blame where need be, and you've got yourself a war. Wowza! If that isn't the ultimate wet dream for some deputy secretary of whatever, I don't know what is."

"But assassinate an American president to keep the plan rolling?" Billie says. "Isn't that somewhat self-defeating?"

"Fucking brilliant if you ask me," Rusty says. "So much niftier than the dawdling defense-budget escalation scheme your imbecile lover here cooked up. Hell, if I were running their scheme, I'd have done the same. Why let one darned elected official stop you when you've got such perfection lined up and ready to rock?"

I feel a form of heartburn heat up in a compact ball just below my breastbone. The line remains silent until I finally get tired of the hiss of the background noise.

"We'll call you later, Rusty," I say, and break the connection.

-54-

ONE MORNING, MANY MONTHS BEFORE the story broke on the Hezbollah-El Salvador arms deal, I received news of record approval ratings. The highest, it turned out, for any such president since such records were kept. And there was a reason for it.

Three days earlier, seventeen American students had been seized in Mogadishu by Somali rebels. After 48 hours of unsuccessful public demands by my Secretary of State that the hostages be set free, I made a decision in five seconds flat and sent in a Blackhawk strike team. The squad rescued all seventeen students and three Somali professors. My popularity, previously hurting in the wake of Rusty's defense-spending scandal, soared and held, pegging the scales at well over sixty percent. The approval numbers stuck right up to the summer of my fourth year, when the economy took a nose dive.

The success of the rescue operation, and my climb in approval ratings that followed, didn't distinguish me from 39, Jimmy Carter, and his flubbed hostage rescue; it only meant my helicopter worked when Carter's didn't. It also meant I was lucky enough to have one of the best operatives on the planet running my rescue team. His name was Whitford Sealy, and following the rescue I immediately held a medal ceremony in the Rose Garden, which we followed with a lavish dinner in the Blue Room, all mere weeks prior to the moment when, on the advice of White House counsel Miles Glinn, I unceremoniously banished Sealy by casting him as the scapegoat in my arms-for-hostages fiasco.

As Miles predicted, Sealy never served time, but was investigated, indicted, and stripped of rank before I then pardoned him, an order I activated on my last month in office. He retired three years later, taking a lucrative gig as an on-air analyst for Fox News soon after.

Hunkered in our seats aboard another Metro car, I'm leafing through my journal to recall my last conversation with Sealy when Billie peers over at my little black book.

"So what exactly does that little journal of yours contain?" she says.

I shrug. "My list."

"Of what?"

"More *who* — people. Friends. Acquaintances."

"Which ones?" she says.

"All of them."

"Every acquaintance you've ever had?"

"Yes," I say.

"Can I take a look?"

"Sure."

I fork it over and she starts leafing through it.

"Jeez," she says. "When you said all of them, you meant it."

I haven't really shown the book to anyone. I've always considered it part of my private, personal world.

"Look at some of these people. You know *him*?"

She's pointing to the name of a famous European soccer star. Freakishly handsome, he's generally seen in watch advertisements, and underwear ads, in just about every magazine published.

I nod. "They're not all famous. Most of them are just ordinary people."

She's shaking her head as she reads. "You mind if I look through it for a while?"

"Probably have it memorized by now anyway. Knock yourself out."

It's early again, around six a.m. Billie's exploration of my black book draws to a close as we reach the Foggy Bottom station. It's a ten-plus minute walk to Georgetown, where Whit Sealy lives in a brick townhouse complex. The buildings, seen from the sidewalk across the street, are to be built in a tight row behind a wrought-iron fence. Mounted on the fence's gate is a callbox, but I'm not interested in getting caught by the camera that's bound to be utilized as part of the security setup.

In a moment, a silver Audi sedan emerges from the garage and eases onto the street. The gate stays open long enough for us to dart into the garage without running. This too will be caught on security camera, but it's less likely our faces will be seen.

"I'm starting to feel like a pair of Jehovah's Witnesses," Billie says as we approach Sealy's door.

It's Sealy's wife who answers our knock. I pick the direct method.

"Morning, Emily," I say. "Is Whit home?"

Emily is blonde and tall, her eyes glassy and flat, as though she's experienced more than she ever wanted and retreated to a deeper place inside herself in search of safety or calm. She doesn't recognize me, but my blunt question yields a reflexive sort of response.

"Um, sure," she says, momentarily confused before turning inside. "Hon!"

Sealy emerges from his kitchen wearing gray sweatpants and running shoes, coffee cup in hand. His T-shirt is darkened by a V of sweat from the roadwork he's already logged for the day — once a Marine, always a Marine.

"What is it you need, bud?" he says, stiff and rough, when he too fails to recognize me. I see a chilling glint in his eyes — a kind of readiness to take me down if I give the first indication I'm as strange and unbalanced as I appear.

"I've come to ask a favor," I say. "Apologies for the early knock at your door and arrival out of the blue."

His increasingly blank stare remains fixed, his body tensed. I'm reminded of the impression I caught on meeting him at the White House — it wouldn't be your preferred seat to be on the receiving end of a vengeful Whit Sealy. Unfortunately, the real person beneath this disguise I'm wearing did more damage to Sealy's career than any unbalanced psychotic could ever dream of doing, save the fame and the resulting Fox News gig.

"Sorry," I say, "figured you'd recognize my voice." I point to Sealy's wrist, where the leather band and chronograph face of a Tag Heuer marks the end of his Popeye-grade forearm musculature. "Happy to see that old Hanukkah present is getting some mileage. May we come in?"

Sealy's eyes fall to his wrist, squint their way back to me, then flare suddenly.

"Jesus, Mr. President — " He nearly spills his coffee as he steps closer to us. "Emily, for God's sake, get them in here and close the door."

I feel Billie's hand on my shoulder as we follow the mother-hen gestures Emily makes and slip inside the house. Sealy and I shake hands, and as he seizes me with his iron grip, he's still eyeing my disguise.

"Good God, sir," he says, "you look like shit."

Both of us have aged since we've last seen each other, the difference being Sealy's body hasn't followed the trend. There's gray powder around the temples, chunkier bags beneath the eyes, but other than these evident symptoms of nearly a decade gone by, Whit looks the way he always has: like a trimmed-down NFL linebacker moonlighting as a soap star.

We settle into the seats at the Sealys' kitchen table, where the retired Marine had previously been occupied with his *Wall Street Journal*, coffee, and slice of whole-wheat toast. Without asking, Emily adds to the operation she already had underway and soon sets out plates of bacon, buttered toast, and mugs of hot coffee for all. I take a sip and the coffee tastes better than I've ever imagined a swallow of liquid could taste after another nerve-wracking night in Rusty's subterranean apartment.

Sealy has learned the hard way not to trust me one iota — in fact he probably learned long ago not to trust anyone. Thus, based on this premise, Billie and I concluded on the way over that any effort to hide specifics would likely result in Sealy calling the FBI before we leave the building. Without preamble, we tell him what's happened. All of it. Knowing we sound like paranoid schizophrenics on parole from downstate, we manage our way through the tale. I finish with our findings on the Venezuelans' plans to disperse *Y. pestis* into the skies along the Potomac and Rusty's theory on why the study group wants the ARD-BW attack to proceed.

When I'm through, Sealy stares at me in silence for maybe three minutes. His look is that of a psychiatrist who's just been told a flying-saucer story by a patient.

"Why should I believe your version of recent events?" he says.

After a moment, during which I fail to devise a suitable response, Billie says, "Because it's the truth — I've been through all of it with him."

Sealy re-targets his thousand-yard stare.

"Billie, is it?" he says.

"Yes."

"Thank you, Billie," he says, "but for all I know you're just as whacked-out as the Bohemian peyote-toker over here. I know that *you* were there, sir, as I've seen the video showing your presence, but were both of you were there when the president was assassinated?"

"Yes," Billie says.

"And the couple in Sonoma the media is talking about," Sealy says, "whom you, sir, allegedly massacred. You maintain that they were actually part of a team of feds?"

"Members of an extraordinary rendition team," I say, nodding, "working domestically. Working illegally as kidnappers, and killers, it turns out."

Sealy continues to eye me expressionlessly.

229

"We'll get to your references to the so-called study group in a moment," he says. "But this Venezuelan terrorist cell, or however you choose to label it — the associates of the people interrogated on the tapes — their shipping schedule, their destination, their weapon. Assuming some or all of this to be factual, this information is known by whom?"

"The analyst, Laramie, obviously knew of it," I say, "but how many others at CIA knew or heard something about what she found is up for debate. There's the interrogator on the discs, for instance. It's anybody's guess who employed him or where he's wound up since. And whoever had the discs before Laramie got her hands on them will have seen the interrogations. Yet according to Walker, no such people surfaced. The part that's clearer is that some of the old buzzards, as Walker called them — study group members — knew precisely what she'd found."

"And you're convinced nothing is being done about it," Sealy says.

"It appears not," I say, "though I'm not exactly tapped in of late."

"Precisely," Sealy says. "Forgive the blunt question, Mr. President, but how would you know how much is being done, or not done, about this intended strike? Further, while rumors persist about a controlling organization, a kind of executive committee within our federal government, I've never been confronted by any such organization, at least not directly or transparently. How could we possibly be certain members of this supposed organization are the bad actors here?"

"That," I say, "is why we're here."

Sealy takes a deliberate swallow of his coffee, bites the last corner of his toast, chases it with more coffee, sets his mug on the table, and settles back in his seat. If the seat is the same sort as the one I'm in, there isn't much cushion to settle back into. After a while of sitting there in a posture that must be killing his back, he eases up into his previous posture, rolls his shoulders — not quite a shrug, but almost — and his eyes find mine again.

"What is it you want," he says.

"We'd like to use the System," I say, "and we need your help getting in."

This earns me a blank stare.

"The System," he says after a while.

"We need to find out whether the attack is proceeding as scheduled," I say. "To do this, we will need someone to visit and inspect the designated container ship in Venezuela without anyone connected to the study group knowing about it. Without resources or trustworthy connections, our options are pretty slim on who the someone to do that might be — so that someone is going to have to be us. Flying commercial is out of the question, and since rides in the System work anonymously, it can give us not only secrecy but mobility and speed. So I'd like you to get us in. I'd also like to ask you to be our escort on the trip."

Sealy takes a look behind us, possibly into his living room, though maybe out into the courtyard visible through the living room windows. Then his eyes return.

"Oh," he says. "That's all."

While in office, I learned something about the System. The term was used during an operational briefing at a staff meeting and I stored it. Later — during that thank-you dinner with Sealy and Emily — I pointedly asked what Sealy knew about it and whether he'd ever used it. Sealy obliged, sharing what he knew between tastes of lobster bisque. A network of seats aboard a wide expanse of military vehicles used to clandestinely shuttle personnel as needed, the System is known by only a scant few, and tracked by virtually no one.

"Assuming," Sealy tells me today in his kitchen, "on the off chance that a disgraced, now retired special-ops guy, today a mere pundit, can even access the thing — where is it you want to go?"

"If the timetable described by Laramie's notes and the interrogation discs she found remains intact," I say, "then the Venezuelans, or whoever they are, are currently loading their cargo aboard the container ship *Maria*

Sandoval in Puerto Cabello. Next stop, Port of New Orleans. If we move quickly, we may be able to intercept and board the ship before it leaves Puerto Cabello."

"So you'd like to travel down there clandestinely, then, say, helicopter in and — what? Pull a fraudulent waterborne Homeland Security inspection with the equivalent of a Coast Guard OTH?"

OTH, meaning Over The Horizon craft, the rubber-hulled speedboats used by drug-interdiction teams to chase down offending vessels on the open ocean. I know Sealy is being sarcastic with his question but, minus a few exaggerations, his summary of our aims is pretty accurate. Of course, there are parts of the plan that that I don't see much reason to share with Sealy just yet.

"More or less," I say.

"And with this access — with this 'interception,'" he says, "you then intend to — what? Apprehend and interrogate the people transporting the biological weapon, like we're conducting some kind of international citizen's arrest?"

"Yes," I say, although that isn't quite the intent of the plan I've been imagining.

"I assume we won't be capable of seizing the device itself," Sealy says, "not on our own at any rate — unless it's smaller than I suspect. What is it you propose we do with the biological weapon once we apprehend anyone who may be accompanying it?"

As Sealy did earlier, I lean back and attempt to settle in against the uncomfortable backrest of my chair, putting on my best poker face. This is the part where I'll have to hold back quite a bit of my intended scheme. But I think my poker face can succeed, since the best lies contain part of the truth, and that's exactly the case here.

"We track it," I say. "My suggestion is we go in with a means of affixing to the container some sort of transmitting device. We confirm the presence of the weapon, apprehend anyone accompanying it, and use this information to confront the study group. Once we complete our confrontations, we phone in the coordinates from the transmitter and the Navy can dispatch a strike team and seize the weapon."

For a moment I suspect he knows I'm bullshitting him, but I don't drop my slack expression. I know how men like him think: it will be hard for him not to assist in a situation involving a direct threat to the country. But whether I'm conning him or not, to Sealy it may not matter: once he confirms the threat exists, he figures he'll do things his way — or, more precisely, the U.S. military way. Which may not be my way.

I'm not concerned with that part, at least not yet. I need his help to get us anywhere close to facing that particular conflict. Without his access to the System, we're nowhere.

Sealy grinds his teeth, causing the heel of his jaw to protrude on each side of his face as his muscles flex. A blank minute goes by, which feels like ten. But then he blinks and refocuses, and I know from the way his lids fall over his eyes that I've got him.

"Not saying I can pull this off," he says, "but why don't I make a couple calls and see about whether the rides in the System still work the way they once did."

PART IV:

THE CONTAINER

-55-

N o matter how many times I ride in them, I never get used to helicopters, and tonight's flight is no exception. Air pocket here, wind
shear there — none of the turbulence holds the response I expect from the
aircraft beneath me. Our windowless, forward-propelled elevator ride from
Caracas to Puerto Cabello is making me sick.

A flight aboard a military L-1011 from Washington to Miami, then
another dark ride in a Avianca Cargo 767, brought us to Caracas, where we
caught the chopper ride after a three-hour wait in a private aviation building
at Simon Bolivar International Airport.

In the same way traditional military personnel have unique travel
needs, so too do intelligence officers and their assets. And just as an Army
colonel might hitch a ride aboard a C-130 if he needs to get from Washington
to Berlin, members of the intelligence community can accomplish the same
feat in a similar manner. Across various federal and private-sector transportation systems — the inventory of which includes cargo planes, express-mail
carriers, trucks, ships, helicopters, submarines — there exist a certain number
of designated seats. And if you've got the credentials, you can get yourself one
of these ticketless, passport-free rides. Very few have the authority to sign
off on the seating allocations, but for those who gain approval, there are no
questions asked. The System: our current mode of travel.

Since their expressions appear unstrained, apparently Billie and Sealy
are impervious to the effects of helicopter turbulence. Inside our chopper,
Billie nudges me. She's fiddling with the transmitter box attached to her
headset. She holds up three fingers and points to mine and I realize she's

changed her channel and wants me to do the same so we can hold a private conversation. I get mine adjusted.

"I thought maybe we could continue our conversation from the orchard," she says.

I nod through my nausea. Not for the first time, I realize I wasn't such a good listener in my marriage. This might be a good time to show improvement in that area.

"Okay," I say.

Billie is giving me a funny look, gesturing to a button on my transmitter box. "Ah," I say, realizing I neglected to activate the mic. "Okay," I repeat, button depressed.

"Want to know when I realized my ex-husband and I had become two distinct entities?" she says into her mic.

Click. "Sure."

"My fairy tale, sorority-pinned, white-picket-fence life had brought me to vodka doubles in a coffee mug by eleven a.m. and, one morning, what I thought was a heart attack — but which turned out to be a nervous breakdown," Billie says. "Once the record-shattering daily dose of anti-anxiety meds kicked in and brought me back around to a semblance of sanity, I elected, without informing my husband, to embark on a cross-country bicycle ride. Alone. Twenty-eight hundred miles — from Southampton, New York, to the Santa Monica Pier. When I got there, I checked into the Fairmont Miramar on Wilshire, registered for a triathlon in Hermosa Beach, trained up and down the Malibu-to–Palos Verdes corridor, and beat all of the women and most of the professional men in the race. I didn't give my husband more than a fleeting thought until I collapsed on the bed in the Fairmont, medal around my neck, two months from the day I left. Want to know what I did next?"

I cross my arms, some of the airsickness sensations easing.

"Asked for a divorce," she says, "then applied to graduate business school and got accepted at Stanford. The only condition I requested in the divorce was a no-interest loan for seventy-five grand — enough to cover a year of graduate school plus living expenses. He agreed. I figured out how to arrange a traditional student loan and paid him back prior to the end of my first year. I finished the two-year program in 18 months and landed a position with a venture capital outfit before I'd finished the last day of classes. Six years of eighty-hour weeks into my VC career, I was feeling somewhere close to how I felt toward the end of my marriage. I started spending a lot more time on my bike, and on one particular Sunday morning ride I stopped into a smoothie shop in Carmel. In talking to the owners, I discovered they were looking to sell."

"And the rest was history," I say.

"Yes."

"That's quite a journey."

Billie crosses her own arms. I notice Sealy sneaking a look at us.

"I'm telling you these things about me for a couple reasons," she says. "I'm doing it partially because I wish I had shared more with you from the first time I'd seen you. I had a sense you were a good listener, a good person, and a possible friend from our first interactions — yoga class among the very first, if I recall correctly."

"You do."

"I'm also sharing to make another point."

When she doesn't elaborate, I say, "That point being?"

"Even during a time of crisis — even one like this, with enormous stakes — even then, women like to talk. Or at least I do. About various things. Some trivial, some not so trivial. So maybe it isn't about how sexes behave but how partners should behave. One example: sharing what you have in mind *before* we ask people for help."

Ah, I think. I click the mic and say, "Ah."

"There are parts of your plan you're not telling me," she says.

I watch her for a moment in the semidarkness, feeling some nausea again. "Correct."

"I would prefer you not do that. Even if you aren't sharing every detail of your schemes, I'll need to at least know what you've got in mind *before* we engage in action. We're partners. I can be of better help if I know where we're headed."

She stares at me for a while — the helicopter jostling us around, Sealy working very hard at not watching the two of us. She's hard to see clearly in the dark, particularly through my haze of looming nausea, but still Billie's eyes shine and there is an energy those eyes emit, as though she holds some sort of glow-in-the-dark powers.

"Duly noted," I say.

After a long, silent moment, she nods.

"Good," she says.

-56-

According to Sealy's Coast Guard contact, the *Maria Sandoval* is a 6,700 TEU-capacity container vessel with a probable crew of fifteen to twenty with primary quarters near the engine room. TEU, for twenty-foot equivalent units, measures the number of 20' shipping containers the ship can carry. As we approach the dark side of the *Sandoval*, moored in the Puerto Cabello shipping terminal, I realize what it means to have a TEU capacity of 6,700.

It means the *Maria Sandoval* is one big goddamn ship.

The official stats call it nine hundred feet long — shorter than most U.S. Navy aircraft carriers, but the *Sandoval* might as well measure a mile from stern to bow, as large as the looming ship appears from the seats in our rubber-hulled Zodiac.

It's just past two a.m., putting us in a noticeably slow shift of dock activity. We're silent and nearly invisible — the Zodiac is black with a whisper-quiet electric outboard. A Venezuela-based former colleague of Sealy's was able to take and text him photographs of the ship, from which photos Sealy then devised his preferred way aboard. He told us he suspected security would be minimal on the bay side of the vessel and it appears he was right: only a single patrol craft has been making its rounds through the port waters, swinging past the *Sandoval* every twenty minutes.

The patrol boat moves out of range along the same course it had taken twenty and forty minutes prior, prompting Sealy to engage the Zodiac's whisper-quiet electric motor. As we cruise from our hiding spot toward the

Sandoval's bow, the ship's enormous hull looms, the stacked, colorful containers stretching endlessly into the nighttime sky.

"Keep low," Sealy says, steering the Zodiac across a short stretch of open water. We're dressed in black garb. There are no wasted seconds as we reach the side of the ship. Sealy pulls something resembling a gray poster tube from his knapsack, drops a coiled length of flat-black cable into the Zodiac, stands with his knees bent, takes aim, and fires the tubular device open-end skyward. It makes the sound a tennis racket does on a forehand return. The thin black cable whistles, unspooling, and catches on the railing of the deck above. Sealy, pleased with his shot, drops the tube, seizes the line, and pulls it taut. The line unfurls with his tug and we see that he's just affixed a makeshift ladder to the side of the ship.

"You first," he says to me, hands gripping one of the ladder's floppy rungs. He means to be holding the thing steady, but the wavering laterals of coiled cable and linking six-inch strips don't look too firm. I work my way up the way an overweight tarantula might scale an ordinary spider's web.

By the time Sealy joins Billie and me on the deck of the *Sandoval*, I've briefed Billie on a portion or two of my plan I hadn't previously filled her in on. When Sealy arrives, we cover the basics of the plan. There are some elements we don't include in our discussion with Sealy.

Down below, our twenty-minute stretch of freedom has elapsed. The patrol boat swings into view near the stern of the container ship as Sealy seizes the rope ladder, spreads his forearms a foot or so apart, and winds up the ladder in seconds. He stows it and ducks beneath the railing; my curiosity on what he did with the Zodiac before coming up the ladder will have to be shelved.

I hear more than see him as Sealy turns to me in our dark niche.

"Alright, Mr. President," he says. "Let's find that container of yours."

-57-

THE BLUE HANJIN SHIPPING CONTAINER we find after an hour of searching — the numerals 11705 painted on its skin — is a forty-footer. Occasional twenty-foot units sit together in rows, but ninety percent of the *Sandoval's* cargo is made up of the longer variety. The front half of the ship is full — containers stacked ten and twelve high, a sea of steel, no consistency of brand among the metal boxes, Maersk, Evergreen, OOCL, APL, many freshly painted, some old and rusty. The deck is no deck at all, but a set of catwalks — looking down, containers are stacked as deep into the hull as high into the sky. There doesn't seem to be any loading operation underway in the overnight hours on any of the ships in the port including the *Sandoval*.

Hanjin 11705 isn't far from our hiding place — it's the second container from deck-level looking up, three rows in from our spot along the starboard railing. Risers, ladders, and tie-down paraphernalia are stored in pockets adjoining the catwalks between stacks. Under Sealy's supervision, we activate one of the risers — part scaffolding, part forklift — until it reaches the base of the Hanjin container. Sealy locks the crank in place and pulls a slim rectangular device from his pocket.

The rectangular device is a military adaptation of a rescue aid called a PLB, for Personal Locator Beacon. Serious climbers, or at least wise ones, bring them along on their trips, activating the beacons when they find themselves in distress. Rescuers are then able to zero in on their whereabouts using the signal, which utilizes satellite technology and is therefore technically accessible from anywhere in the world. According to Sealy the military version allows for tracking rather than simply for SOS emergency notification use, utilizing two units — beacon and receiver — that ride on the satellite signal in what is basically a closed-circuit cycle. Sealy pulls a plastic strip from the PLB, reaches under the bottom lip of the container, and affixes it in place. He rises and brushes off the scaffolding rust from his black fatigues.

"These containers open from the outside," he says. "They're basically truck trailers." He grasps a padlocked handle on the exterior of the container door. "This padlock may be aided by an additional interior lock, and possibly some kind of alarm sensor. Option one would be to cut the padlock, then use the leverage of the handle here — " he mimics the act of yanking open the latch — "to jerk the door open and snap any interior lock with the momentum of the swinging door."

He points toward our previous hiding spot near the ship's railing with a thumb.

"Option two is we cut our way inside. I brought a portable arc-welder in my pack. This option would take longer, and might avert the alarm, but we'd also lose the element of surprise — "

"You hear that?" I interrupt.

Sealy listens. Ocean, distant diesel crane engine, the squawk of a seagull — then his face registers the fact that he's heard what I have.

Music.

Barely audible — sounding like the tiny speaker of a transistor radio — we listen to the vaguely Latin music playing behind the steel walls of Hanjin 11705. The tranquil tune is then harshly interrupted by the sudden sound of a hacking cough and what sounds like a man spitting to expel the phlegm from the cough.

Adrenaline courses through my veins.

For the first time since encountering the note hidden in my bike's tire-repair kit, there now exists the opportunity to be proactive against the people responsible for the kidnapping of Rachel Estrella and the mayhem that followed. We have found our way to what is likely the biological weapon — and somebody in there guarding it for the device's ride to New Orleans.

"Come on," I say, climbing down the scaffolding. I wave for Sealy and Billie to join me. When they arrive to join me at the base of the platform, I say, "You suggested two ways of accessing the interior of the container."

"Correct," Sealy says.

"There's a third. A way I'd like to try."

"What way is that?"

"We knock."

"You want to knock," Billie says.

"Yes."

"Mr. President," Sealy says. "There is a one-hundred percent chance the escort inside that container is armed. There is a one hundred percent chance he is not expecting nor interested in receiving company. There is a ninety-nine percent chance he's been trained and instructed to kill any intruders, along with a ninety-eight percent likelihood he'll take his own life if the operation is compromised, but not before attempting to take yours — "

"All the more reason," I say, "not to cause an overreaction. A simple knock will allow him to feel that he's in control."

"You can't expect — " Sealy says, but then he stops and shakes his head. He ducks down, staring into the canyons between containers. In a moment, he breathes in deeply, lifts his head, brings his assault rifle around with one hand, digs into a shoulder holster I hadn't realized was there with the other, and comes out with a handgun. I read this as his recalling how stubborn I've always been but that the results have usually turned out to be effective — with perhaps one glaring exception.

"It's your mission, Mr. President," he says.

Sealy turns to Billie, reverses the gun he's just withdrawn, and hands it to her. "You may need this," he says. "Wait here, at the deck level. When this person attacks us, which he is likely to do, and if we are shot, which we are likely to be, he will come after you next. Don't wait for him to shoot at you specifically before defending yourself. Bottom line, if a gun is fired, or even if a gun appears, point and pull the trigger. Be fast and shoot first. This person will be practiced with whatever guns he or she is armed with."

"Copy," Billie says.

He fires a sharp look my way then points to the riser.

"I assume you will want to be the one doing the knocking and talking," he tells me. "When you do so, stand with your body behind the metal door, so that you'll be able to hide yourself quickly in the event it's bullets that answer your friendly knock. I'll be behind the door as well; if you get shot, if you don't like what you see — even if you have a bad *feeling* — jump behind the door and drop to the ground. I will come in over the top of you. All right?"

I look up at the doors of the container, determining how what he's saying will work. It sounds, and looks, simple enough.

"All right," I say.

He pulls what appear to be miniature bolt cutters from his utility belt. "I'll go up ahead of you," he says. "Tell me when you're ready and I'll cut the external lock off the handle. At that point he'll be in control, so don't wait. Do your knocking and get on with it."

We start up the riser.

As I hit the top of the platform, I feel the bottom of my stomach drop — wondering, as I approach the doors to Hanjin 11705, whether this latest in my newfound string of five-second presidential-grade decisions will be my last.

-58-

IT DOESN'T TAKE LONG TO get an answer.

Barely audible through the metal skin of the container, a man's voice calls out in response to my knuckle-raps on the door, seconds after Sealy has cut the bolt.

"*Eh?*"

It's a deep, gritty male voice.

"Open the door! We're here to talk!" I say loudly.

"Jesus," Sealy whispers from behind me.

"Eh? Who's this!" comes the voice. It's ridden with a heavy accent that's difficult to place.

"Open the door and I'll explain!"

An extremely long silence is finally broken by the dull sounds of a jangling chain behind the metal door. When no further sound comes, I crank and pull the handle. Sealy hovers behind me. The door is heavy, so I have to pull hard. When I get it open, the hideous stench of decomposition blasts me in the face like a brick wall, and I have to fight to keep from vomiting, which I barely manage.

Within the darkened interior of the container appears a sinewy, powerfully built man with copper skin and the distinct, high-cheekboned look of an indigenous South American. A lit cigarette dangles from his lips, and clutched in his right arm is an assault rifle. The gun looks like an AK-47, though it's hard to tell in the shadows.

The music is louder now that the door is open. The man's matted black hair is pressed to his scalp and appears wet. Beads of sweat protrude from every pore on his face.

"You want what?" he says, his English good, but stiff, sounding to me like the product of recent ESL training. "Is this inspection?"

I sense Sealy coming around behind me and I move my body to block the way. I can feel the crackle of his energy — the coiled spring of a frustrated man ready to explode. The man in the container has taken note of the armed person behind me, but shows no sign of panic, his eyes soon affixed to mine again. I hear the muffled whisper of Sealy speaking to me over my shoulder. "Say yes," he utters hoarsely.

"No," I say. "It's not an inspection. I'm here to help you."

"I am in need of no help."

"I think you are," I say.

"Why is this?"

"Because you are doing exactly what your enemy wants you to do."

"America is my enemy," he says. "You look American. Familiar. Famous American? Sean Penn. George Clooney. Hah — I don't need famous American's help."

He waves the barrel of his AK-47, pointing it at my stomach. This prompts Sealy's body to press against mine — ready, I assume, to throw me out of the way as needed.

The gun rises, now centered on my chest.

"Since I'm an American," I say, "famous or not, don't you wonder how it is I've found you? How I knew you were on this particular ship, at this particular moment?"

His black eyes pass lazily over mine and across Sealy as the deep rumble of a cough starts up and results in a loud series of hacks. I concentrate on being very careful in choosing my next words.

"I know that you are going to Washington, DC," I say, "and I know what you are going there to do. I know what you have along with you in this container, and what you intend to do with it once you reach American soil. I know the container's destination in Washington — the 14th Street Bridge — and I even know where you trained."

Recounting the specifics from Laramie's potentially dated intel was a risk, but not nearly the kind of risk I've already taken to gain admission to the container. For all we know, the plans have been drastically altered since the interrogator fished the information out of his subjects on Laramie's tapes. But as I study the man's eyes, lids mostly obscuring his pupils, I know that the risk was worth taking.

He observes me for a long moment before speaking. His lips tremble, maybe forming a smile, the cigarette dangling there reduced entirely to ash, an impossibly long ember refusing to disintegrate and fall from his lips.

"You know this how?"

"I know more. I want to talk. Inside, so our presence isn't revealed to the security personnel patrolling the ship. I want to talk about why you're doing this." I feel a small hot cloud of air brush my neck as Sealy grunts in disgust.

"Why? What to discuss?" the man says.

"There's a problem we need to handle."

The man's eyebrows cut down in the center of his forehead to form a deep V. The aim of his gun has inched up further, its barrel now aimed at my chin.

"What problem?"

"It's the problem of how I know what you're doing," I say. "Of how I know what your schedule is. The problem of how I'm American, and that I know these things. The problem of how I am a former government official of the United States, and I know these things. The problem that I learned of what you are doing from a *current* official of the American government. Do you understand what I'm trying to tell you?"

He fixes on me with those smart, black, angry eyes. "But they did not send you. You do not work for them any longer."

"No."

"They did not . . . " He looks at Sealy, then back at me again. "They have not sent anyone. And yet they know of this. You learned it from them."

"Yes."

He shakes his head. "I understand point you are making. But they cannot know the extent. Even you do not."

I lift my hands, an involuntary gesture, which causes him to tighten his grip on the AK-47, which in turn causes Sealy to use my shoulder as a tripod and take direct aim. I lower my hands.

"Yes, they do, and so do I. They know when, and how," I say, "and yet they're not stopping you. You understand the reason, right?"

He shrugs.

"The reason is that what you're doing suits their purposes," I say. "They want you to do it."

A rumbling cough builds and erupts. The long ash breaks from the cigarette and falls to the floor of the container, scattering as it strikes the naked steel. There is a tension in this man's shoulders, biceps, his sinewy neck — and his trigger finger. I wonder whether I've gone too far. I suddenly doubt that Sealy will have any ability to do anything about it, and doubt myself for having tried to hold a conversation with a person like this in the first place, obviously the lowest level trooper in the mass-killing chain. Then the gunman's piercing stare breaks, the tension of his musculature eases, and he motions in Sealy's direction with the AK-47.

"No weapons," he says. "He must leave gun outside."

I'm assuming Sealy's spindly assault rifle is only the tip of the armament iceberg he's brought along on his person. I say, "No problem."

"Her too," the gunman says. "No gun."

I turn, and Sealy kind of half-turns, careful to keep the gunman in his peripheral sight — and we're both able to see Billie standing behind us on the platform. Pistol in hand. Sealy shakes his head.

"Got it," I say. "No problem."

"Goddamn it," Sealy whispers as the gunman moves aside, keeping the AK-47 trained on me while Sealy and Billie deposit their evident guns on the platform.

The inexplicable, untenably foul stench of the container is overwhelming as we come inside.

-59-

THE PRIMARY SOURCE OF THE odor is a dead man in the rear corner of the container. The body is challenging to make out, but it appears a knife is protruding from the neck. An argument between escorts? Another visitor whose conversation took a wrong turn? Either way, it's hideous that the gunman has been locked in here from the outside, while this dead human being lies in here with him, no matter the reason or duration.

Less intense, though still foul scents waft from the latrine, a standard, blue plastic port-a-potty standing against a wall of the container. It reminds me of a misplaced phone booth.

The gunman reaches over with his free hand and clicks off the portable transistor radio resting on a cardboard box, and I see behind the box that the container's primary cargo is a massive wooden shipping crate, propped on a set of pallets. It occupies nearly half the container's floor space. Garbage overflows from an iron barrel, food waste is strewn about, and I spot a resident rodent. A pair of cots rest along the wall opposite the port-a-potty. The entire space is lit poorly by a battery-powered lantern.

Following the gunman's lead, we sit in a semi-circle on the rusting metal floor. It is a rusty, cold, wet place to sit. Refusing to ponder the source of the dampness, I kick into the meat of my confrontation.

"The weapon you have in that crate," I say, "is going to be used to justify an American invasion of your country."

After a very long examination of my face, the gunman nods, finds a pack of cigarettes with his free hand, pops one into his mouth, sets the pack beside the transistor radio, pulls a lighter from the breast pocket of his shirt, fires up, and inhales deeply.

"Maybe that is good thing," he says. "Like Iraq war grew ISIS."

My knees are already beginning to hurt from the cross-legged position I've assumed on the floor. "Maybe," I say. "But then why all the security?"

"What do you mean?"

"Why smuggle the weapon inside a container? Why guard it with personnel, risking your life in transit? Why take all possible measures to keep from being detected? And I have a question: is your identity real or assumed?"

"You think me a fool?"

"The whole idea here," I say, "is to attack the enemy without accountability. A surprise, secret attack inflicting the most possible damage on the largest number of people in the least amount of time. But if your ties to your homeland are being intentionally tracked, and are easily revealed later — if officials in the American government already know everything you're doing and who you're doing it for — then, in the end, you're just killing your own."

"Your theory is that this box and I are evidence?"

I nod and the gunman coughs again. It's a deep, phlegm-ridden cough that sounds like the advanced stages of a bad case of pneumonia. He drags on his cigarette, staring at the damp, cold floor. Then his eyes rise to meet mine and I see a familiar look on his face.

"Now I remember who you are," he says. "You were not just ordinary government official." The barrel of the rifle comes back up. "Do you know what your policies did?"

"It was a long time ago," I say, "but yes."

"You sent commandos," he says, starting in on a sermon that I sense will not be dissimilar from the one Gomez and I laid on Billie's cycling dude. "Soldiers with no uniform."

The trick, I've learned, in occupying the other side in these conversations is to follow the path of least resistance, a path that doesn't include much dialogue from me. I note that his muscles have tensed up again — including his trigger hand.

"Your commandos have been exterminating my people," he says. "Not many remain! Only very few, with no lands or home, like me. And him." He points to the decomposing body at the base of the wall. "I am survivor of American-led genocide. Our people prospered for thousands of years. Apart from the cities. Apart from government. But government forced rebels into our lands and say we too are rebels."

The rat skitters from the shadows near the wall to the body, then back again.

"You'll find no argument from me," I say. "Instead, I've come with a solution."

The tip of the AK-47 rises until the gunman brushes it roughly against my nose, which hurts. I try not to flinch.

"I should kill you here and now," he says, his throat sounding raw. "American president?" He spits. "*You* are the enemy. And now I have you. We will win on July 5, and I will start the win tonight."

He shoves hard, jamming the AK-47 forward so that it scrapes across my nose, slips, and slices my cheek. A sharp hit of pain bangs through my cheekbone. It is at times like this I am forced to face it — the past. With a creeping sense of dread, I occasionally realize that nothing I can do now will remedy my sins. That in all likelihood, I am destined for a trip to hell, thanks to many such five-second decisions made over a single four-year stretch of my life. Had I been president of any other nation, I'd probably stand trial for crimes against humanity and be executed. But we are the beacon — America, the leader and champion in the pursuit of liberty. A peaceful transition of power remains the dynamic, even for a war criminal such as myself.

My skin has split, and maybe he's cracked something too, but I don't reach for my face, or anything else. I reach only for Sealy's knee, a gesture meant to keep him from responding.

"Speak!" the gunman grates out. "What do you have to say? *Nothing*! You have *nothing* to say!"

I nod, which causes more than a token amount of pain. "You're right. There is nothing for me to say. Not as pertains to the decisions of my past. Whether you choose to believe this or not, I am ashamed. But it doesn't matter."

He coughs and spits and lifts the stock of the AK-47 until it rests against his shoulder. Lining up perfect aim for my forehead. Positioning his body to properly cushion the recoil.

"What is *solution*, then?" he rasps.

I rub my fake beard. Flick my eyes to Sealy, then Billie. "My knees are killing me," I say. "Do you mind if I stand?"

His eyes watch me but he doesn't refuse the request. I rise slowly. Sealy and Billie follow suit. I'm suddenly relieved not to be sitting in the moistness.

There is a pen and scrap of paper in the knapsack I asked Sealy to procure for me prior to our helicopter ride. Now able to access the knapsack more freely, I dig for them, careful to do it slowly, my eyes on the gunman as I pull them out. Then I look at Sealy.

"Give me your cell number," I tell him.

"There is no fucking wa — "

"*Give me your number.*"

Slowly, Sealy levels out. He states the number deliberately. I copy the digits onto the paper and hand it to the gunman.

"A phone call," I say. "That is my solution."

The gunman eyes me down the barrel, his off hand now holding the slip of paper.

"Members of your group were compromised," I say. "They revealed your entire plan to an American interrogator. Certain leaders in the American government decided to allow your plan to go forward, intending to use your mission to justify a counterattack. The counterattack will come in the form of a war they had already been looking to wage."

I zip up the backpack and strap it back over my shoulders.

"I too am allowing your plan to go forward."

"Now hold on, sir – "

I ignore Sealy's comment, knowing I'll need to take this up with him if we make it out of here. At least I briefed Billie in advance, so I'll only have to overcome one primary skeptic for approval of the strategy.

"I'm allowing it to go forward," I say, "because I believe you will come to agree with me. When you do, and you arrive at your final destination, we ask that you call and tell us where that is. Once you confirm the location, we will use that information to remove the justification for war, and extract justice from the people who have allowed your mission to go forward for their own ends. A call from you will stop a war. A war in which your people will pay the harshest price."

There is another part of my plan I'm not revealing to the gunman, a part that hinges on the gunman *not* figuring it out.

After a moment, the he pockets the slip of paper. His freshly lit cigarette down to embers again, he removes it from his lips, flicks it across the container, and fires up another, all one-handed, the assault rifle never leaving its one-eyed stare-down with my forehead.

"It's true, then," he says.

"What is?" I say.

"You are as crazy as they say. The Bohemian. Eh?" He chuckles, taking a deep drag on the new cigarette. "You are prepared to risk the detonation of this bomb on the chance I choose to call? To become double-agent for you?"

"Yes," I say, and suddenly there is movement, and my eyes are caught following the arc of the gunman's fresh cigarette, which he's tossed from his lips —

And before any of us, including Sealy, can react, the gunman turns me around, bear-hugs me with his cigarette-arm, and jams the cold steel of the AK-47's barrel into the soft expanse of skin beneath my chin. Sealy's eyes are fired up and his hidden snub-nose is out and aimed at the gunman's head. But it's too late: the gunman's got me.

"Maybe instead," the man says into my ear, "I run my own plan. Maybe in my plan, I pull this trigger. Maybe that is better solution. Maybe I prefer to see my cargo delivered. Our mission accomplished. Venezuela and its allies invaded." He jams the barrel up hard, bruising my jaw and splitting my skin again. "Eh?"

I can see from Sealy's stance that he is about to take a shot. I catch his eyes and shake my head. His eyes return to their target and he offers no change in expression.

"I don't think you'll do that," I say, "and I don't think that is your preference. I choose to put faith in you. I choose to treat you with respect, and honor the reasons that have brought you here. I'll let you decide. I believe you will let me go. And that you will call us and help stop another pointless war."

For a moment there is no motion — a standoff — but then I feel the gunman's grasp on me loosening. He pulls the gun from my chin, pushes me away, takes a long step toward the back corner of the container, and pulls the trigger of his gun. Set on full automatic, the assault rifle lets loose a stream of rounds into the corpse on the floor.

"Jesus!" This, from Sealy.

The noise is deafening, the bullets chattering as they knife through the soft, swelling flesh of the decaying body, striking the container floor beneath. Some ricochet, bouncing in deadly arcs past our mortal bodies. Billie and I duck and cover. Sealy does not.

The gunman spins and trains his gun on Sealy.

Not nearly as discombobulated as his civilian companions, Sealy has long since drawn a bead on the gunman's head, pistol held firmly in his right hand, left hand supporting his right for greater accuracy.

But Sealy doesn't shoot and neither does his target.

"Leave," the gunman says.

He lowers his rifle, sits, turns, and clicks on his transistor radio. The music, full of static, wafts again through the confines of the container.

-60-

W<small>E'RE IN THE PRIVATE REAR</small> cabin of another ship in The System seating inventory, an oil tanker nearly as large as the *Maria Sandoval*, whose course matches the container ship's path on a similar schedule, running about seventy miles behind. The cabin has baseboard heaters that make for a fairly comfortable ride. The PLB receiver is flashing green every twenty seconds, coordinates on its screen shifting in synch with the flashing light. Tracing the *Sandoval*'s path.

None of these factors have the slightest positive effect on the attitude of Whit Sealy, who continues his glare at me, seated upright on the cot four feet across from mine. I've been waiting for his pent-up frustration to spill out, and this is the first moment we haven't been running, hiding, descending a ladder, or darting across a gangplank to our latest seats on our clandestine journey. Billie, leaning against a cabin wall, looks on.

Sealy's jaw muscles bulge. He speaks deliberately.

"Ignoring the fact that you chose not to reveal the most ludicrous and dangerous aim in your half-baked plan until I agreed to help and got your ass down here," he says, "let's take up question number one: How is it that by allowing these terrorists to import, and — what — possibly *detonate* their weapon too — you would be *stripping* the study group of their power?"

He scratches his cheek roughly, jaw muscles still bulging.

"Question number two: How is it you plan to expose them? The risk-reward equation is not favorable here, Mr. President, and I have only temporarily elected not to call in a strike force to seize the weapon, pending the result of this conversation. I agreed to go along with the changes to the plan in the heat of the moment in the container, but let me be clear that I only did so to avoid further distractions in the operational execution and in my ability to protect you two from getting killed. I have not agreed to allow that weapon's egress into our nation. Answers, please."

I nod. "I appreciate your cool demeanor in the heat of the moment appreciate further your skill at protecting us, and appreciate most of all your granting the temporary reprieve on the strike force maneuver."

I sit up a little straighter.

"Here's the logic. If we seize what's inside this container and put an end to the intended attack this early, the bad actors will just repeat what they're trying to pull off now, but in another form, with none of us the wiser. However, if we delay seizure, allow the ARD into the U.S. and track its path with our PLB, we can use it to publicly expose the study group's knowledge and approval of its arrival, thereby incriminating the significant players in their organization. If we do this properly, the study group leadership will no longer be clandestine power brokers – they'll be the topic of every cable news primetime telecast and likely imprisoned. Broken."

"With all due respect," he says, "I haven't always done well leaving my destiny in your hands. I'm not even convinced you know how you're going to do it. In fact, I'm convinced you *don't* know how you're going to expose these bad actors. Do you even know who they are — the names? The individual people in the study group? I doubt you do. Under the assumption the organization actually exists, very few people if anyone knows who's in on the act."

He shakes his head like a mosquito is buzzing in his ear. "There are too many variables. The people transporting the bomb could find the transmitter. The PLB could malfunction or suffer damage. I'm all for disrobing the study group — let's put it this way, our current predicament isn't the first time I've been aware of anti-American acts by these people. But this concept of yours, this theoretical method of exposing them, is far too dangerous from an operational standpoint. There just isn't enough control. The bomb is not theoretical."

What he's saying is perfectly rational and wise, but won't solve the issue that needs solving.

"I'll grant you it won't be easy," I say, "and there will be huge risk at every stage. But if we don't take the risks now, when we have knowledge of their actions, they'll be free to move on to the next mission. We are not likely to get another such chance."

"My preferred course of action is to seize the weapon and end this attack now," he says. "Then we work, with the help of others, to present the evidence of the study group's culpability to the new president's administration or the DOJ. We advocate for the establishment of a task force to root out the study group's leadership and take them down before their next operation can come together. I can talk about it every night on television."

"If they retain power," I say, "no task force will be established. Not with any teeth. No players in the administration will listen. We only stumbled across this scheme through a chain of wild luck. Mostly bad luck, but still it came through chance, and we can hardly count on being that fortunate again. It's bring them down now, or not at all. And if it's not at all, they'll soon come after me, Billie, Rachel, Elena and, now that you're in the mix, I'm sorry to say that you'll be on that list too."

Sealy's jaw is doing its muscle-bulge thing again, telegraphing what he's about to say before he aims his stare on me and says it.

"Let me ask you a question. Are you sure," he says, the words measured and gritty, "are you *absolutely positive*, that this has nothing to do with the fact that you are personally screwed by your current circumstances?"

I stare back at him.

"That if you don't expose this fucking study group," he says, "instead of saving however thousands of lives this weapon could take, that you and your girlfriend here will never be able to return to the life you had before?"

I watch him, feeling an inkling of doubt but instantaneously dismissing it.

"I want you to tell me," he says, "that you aren't risking hundreds of thousands of American lives — that you aren't *sacrificing* them — in order to simply help acquit yourself of this bogus murder rap and pull yourself off the most wanted list. I want you to tell it to me. If you don't say it, or I don't believe you, game over. I'm pulling the plug and calling people in. *I'm* saving lives. Now. Not in some hypothetical future."

His eyes, unblinking, pierce mine.

After a moment of silence, Billie says, "He isn't," from her position against the wall.

Sealy doesn't turn, blink, or adjust. He wants to hear it from me, and I don't blame him.

"I'm an old man," I say, looking into the maw of Sealy's thousand-yard stare. "Not so much in age, but in absolute experience. I've seen as close to the entire world as a person can see. I've met as many people as one person can meet. I've had love, and I've blown it, and found it again. I've got knees that barely work, a mind that's all but gone. Mr. Sealy, in terms of my life yet to be led, I am worth practically nothing. My existence has already been lived to fruition and beyond, in its pleasures and failures both. Considering some of my failures, in many real ways I deserve to die. Do I nonetheless want to continue to partake of life? Affirmative. Does that make my existence any more worthwhile relative to any potential casualties that could result from a detonation of the weapon? No. What I'm telling you, Mr. Sealy, is that I, sir, as a human being, have spent from my life bank and gotten more than my money's worth. I am expendable. This has nothing to do with me."

"Expendable," he repeats.

He holds my gaze for a long time. I read his expression in the dull fluorescent glow of the lights in the cabin. Despite the dim light, it's a simple read: *Even if I agree to go forward with his half-baked plan, I will decide for myself when that forward motion ceases. I will make that call. If I so choose, the plug will be pulled. If I choose to save lives in the moment, rather than later, the plug will be pulled. I will decide, and I'll do so when and only when I feel the time is right. Not when you tell me, Mr. President, whether or not I elect to go along with your half-baked plan for now.*

What I'm counting on is Sealy's conviction that as long as we're following the weapon and remain in monitoring range, he could bring its voyage to a halt with a single phone call. That he could choose, as the container is lifted from the *Maria Sandoval* to the dock in New Orleans, to call in the authorities. Or sometime during the next step in its voyage to Washington, if the original destination holds. If he believes he has a modicum of control, there's the chance he'll go along with my plan an inch at a time.

You've lived your life to fruition? I see him thinking. *The hell with you. I reserve the right to do things my way.* It's his right to make whatever decision he makes, and he's certainly capable of pulling the plug. At least he is for now.

He concludes his reverie, and for a second time, I know that I've sold him.

"Mr. President," he says, "you've spent your professional life dealing in scenarios. What-ifs. Theories. In my line of work, there's no affording that state of mind. In my world, we deal with the here and the now. We will operate according to your theory and strategy, but only for the moment — and I mean literally minute-by-minute. That is all I will agree to. Here and now only. No guarantees for later, for tomorrow, for ten minutes from now."

Holding his stare, I nod. His face is stone, offering no nod in return.

"Understood," I say.

And now it's on me.

-61-

THE NAPOLEON AVENUE CONTAINER TERMINAL in the Port of New Orleans appears more fluid, efficient, and active than the relative dock-side inactivity we witnessed in Puerto Cabello. Container-terminal work isn't particularly labor-intensive any longer — it's all about massive cranes and vehicles, some controlled remotely, some clocking in at fifteen stories high and thirty yards wide while being run by a single operator — but there is far more activity here.

A gray Chevy Malibu is parked on the road outside the terminal's perimeter fencing, left there by another former colleague of Sealy's. We find its keys on the right-front wheel, climb inside, and discover we don't need to take it anywhere just yet. From the sedan's place on the curb, we have a clear view of the *Sandoval*'s rainbow-hued containers, including ours, bathed this early morning in the dock's 24-hour lighting.

It wasn't long after our own ship docked and we made our way here — around four a.m., the sky just showing some purple — that Hanjin 11705 was snatched by the giant orange crane offloading the ship. The crane's magnetic claw stacked the Hanjin container with its brethren on the tarmac.

We've seen only a single, incomplete security sweep of the *Sandoval*'s cargo before it was offloaded to American soil. A randomly chosen container here and there appear to have been set aside by the cranes for inspection. Hanjin 11705 was not one of them.

Whoever procured the car also left a modicum of surveillance equip-ment for us in the back seat — binoculars, a digital camera with a long zoom lens, a couple of less traditional gadgets. Sealy uses the camera while Billie and I trade off with the binoculars. For a couple hours there isn't anything to see, until a smaller mobile crane, operating on tracks, begins transferring containers from the asphalt to waiting truck trailers. Some of the trailers are already hooked to cabs, and pull out as soon as their respective containers are secured.

Hanjin 11705 is deposited on one of these tractor-trailers, and we watch through our long-range lenses as the semi starts up and crawls toward the terminal's exit gate. The simple white lettering on the door of the cab is visible: American Intermodal.

Most American ports have Geiger counters, drug-detection equipment, and other security paraphernalia positioned at the front gate. Trucks or trains departing with imported cargo are ostensibly scanned on departure — but at last check, these exit detectors aren't sensitive to *Yersinia pestis* bacteria. The rig's exit is simpler and quicker than a trip through the EZ-Pass lane on a highway toll plaza: the driver hands a yellow slip of paper to the guard manning the exit booth, the guard checks the paperwork, makes a notation on a clipboard, then waves the container truck, its spinner bomb, the gunman, and his dead comrade into the city of New Orleans.

"Homeland security at its finest," Sealy says from behind the viewfinder of the camera. He snaps a final set of pictures before depositing the camera on my lap and starting up the car. Leaning forward from her position in the back seat, Billie taps the PLB receiver. It resembles a thick iPhone in size and appearance.

"Signal's loud and clear," she says.

From all indications, Hanjin 11705 has yet to be opened or otherwise tampered with outside of our earlier infiltration, which we reset in Puerto Cabello, securing the chain and padlock to its original state minus the snipped link. The truck, one of about a dozen simultaneously leaving the terminal, turns right onto the adjoining arterial and after waiting at a red light, continues around a long bend past a sea of unused industrial buildings until it vanishes from sight.

Sealy, shaking his head, pulls the Chevy off the curb and gets us moving. I see on the dashboard clock that it's now 7:03 a.m.

"I don't like this," Sealy says. "I don't like it at all."

I'm not sure I do either, but for the moment, my plan — incomplete though it may be — is proceeding on course.

-62-

A CCORDING TO THE PLB, THE container truck is five miles ahead of us on I-59 as we approach Tuscaloosa.

"This route could take us to Washington," Sealy says from behind the wheel, "but it's far from clear that Washington remains the weapon's final destination. And we don't even know if that son of a bitch survived the conditions inside the container for the journey across the Gulf." Sealy has been growing increasingly vocal with his agitation with every passing mile. "And even if he *did* survive, I can't imagine somebody from the domestic terror cell, or whatever those assholes driving and ultimately receiving that truck call themselves, isn't going to kill him the minute they open that container and confirm the weapon made the trip. He can't call you if they've killed him first."

"We've still got the PLB," I say. "Besides, they won't kill him. They can't."

"Why not?"

"Because it's too early for him to die," I say. "He needs to make it to the detonation site. With his partner dead, he's the only surviving foreign national accompanying the device. Having him die, or be shot, unceremoniously dumped on the side of the highway — if they don't get him all the way to the blast site, or near to it, and aren't able to 'discover' him there, the study group's investigation won't be properly teed up."

"They could bring him dead to the final destination," Sealy says, "the same way his dead buddy is being transported: as a corpse."

"You see that?" Billie says, peering out the window. "I think I've seen that same car a few times on our drive."

She indicates a gray Chrysler sedan, one lane over and a hundred yards ahead.

"I've noticed it too," Sealy says. "It's been ahead of us the whole way, rather than behind. It's unlikely but it could be tracking us, could be tracking the container, could be a family driving the same route up to their lake house."

Billie jots down the car's license number on a rental-car slip. Sealy keeps on.

"The domestic appeasers," he says, "whether they're study group members or hired hands, could ace your man in the container and keep the body around." That jaw muscle flexes. "That satisfies your condition. So what you're saying doesn't hold water. There's no assurance this shithead is going to call us, or even be *able* to, on the off chance he wasn't bullshitting us back in the container to begin with."

Another mile comes and goes with just the noise of our tires on the road and the engine beneath.

"He'll call," I say.

The words sound and feel hollow to me, so I'm relieved when the road noise overtakes us again without further comment from Sealy.

-63-

We've pulled into a service plaza in Tennessee, the tractor-trailer seven miles north of us, when Sealy gets out his cell phone and makes a call he doesn't intend for me to see. We've been on the road for over twelve hours and it's growing dark. He's just gone to procure snacks, leaving Billie and me in the car, and I see through the window of the fast-food complex that he's got the phone against his ear. Lingering near the restroom but making a phone call while we're meant to think he's relieving himself. I can only spot this thanks to the binoculars, but with them I can make out Sealy's body language during the call.

Agitated, he waves a hand as he talks, likely expressing the same frustrations he's been laying on me for the past few hundred miles. For all I know he's talking to an aunt or uncle and explaining that he'll miss a family event tonight, but I'm growing increasingly uncomfortable with Sealy's disquiet. He could, just as easily, be talking to a colleague in the Pentagon, teeing up a bust of the rig and its occupants a few miles up the road. And while I haven't slept in far too many hours — and didn't exactly begin my sleep-deprivation phase with a clear head — an idea that crystallized back near Montgomery now flips into view in my mind's eye. It's a very bad idea in its way, but if I believe my big-picture plan is the one we must follow, then I'm starting to think I've got no choice.

When Sealy returns, I announce I'm headed for the restroom too, and that I may as well buy a couple of snacks for myself while I'm at it.

"I thought we were keeping you out of sight," Sealy says, munching on a granola bar.

"We are. But I'll keep my head down. The disguise should be sufficient."

"I can go back and get it, whatever it is you want," he says.

"Can't take a leak for me, though," I say, and climb out of the car, feeling both his and Billie's eyes on my back as I cross the asphalt.

After a slouched, careful visit to the high-traffic restroom, I duck into the plaza's convenience store and buy a few things with the last of my cash. I make sure to add a pack of Advil and a hot dog to the more mal-intentioned purchases I set on the counter. I do my best to hide the contents of my second bag as I climb into the car.

"Get what you need?" Sealy says. I open my 2-pack of Advil, pop 'em, and start munching the foul-tasting hot dog I have no interest in eating.

"Couldn't resist a convenience-store dog," I say, taking another bite and chowing down on the flavorless, overcooked meat and bleached white fluff of bun.

"Not exactly a Kale Sunrise Smoothie," Billie says, echoing my thoughts as Sealy merges back onto the highway.

-64-

I<small>F I COULD ASK</small> B<small>ILLIE</small> her advice on how to pull off my very bad idea, I'd do it. But there isn't a private moment in which to corner her before the opportunity I'm looking for arises. It's been three hours since our last roadside stop. A blue sign on the side of the highway indicates that gas and lodging are available at the upcoming exit. I gesture at the sign.

"Anybody else need another pit stop?" I say.

"I'm okay," Billie says in the back.

Sealy turns to me. "Remind me not to take you along on my next surveillance assignment," he says. "You've got a bladder the size of a pea."

As I suspected from the rural nature of the area, the blue sign turns out to be false advertising — after exiting, it takes at least a mile on the country highway before we hit any businesses. An old service station appears ahead on the right. I see a splash of light a half-mile ahead — probably the more modern Mobil or Chevron advertised by the service sign on the throughway. The old service station we're approaching has long since gone to seed, maybe with a few attempts at an antiques or furniture-repair business along the way. But it's clearly abandoned now.

"Pull over here," I say. "Safer to do it off the beaten path."

Sealy parks in the gravel lot beside the old station, sighs, and then says about what I anticipated, given that he skipped the restroom in favor of a clandestine phone call on our last stop. "Since you and your pea-sized bladder are at it," he says, "I'll join you."

271

As Sealy exits, I dig through the plastic bag, find what I'm looking for, and open my door to get out.

"What are you doing?" Billie whispers, seeing what I've got in hand.

I'm out of the car before it turns into a conversation or debate.

Sealy's already doing his business as I approach from behind — this special-forces vet to whom I owe much of the success of my presidency. He hears me approaching and turns his head slightly to speak.

"We're closing in on Washington," he says. "We need to talk ab — "

Armed with the snow-globe I bought in the convenience store, the heavy, hard sphere tucked tightly in my palm, I take a short, quick swing and smack Sealy across the side of the head. I've spent enough time in martial-arts studios in my retirement routine to have a decent sense of the points on the body that, when struck, will knock out a man without inflicting permanent damage — but it's questionable how accurate I've been with my strike.

He whips toward me suddenly, eyes ablaze, the soldier realizing he's being attacked, and wondering if I've missed the target, I hit him again in the same place.

"What the f — "

His voice fails as his knees give out and he drops to his knees, body slackening. I do my best to catch him so he doesn't hit his head on the hard gravel of the driveway. He mumbles something but can't hold the word, and I know I won't have long before he comes around, at which point he will kick the living shit out of me — and my very bad idea, at best suspect in the first place, will have gone nowhere and then some.

I jog back to the car and get the convenience-store bag. Billie is out of the car and follows me back to Sealy while she talks.

"Jesus, what are — you just knocked him out!" she says.

"I did," I say. "I'll explain in a minute. Meantime I'm going to need your help."

I hand her the bag, get my forearms under Sealy's armpits, and drag him behind the buildings. He's much heavier than I expected.

Most of the windows in the rear of the service bay are busted. A door hangs half-open on its hinges. It's hard to see without a flashlight, but I decide this is where Sealy is going to stay for a while, so I go ahead and open the broken door. Billie has arrived with my bag, and I remove from it the packing tape and ball of string I bought with the snow globe.

"Time to tie him up," I say. "Hold his arms while I tape him."

"You're in never-never land," she says, but helps while she vents. "What are we supposed to do without him? What did he do wrong?"

The tape unspools noisily as I wind it around wrists, ankles, and mouth, but not his nose. "If I hope to stick to my plan, then this was the only choice I had. And I apologize for not informing you in advance, but I didn't see an opportunity to do so this time."

"So, KO'ing your friend, who's done everything we've asked him to do, so we can, what — continue with a plan we haven't even formulated yet — that was your only choice?"

"I prefer to see it as the most effective way possible, under the circumstances," I say, "to prevent Sealy from calling in the Homeland Security Administration and arranging the seizure of that truck and cargo. Which would prevent us from exposing the study group. I'll need to secure him to something so he can't bang around and make a racket."

"Aren't you worried that no one will find him here?" she says.

"A man with Sealy's physical conditioning can live without food or water for close to a week if he's got shelter. Which he does. As long as we check in on him four or five days from now, he'll be fine. Tired and thirsty, but fine. If we run into problems in Washington, we call the local police with a tip and they can come get him, but if all goes well, we come back and free him ourselves."

"He's going to kill you," she says, "when you untie him."

I get some extra string wrapped around his arms and legs and tie and tape him to a workbench that's built into the wall. I reach into his pocket and find his car keys and mobile phone. When Billie sees I have the phone, I hand it to her.

"Take this," I say. "And I'm sure you're right — he will kill me. And probably should."

Billie pockets Sealy's cell.

"I've had some time to think this through," I say. "I've come up with the broad strokes on how to go about this. Among other facets, my idea involves the notion of removing the majority of spinners from the bomb but otherwise allowing the detonation to take place."

I think of something, find Sealy's wallet, and swipe the remainder of his cash — ninety bucks. I look up at Billie.

"That's the key part," I say, "but there's more to it, and more still to be figured out, such as the need to identify and confront the study group leadership and determining exactly how to coax them into admitting publicly their knowledge of the bomb. But we'll get to those parts of the plan soon enough. The key is to allow the weapon's passage and to continue tracking it."

"Sounds neither thoroughly thought out," Billie says, "nor easy to accomplish."

"Correct on both counts. And we're going to need the help of a significant number of people. But there are quite a few such people I believe who will be willing to join us. Off-the-radar people."

"From your little black book," Billie says.

"Yes," I say. "First problem being, we've got no way to get any of those who reside outside of Washington into the nation's capital. And then there's the Sealy issue. Among the recruits, we're going to we need someone like him — a paramilitary type. And obviously he's now indisposed."

"Do you think you might have considered that before assaulting him with the snow-globe?"

"I believe he was on the verge of phoning in a strike to seize the weapon and have its escorts taken down. The call he made in the service plaza was probably to a mentor. Maybe checking his instincts. It was only a matter of time before he made the next call."

I kick a bunch of garbage clear of Sealy's new home on the floor. It won't be cold in here on a summer's night, so I figure he'll be all right. The biggest threat to him will probably be mosquitoes and wildlife — an ornery raccoon or fox could do some damage if Sealy isn't able to scare the creature off. I roam around the structure, checking for any obvious ways in or out. Finding some broken panes of glass, I cover them with a squat metal file cabinet. I return to the door at the back of the bay, close it tightly, and rejoin Billie outside, feeling good about the wildlife situation.

At the car, Billie says, "Probably be tough for Sealy to kill you, anyway."

"Why's that?"

"Because," she says, "by the time he has a chance, I may have killed you myself."

I climb into the passenger seat. When Billie slips behind the wheel, I say, "If I screw this thing up, neither you, Sealy, or anyone else will get the chance to take me out. Either the biological weapon or the study group — or both — will have beaten all of you to the punch."

Billie slams her door shut and fires up the ignition.

"Don't screw it up, then," she says.

-65-

I T'S 11:15 P.M. AND PITCH black in Virginia, two hours from the Beltway, when the low-fuel indicator illuminates. We've consistently maintained a seven-mile tail with the container truck. Billie pulls into the first service plaza that comes into view.

She heads over to pay with Sealy's cash and make a civilized restroom stop while I pump. Inside, from the counter, she signals she's paid.

I get the gas flowing, then make the mistake of looking at the minivan on the far side of the pump. There's a man, presumably the husband in this arrangement, standing obliviously at the rear fender pumping gas just like me. But a woman — his wife, perhaps — catches my eye from inside the vehicle. I get the idea she's been watching me all the while, and I see it in her expression. That familiar look . . .

Except this time the look is laced not with the usual head-shaking dismissal or precursor to snapping a photograph with her phone — but instead, fear. I turn my back to her as casually as possible, but by the time I'm topping off the tank I know it's futile. Maybe she's an avid viewer of CNN or Fox News. Could be my makeup is melting away; could be somebody we ran across tipped off a law enforcement organization about my disguise. If so, police composites of my modified face would be plastered all over the media. Could be I'm just paranoid — but the woman's look tells me otherwise.

By the time Billie returns from the restroom I'm at the wheel, the engine running.

"What do you think you're doing?" she says.

"Hurrying us out of here," I say. "Come on, get in. You can take over again in a few miles."

Easing away from the pumps, I slip a look through the rear-view mirror. Confirmed: she's on her phone. Watching me watch her through my mirror.

I lose the minivan as we merge back on the highway, but there's no longer any need to see it, or the woman inside. I can imagine her actions just fine — squinting and straining, looking carefully out the windshield, making sure she has it right as she relays the digits of our license plate. *Chevy Malibu*, she'll be telling the operator at the TMZ tip-line. *Louisiana license plate number...*

I accelerate into the fast lane, knowing, as I act to outrun the sinking sensation that's caught hold of me, that our speed will be useless against it.

-66-

I T's TWENTY MINUTES LATER, IN a woodsy, rural stretch, when I see what I've been expecting in the nighttime sky. I open my window, trying to hear over the noise of the wind and road.

"What's the matter?" Billie says. "And when do we switch seats?"

"Just getting some air. Back at the service plaza, I was worried a woman may have recognized me," I say. "Didn't want to give her a chance for a closer examination. We can switch seats in a couple minutes — I'll look for a safe spot where we can do it."

What I'm seeking to hear would be hard to detect even if I weren't zipping along at 70 mph. Still, I think I hear it. Then I know I do. I shut the window. Close my eyes. Open them.

"What is it?"

"Just a little carsick."

I know how this works. I've had it shown to me before, watched two or three of them live, involving significant fugitives. If it's important enough — if the person of interest matters enough — there's a few tricks the authorities have got up their sleeves. One of the tricks is the helicopters – they fly without running lights and are equipped with whisper-quiet turbines, video feeds, infrared scopes, cutting-edge heat sensors. They're watching you, closing in, lining you up, and you've got no idea and no way out. No matter how fast you drive, how many turns you take.

The highway ahead is lined with trees, bereft of the kind of streetlights we've seen in the busier stretches. It's late, so traffic has thinned drastically

— there isn't a car ahead or behind in visual range. A bend in the road is approaching. The turn isn't sharp, but with the trees, the lack of streetlights, and the curve . . .

I change lanes without using my blinker. Decelerate without touching the brakes — getting down to 50, then 40. I try to keep Billie from noticing it.

"What's going on?" she says.

I lean over and Billie gives me this weird look. Understandable, since I'm probably sporting an odd expression of my own, and the way I now reach across her is awkward, even aggressive. I try to do everything in the most confusing rush possible.

"Just pulling over to switch seats," I say, and unbuckle her seatbelt. I know she's been keeping the items that matter to us in her pockets. In the heat of the distraction of the unbuckling maneuver, I slip my little black book into one of the pockets too. I know I'll only have a second or two at most to catch her by surprise.

"Why are you unbuck — ?"

"I should probably tell you that I love you," I say. I kiss her while reaching across her body, pull her door handle, open her door, and bump her shoulder firmly enough to ensure that she falls out of the car.

Billie is strong and wiry, but she's a lot lighter than me, and she doesn't have any leverage, so by the time she realizes what's happening and tries to grab hold of something — my sleeve, the seat belt, the head rest — it's already too late, and she's gone, and I'm left hoping my assumption was correct about the occasional spill on her bike having built some skills on how best to roll so she doesn't break any bones. The speedometer tells me I'd gotten the speed down to 25, so she shouldn't have too much difficulty with the fall.

I yell out the open door.

"I'll call you on Sealy's cell!"

I hear her yelling back at me as I close the door. "No! You're making a mistake—!"

Since she's yelling at me, I'm assuming she'll survive, and she passes quickly out of earshot. I pull her door closed and floor it to get the car back up to speed. In the rear-view mirror I see her stand. In the pale red glow of the Malibu's taillights, she's still screaming and waving at me from the shoulder. I can make out no approaching headlights from behind.

Less than two miles ahead, the inevitable happens.

-67-

I SEE A GLINT OF STEEL, or maybe it's a flash of reflective taillight, exposed by my high beams. It's on the side of the highway, back from the shoulder, and then there are high beams in my own rear-view mirror, and then there are two, then three, then six sets of headlights. Like a fool I accelerate, instinctively shooting for a way to outrun my gauntlet, but then I come around the slow bend and it's over. I count five state cop cruisers ahead of me plus the six behind. The units ahead skid sideways across the two northbound lanes, the screech of their parking maneuvers loud and shrill even from inside my car. Their blue-and-reds whirl —

And then the whole place lights up.

I know it's the helicopter, but it doesn't matter if you know where it originates — it's still surreal and it shocks you into a primal state of fear. One second the endless black ribbon of highway stretches blankly ahead into the night — and the next, it's a blinding, white-hot construction zone. It kicks up your adrenaline, and my instincts are to make a run for it — where, I don't know — but then I feel the bounce underwheel and there's no more running. The Chevy's power-steering turns sluggish and the ride gets rough, the nail-strip I've just run over doing its job.

I lose control, correcting then overcorrecting. The brakes ignore my pleas. The Malibu spins and I lose perspective on which lights are where, hoping the car doesn't catch on the pavement and roll, until the ordeal ends in an anticlimactic backwards skid.

Voices blare — crisp, piercing, megaphone-enhanced, but I don't think of it this way, I'm just *targeted* —

"Out of the car *now!*"

"Open the door and put your hands where we can see them!"

"*Now!*"

"*Do it now!*"

I don't know whether it's one voice or ten, coming to me over a megaphone or from the helicopter or from *God*, but in my shock I do my best to comply. The voices are deep. Baritone. Enraged. I am criminal, I am enemy; I am nothing. They are authority; they are everything.

I'm prepared to surrender, unlatching my seat belt and slowly opening the door, one hand extended showing my empty palm —

When I see the one thing I cannot possibly be seeing.

I know immediately this is the mistake Billie was yelling about. The mistake that will mean death, mayhem, destruction — a guarantee, thanks to my cascading set of cataclysmic errors, that the study group will fulfill its every dream of violence and tyranny. In the cylindrical depression of the drink-holder between the front seats of the Malibu, resting inanimately — symbolizing my failure despite its inertness —

Is the PLB receiver.

You can't be here! my mind says. *You can't!*

Billie had been religiously tracking the container truck, always replacing it in the pocket of her jeans. How could I not have noticed? I tossed Billie from the car to spare her the fate I'm meeting now. I knew the woman in the minivan had phoned me in. I knew from the sound of the helicopter that they were coming for me. And Billie being out there with the PLB remote, out of the study group's hands — as free as I was a minute ago — was my sole hope of keeping some semblance of my plan intact.

Now the gunman in the container — presuming he ever comes around to my way of thinking at all — is the *only* hope. Billie at least has Sealy's mobile phone — assuming it survived her 25 mph tumble out the door. But the wafer-thin, supremely flawed insurance policy Sealy was wisely objecting to is now all that stands in the way of the detonation of the bomb and the release of its deadly pathogen on the citizens of Washington.

A bomb that the study group intentionally allowed into our country — and now I have too.

The police will seize the PLB . . . *but maybe I can hide it in a pocket.* Or even if I can't, I could try to convince one of the local constables that the device must be read, the transmitter and container tracked. As Sealy would see it, lives would at least be saved. There's got to be someone on the police force who isn't held in the study group's grip and can sound the alarm for me.

"*Out of the car!*"

"*You will get on the ground now, asshole!*"

It looks through my windshield like a military operation, and I suppose that's what it is. Police in riot gear, armed to the teeth, sprinting to my car, eager to shoot or tackle or maim — and now I've hesitated, and they don't like that.

I need that PLB — and so I reach for it. I stretch and almost get it, my fingers brushing against its smooth surface —

Gloved hands are on me. Descending troopers snatch at the fabric of my shirt, pants, belt, and I am bodily extracted from the car and heaved to the asphalt. I hear more than feel the *oomph* as air expels from my lungs on impact.

"On your face, *now!*"

I don't need to be told this, since at least three large men have just tackled me to the ground. I feel the dull scrape of my jaw losing its confrontation with the asphalt. My back and torso fire missiles of pain in every direction. A chorus assaults my ears — "*Get down! Eat the pavement!*" "*Spread your arms and legs!*" "*Hands on top of your head!*" "*Hands behind your back!*" "*Don't move! Do not move!*"

The side of my face grinds against the grit of the road, sandpapered raw before they pull me to my feet. As I'm starting to find some oxygen, I see the approaching hood of a police cruiser and I'm driven into it.

Like every target of law enforcement does, I want to say, "I'm innocent," "You've got the wrong guy," or "You've got it all wrong, you can't take me in" — but it doesn't really matter what I want to say, because I can't even breathe, and it wouldn't matter if I could say anything since nobody would — or should — believe a word out of my mouth.

Innocent until proven guilty, my ass: I'm as guilty as Charles Manson and every cop in this brigade knows it beyond a reasonable doubt.

PART V:

WASHINGTON

-68-

T HE INITIAL VERSION OF THE Hotline — the red telephone created to establish direct communication between the leaders of the Soviet Union and United States memorialized in various Cold War movies — involved no voice transmission. Technically, it wasn't even a phone. It was a redundant telegraph, connected through two routes utilizing a newly installed sub-Atlantic cable.

On the most crucial day of the Cuban Missile Crisis — October 26, 1962 — our countries were on the brink of nuclear war. On that day, a letter was sent from Nikita Khrushchev to 35, offering Kennedy an out from the standoff involving Soviet missiles in Cuba and a U.S. naval blockade of the island nation. It took so long for the letter to be transmitted over traditional teletype, then subsequently translated — 12 hours in total — that before the U.S. was able to generate a response, a second, more ominous letter had already arrived from Khrushchev. It was only due to Attorney General Robert Kennedy's suggestion that the president ignore the second letter and proceed with the planned response to the first that an agreement was reached and direct military engagement averted.

In the wake of the crisis, both the Kremlin and White House perceived the need for a more direct and faster mode of communication. On June 23 of the following year, this yielded the Hotline. Upgraded every U.S. presidency, and used with increasing frequency on ever-milder crises, the device had begun to function as a full-fledged media hub by the time I took office. Its signal ran through geostationary satellites, could transmit virtually any sort of communication of that era — fax, email, voice, even limited video — and

287

was staffed on both sides with dedicated translators. Had I needed to speak to my Russian counterpart, there was of course a process by which he would be located and summoned, but the Hotline had come to be used primarily by high-ranking White House or State Department personnel and their Russian Federation equals as a general-purpose diplomatic tool.

For the single occasion on which I personally put the Hotline to use, my call was routed not to Moscow, but instead to Russia's Ambassador to the U.S., Anatoly Stanislav, working down the street from the White House at their embassy in Washington. Anatoly was a seemingly ageless man who persevered through shifts in Russian leadership and managed to maintain his seniority as effectively under Putin as when he worked for Yelstin and Gorbachev.

My dicey moments in U.S.-Russia relations came via regional proxy wars.

These were literal battles and wars, but not ours or Russia's — at least not directly. In the superpower chess game, local influence mattered almost everywhere. The knights and rooks with which we played were not literal U.S. or Russian army battalions, but still these were wars, and we each had people there, which we preferred to call *advisors*, supported by *aid* and *materiel*. Call it what you want, American and Russian citizens were fighting against each other with live munitions, *supporting* local troops on our respective sides of the conflicts.

Afghanistan seemed to garner all the headlines, but active proxy wars were waged during the Cold War in Malaysia, Angola, Syria, Cambodia, Libya, Chad, Laos, Tajikistan, Northeast India, and Turkey, naming but a few.

The reason for my call to Anatoly on that particular morning was that we'd been caught with our hand in the cookie jar in one of these conflicts and were now, for lack of more precise military jargon, completely screwed.

Two weeks prior, with the clandestine promise of our military support, Somalia had invaded Ethiopia, whose citizens were being repressed by a Russia-engineered dictatorship claiming to be socialist in its bearing.

Unfortunately, in this endeavor we'd gambled and lost, placing insufficient numbers of unmarked American troops and tanks alongside Somali forces in what was supposed to be a surprise attack. Turns out Russia outguessed us and brought even more firepower to the defense of their Ethiopian ally, resulting in the ambush and looming annihilation of 2,850 American soldiers who weren't supposed to be there.

If we didn't engage Russia to sanction our side's safe retreat, local forces would slaughter our unofficial troops in a matter of hours.

"Hello, Mr. President, how is the weather in Washington today?" came Stanislav's thick Russian accent over the Hotline. He liked to maintain the ruse that he could be anywhere in the world, from Moscow to the Mediterranean, thanks to the technology of rerouted phone lines. The ambassador spoke in lightly accented English.

"Same as it is around the corner at the embassy, Anatoly, but thank you for asking," I said, and got directly to it. "Your military has clandestinely expanded its presence beyond the levels we consider reasonable in the Horn of Africa."

"Really?" Stanislav said. "I will have to look into this claim. Thank you for alerting us to this apparent misappropriation. Yet I am told there are unauthorized American forces in the region as well."

When you need something from Russia, I've found it is best to wield a very large hammer augmented by the presence of an appealing carrot. In this case, I didn't have much of a carrot to offer, so the hammer had to be as big as they came.

"Regardless of respective deployments, official or unofficial," I said, "I'm calling for a more pragmatic and urgent reason."

"Urgent?" Stanislav said. "For whom? Perhaps urgent for your American advisors, eh? But, I suspect, not for us."

"Unless I am mistaken," I said, "the Hotline is intended for direct communication during times of potential or imminent use of nuclear weapons."

In the silence that followed I thought I detected a low rumbling, as though the heavyset Stanislav may have been growling on the other end of the line. If he was, he had good reason to be: I knew that Stanislav and his superiors had recently learned of our capability in the Africa region to deploy battlefield nuclear weapons, also known as "theater nukes," so named for their tactical functionality within the limited theater of ground battle.

"We will not lose three thousand American lives," I said. "Therefore I am calling to alert you that our Secretary of Defense has ordered our advisors in Ethiopia to utilize the highest and most deadly form of theater armaments to defend the Somali position."

Another silence, punctuated by a "Hmph." Then, "An escalation of this sort would surely result in like-for-like retaliation, Mr. President. I can't speak for my superiors yet, but I estimate their position will be similar to yours: we would not tolerate the loss of . . . *six* thousand Russian lives any more than you would accept the demise of your *three* thousand."

"Then we are in a bind," I said.

"You will not use these 'most deadly theater armaments' in Ethiopia. The political fallout would be too great for your administration to bear. Eh?"

"Where you are mistaken," I said, already prepared for this argument, "is that if it were discovered that I positioned and *lost* three thousand lives, the fallout would be equally damaging. I am no worse off through escalation."

I left it at that. After a long while, Stanislav spoke.

"What is it you suggest that you and I do?"

A twinge of icy satisfaction coursed down my spine. Time to convince him to eat the carrot he already holds. "I suggest you deliver your side a win. Perhaps you can take a proposed settlement to your superiors. Under the terms of this settlement, I would advise the Somali military to withdraw its troops and, for an agreed upon armistice period, respect the sovereignty of the Ethiopian state and its current regime. Your side would, in turn, recommend to the Ethiopian military that they allow the Somali troops and their accompanying advisors to safely retreat. You win, we lose."

I counted four seconds of silence before Anatoly answered. "I believe I understand what you are suggesting," he said, "and I will call you shortly with an answer."

"I look forward to the call," I said.

There was a long crackle of silence over the Hotline. Then the ambassador said, "Someday we shall break bread over a bottle of fine Russian vodka, and you will tell me the truth of this call today."

-69-

TWENTY-FOUR HOURS TICK BY. HUNDREDS of times, I summon the guard to my "hole" in solitary confinement. Though he duly appears every time, he ignores me as I try every way I can think to explain that he and his superiors need to get their hands on the device that was left in my car. That it's tracking a weapon of mass destruction, headed for Washington, and he's got to tell his commander, *anybody*, to get somebody, *anywhere*, looking for the threat to our existence I accompanied across the Gulf, then lost. Back at the port, we took down the license plate of the rig and I remember it clearly. I relay it to the guard, knowing that he can inform his superiors and they could put out an APB. A sweep of the entire Washington area should find it, unless its driver has already deposited the container and fled the scene.

The guard says nothing, and shows no shift in facial expression, in response to my theatrics.

At least Billie's out there.

Maybe she's gone back for Sealy. Maybe our man in the container will call. Maybe the gunman has bought into my dubious wisdom and the faith I put in him. But this is a lot of maybes. Any optimism feels more like a Hail Mary with every passing minute. I've lost track of the weapon. The evidence lab or, worse, the study group now has the PLB receiver. I tax my concussed brain to produce a strategy — *any* strategy. No solution comes.

In the end, Sealy had it right.

If I've correctly counted the clock since our round-trip journey across the Gulf by various means, it's nearing 1:00 p.m. and today is July first. The weapon, if its shepherds intend to keep their schedule, is set to detonate in four days and six hours from now.

A voice sounds out, then a buzz, followed by a metal-on-metal *clang*. My cell door opens and light pours into the room for the first time in hours. The typically mute guard's hulking body looms, cutting a monstrous shadow within a doorway of blinding light. I'm readying to make my pitch to him again when he speaks — his first words since my arrival.

"Get a move on! Somebody here to see you."

He latches a pair of handcuffs to my wrists, gestures down the hall, and follows as I obey his gesture. In due course he tells me to stop, opens another door, and pushes me into an interrogation room. The room is empty save a table, two chairs, and a pair of wall-mounted video cameras.

"Sit."

I do and discover that I can see myself in the room's wall-length mirror. Of course it isn't a mirror at all, but a window through which observers can watch my interrogation. Suffice to say that with the disguise partly peeled from my face and the bruises and scabs scarring my complexion, I look as bad as any living person could. I'd give a few John Does in the morgue a run for their money.

The guard removes the cuffs before re-attaching my wrists to another set of restraints, secured to the table by bolts and chains.

"Wait here," he says, which seems sort of unnecessary.

Alone, I find myself wondering just what the study group has decided to do with me now that they've got me in their clutches.

"Who gives a shit?" I say.

Confused from my extended time alone, I'm beginning an interior debate on whether I've said this aloud, or the thought has simply banged around the interior of my skull, when the door opens.

Head bowed, the visitor closes the door with his back to me. Clad in a pinstripe suit, it's a man who's mostly bald save a comb-over, and stands semi-hunched, his posture suggesting old age is gaining on him. Yet even with his back turned, the unfamiliar clothes, and the reduced volume of hair, I sense this is someone I know. It's hard to tell from where or when, but I feel I know him just the same. When the visitor finally turns and reveals his face, my eyes and brain confirm what instinct has already told me.

The man who has just arrived in the interrogation room to pay me a visit is Anatoly Stanislav.

-70-

THE FORMER RUSSIAN AMBASSADOR HAS brought with him an unlabeled bottle of clear liquid and two shot glasses. Besides the evident fact that he's come to share that long-promised vodka, something is starkly clear from Anatoly's arrival.

The study group wouldn't have allowed word of my seizure to escape to the general public. Only someone on the inside would know that I'm in custody here. Thus I'm left with a simple conclusion: that the former ambassador is still an ambassador. All that's different now is the organization he represents.

"Mr. President," he says in his subtle Russian accent, which has become even more refined. "It is so good to see you again."

I watch him, in no mood to speak. *This isn't an Oval Office photo op — think I'll skip the pleasantries.*

Taking the seat opposite mine, he cracks the seal on the bottle, pours the shot glasses full, and leaves the bottle open. Checking the video cameras, I note that no little red lights are illuminated.

Doubt they'll want this session on tape.

"*Budem zdorovy,*" he says, lifting one of the glasses as he toasts. "Finally we enjoy that vodka together. So tell me. You *were* bluffing. You did not have theater nuclear weapons in Ethiopia. Eh?"

I take my glass and accept a bruising toast that spills vodka from both glasses. I then set my glass on the table, seize his, push mine across to him, and offer a repeat of the toast, waiting for him to drink first. He nods and acquiesces to the new toast and its poison-protection measures.

Once we've drained the glasses, he refills them immediately.

"Russians are so predictable," I say. "I knew your response before I made the call. Of course we didn't have them. And guess what? You're just as predictable now. Former despotic so-called socialists always seem to make the most fervent capitalists. Sell yourself to the highest bidder, no particular principles required. In this case, the highest bidder being the study group, I assume. At least you still know your vodka."

"*S otyezdom*," he says, and drains his second glass.

I leave mine full.

"As was always the case when we conversed," Anatoly says, "we can skip the unnecessary burden of pleasantries where we lie to each other for a time before 'talking turkey.' Eh?"

I say nothing.

"So, then," he says, "we know that during his time with you, President Walker revealed a great deal of sensitive information."

I study his mannerisms as he speaks. Capitalism has been good to him — despite his advancing years, he's gained some weight. No surprise — so have I.

"We know additionally from Mr. Skeel," he says, "and from Deputy Director Rudd, that you probably know all that President Walker knew, if not a great deal more. So we have but a single question."

I find myself doubting that the CIA man was a turncoat. They probably abducted him and whipped Saran wrap around his head. "To whom does your royal 'we' refer?" I say.

"The question is simple," he says, ignoring mine. "Why the change?"

I take a minute, but still don't get it.

"What change is that?"

"When the commission and its . . . international allies," he says, tossing me either a facial tic or wink, "was in its infancy, I've been told that you were more than willing to, as they say, go along with the program. I'm also told some felt this was because you understood the value of the program you were going along with."

"Ah," I say. "The commission. Band of buzzards. Study group. What other names do you like to use? Deep state, maybe? — though I imagine that's an insulting one, like you're a bunch of Internet hackers living in their mothers' basements. Regardless," I say, coming back to his question, "what you posit was not the case."

"No?"

"While I held office," I say, "your colleagues weren't more than aspirants to the power the group now seems to wield. So it occurred to me back then that the wisest course was to go along with the program here and there, and focus on what I intended to achieve rather than fighting the JV team's aspirations. Put differently, I chose to remain clean and avoid wrestling with the pigs."

"Confusing American phrases," he says after a moment of consideration, "but if I understand the meaning, your approach was sensible." He pours himself another glass and downs it. "But again, the same question, put differently: Why do you insist now on going against the program to which you acquiesced before? Why, now, are you wrestling with the pigs?"

As he used to, Anatoly wears wire-frame glasses. I stare through them.

"I realized I was wrong in the first instance," I say. "Walker, as it turns out, showed a little more wisdom than I managed in my time. He was right to try and throw a wrench in the machine. Now it turns out I'm the one holding the wrench."

"Lucky us." Anatoly levels a cool, closed-lip grin at me. "Incidentally, we have the tracking receiver. Its duplicative monitoring function has proved productive, since the Venezuelan cell seems to have shifted the detonation site. Their scheme will of course be allowed to proceed, but our evidence-gathering will remain more efficient thanks to the transmitter you placed on the device. Without your help we might not have known the weapon's revised destination, nor been able to accumulate the proper evidence against the perpetrators of this heinous act."

My stomach feels heavy. Did our man in the container know the alternate detonation site? If so, he played along as though I'd told him the location as he knew it. Letting me show my cards while he heard me out. Not sure whether that makes him more or less likely to call.

Anatoly fiddles with his empty glass as though fighting the urge to pour it to capacity yet again. I continue to ignore my full glass.

"Back to the point at hand," he says. "There was greater wisdom than you realize in the approach you once took. In the years that followed your administration, our organization's pooling of Eastern European and North American personnel benefited the global economy in ways that lasted well into the new century. Now, the program is similar, but for a new frontier. As you might imagine from what you have learned, our studies now call for a unified North and South America to prepare for the coming struggle with the Far East."

No matter the version, it's always the same — everyone's an enemy if you choose to look at the world as a place full of combatants. The bigger the region, the greater the potential threat. Current case in point, China.

The fact that they've got the PLB . . .

Ignoring for the moment his fairly frightening reference to collusion of study group members across the Russian and American bureaucracies, I try to conceive of any last-ditch means by which lives may yet be saved. If they've got the PLB, my chances of rescue, and the saving of American lives on July fifth — let alone halting the progress of this global deep-state cigar club — have plainly been reduced to Billie-and-Sealy or nothing. And the only way *they'd* be empowered to get a goddamn thing accomplished is by way of a call from our man in the container.

Then I think of one more person. Though without any means of contacting her, the thought is an empty one.

"Quite a strategy, and why not?" I say, coming back to his stated trans-regional warmongering scheme. "Suppress the socialist factions currently ruling most of South America and you've got a united, capitalist trio of continents, joining hands against the semi-communist, anti-capitalist Chinese. It will create an even more compelling storyline than the Cold War we enjoyed with you. Listen, why don't you get to the point? I'm not a regular vodka drinker. I've had enough."

"Which point is that?"

"Since you now operate under some kind of bilateral dictate, I'm assuming you're planning on leaving me with an ex-KGB torture expert," I say, "or possibly a Langley-based zero-anesthetic surgery team. So let's get on with it. What is it that you want to know? Though I can't actually fathom what you think you could learn from me at this point — unless you're interested in the subtleties of pruning Zinfandel vines in February, or the frustrating number of cloudy days in June along the California coast."

"We already know what you know," he says, flipping his hand in the air dismissively, "or what you think you know. No torture necessary. Interrogation is not the purpose of my visit. Instead, I'm here to offer amnesty."

"Ah," I say. "Amnesty — from what offense?"

He flips his hand for a second time.

"Put differently," he says, "I've been sent to offer you a position on the commission. Or to use your nomenclature: a seat within the study group."

Something clicks in my brain.

"Call it what you want — we are offering membership," he says. "I recommend that you seize the opportunity. You're fortunate to receive this, something to which I can attest that many have not. To put this bluntly, I will accompany the offer with some advice: go along with the program, Mr.

President. I assure you that the alternative is not pleasant, nor is it an empty threat, like your 'theater nukes.'"

I might have expected this. Clearly, it's something the man sitting in front of me was offered some time ago. And I imagine Walker would have seen the same membership invite, possibly as a last-ditch effort to shut him up. Still, I find it hard to believe they'd consider *me* an acceptable risk, even if membership would allow them to keep me as near-and-dear an enemy as possible. A new kind of Bozo detail.

"What could keeping me alive," I say, "let alone recruiting me to join the fight club, possibly do for you people?"

"It buys us your silence, of course," the former and current ambassador says, "while also retaining for the commission the strategic mind of an effective former politician, as needed."

For the second time in a month, I find myself thinking the same thought: *You've got the wrong president.* Meanwhile my mind has almost finished plugging away at the deeper meaning here. I decide to keep Anatoly talking to give my head more time to solve the riddle.

"Killing me buys the silence you're looking for," I say. "So why don't you just do that?"

"We can only kill so many former presidents," he says, and then he winks, "before the world goes to hell."

"Bullshit. Leaders are assassinated all the time. America has just been insulated from it for the most part."

Anatoly shrugs. "In point of fact, there is a rule in our constitution to this effect."

Relenting in the face of undue temptation, he pours another glass of vodka and downs the shot.

"Whose constitution?" I say.

"The . . . entity's. The commission's."

"And that rule is . . .?"

"Except by a special vote," he says, "approximating a version of America's constitutional amendment process, the commission is not permitted to cause the assassination of a president, current or former, of any of our member states, more than once every fifteen years. The logic is obvious: anything more frequent would result in chaos. Chaos," he adds, "being the very state of affairs we are committed to avoiding."

I barely hear his explanation. The rule, if it runs according to Anatoly's explanation, actually *allows* for the murder of a president from time to time. *When convenient — as needed — just keep it to a minimum.*

But it also means something else, allowing the puzzle piece my brain was trying to fit to click into place: *This is the real reason President Walker picked me as his chosen one. There were no other teams. No eight helping hands to match the supposed extraordinary rendition teams he and Rudd had identified. There was only one abduction team, and one chosen helper. They offered him amnesty too, and whether he gave them the impression he accepted or not, he learned what I've just learned, and he picked me because he knew if they'd make a play at killing him, I would be his insurance policy. Unfortunately for him, it turned out the other way — he's become mine.*

Whoever they killed first didn't matter— one of us would wind up with immunity. *Two presidents are better than one.*

This also answers Billie's question: it's the reason they didn't take me out with a bullet at Lou Ebbers' house while they were busy assassinating my former DCI. Given I'm a former head of state, they were only permitted to capture me, lest a foot soldier burn through the constitutional assassination rule without proper study group authorization.

I nod, scratch my cheek, and offer my looniest grin to Ambassador Stanislav. "Here is my answer to your offer," I say. "*Poshol nahuj.*"

I've just told the former Russian ambassador to go fuck himself.

He nods. "We weren't expecting you to be cooperative."

His back straightens, Anatoly no longer my companion in this discussion. "Just so you know, you are going to be 'disappeared' now. I hope you are enjoying your time in the cell you currently occupy, since soon, you'll commence to passing the remainder of your years in one with far less hospitable confines."

I smile another madman's grin. "Can't wait."

"Officially," Stanislav says, "you will escape from the Rockingham-Harrisonburg Regional Jail. A massive manhunt will follow, to no avail." He keeps a thin, cold smile on his face. I wonder whether he's stone drunk by now. "The public will probably root for you. Journalists sympathetic to our aims will speculate you took on a new identity in the face of your heinous crimes, and are ensconced on an island in the South Pacific. If we come to need you for something, we'll show your face here, release a current photograph there. But in the meantime you'll lead a life of . . . veal."

He stands, and I reflect that I'm now destined to play the role the study group once had me engineer for Carlos the Jackal.

"I'll say that you should — " he flutters a hand through the air again, butterfly-like — "prepare yourself."

"How exactly does one go about preparing one's self," I say, "for a couple decades of solitary confinement?"

He shakes his head. "*Nyet*," he says. "Not for the cell."

"For what, then?"

He lobs me a final grin.

"For the temperatures. I'll leave you the vodka so you can warm your belly. Solitary confinement in Siberia is much colder than the equivalent here."

-71-

IF YOU LIVE IN CALIFORNIA and find your bed rattling, the vibration escalating to an eruptive impact, and the wall supporting your roof shedding their coat of paint and disintegrating to bare cinderblocks and mortar, you typically conclude the obvious:

Earthquake.

Rockingham, Virginia, however, is not known for its temblors. As the walls of my jail cell cave in and the world implodes in the semidarkness of yellow safety lights, my reflexive thoughts shift.

Can't be an earthquake. Not here.

The roar is overwhelming. Soldiers in masks and flak jackets burst through the cascading rubble. Their arrival is too quick on the heels of the ruckus for them to be emergency responders of any kind. The soldiers push through chunks of busted cinderblock, beams of halogen headlamps cutting through the haze of concrete dust, and then one of them is on me.

It's Anatoly's way of initiating my attempted escape, feeding the study group's propaganda plan for America's most wanted former president.

The commando grabs at my shirt and pulls my face close. I see the glint of the safety lights in the soldier's eyes, but that's all — a ski mask covers nose, mouth, ears, cheeks, forehead, hair.

"Got him!" he says.

Another soldier has my legs, and then the two of them are carrying me through the crushed wall and we're outside in the night. A miniature frontloader is parked beside the exterior of the jailhouse. Equipped with a kind of drill head, the vehicle is half-buried in a pile of cinderblocks formerly comprising the exterior wall of the county jail building. I'm swung onto the back of a motorcycle, one of two parked near the front-loader. One of the motorcycles carries a soldier and me; the other seats the other two soldiers — presuming that's what they are. Given the sparse inventory of equipment deployed in the operation, my assumption of this extraction as study group-driven paramilitary action is fading as quickly as my initial earthquake suspicion.

Six or seven minutes on the motorcycles in the warm, humid night delivers us over the rough lip of a driveway into a parking lot. The lot is bordered by a chain-link fence; distant sirens sound out. One of the soldiers throws something at me and I catch it; I look down to see that I've just caught a key ring. On the ring are two car keys plus a clear plastic rectangle encasing a white slip of paper with a license plate number and other markings.

Rental car.

I raise my line of sight to take in the pair of blue sedans parked in the lot. The soldiers from the other motorcycle climb into one of the cars. The man I rode with looms into my field of vision, ski mask still covering everything but his eyes.

"You've got a map on the passenger seat. Follow the directions printed on it. And I recommend you get going. Quick." He motions in the direction from which we came. "Dragnet won't be far behind."

I recognize the man's voice.

"I know you," I say.

I see some crinkling of the wrinkles around his eyes, and then he salutes, says, "Goes around, comes around," turns, and jogs to the cars. He climbs behind the wheel of the one loaded with the others and they bounce down the driveway and out of the parking lot.

I hustle to the other car.

-72-

THE DIRECTIONS ON THE PASSENGER seat in the car take me to a hulking fortress of shadows minded by another chain-link perimeter fence. No light emanates from the confines of the vast property. According to the printed map and directions, I'm in Berryville, Virginia, 70 miles or so from my starting point.

The gate beside the vacant guard booth is unchained and opened wide enough to admit a car. Pulling through deliberately, I enter a parking lot the size of an ocean, bereft of vehicles. Bereft of anything. Moving slowly, I explore the lot from behind the wheel of the rental car, learning that the asphalt swath is not completely empty, at least not if you count a few dozen beer cans, soda cups, and Burger King hamburger wrappers, all of which conspire to make me hungry. I swing back near the guard booth and, still inside the confines of the lot, pull the emergency brake, kill the lights and engine, and sit in silence with the windows open.

Examining what little I can see and hear of the abandoned buildings in the darkness, I think what I always do when I see places like this. Whatever was once made here is probably being made in China now, or Indonesia. Manufactured for half the cost, even after the write-off it took to leave this environmental time bomb in the dust. Despite the benefits of global capitalism I once espoused, the fact remains that all those jobs keeping families in nice homes in Berryville are long gone. Pension plans, too, presuming the company that abandoned the plant also worked a strategic bankruptcy into their scheme. You'd think no American would buy this company's products anymore, yet the opposite is probably true. Sales and profits have likely soared since the jettisoning of this hulk.

The sound of a rusty old metal hinge comes from the building.

The noise is followed by the appearance of a figure in a doorway of the old structure. The figure holds a flashlight that illuminates the ground ahead but keeps the figure in shadow. Difficult to make out in the night at a distance, the shadowed figure appears slight, feminine, and wiry — then familiar.

I pull the keys from the ignition, climb out, and lean against the hood of the car as Billie clicks off the flashlight on her approach. I'm not sure what to expect, or say, or do. The last time I saw this woman, she was flying out the passenger side of a speeding car, thanks to a nudge from me. And in the meantime, it appears she, rather than Anatoly Stanislav, has seen to my extraction from the Rockingham-Harrisonburg Regional Jail.

She stops a few paces off. "Hi."

"I really owe you an apology," I say, laying into it. "I had a sense it was over, that the road block was rightly up ahead. Pushing you out — "

"After I cooled off, I realized it was a nice move," she says. "It was the only option if we were to hold any chance of tracking the container."

I nod.

"Except that the PLB didn't make it with you as you rolled out of the car," I say.

"No."

"Tell me about the people who broke me out."

"We found someone with the words *escape specialist* written beside his name in your little black book."

"Escape specialist," I say, then make the connection between the voice of the masked soldier who sprung me and Billie's explanation. "Rudy. That was Rudy Simmons."

"Yes."

A Louisiana prisoner originally sentenced, at age 15, to a hard-labor chain-gang for "knowingly purchasing" a stolen engagement ring for his high school sweetheart, Rudy subsequently escaped, was recaptured, escaped again, and so on, a total of seventeen times. Each escape earned him another five-year stint, thereby quashing any hope of legitimate release during his actuarial life expectancy. The final lawyer in Rudy's otherwise failed chain of legal representation was a former associate of Miles Glinn, who ultimately presented Rudy's case as a potential presidential pardon.

Possibly the world's greatest escape artist, he had twenty years remaining on his multiple sentences — and yet he never should have been jailed, nor tried as an adult for that matter, unless buying an engagement ring for ten bucks from a pawn shop was a new sort of federal offense I hadn't tracked.

I pardoned him immediately.

Goes around, comes around.

"My black book," I say to Billie. "You went through it. Made some calls."

She nods again, but even in the dark I catch the odd expression on her face.

"What is it?" I say.

"That book of yours," she says.

"What about it?"

"It's pretty accurate. You know, the phone numbers, and so on. Almost all of them, in fact." She motions toward the factory with the flashlight. "Come inside."

I follow her through the old metal door, its rusty hinge objecting to its continued use so late in life. We move through a cobwebbed entry lobby of sorts before turning into an enormous, cavernous space stretching far into the darkness. Chunky, mechanized shapes loom then retreat in the darkness of the abandoned factory's interior as the beam of Billie's flashlight splashes over them on our walk.

"Listen, I have questions," I say. "Do you still have Sealy's cell? We'll need to pull him out of that service station. And it all depends on that phone now: I was visited in jail by a member of the study group. They've got the PLB, and with it they determined that the Venezuelans changed the location of the detonation site. We'll ne — "

"I've got Sealy's cell," she interrupts, our voices sounding miniscule in the cavernous room, "and you don't have to worry about Sealy. Not yet. The most important thing you need to know is that we also learned that the detonation site was changed. We don't yet have the new location, but we believe we are getting warmer."

"Getting warmer — ? Did the gunman from the container call?"

Billie shakes her head. "Neither he nor Sealy nor I can take the credit on this one," she says, and gestures ahead of us with the flashlight. "I've got somebody here I think you'll want to meet. She deserves most, if not all of the credit."

Fifteen or twenty paces toward the back of the room, another flashlight clicks on, and with the double dose of light, I'm able to make out a fair-skinned woman in jeans and a white Oxford shirt, sandy hair cut to her shoulders.

She's just flicked on her own flashlight, and looks mildly familiar as she approaches, but I can't yet place the face.

She reaches out to shake my hand.

"Evening, Mr. President," she says. "My name is Julie Laramie."

"How did we find you?" I ask Laramie.

"It involved a little finding in both directions," Laramie says.

"Tori Fleming was one of the people I called," Billie says. "When I pressed her, she realized that one of the items in the boxes gave a clue on how to contact Laramie — at least, how to leave a voice message for her that she could retrieve."

"When she left me a message," Laramie says, "and I called her back, she caught me up on your story. Not that I hadn't been tracking it. Saw far too much coincidence in the timing of your very public problems, Walker's twin assassinations, and the proximity to July fifth. It seemed to me that we would see eye-to-eye on what needs to be done."

"Tori then put us together," Billie says.

"How were you able to discover the alternate location of the weapon?" I say.

"You heard I came down with the flu."

"Yes."

"I staged the illness to protect myself from the same fate President Walker suffered," she says. "Based on the sequence of events following the delivery of my memo to the president, it was clear nobody of weight intended to do anything to stop the July fifth strike. I also suspected that the Venezuelans — having had numerous members of their group compromised or killed by CIA contractors such as the interrogator you saw on the DVDs — would shift the detonation site, time, or method. So I went to Venezuela.

Took me a while, but with some work, I uncovered the location that I believed they planned to use as the new ground zero. As it turns out, their operation was fundamentally too crude and thinly funded to alter much more than the location, and even that they only shifted by a few miles."

"Billie said we're getting warmer on finding the new location," I say. "What did that mean?"

"In my investigative work down south," Laramie says, "words like 'plant' and 'yard' came through repeatedly. In checking maps of Washington, I was able to think of those terms through a different lens: there's an abandoned passenger-train maintenance facility in the Ivy City rail yards. We haven't visually confirmed the bomb is in the building but we have a supporting clue."

"Remember the car from the highway?" Billie says. "Gray Chrysler?"

"Yes."

"Once Laramie told us what she believed to be the new location, we worked together to survey the area. Looking for sentries, pieces of the shipping crate — anything. We hadn't made any progress until we passed a gray Chrysler parked on the service street north of the building. Plates matched the number I'd written down on our drive."

My mind firing on most of its cylinders by now, I reach the same conclusion Billie and Laramie obviously had. "Car wasn't following us at all," I say. "It was somebody, possibly from the study group, monitoring the progress of the container truck."

"Right."

"And they've continued the monitoring post-delivery," I say.

"We think so," Billie says.

I look around the building. "And this place?"

"We picked this old factory from a few choices a location scout from your black book identified," Billie says. "This one sees no visitors. It's close enough for access, far enough away to allow us to remain hidden."

I can't remember who from my black book does location scouting for a living, but that's why it's said that a short pencil is better than a long memory — the very reason I write everyone I meet into the book. I've got another question for Billie.

"You keep saying 'we,'" I say. "Does that mean you already got Sealy out?"

"Yes," Billie says. "And you can see him in a minute. But that isn't really the 'we' I'm referring to."

"Explain."

"This way," Laramie says.

I follow the two of them through an archway into the rearmost half of the giant hall. From the glimpses of the machinery in the muted illumination of the flashlights, it appears we've arrived in the heart of the old production line, though it's difficult to surmise what products were made here. Maybe textiles. The room is nearly the size of a football stadium.

"I mentioned in the parking lot," she says, "that I called some of the people listed in your little black book. Many of them agreed to help."

"In what capacity?" I say.

Billie shrugs. "It's your plan," she says, "so you tell me. Or just tell *them*."

She and Laramie turn to face the wider part of the room. There's a rustling, which either wasn't audible until now, or wasn't something I'd noticed. The shuffle of a foot or two. The sighs of a few sets of lungs. Then a loosely collective *click* sounds out, and the beams of fifteen flashlights flick to life. The flashlights bathe the decrepit production line in an amber glow, allowing me to see more than just the shadowy machinery.

Seated, standing, reclining on the equipment, leaning against the walls — arms folded, draped over others, holding and pointing their flashlights —

Are nearly two dozen friends of mine.

Counting, I see there are twenty-three including Billie and Laramie. Twenty-four, if Sealy has in fact been pulled from the service station, since

I don't spot him in the crowd. I see Elliott Woodruff and Rachel Estrella. Luciana Gomez, my Colombian mine-clearing friend. Tori Fleming. Rudy Simmons, Rusty Kincaid. Bob and Gloria Hansen.

The tableau of colleagues, friends, acquaintances — each representing a moment of my long, strange trip, my time in office, or my days since receiving the patch-kit note — slowly proceeds to animate. Standing, rising, extending a hand, the people Billie has summoned approach from their places around the room.

Before I shake a single hand, my sense of euphoria yields to an overwhelming fear.

Now what?

-74-

WHEN THEY TAKE ME TO Sealy, his eyes find mine before I've completed my turn into the room. He's secured to a chair with a fresh batch of rope and duct tape.

"He agreed to keep quiet if we took the tape off of his mouth," Billie says. "None of us were too comfortable keeping him tied up, but we figured you two might need to catch up and . . . come to an understanding before we proceed."

I examine him from a few feet away. He seems relatively undamaged. His eyes don't move off mine.

"I were you," I say, "I'd pummel me the minute I got loose."

"Me too," he says flatly.

"I was a little overzealous," I say, "but I do have an explanation. I didn't want you to do what you were about to do. You were talking on your phone at the rest stop. If you went to the authorities before I figured out how to expose these people with what little leverage we'd gained, then my battle was lost. Walker's battle was lost. And not to get melodramatic, but the people's battle was lost."

"Which people would that be? The people who won't already have been killed by the biological weapon you've allowed into the country as part of your strategy?"

"Right," I say. "Them."

His stare holds.

"What is it you want?" he says. "I'm not sure I'm all the way to forgiveness, if that's what you're looking for. *Sir.*"

I shake my head and attempt to meet his thousand-yard stare.

"No need. All I ask is that you participate in the meeting we're about to hold," I say. "I'd like you to participate and agree to a democratic form of participation. Meaning that you'll have a say. Same as everyone else. When we're making our decisions, you'll have your vote. But you'll need to go along with whatever the group decides as a whole, including wherever we need your help. We'll make decisions and follow through with them as a sort of congress, and none of us can go rogue for it to work. You agree, and we cut you loose. You don't, you can wait here in this room until we complete our vote and finish getting on with the things we'll need to do. Then you can head back to your day to day."

He shakes his head in a herky-jerky fashion.

"I don't really grasp where you're headed with all this," Sealy says, "but if you remove this fucking rope and tape, I'll agree. *Sir.*"

I hold his stare, decide I at least partly believe him, and get started on freeing him. Billie helps. There's a moment of inaction as Sealy's body seems to relax, adjusting to its newfound liberty. Then he pulls his arms from his sides, leaps to his feet, and grabs me by the neck. His leering face brushes mine. Up close, I smell the service-station grime. Making me wonder how much worse I must smell in my half-decayed disguise and no shower for as long as I can remember.

"Maybe I lied," he says. "Maybe I don't agree. Maybe I ought to tell you, your friends, and your plan to taking a flying leap at a rolling donut, and do whatever I feel I need to do to stop the weapon from being detonated. Maybe that's how *I'll* fight the people's battle."

He lifts my full weight slightly from the ground. Air is cut off from my lungs and black spots begin to invade my field of vision.

"Anything you can think of would stop me from doing this?" he says.

The look in his eyes, seen from up close, is not one you want to see. Not when it's aimed at you.

"Loyalty to an old friend?" I say.

His grip tightens. "Goddammit," he says, "I was talking to my *wife*. On the phone. You know something? Maybe — maybe, *just once*, Mr. President, you might quit hanging me out to dry in the thick of a crisis."

After a very long moment, he shakes his head in disgust, drops me flat, and walks out of the room. Landing hard on a knee, I catch myself before toppling entirely. My clarity of vision and breathing return. The room sounds loudly silent.

"You okay?" Billie says.

"Taking me a minute," I say. "But I'll make it."

"You think he's bolting or sticking around?"

I lift myself off the floor and straighten my shirt.

"Only one way to find out."

-75-

I'VE GIVEN A LOT OF speeches, to audiences as varied as three heads of state to crowds of two hundred thousand spectators at a music festival. But never have I felt as awkward as I do today before our hastily assembled congress. It's an eerie setting: the faces of my audience just visible in the diffuse glow of the flashlights, dust and cobwebs everywhere, the hulking, bulky shadows of abandoned industrial equipment looming behind all.

Though each will have have heard portions from Billie, I describe the extraordinary-rendition abduction of Rachel, the effect it was meant to have on Walker, what it was that Walker had seen in Laramie's memo, and what it was that Laramie had learned. I hit the highs and lows of the journey Billie and I have taken these past three weeks. I lay out the spinner-detonation plans by the Venezuelan terrorist group and cover the existence of the study group. I describe how the organization viewed Laramie's intelligence on the intended strike and subsequently allowed it to proceed. Before getting to the meat of my speech, I peer into the shadows in search of Sealy, and find he's half-visible, lurking at the back edge of our ring of light.

"Billie went to great lengths to track each of you down," I say, "and I know many of you went to extremes to get here. And she probably believes, and therefore will have conveyed to you, that I have a detailed plan on how to bring the study group to its knees."

This is where I will lose them briefly.

"I don't."

Time to bring them back — but as vested partners, rather than an audience. It's the most important beat in every speech a politician gives.

"The fact is, I haven't solved the reality of how to expose the study group, all they've allowed to happen, or all they have in store. I do know that we've got our knowledge of the planned July fifth incident to work with. And while it's thinner than we would like, we've got a strong suspicion on the altered location of the device. Our colleague Rusty Kincaid informs me that he has established with a reasonable degree of accuracy who in the Washington area are believed to be the more influential members of the study group, where they work, where they live, and where and when they go in their daily routines. Finally, it's my view that if we don't stop these people now — exposing them to a degree that will allow legitimate prosecution — then we are likely to see another bombing down the line of the sort we're faced with now. Another allowed strike, an alternate excuse for another war."

I lean forward and speak with as much intimacy as I can muster in the strange room.

"I'm a little out of practice, but there's something I was once very good at. To whatever degree I delivered positive achievements for this country, I did so on a very basic principle: get a group of very smart people together in a room and empower them to make decisions."

I carefully make eye contact with every single person in the room. "I hereby suggest that you appoint yourselves as our country's emergency executive cabinet. As this cabinet, you are the world's only representatives in this matter, since only the corrupt officials that make up the study group know what I've told you tonight, and most, if not all government officials not allied with the study group are compromised to them in some way."

I straighten my shoulders.

"If you tell me we should simply go ahead and pull the plug and alert the authorities to the bomb's location, then that is what we will do." I turn my look to Sealy. "Whit Sealy, a decorated military veteran, has felt for some time that we should call in the FBI and U.S. military and seize the weapon. If you all agree with him by a majority vote, then that is what we will do. Same goes for any other suggested strategies we devise. But whatever the decision of this congress, that is the plan we will then run with together. We discuss, decide, and execute as a group."

I check my watch, find it's missing, and realize it's probably sitting in a box in Rockingham county lockup. But I know that we started this session in the small hours of the morning.

"Don't know the hour exactly, but it's well past midnight," I say, "meaning it's officially July second. We've got three days. We're outcasts; we're operating under the radar. We're as far from the halls of government power as a cabinet can get. But we are all there is. I ask for your help and I can offer virtually nothing in return. A great number of lives depend on what we do here tonight and in the coming three days. I ask that you consider accepting your position in this executive cabinet and we get to work."

I search faces, hoping to connect with my old pals — man-to-man, man-to-woman. Friend-to-friend. My eyes have adjusted and I can see them now, but I'm only met with stares, reactions unreadable. When the long silence finally concludes, it's Whit Sealy's figure that leans forward into a shaft of light to break it.

"Former president or not," Sealy says, "the Bohemian here is crazy — certifiable, in fact. That much is clear. And trust me, I've got more first-hand experience on the topic of his sanity than any of you. All that aside, I'll share with you that my position has shifted. I think there may actually be a way to accomplish what he's suggesting."

The room rustles. People shift.

"Considering this is a congress," he says, "I think there's a way you're supposed to go about this. I'm not currently on any boards or committees, so I'm not sure if I have it right, but I'll give it my best shot."

He inclines his chin.

"I move that we call this cabinet meeting to order," Sealy says.

PART VI:

THE PEST

-76-

URGENT BUSINESS REQUIRES FORMER-AND-CURRENT AMBASSADOR Anatoly Stanislav to attend a meeting in Los Angeles, or so Rusty Kincaid has determined. In fact, Rusty has similarly established that every name on his list of suspected Washington-based study group members has urgent plans, all plausibly legitimate, to leave the city for the holiday weekend.

Anatoly is known to travel with a bodyguard and, as anticipated, the assigned Lincoln MKZ car service has reached his neighborhood early.

It's nine a.m., July 3, in Alexandria, Virginia — 58 hours and 5 minutes remaining, but who's counting — and I'm seated in the back of a panel van outfitted with signs declaring it to be the property of an obscure cable company. Our team is equipped with walkie-talkies plus some more sophisticated eavesdropping gear, all purchased at a Washington spy shop courtesy of stash of cash Elliott Woodruff pulled from his basement to contribute to the cause. In addition to these tools of the trade, we've got a tree-trimming truck and a beige Toyota Corolla, both rented for the day along with the panel van with the aid of a few friends' credit cards. None of our equipment has been blocking traffic. Our set-up appears as nothing more than a crew getting prepared for a day of tree-trimming while the cable guy does his thing farther up the block.

Until now.

Our driver of the tree-trimming truck pulls awkwardly into the middle of the street, the wood-chipping trailer he's towing getting jammed up based on his faulty attempt at a K-turn. One of a short roster of freelance professionals recruited by Sealy — this guy a bearish, bearded giant named Kamik — climbs from the driver's side of the Toyota and grabs a set of orange cones he'd stacked earlier behind the car. He sets to laying out the cones until he "notices" the approaching Lincoln, whose route is now blocked by the truck.

Kamik ambles to the Lincoln, yellow reflective vest announcing him as the designated traffic-flow supervisor. The car service driver zips down his window. Kamik is wired, so I can hear the conversation over the headphones in the van.

"Yo, sorry," Kamik says in something resembling a Brooklyn accent. "He's gonna need a minute to turn that rig around. Can't drive for shit."

"How long?" the driver says, gruff and impatient. "If it's longer than a minute, I'll need — "

Thuk.

The sound cuts off the driver's words and an abbreviated moan follows, the man's now-sluggish brain objecting to the equine-strength tranquilizer Kamik has just fired into his shoulder with a CO_2-powered pistol. The driver falls silent and slumps against the wheel.

Kamik has instructions to survey the interior of the vehicle for other occupants, namely a bodyguard, which he does. I see him glance around, checking for any passersby examining things too closely. Satisfied nobody is watching, he reaches in, opens the door, unbuckles the seat belt, pushes the driver into the passenger seat, removes the yellow vest, throws it inside, climbs in, closes the door, backs up, turns around, and drives away.

Our hired driver re-parks the truck, retrieves the cones, and gets behind the wheel of the Toyota Corolla. He drives off in the opposite direction Kamik has just steered the Lincoln, leaving the tree-trimming rig behind for now.

"Your driver was packing," Kamik says over the headphones without the Brooklyn accent, "but he was alone."

Outfitted in a fresh disguise and ID supplied by Woodruff — again with more 70s attire, this time a suit, wig, and moustache that has me looking something like Mike Brady from *The Brady Bunch* — I'm emboldened sufficiently to risk exposure from the driver's seat of the van. I start the van's engine, pull up the road, and park fifty yards from Anatoly's elegant house. Ninety seconds later, Kamik appears around the corner in the Lincoln. He pulls into Stanislav's driveway and pops the trunk, leaving it open while he remains behind the wheel, same as any courteous, unassuming car-service driver might.

It takes an excruciating seventeen minutes before the door to Stanislav's house opens. During this time, I count four women and one man walking their dogs; two joggers; and twelve passing cars. No police, but the dog-walkers haven't seemed too trusting of my cable-company van, parked with its tinted windows on their quiet, safe street.

The rest happens fast.

Anatoly is talking on his cell as he comes out the front door, laptop satchel strapped to one shoulder, garment bag slung over the other. As rehearsed, Kamik waits as long as he can, until Anatoly has almost reached the car. Maybe it's because Anatoly was using his phone — studies show a gorilla can pass unnoticed across a person's field of vision during mobile-phone use — or maybe it's because Sealy hires well. But either way, Stanislav doesn't seem to catch anything out of the ordinary until Kamik courteously opens the Lincoln's rear door, at which point Anatoly turns his head, pulls the phone away from his ear, and ogles the big man.

"Will call you back," he says into his phone, then disconnects it. "Who are you?"

"Your new driver, sir," Kamik says, taking Stanislav's garment bag and laying it on the roof of the sedan. He shoots Anatoly in the neck with the tranquilizer gun, pushes him into the back seat, and closes the door he only just opened.

Kamik retrieves the garment bag, encloses it in the trunk, climbs behind the wheel, and with the comatose Anatoly Stanislav splayed in the back seat, pulls out of the driveway and away down the tranquil dog-walking street.

S OME YEARS AFTER MY PRESIDENCY, I was giving a speech at the U.N. at the invitation of Luciana Gomez. I spoke on the need to ban land mines in current military conflicts due to the danger they pose to civilians for decades beyond. After my speech, a young MBA grad, serving at the time on the American U.N. ambassador's staff, told me he didn't much like me. Actually, the way he put it was, "You know how I've come to see you since your departure from politics? Like some pathetic bowl of mush."

The young MBA grad's name was Stuart Ackerman, and he's since risen through bureaucratic ranks to become a deputy director at the National Security Agency — while also, per Rusty Kincaid, rising up the ranks of the study group. At the moment, Ackerman is riding in the back seat of a Cadillac Escalade, his shock of red hair visible from a car length behind.

Billie has the wheel of the cable-company van. I'm riding shotgun.

Our multiple kidnap squads have seized eight members of the study group so far, and we're after ten more — including this red-headed buzzard in the Escalade, moving through rush-hour traffic ahead of us in the right-hand lane of Walter Reed Drive in Arlington. Kamik and our hired driver accompany us again; Sealy and Bob Hansen are also in on this one. It's 3:15 p.m.

We've got three vehicles in the mix. Our second is a taxi, actually a rented Toyota Camry falsely outfitted with all the legitimate markings of a local dispatch company. Our driver from this morning is at the wheel, with Sealy riding in the back seat. The cab occupies the lane to the left of our van, hood running about even with the rear bumper of the Escalade. Our third vehicle, a Honda Odyssey minivan driven by Bob Hansen, changes lanes from left to right, crossing to settle in front of the Cadillac. We've now got the SUV boxed in.

My walkie clicks.

"Stand by," Sealy says over the radio. "Few more seconds."

Shortly Sealy's voice crackles again. "This is it," he says. "Stand by."

The traffic flow has picked up some speed; we're moving at 30 mph. An intersection, Columbia Pike, is immediately ahead. The light at Columbia is green. A right turn here will take us straight onto the Beltway, visible two long blocks to the right.

"Bob," Sealy says, "you're on."

"Roger that," comes Bob's voice over my cell as the Odyssey's brake lights flash. Slowing rapidly, Bob forces the Escalade, and us, to ease down to 15, then 10 mph. Sealy's cab slows at the same rate, holding position directly alongside the Escalade.

The driver of the Escalade leans on the horn — and Bob stands on the brakes. Ackerman's driver, intent on getting his client to the train station, isn't ready for the dead-stop and plows into the rear of the Odyssey. Sealy's driver, meanwhile, floors it while making a hard right, smashing the right-front fender of the Camry into the driver's-side door of the Escalade. Billie pushes on our van's accelerator until we make contact with the back bumper of the Cadillac. Kamik, already out the side door of the van, leaps at the Escalade, tire iron in hand.

Then it goes all wrong.

I watch, feeling slow and useless, as Ackerman's driver zips down his window, takes aim with a 9mm pistol, and fires off two rounds with practiced speed. The cab's front windshield shatters, Billie exclaims something beside me, and an explosion of blood sprays the dashboard of the taxi as our hired driver is struck by the shells. His body slams against the steering wheel and the cab's horn blares.

The rear passenger-side window of the Camry shatters next. Billie says, "Sealy!" and I'm thinking he's been shot until I see the gun fall from the hand of the man driving the Escalade. Sealy's own automatic pistol now protrudes from the cab's shattered window.

Kamik smashes the window of the right-rear door of the Escalade with the tire iron as Ackerman's head bobs away from the flying glass. The big man drops the iron, reaches through the shattered window, unlocks and wrenches open the door, and with both hands, seizes Ackerman and yanks him out.

In two long strides he's back with us in the van. Ackerman screams, wild-eyed, as Kamik shuts the door behind him. "Do you goddamn well know who — "

Kamik's right cross silences Ackerman and he slumps to the floor.

Billie reverses, pulls to the right, and bounces us forward over the curb. We pull around the Escalade and onto the sidewalk, then bump back down onto the street ahead of the Cadillac, clipping its right-front fender on our way off the curb. Bob floors it ahead of us, leaving open asphalt in his wake.

Billie keeps the pace slow until Sealy finds his way to us, pulls it open the left rear door, and climbs in on the fly.

Kamik's already got Ackerman blindfolded, handcuffed, and shackled as Billie takes the corner onto Columbia Pike and we're up the cloverleafed I-395 on-ramp in seconds.

-78-

"Including my driver," Sealy says, "we lost six."

We're approaching Berryville, our bound-and-gagged captive stored in the rear of the van. It's almost 5:00 p.m. — T-minus 50 hours and change — and our eighteen abduction attempts have all been conducted. Sealy has been on his phone, receiving status reports on the remainder of our second wave of strikes.

"Went fifteen for eighteen," he says. "Fifteen study group members are now in our custody. Twelve are already at the factory."

"Who else besides your driver did we lose," I say.

"Two others were among the professionals I hired for backup." These were people too, but I can't help feeling relieved. Sealy seems to read my mind — his eyes turn hard. "I knew these men. I didn't just hire them out of the phone book. But they understood the risks inherent in the assignment. It's the nature of their profession. Unfortunately we also lost one of our civilian members in each of the three failed rendition attempts."

He states the names. These were my friends; they came here at my behest. The parade of people I've seen off to death in recent days continues.

"They're gone," Sealy says. "As with my professionals, bodyguards or police opened fire on them. We made mistakes, but there was probably little to nothing we could have done differently. Some of the study group members are better protected than others, and all of them were on high alert after our morning renditions, which probably weren't fully documented or understood, but caused confusion and a state of caution with our targets."

"Suppose I shouldn't have expected it to go any better," I say, "but I did."

"Operationally," Sealy says, "we got results. It's what our cabinet voted for; we accomplished it."

I shake my head quickly. "There's always a price to pay," I say, "and we paid ours. Six lives. But we gained ground. Fifteen of them. Fifteen to six. We've taken the lead."

The words stream from my lips as though on auto-pilot, but as my friends and colleagues perish with increasing frequency, it's becoming more difficult to adhere to the kind of logic on which I used to thrive.

I feel Billie's eyes on me. Not for the first time, I wonder, but can't find enough energy to concern myself with for now, whether she disapproves of the way I've come to see the world again. *Fifteen to six.*

We pull into the abandoned factory's parking lot, Sealy climbing out and sliding the busted chain-link fence into place behind the van as we enter the property.

-79-

CONTRARY TO THE COMMON MISCONCEPTION that NASA is based in Houston or Cape Canaveral, the agency's headquarters building is set in the heart of Washington. The businesslike structure is on E Street SW, a mere ten blocks from my former residence. NASA's current administrator — this being the oddly bureaucratic title the agency uses for the position Bob Hansen once held as chief of the agency — commutes 40 minutes to the E Street facility from his residence in McLean, Virginia. It's in McLean where I presume he is accustomed, at the end of his long workdays, to warm greetings from his wife and two children.

Not tonight.

As part of the strategy coming out of our all-night congress, it was decided that a nineteenth abduction attempt was in order, this one a two-parter: a true abduction followed by a surprise visit. Neither involves a single study group member, and in fact, all four victims of this final abduction effort are innocent bystanders comprising the nuclear family of the current NASA administrator.

His name is Sean Griffin, and on this evening in McLain, he steps into his air-conditioned kitchen through the garage door to find a motley crew of five men facing him astride the room's L-shaped island.

Routinely setting his briefcase on the stool beside the fridge, Griffin senses our presence before spotting us, turning sharply to find Rusty Kincaid, Bob Hansen, Whit Sealy, and myself occupying the stools at his island. Kamik sits at the eat-in kitchen table.

"The hell — "

Despite the exclamation, Griffin isn't too sure what to do with his physical self. He steps backward, toward the door, but otherwise stands frozen in miscomprehension. After all, he isn't exactly stumbling in on a gang of burglars. Woodruff removed my disguise before our group departed Berryville, meaning the look on Griffin's face quickly transitions to the one I'm so familiar with.

"Mr. President? You're . . . "

"Yes," I say. "It's me, and I'm in your kitchen. And yes, I'm a fugitive from justice wanted on a double-murder charge out of Sonoma. And unfortunately for you, you're now a victim of my latest in a series of activities taking me afoul of the law."

Griffin's eyes flick to Hansen, a fellow NASA man.

"Bob — ?"

"Sean," Bob says.

"What do you — " Two things seem to come over him in quick succession: first, composure; second, a realization. "Where are — "

"Your wife Molly," I say, "and your sons, Roger and Sean Jr., are in our custody. *My* custody."

"Your — *where!*"

"Elsewhere," I say. "They're safe. For now. The good news? They'll stay safe if you agree to our demands. In point of fact, we actually only have one demand, requiring a single act from you. If you don't agree to what we're asking you to do, or if you screw it up while trying to make it happen, we cannot and will not guarantee Molly, Roger, and Sean's safety."

This part isn't an act — there are at least a couple factors that would place his family in harm's way if we can't pull off our plan from start to finish, unless of course we were to immediately transport them out of the region. But Griffin couldn't possibly grasp the subtlety of my meaning, and his eyes turn white-hot, mouth dropping halfway open, breaths becoming shallow.

He's more a boardroom kind of guy, but if he were a fighting man, or even if he weren't outnumbered no matter his type, Griffin would be lunging at me.

"Have a seat, Sean," Bob says, motioning to the stool we've set against his side of the island. Griffin keeps his eyes on me, eyebrows forming an enraged V, mouth still half-open, as he pulls the stool beneath him without looking down.

"I want to know they're okay," he says. "How do I know they're safe?"

I nod to Rusty who taps a command on the screen of his iPad, which he rotates for Griffin to see. Onscreen is a live FaceTime feed of his wife and kids, awake but bound and blindfolded on three chairs in the same room in the factory that previously held Sealy. The lighting is adequate for Griffin to see movement from them in the chairs.

"This could be taped," he says. "I need to know that they're — "

"Honey? Sean!" comes his wife's voice through the live feed. Her head tilts, since, blindfolded, she's unable to see the iPad on the table before her. "Sean, where are you!"

"Molly! I'm with the people who took you. Stay calm. I'll get you out. I'll goddamn well get you all out of — "

Rusty closes his iPad case and pulls it back to his side of the island.

"Any idea what's going down two days from now?" I say.

Griffin, wild-eyed, says, "Two days?"

"Venezuelan Independence Day," I say. "July fifth. Further to the point, just after seven p.m. on the fifth — at 7:05, to be precise — a biological weapon is set to detonate in Washington. It has been brought here by a small and vengeful Venezuelan terrorist cell. The device is probably only powerful enough to destroy a building or two, but more significant is its 'bio-dirty' element. It's equipped with an aerosolization feature that will distribute a bacterial mist across the city. The bacteria are a genetically engineered version of the plague, also known as the black death and several other nasty terms. If the device is allowed to go off as planned, it's likely that hundreds of thousands of Americans will die within two to three weeks, before adequate infectious disease control measures are undertaken."

The aim of Griffin's gaze has slipped south to settle somewhere in the middle of the bar's countertop.

"For reasons we'll skip for the time being," I say, "a very powerful faction within the U.S. government has decided to allow the detonation of this biological weapon — brought here by an otherwise irrelevant, ineffective, and easily compromised so-called terrorist group — to go forward. The ulterior motive of the U.S. government faction matters not, but suffice to say their intended counterattack will likely result in geometrically more casualties if the Venezuelans' device is allowed to detonate. To the point: the sole act we ask of you tonight will play an important part in reducing casualties. Your compliance will contribute to our potentially saving as many as millions of lives, will harm no one, and will also ensure that my team proceeds with the safe release of your family."

Griffin's white-hot eyes zero in on mine again.

"What is it you want," he says without inflection.

I turn to Rusty, who pulls a folded sheet of paper from the pocket of his shirt, flips it, and pushes it to Griffin.

"Printed on this page are four lines of information," Rusty says. "From top to bottom, we've written, first, an internal server name, called 'EOS,' which you are able to access from the desktop in your office — "

"I know good goddamn well that I've got access to the Emergency Override System."

Rusty nods. "Excellent. Second line on the slip of paper is the password that opens the EOS directory." He puts a hand up to intercept any objection from Griffin. "You may already know it, but I've confirmed that this is the correct and current password that will grant you the access we require. Use only this password. The third line of information is the name of a file within the EOS directory."

He shifts his posture and points at the slip of paper.

"On July 5, at exactly 6:15 p.m., we want you to open that file. You will see a series of prompts asking if you want to activate the EOS," Rusty says. "We will need you to answer all the prompts *Yes*. The fourth and final line of data on the slip of paper contains the coordinates you will be asked to enter at the very end of this series of prompts. The dual coordinates represent, first, the capture of a satellite television uplink signal, and second, the destination to which you will in turn forward that signal. Nothing more, nothing less."

Griffin blinks and rotates his eyes back to me.

"You want me to activate a satellite signal through the override system."

"Yes," I say.

The frown creasing his forehead eases, though only slightly. "You're putting something on television," he says, "and forcing every major network to carry it through the EOS override."

Rusty nods and pushes over a second slip of paper. "Once you've entered the coordinates, we'll then want you to back out to the EOS login page and select the option to change your password," he says. "You'll need to return to your opening login page and create a new password there. You'll tell no one the new password, and you will not write it down. You will then leave your office and make yourself unavailable, answering no phone calls, emails, texts, or other communication from anyone besides the cell phone number written here, for a minimum of two hours. At the conclusion of the two-hour window, you can return home. We will then contact you on the logistics of the return of your family."

"I'll lose my job," Griffin says, "let alone be prosecuted for illegal use of the emergency system."

I shake my head. "Under ordinary circumstances that's true, but we're well out of that space now. If we succeed with our efforts, you'll be lauded as a hero. If we fail, you'll likely be infected along with the rest of us."

Sealy says, "Starting now and up to and including the two-hour no-contact window, we will assign you a security detail. Our associate, Mr. Kamik, here, will be the lead observer on the detail." He motions to Kamik, sitting at the tiny table near the window. The big man nods.

"Observer," Griffin says.

"There will be two men in the security unit," Sealy says, "working in six-hour shifts. One of them will accompany you everywhere, every minute, ensuring both your safety and silence, and by extension the safety of your family, during the next two days. You are not to contact the police or any other authority, in fact you are not to contact anyone or take calls or receive visitors from now until the end of the no-contact window. Nor will you leave your house during this time, except to accomplish your assigned task at NASA headquarters."

Griffin doesn't look at Sealy, just that spot in the middle of the counter. "Your observer," he says, "won't be allowed to accompany me into headquarters."

Sealy shakes his head. "Wrong. You'll arrange a visitor's pass."

Griffin looks sharply at Sealy, then brings his glare back over to me.

"If I refuse to do your assigned task," he says, "there's no way you won't try to stop the detonation. If I contact my colleagues at the FBI and report all this from my desk at headquarters, you'll still try to stop the bomb from going off. And you wouldn't dare hurt my family. I know who you are — " — he stabs his right index finger at Sealy, "and I know you — " — same at Bob, "and you are not criminals, nor kidnappers. You wouldn't dare."

He doesn't quite sound hysterical, but his words are shrill, his volume and tone thin and devoid of conviction. It's like he's trying to rev himself up for a fight, but doesn't quite buy his cause.

I've had plenty of practice selling my nut-job look — that Brian Wilson hollowness-of-eye following the breakup of the Beach Boys — which has proven highly useful in discouraging the press from hounding me on my voyages. I give it to Griffin now.

"It's funny," I say, chucking out a creepy laugh, "what crisis does to people. When people reach the end of their rope. You can roll the dice. Take the risk. It's your call. But I've lost a wife. I know how it feels. It's a feeling that never leaves you. If I were in your shoes," I say, "leaving to chance the question of whether we would dare — we being an accused double-murderer and his comrades, who as a team have intentionally allowed the device to complete its journey to America — suffice to say isn't a risk I recommend taking."

I step back and push my stool beneath the lip of the island. "We'll be in touch, Administrator Griffin," I say.

We move as a group out of the kitchen, through the family room, and out the front door, leaving Griffin alone in his house. Alone, that is, excepting one very large observer.

-80-

"I'VE BEEN DOING SOME THINKING," Billie says.

It's 9:00 p.m. on the Fourth of July – T-minus 22 hours and 5 minutes. Billie and I have found a couch within a distant room, far enough back in the factory to give us a modicum of privacy. It feels like a manager's office, long since overtaken by cobwebs. We sit side-by-side on the couch the manager probably used for visitors. A flashlight on the floor serves as our sole source of light.

"Chances are," she says, "this plan we've devised will fail. Chances are you, or me, or more of your friends, or half of Washington, DC, will get hurt between now and 7:06 p.m. tomorrow. And even if we pull it off without a hitch, you've still got the charges the Sonoma County district attorney filed against you."

I nod. I've been thinking some of the same things.

"What occurred to me, though," she says, "was that on the off chance everything comes together ... "

Close to a full minute passes without her finishing.

"Yes?" I say.

"I thought that we could consider moving in together," she says. "And I have some reasons for this."

I hold her eyes as I feel my face flush — a sensation I don't remember feeling since I was fourteen. My throat seems dry. For this moment, the rest of the world and its circumstances are blotted out. "Reasons," I say.

"I like it when we're together. I like me when we're together. I want more time with you. And the past few days brought me to the realization that no matter how much time I've got left, I want you with me for it. But I want to make sure you understand something."

I swallow.

"I'm not really interested in . . . marriage. Or at least the traditional kind," she says. "I want to make sure you're okay with that. That we don't go into this with an expectation that I'm going to become — you know, a *wife*. Been there. Done that. Failed. I'm good at a few things, or maybe I should say there are a lot of things I like to do and I've done all right at some of them, but the deal is that I'm going to keep doing those things or something like them. I'll keep being the way I am, and marriage isn't part of the package of things I'm good at. Moving in or no. Do you understand?"

I start my response, which may, were it to complete itself, have commenced and concluded with little more than "Um," but she keeps on before I can get anything out.

"Also, don't expect me to be the only one making the bed. And/or performing related domestic chores. I think you like to cook, I know you like to do some gardening, and you probably even like to vacuum and can certainly afford an army of maids and you've used a caterer here and there. But still."

I attempt to clear my throat. "You're saying you want you to stay you," I say, "even in our becoming permanent."

"Yes," she says.

We stare at each other for a moment. She looks good in the half-light, even with Woodruff's latest disguise affixed to her face.

"So?" she says.

Focus, man.

"I didn't actually answer you," I say, "did I?"

"No," she says, "you didn't."

"Unless, like most of the world, you consider me certifiable, you already knew my answer before raising the topic."

She smiles and shrugs. "Still want to hear it."

"Well, then," I say. "I think it would rule if you moved in with me."

She's still smiling, and I'm pretty sure I am too.

Billie sets her palms on the couch, one hand on either side of her thighs, and pushes down into the cushions, the way you might test a piece of furniture out in a store.

"I've got a question," she says.

"Yes," I say.

She juts her chin toward the door. "You think your cabinet of advisors would be able to hear us if we . . . "

I'm already shaking my head before she gets halfway through her sentence.

"What?" she says.

"You think I give a flying leap about that?"

I reach down and flick off the flashlight.

-81-

IT'S A JARRING NOISE THAT makes me wonder what the hell it could be —

And then I realize where I am, and that somebody is knocking at the door. Along with most of the surviving members of our cabinet, I slept in the abandoned factory. Billie and I are in the office we found the night before. It appears we managed to pull some of our clothes back on in the night, but not all.

"Come in," I say.

Sealy pushes open the door, arm extended. In my morning haze I'm still not sure what he's up to until I see what he's holding: his cell phone.

"It's for you," he says.

Jesus.

I sit upright and grab the phone.

"Yes?"

When the heavily accented caller rattles off the word, "Ivy," then repeats it, saying, "Ivy City," I immediately place the voice as the gravelly vocal cords of our man from the shipping container.

My eyes fire to Sealy, and he gives me a look — *you were right.*

"Repeat that, please," I say.

"Ivy City Yard!" he rasps, impatient and annoyed. *He's confirmed it.* "That is new location. You are not to be trusted," he says, hacking out a cough. "I am a fool. But now I have fulfilled my end of this bargain. Maybe I have made the right choice. Maybe I have not."

The line clicks and crackles, but the connection's still there. He hasn't left. Maybe he's waiting for some kind of reassurance.

"It's a good decision," I say. "The right one."

The crackling hiss rises again. Then —

"Maybe yes," comes his voice. "Maybe no."

The static gives way to silence as he breaks the connection.

-82-

THERE REMAINS A PORTION OF every urban center overlooked or ignored as a matter of routine by the general populace: the rail yard. Maintenance crews, freight or passenger train operational personnel, and equipment delivery drivers populate portions of them. Other areas of within these properties are utterly neglected, often for a decade at a time, as aging buildings are abandoned in favor of more modern facilities and left there for a period before meeting their fate. That fate may mean demolition, or commercialization, or environmental remediation, but until then, the ill-used buildings lay in wait, generally only loosely protected, if at all. Along with the neglect of these dated buildings comes a years-long, low-grade construction presence, with few personnel present.

Washington, DC's version of this urban phenomenon is the Ivy City Yard. Functioning as Amtrak's regional maintenance facility, hulking warehouses enjoined around legions of tracks allow for locomotives and passenger cars to be brought directly into repair bays. Much the way hangars occupy land across the runways from the passenger terminals at airports, the Ivy City Yard sits apart from its public-facing sibling, some two miles northwest of Washington Union Station. Within the maintenance area — in a burst of optimism amidst its crumbling passenger rail infrastructure — Amtrak recently succeeded in gaining funding for a state-of-the-art maintenance structure, and the new building, sleek in appearance and brimming with state-of-the-art mechanicals, sits in contrast alongside its neglected predecessor. The grounds of the abandoned building contain the usual detritus of quasi-construction — a place where it would go unnoticed were you to store any manner of trucks, cars, or stacks of equipment, for months, or even years.

A biological weapon of mass destruction could be hidden here too.

Finally, neither would you capture any particular attention by parking a pair of high-definition TV production semis in a sea of two dozen dilapidated semi-trailers in the construction yard fringe.

One of Sealy's hired pros drops me off at the semis and takes off in the cable-company van. I knock on the door near the back of the first trailer and wave at the closed-circuit security camera eyeing me from the roof of the truck.

Billie opens the door and leads me in. The interior, much like a casino, would look no different day or night. In here, it will always be halogen track lights, blue-tinged TV monitors, soundproof paneling, electronics gear embedded in every visible surface. The temperature is a permanent seventy degrees.

We reach a section of the truck where an entire wall is occupied by a bank of monitors. Each screen on the wall of images is tuned to a different news channel. Some display mainstream broadcast networks, but even these stations, save one or two without news departments, have broken in with live news programming covering the abductions along with a continuation of the other stories of national crisis from the prior three weeks.

"It appears that whoever remains active among the study group's leadership ranks," Billie says, "is already out to the news media with their pre-detonation talking points."

Rachel Estrella looks up from her director's seat at the truck's control board as we arrive. "Yes," she says. "The spin doctors are at work."

I check a digital clock at the top of the television bank: 12:50 p.m.

T-minus 6 hours 15 minutes.

There's a low cacophony of noise, with each of the monitors turned up just high enough to drown out the others. "Can you isolate that one?"

I ask, pointing at one of the screens. Rachel turns a knob and we hear the CNN signal in surround sound. Anderson Cooper has just come back from a commercial; the anchor's head-and-shoulders profile is practically dwarfed by top-and-bottom **BREAKING NEWS** graphics, most notably an ominous, scarlet-hued box with white block letters saying **THREAT LEVEL: IMMINENT.**

In April 2011, the U.S. government disbanded the color-coded Homeland Security Advisory System put into place in 2002 by the Bush administration. The new protocol, renamed the National Terrorism Advisory System, continues to function primarily as public announcements from the Department of Homeland Security, with the threat levels now referred to as "Elevated" (if there is no specific information on timing or location) or "Imminent" (when Homeland Security believes the threat is impending).

Anderson Cooper declares today to be the first time the federal government has issued the "Imminent" advisory before continuing with the story.

"Here is the statement issued to the media by the office of the Secretary of Homeland Security," he tells viewers, "just after noon eastern today." A blue background consumes the screen as smaller white letters, in quotes, lay out the government's statement. "'Current and credible chatter and other intelligence reported by multiple law-enforcement agencies indicates an imminent risk of a domestic terrorist attack in the coming 24-hour period,'" Cooper says.

He reappears on screen amid the **BREAKING NEWS** boxes.

"The statement details that the agency is in possession of 'intelligence indicating that members of an organized foreign terror group may already have entered the United States.' And while their current whereabouts are unknown, sources tell CNN it is believed that the alleged terrorists may have illegally imported items into the U.S. aboard a container ship in the Port of New Orleans."

The telecast switches to a split-screen. "Here with me in our studio to discuss the possible identity — "

A knock on the exterior door of the truck interrupts; Rachel points to one of the monitors on the TV wall, where the faces of Bob Hansen, Rusty Kincaid, Luciana Gomez, Whit Sealy, Elliott Woodruff, and Julie Laramie are revealed to be waiting outside the door.

Rachel kills the volume on the CNN feed. Billie points to the front of the truck on her way to open the door for the team.

"This way," she says. "We'll use the conference room."

-83-

"WE'VE DETERMINED THERE ARE FOUR sentries keeping watch on the weapon," Sealy says from his seat at the table in our truck-based war room. "They work in teams of two. The alternate team stays at a motel two miles from the building. They've been switching off every four hours. The way they loop around the perimeter of the building and the rail-yards, there are predictable five- and ten-minute gaps during which we can access the device. There could be cameras inside, though none appear to have been installed on the exterior of the structure."

His eyes find Gomez. "Gomez, during one of these windows, it will be up to you and your team to determine whether the detonating mechanism can be operated by remote control. If it can — by somebody holding an activation device in the motel, for instance — then you'll have five to ten minutes to do your work. Any longer and we risk the sentries spotting you."

"But if it isn't remote," Gomez says, "I'll have much more time, correct?"

Sealy nods. "If you're able to confirm the device doesn't have a transmitter-receiver, my contractors will neutralize the sentries. At that point, in theory, you'll have as long as you need. Unless we trip some sort of alarm or a sentry is able to call in a warning signal."

"Assuming you can extract all of the spinners and ensure that the conventional explosive remains live," Laramie says from her side of the table, "we'll have you place two of the disconnected spinners near the device as evidence. Investigators can use them to corroborate the story of government officials having tracked and allowed the detonation of this biological weapon — which we hope America will by then have heard all about."

"Understood," Gomez says.

Sealy nods at Rachel, who holds aloft a tiny white spherical oval featuring a hole on one end. It resembles an elongated AirPod.

"Mr. President — the production side of things will work the way any ordinary live news or talk show would," Rachel says. "You and Sealy will wear these in your right ear. It's an unobtrusive way for us to talk to you while you conduct the interrogations." There's a small dry-erase board on the table in front of her and she turns it so Sealy and I can see the drawings on the board. "We'll have a three-camera setup. Obviously most productions go to a great deal of trouble to ensure that the host is front, center, and looking good. In our case, we're doing the opposite — being very careful to keep you and Mr. Sealy out of view. As far as audio goes, whenever your voice becomes necessary to include — when you ask a key question, for instance — I'll be electronically distorting the signal."

I see that the dry-erase board includes sketches of cameras, people, lights, and chairs, with dotted lines connecting these elements to a truck with a satellite dish on its roof, in turn to a satellite, then back down to a building and finally to a television.

"We're going to be shooting as though we're live, but the plan is to output our signal on a two-minute delay. This provides time to insert a show open and have B-roll and voice-overs handy for edits, which my camera crews are shooting now. The delay will also allow us to condense your first couple of interviews or eliminate any answers you don't like. I'm hoping that after the first interview or two, you won't even notice the cameras. If I need to guide you one way or another, away from a camera and so on, I'll talk to you over the earpiece."

She pushes a typewritten sheet of paper across the table.

"This is the rundown," she says, "a loose outline of how I see the show working. I've secured all the relevant 'Breaking News' and 'Live' banners and graphics and music which should mimic the Fox News channel fairly seamlessly. Network execs and viewers on other channels might be confused initially, but we figure it's better to make it feel legitimate to get momentum rolling off the bat. Short version: you just ask the questions you want answered and I'll do the rest. The viewing audience will believe they're watching some of the greatest investigative journalism ever broadcast."

"As long as our captives answer the questions," Billie says.

Sealy's expression darkens in a delighted kind of way. "Oh, they'll answer the questions," he says, before changing gears. "On the NASA side of the operation, if Administrator Griffin logs in as ordered, our Emergency Override System connection should sync up just ahead of 6:20. The satellite Rachel's pinging with her uplink will feed our signal to the facilities normally functioning as network receivers in a relay chain destined for viewers' home cable boxes or streaming feeds, so that the program you're making should be broadcast on every network that's physically tied to the EOS, no matter how these networks are brought to viewers. The larger networks are required to maintain the emergency chain, but dozens of smaller cable networks are not mandatory channels in the system and therefore wouldn't be automatically taking our signal."

"Something to think about while you're conducting your interrogations," Bob Hansen says, "is that the EOS override is something of a dinosaur. It's unlikely that anyone but the most senior executives at the networks will know much about whether they're permitted to turn off the EOS feed once it's running. Some may cut their network signal entirely, some may switch to other programming, but we believe most will keep the signal running until they're able to reach an FCC or other government official and receive permission to cut the feed."

"So the more we get in off the top," I say, "the better."

Bob nods, and with that, there is silence, the low thrum of air conditioning consuming the room. Eyes ping back at me.

"That's it, then?" I say.

"That's it," Rachel says.

"Affirmative." This from Sealy.

It's just after one-thirty p.m. — T-minus 5 hours 35 minutes — as I stand.

"It's just about showtime," I say, and lead us out of the war room.

-84-

"**C**AN YOU GET THE CASING open?" Sealy says into his walkie.

"Yes, it's open already," Gomez's voice comes back over the speaker. "It's fairly sophisticated. We'll need a significant period of time to remove the canisters. There are at least twenty-four that I can see, and potentially twelve more underneath. I'd estimate forty minutes."

Billie and I sit with Sealy in the cab of the second truck, parked alongside the TV rig. Sealy's behind the wheel, Billie in the middle, and I'm on the passenger side. The study group hostages are housed in the trailer behind us. The digital clock on the dash reads 5:48 p.m.

Gomez and her bomb squad kit, accompanied by two expensive freelance experts, have been secreted into one of the loading docks along the back of the abandoned building. She informed us prior to Sealy's question that she had found and begun her work on the device. Per her narrative it was no longer inside of a steel container, but did remain housed in its original wooden crate. She told us the device is oblong, some four feet by eight.

"Incidentally," Gomez says, "I don't know if it is of consequence, but there are two dead bodies here on the floor near the crate."

Billie says, "Our man from the container and his travel companion?"

"Most logical explanation," I say.

"With two teams of sentries," Sealy says, "we've got no room for error on the question of a remote control. Are there antennas? A small black box of any kind? I'm guessing you'd find the receiver, in whatever form, in the same general area as the detonator."

We wait in silence for what feels like forty years, but based on the clock in the truck, adds up to three minutes. Gomez's voice crackles back over the radio.

"I'm not seeing one."

Sealy turns to me. I know what his look is asking: *Can we trust her read?*

I take the walkie handset from Sealy's palm. "You've checked everywhere? Is there any portion of the device you need to open, or access, to make a more thorough check?"

Another silence — only two minutes this time. "I don't see anything that could be a remote control," Gomez tells us, "and I've checked almost every inch."

"We'll never know," I say to Sealy, "more definitively than we do now."

"Hold on," Sealy says over the walkie. He rotates the knob to a second channel, hits the button, and says, "One-A, Two-A, it's a go. Repeat, green light."

The words "Roger, One-A green," and, "Roger, Two-A green," come back over the radio, to which Sealy answers, "Copy," before another four empty minutes snick by on the truck's clock.

Then Sealy's teams report in again.

"One-A, targets down," comes the first voice, and then, after another interminable silence, "Two-A, targets down."

Sealy switches back. "All clear," he says. "Do your thing, Gomez."

"Copy," comes the response. "Thing being done."

-85-

W E RIP OFF THE BLINDFOLDS.

Perched on the second-floor foreman's loft, with an interior view of the cavernous old Amtrak maintenance building, sit our fifteen captive commissioners. Their view features a sea of train tracks, a pair of forgotten passenger coaches, and rusting repair equipment dotting the interior of the building in a seemingly random pattern, all beneath a vast roof that's broken in places, the early evening light prodding through at irregular intervals.

Each commissioner is duct-taped at the ankles, wrists, waist and neck to a chair. Almost sixty feet across, the ledge of this foreman's loft overlooks the eight-track, hangar-like repair grid below. Windows, some broken, all dirty, line one side of the foreman's loft, offering clouded views of distant monuments and, in the foreground, the outdoor set of tracks backed by an industrial neighborhood. Before we brought in our captives, Rachel ran us and her camera operators through a set of rehearsals, so we have them all set out according to the proper blocking on the platform.

In these positions, the commissioners face the interior tracks below. Sealy and I watch as the faces of the fifteen formerly powerful study group members reveal differing degrees of confusion, frustration, rage, or fear. Many of them appear childlike in their expressions. They've been held in total darkness, without food or water, for the past forty-eight hours. Studies show they will now crave human contact — even abusive contact.

A strip of the tape covers each commissioner's mouth. Each will have it removed and be permitted to speak only on a pre-arranged cycle. Sealy, a trio of his professional gunslingers, and Rachel's crew of camera operators have joined me for the occasion. NASA Administrator Sean Griffin's activation of our satellite-hijack is scheduled to take place momentarily. The only part I'm concerned with now is the mindset of our captives.

Step one: time for them to absorb the view.

I hover behind them, out of visual range, while they soak in the sights. Each man wondering, I imagine, who has seized him; why; what the view is supposed to mean; and possibly whether he's about to be tossed over the edge of the loft to his death on the sharp edges of track, skewed railroad ties, and machinery below.

"Ring a bell?" I say.

Heads swivel to take in my face, now clean of disguises. Expressions shift, recognition apparent, some of the slackened features of our captives' faces firming up with rage. It's gray and dim in the broken, cloudy patterns of evening light, but bright enough for the commissioners to recognize their captor.

"May not hit you at first glance," I say, "but you are currently seated on the foreman's loft of the abandoned Amtrak maintenance facility in the Ivy City Yards in Washington."

I pause again, since if we've captured the right people, each of these men will know what that means. I see that Anatoly's poker face is revealing nothing; the others seem less self-assured.

"Examine what you can of the facility from our perch here," I say, "maybe have a look out the windows there to see the city, and confirm it. The supposition that should now occur to you is correct: you are seated one story above the relocated site of the biological weapon of mass destruction. It is stored, of course, in one of the loading bays approximately twenty-five feet beneath your chairs."

I see from their faces that they're almost there — their minds have taken them three-quarters of the way to my intended destination. They're still trying to hide it, but they've begun to compute the facts of their predicament.

"I can see each of you trying to explain off the coincidence," I say. "But you know it can't possibly be coincidental. Your gut is right. Your fear. It's no coincidence at all."

I check the time on the miniature screen of the iPhone that's come with the package of spy and broadcast paraphernalia we're using tonight.

"You may have become disoriented in captivity, so perhaps this will help. It's now 6:12 p.m. on July the fifth. Venezuelan Independence Day." I walk along the row of chairs, holding the iPhone directly before each man's eyes long enough for him to read the screen. "You see the bars on the face of this phone. The signal is live. The date and time are current. Incidentally, we're sorry that none of you were able to keep those travel plans you conveniently booked a day or two before the detonation."

When I've finished my stroll, Sealy and two of his gunslingers swivel the fifteen chairs so that the bound-and-gagged commissioners now face me and the interior offices of the loft.

"For the sake of clarity," I say, "I'll spell it out for you."

Time is at a premium, but this next moment is the one that will drive the rest. I check the face of the cell phone.

"It's now 6:14," I say. "In fifty-one minutes, the biological warhead planted in the loading bay below will destroy this building and a significant section of the rail yards that surround it. More important, at least in terms of the discussion we're about to undertake, is that fifty-one minutes from now, your bodies will be shattered by steel, concrete, glass, and other industrial-grade shrapnel as this platform explodes. The biological pathogen the bomb's intended to disperse won't even matter to those of you here at ground zero. You'll just be gone."

I pocket the phone.

"You can choose to believe what I've just told you, and trust the fear you now feel," I say, "or not. I don't care. What I am going to do is ask each of you a short set of questions. You will be taped by our cameras as you answer."

By design, I omit the fact that the cameras will actually be broadcasting live. I jerk my thumb backward. "You will answer the questions alone, in a room behind me."

I concentrate on standing utterly still. Offering them no distractions.

"For those of you who answer the questions correctly — for those of you who tell the truth — my companion and I will provide your ticket out. We will transport you out of the area and, if you say so, make all necessary arrangements for you to vanish into the equivalent of a witness-relocation program. You'll wile away your days in some suburban housing development, with none of your study group colleagues the wiser."

This is a lie, but an important one to sell to them. I shrug.

"For those of you who answer incorrectly, or don't answer at all," I say, "my associate here will first shoot you in the knee. If at that point you still choose not to respond, we will toss you, fastened to your chair, in the back corner of this floor and leave you here. Left to face your skepticism, or perhaps your misguided loyalty to your commission's aims, alone with the *Y. pestis* spinners and their conventional dispersal device — all of which you know more about than I do as to its predicted blast zone."

I incline my chin toward Sealy.

"My companion and I already know the answers to the questions we'll be asking. We're not interested in what you have to say, since we already know what you've done, what you've got in store, what has occurred to date, and how you've forecasted that events will play out looking forward. We're only interested in having you describe what we already know, in your own words, memorialized on camera. We will then keep the video files in our possession, able to reveal them to those we feel need to see the material."

This is another lie, of course, in that I've neglected to mention the live component to the interrogations. I take one step toward my captives.

"This is the only warning you will get," I say. "Do not fuck around. Hem and haw for two seconds or more, answer a single question with half a lie, and you'll take a warning bullet. Second instance, you're gone. In the corner. We'll be on to the next man, and I'm sure enough of your colleagues will be willing to save their own skin to make your obstinance pointless. The study group, the board, the commission, whatever you prefer to call the organization as you've known it to exist — as of today, it's dead. The only question each of you therefore faces is a simple one: whether to save your own ass."

Slowly, I scan the entire row of men. Staring into the eyes of emasculated authority I know they are hoping they can, in some way, resuscitate, but which I want them to believe, more and more with each passing moment, is gone forever.

That only their lives are left to trade.

I point to the nearest captive in the row of chairs.

"Him first."

-86-

I STARE BLANKLY AT MY FIRST interrogation subject.

Until we know our signal is up and active, any questions are point-less. The instant we've got the EOS link, it's on: the threats I just delivered can pay their dividends. In the higher-risk portion of our agenda, if Gomez can succeed with her surgical spinner-removal work, the bomb will detonate on schedule, but will fail to release more than a modicum of its biological patho-gen cargo. Evidence — corroborating the confessions it is now my job to elicit.

But without the satellite connection, we'll just be a bunch of people having a chat in an abandoned room thirty feet above a very large bomb.

I know that the monitors in the truck, playing before Rachel and Billie, display not just our three-camera setup, but all the major networks. Sean Hannity's face may be adorning one of the screens. Or Anderson Cooper's. Whatever Rachel and Billie are seeing now, they're watching for only one thing: a change in the signal. In my mind's eye I envision Hannity's face flick-ering, fading, maybe turning to static — followed by this channel, featuring our cameras spliced at Rachel's direction, broadcasting with sudden clarity over the network's band waves. When all the network feeds match on the monitors in the truck, we'll know that Administrator Griffin successfully hacked into the EOS on our behalf, and we will be on the air.

A sharp click of static stings my ear and Rachel's voice comes through the wireless transmitter.

"They did it," she says. "We're now broadcasting. I'm running the 'Special Report' graphics and music as we speak. You might have five min-utes, you might have twenty — but you're now live, or almost-live, recorded and transmitted on our two-minute delay. Please do what you need to do, as efficiently as you can."

I nod short and tight, trying to mask the surge of adrenaline while maintaining a blank stare for the first man in front of me, strapped helplessly to the chair in this forlorn room.

I check the iPhone screen for the time: 6:23 — T-minus 42 minutes.

I've thought through the points I'll need expressed on camera. I've got fifteen study group commissioners to interrogate to dredge out the points. I've memorized Rachel's show rundown and we've rehearsed the choreography Sealy and I will execute on the platform. But it still remains to be seen how effectively the isolation, revelation, and threats will be in triggering the commissioners' instincts of self-preservation and give us what we need.

Only one way to find out.

-87-

COMMISSIONER NUMBER ONE GIVES US nothing. No answers to my first questions, no response to our hasty threats of a bullet to the knee.

We quickly use him as an example. Sealy doesn't hesitate, taking out his kneecap from close range with the assault rifle. When he remains silent outside of the screams resulting from the bullet to the knee, we pull him from the interrogation room and drag him across the platform in full sight of the other commissioners. We conclude his journey by heaving him, arms and legs still strapped to the chair, into the grungy, littered corner at the back of the platform, whimpering, prone, bleeding, and useless.

The second commissioner appears ready to be more forthcoming — at least if the look of unadulterated fear on his face is any indication — as we drag him on his chair into the room.

"Why are you afraid?" I say.

"What?"

"Go please — "

This is my cue to Sealy, who lifts the assault rifle he's holding and takes aim.

"No! I'm saying I don't know what you're asking! Be specific! Please!"

I nod and Sealy lowers the rifle.

"Going forward," I say to commissioner number one, "I will need you to answer whatever it is you think I have asked. One more instance of stalling, and your kneecap is gone, then you'll be too. Got it?"

"Got it," says our captive.

"Let's step back," I say. "Tell us who you are and what your role is within the study group. The commission."

He does. His name is Thorpe and he is an undersecretary of the Navy. In the study group ranks, he reveals himself to be what is known as Second Order. He explains that First is highest, Fifth entry-level.

You learn something every day.

"Now the first question again," I say. "Why do you seem fearful? At this moment, in this place? Be as specific and descriptive as possible. When appropriate, clarify how you know what you know."

A furtive glance in Sealy's direction lasts half a second at most.

"According to, ah, our intelligence findings," the commissioner says, "there is a biological weapon set to detonate in a loading dock of this building. The, uh, Amtrak maintenance facility in Ivy City."

"Set to detonate when, and be precise on time and date!"

"It's, tonight, it's — the weapon is scheduled to be set off at seven-oh-five tonight, July fifth — "

"In what city are we?"

"Washington, DC," he says.

"What is the significance of July fifth?"

"Venezuelan Independence Day," he says.

"How did the bomb get here?"

"The device was smuggled into the country by a Venezuelan terror cell."

"Smuggled how?"

"Aboard a container ship, approximately one week ago — "

"How do you know what you've just told us?" I say. "All of you — you and your fellow study group commissioners, whatever order they may be."

I know that I've made a mistake in bringing up his fellow members. This might cause him to reconsider the consequences of his answers. My hope is that he'll remain more concerned with the immediate notion of self-preservation.

"CIA unearthed the operation," he says, "and our organization decided to bury the intel. To allow the terrorists to proceed, and to backload a paper trail."

Check: first points delivered.

I wave, a dismissive gesture I fleetingly realize I may have picked up from Anatoly Stanislav. "Pull him out," I say.

Sealy and his gunslingers comply. As he's being lifted out the door of the interrogation room, the departing commissioner cranes his neck to look back at me.

"I'm getting out, right? And the witness program — I'd like to exercise the — "

Sealy slaps a fresh rectangle of duct tape over his mouth as they turn the corner and vanish from view.

"Next!" I shout.

-88-

"THE STUDY GROUP, BOARD, COMMISSION. By any name, what is it? Be thorough."

I've already issued a fresh round of threats to this, the fourth commissioner in line, our pal the red-haired deputy director at NSA, Stuart Ackerman. Sealy was forced to shoot number three in the knee and deposit him in the corner of the platform. Like the first one, number three also refused to answer my questions even after taking the shot, but we assumed at least fifty percent of our hostages wouldn't yield. Meaning so far we're behind, going only one-for-three.

But all we need is one good answer on each important topic, with half a dozen key points on the list. We're seven minutes in. T-minus 35 minutes.

"Our commission," Ackerman says, "is a membership organization within the United States government and other member countries, which makes and puts into effect policy decisions, foreign and domestic, through its members' positions of influence, as well as through other methods — "

"Such as?" I say.

"Surveillance, intelligence-gathering — "

"You forgot bribery, blackmail, extortion, and murder," I say, which earns a click and comment from Rachel in my ear.

"Don't forget, Mr. President," she says, "you want to get the words coming out of his mouth, not yours."

Ackerman is silent, unsure how to comment on a non-question. I nod as though Rachel can see me and work at getting back on track.

"So you make and put into effect government policies," I say. "What of the elected officials and their appointees?"

Ackerman eyes me, partly defiant, partly cowed. A former bully unsure of how resistance or compliance will best serve his interests.

"I'm not entirely clear on your question, but yes, we make the decisions. The officials we assimilate with comply and execute on the results and recommendations of our studies."

"Who's we?"

"The commissioners. The members of our organization."

"Confirm the other names used by this organization," I say.

"The commission or the study commission are the terms I've been instructed to use. I don't refer to it as the board but some do."

"How many of you are there?"

He blinks, but answers — "In the United States? Thirty-four."

I try not to look at Sealy, who, like me, has heard from Rusty Kincaid that he had estimated there to be twenty-eight active members.

"And what gives you the right to make policy decisions for this country, rather than the elected and appointed officials?"

"The formation of the Policy Study Commission by presidential executive order in December of 1952," he says.

This time I can't avoid looking at Sealy. It seems the commissioners have believed my ploy — a ploy I believed to a degree — wrongly. We *didn't* know the answers to all of our questions.

Again: you learn something every day. Apparently *more* than one thing.

"Describe the study group's guiding principles," I say, "as outlined in the executive order and as adjusted over time, if needed."

"We act to defend the right to own private property," he says, "and the right to operate businesses with minimal government regulation and taxation, and the principle that Christianity was intended as the sole allowable religion by the founding fathers and omitted in the drafting of the U.S. Constitution only due to the fact that this was commonly understood to be the case at the time."

I wonder whether the late President Walker knew these things. My earpiece makes a clicking sound and Rachel comes on again.

"You're ten minutes in," she says. "Thirty-two minutes until the detonation. If you've gotten what you want out of this one I suggest moving onto the next."

It doesn't sound like a suggestion, but since Ackerman is being talkative, I fish out of him another of the points on my list before having Sealy drag him away. We've decided to leave those who've answered our questions in the opposite corner from the garbage pile, as I'm coming to think of the site of the silent ones. We do this with Ackerman: left upright in his chair, we put a fresh strip of duct tape over his mouth and drag and place him, strapped to his chair, facing away from his colleagues, in its way an incentive representing a shot at survival for those yet to enter the room.

-89-

OUR BATTING AVERAGE HAS BEEN running about .400 — just under half of our interrogation subjects are giving me the points we want the American public to hear. A good average in baseball, but the progress feels painstakingly slow against the ticking clock, and I've yet to make any progress on our final two points: the study group's warmongering motive, and an accounting of their actions against Walker and Rachel.

Commissioner number twelve is in the room.

"Once you pin the bomb blast on Venezuela," I say, "what happens next?"

I try not to reveal my inner sigh of relief at his willingness to answer.

"Counterattack, of course," he says. This one speaks like he's at a press conference, delivering assigned talking points aimed at his party's base — which could prove useful considering that he happens to be on live TV. "After this devastating strike on our home soil, America will accept nothing less than regime change in Venezuela and the defeat of neighboring governments who have provided operational support to Venezuela."

"After you've manipulated them," I say, then regret it.

"Try to let him say it," comes Rachel's voice in my ear.

"What's the question!" commissioner twelve says, panicked he'll be shot for the delay.

Stick to the program.

"You're saying Americans will accept nothing less than a counterat-tack," I say, "even though you've actually manipulated them into believing Venezuela's government is responsible?"

"Well, correct — "

"Say it that way! The full statement!"

After a very brief beat, he does.

"Next question," I say. "Why?"

"Why do we want the counterattack to take place?"

Sealy's gun stock elevates, and I lean in until my nose almost touches my latest interrogation subject.

"Yes, that's the question," I say. "And don't use 'we' in your response, or otherwise truncate your answers. If you mean the commission wants war, then say that. Full answers, leaving no room for differing interpretation. Now: American vengeance aside, why does the study group want war with Venezuela specifically, and South America generally?"

Twelve clears his throat — and then, seeing the end of the barrel of Sealy's gun inch closer to his forehead, answers quickly.

"The study commission," he says, "believes that an invasion of the offending nation is likely to escalate into a regional conflict involving its neighboring South American allies in the International Socialism Alliance. The engagement will serve to stem the rising tide of socialism, and its defi-ance of private property rights, a free-market economy, and our, eh, the commission's view of the proper place of God and religion in the governance of society — "

He appears to have stopped himself from saying any more.

"Go on!"

"It's, our, eh — the commission's analysis also posits that a pro-longed engagement will stimulate corporate profits, shareholder wealth, the American and European economies, and provide real-estate price escalation in the countries in which security and private property rights are securely protected."

I stare at him, thinking of Rusty Kincaid's own analysis during the time Billie and I spent in his basement; I also think of our dinner with Luciana Gomez and Billie's cycling dude. The Banana Massacre and all that came after were nothing — a prologue, told over the course of a hundred years, but merely a preview of the main event to come. With war, murder, mayhem, and destruction referred to in study group circles simply as *engagement*.

Distracted, I buy time with a repeat question.

"Summarize for me again — simply please, like you're speaking to reporters in need of sound bites — tell me the paper trail of tonight's act and the strategy that follows."

He blinks, unable to avoid looking at the gun, then says, "The evidence that will be discovered tonight, and in the fallout that follows, will implicate the Venezuelan government in the sponsoring and planning of the terrorist acts, and will — "

"What? What did you just say?"

Sealy raises his gun in response to my tone.

"What are you asking!"

Rachel's voice comes through my earpiece. "Try to keep that emotion out of — "

"You said *acts*. Plural," I say. "What acts are you referring to?"

He stares at me. It only lasts an instant, but in that moment I can tell he's realized I don't know the answer to my question. I asked it wrong, so I may never get this out of him. He looks away and answers.

"The other terrorist act," he says, "was the assassination of President Walker."

His gaze returns to me, but he's failing my patented stare-down lie detector test. He just lied. Venezuelan terror cells, real or fabricated, had nothing to do with Walker's killing.

He was referring to a separate terrorist act.

Another crackle of static is followed by the voice of Rachel in my ear.

"Positive news from the loading dock," she says. "Gomez believes she's succeeded in extracting all thirty-six spinners from the bomb. The conventional explosive is still active and she says it's large — she predicts it will still take most of the rail yards out, more than just the building you're in. And you're running low on time — you and Sealy are going to have to get out soon. The bomb will detonate in twenty-five minutes. FYI, there are three helicopters circling the rail yards. One is the media, two are police or military. But you're still on the air."

I press commissioner twelve with three different questions coming at the same point, inclusive of a knee-shot after the second, but he doesn't give me anything more. Whatever he's half-revealed about another terrorist act, he's leaving it at that.

I wave to Sealy.

"Put him in the garbage pile," I say. "Let's bring in thirteen."

-90-

"DESCRIBE THE PROBLEM PRESIDENT ANDREW Walker presented to the study group's plans," I say. "And what was done to address this."

It's the third consecutive time I've opened with this question and I've got my old adversary Anatoly Stanislav as my last hope to get the answer. Commissioners thirteen and fourteen used different ways to tell me to go screw, and Sealy used the same method as always — a shot to the knee — in our vain attempt to dredge answers out of them. I also pushed fourteen for answers on another terrorist act but either he was genuinely unaware of any such plan, or the best liar of the bunch. We tossed these last two in the garbage pile too, and I'm now left with my interrogator from Rockingham County lockup, our fifteenth and final hostage, and we've yet to glean a confession on the study group's culpability on the assassination of Walker and abduction of Rachel.

I get a crackle and some words in my ear.

"Another FYI," Rachel says. "Bob Hansen says we've lost two broadcast networks and three cable channels. More importantly, you've got twenty-two minutes to evacuate. A police SWAT team and at least six black-and-whites are now outside. They haven't located our trucks but they're in the railyard and I expect they will break into the building or this trailer any moment."

I again nod as though Rachel can see me — though with the trio of cameras in the room being fed through her board out in the truck, she probably can. For the first time I hear one of the helicopters outside.

"Send your hired guns downstairs," I say to Sealy. "Have them hold off the authorities as long as possible."

He juts his chin at the two men. They disappear down the stairwell.

"Tell me what happened with Walker and his daughter Rachel," I say, repeating the prompt to Stanislav.

Anatoly looks me in the eye without speaking or moving. When Sealy steps forward and pushes the barrel of the assault rifle against the bone of his left kneecap, the former-and-current ambassador doesn't flinch, holding our look instead.

Unable to tell whether he's attempting to convey one last threat, silently appealing for clemency for any answers he may offer, or he's working on coming to some sort of decision before proceeding, I decide not to interfere with his process or prompt Sealy to make any move. I see the wiggle room as a way of providing my old adversary with a victory to take home to his superiors like before — even if his superiors this time are his own pride and ego.

"President Walker received an intelligence memorandum late last year," he says, internal process evidently concluded. He speaks deliberately at first, then picks up his pace. "The memorandum informed him of the predicted event of July fifth. We discovered this and suggested that he leave the follow-up in our hands."

"Whose?" I say. "Whose hands?"

" — the commission's hands. He didn't respond well to this suggestion, so the commission placed him under surveillance. Specifically, two members of the Secret Service were assigned to this role and it was determined that Walker was proceeding with his own investigation into the matter."

Our police state at its best.

"And what did you do about that?"

"We activated two measures," Anatoly says. "President Walker had an illegitimate daughter named Rachel Estrella, living with her husband in California. Walker had her from an affair during the early part of his political career. Neither his wife nor the media discovered this or ever became aware of Rachel, but we did."

"And you did what with this knowledge?"

"We — the commission contracted with a seizure team and apprehended Rachel and her family. A cadaver resembling Rachel was arranged to be discovered in a landfill. Authorities declared Rachel dead."

The very alive Rachel's voice crackles in my ear. "Twenty minutes till the bomb goes off. It's 6:45," she says. "The police are outside the truck. They're coming in any second. I'm attempting to lock up the board so they would need to cut the power to cut off the signal."

"What did you actually do with Rachel and what became of her," I say to Stanislav, trying to sound calm, cool, and collected.

"She was held as leverage against Walker."

"But that leverage didn't work."

"No. Walker arranged through . . . unexpected means," he says, "to recover Rachel and then stage his own assassination, believing it would eliminate the commission's leverage over him."

I leave alone his non-reference to me and my actions up Nuns Canyon Road. My personal predicament will be a battle for another day, if we make it through this day at all.

"Yet the commission," I say, "was determined that the July fifth incident proceed as planned." I say as deliberately as possible, not an easy feat given the ticking clock that's about to expire. But I've reached the last of my questions and I come with it now. "What did you do when Rachel's rescue and Walker's survival came to light?"

Anatoly resumes his stare and, with it, his silence. Long seconds tick by. I hold a hand out in Sealy's direction, indicating he should hold back with the rifle. It takes nearly a minute — time we surely don't have — but then Anatoly drops his eyes.

"The study commission," he says, "arranged for the actual assassination of President Walker in order to maintain secrecy to the public and allow the July fifth event to proceed."

Final point delivered.

"We're done," I say, intending the words for Rachel in the truck more so than for Sealy or myself.

"We're still on the air with a few smaller outlets," Rachel says in my ear. "Probably won't last another ten seconds, but it doesn't — "

Sounds of a headset scraping and dropping reach my ear, followed by muffled sounds of footsteps, law enforcement shouts, and more scraping and scuffling. Then the signal goes silent. I take some comfort in the fact that no gunshots could be heard, at least not before the signal was cut. My hope is Rachel and her crew will be taken into custody and taken away to safety.

Billie was in that truck too.

I pull out my earpiece and refocus on Anatoly. His eyes have not left mine. "Mr. President, there is something I believe you do not yet — "

Sealy rips off a piece of the duct tape from the roll and begins covering the ambassador's mouth. Anatoly whips back and forth in his chair, doing all he can to resist the application of the tape.

"*Nyet!* What time is it!"

"Get him out," I say.

Sealy lifts Anatoly and his chair out the door.

"*Govno!* You're not getting it! *Any* of it! There's — "

Sealy gets the tape slapped over his mouth and all that's left are the sounds of the chair scraping along the platform's floor as he's taken away.

-91-

"**K**EEP YOUR GUN ON THEM," I say.

I feel the heat of Sealy's gaze on my back.

"The hell are you doing?" he says.

We've got all fifteen commissioners near the loft edge, including those from the garbage pile. Using a knife I've borrowed from its sheath on Sealy's belt, I've begun slicing the rope-and-duct-tape assembly holding the commissioners to their chairs.

"I'm removing their bindings," I say. "Setting them free."

"Are you insane? Why would you do that?"

"Because they've served their purpose," I say. "Our plan worked — it won't matter whether they return to their jobs. They've been exposed. They'll soon be deposed, indicted, convicted."

He shakes his head. Angrily.

"We leave them here," he says.

I've got the bindings off the ankles, but not the wrists, of four of them now. I turn back and get to work on the ankles of the fifth.

"No," I say.

"We've taken the biological materials from the bomb," he says. "It will be a conventional detonation now. Gomez has left a spinner on the floor near the bomb to corroborate the pathogen's inclusion in the bomb. Our plan requires an explosion, proving the answers these people have just given to be true, so yes, we are allowing the detonator to go off beneath them. But this is *their* plan. *Their* detonation. *Their* bomb. They should stay and enjoy it."

We both notice — it's impossible not to — that Anatoly, last in line and closest to Sealy, is still frantically trying to motion to us, still trying to say something. His actions are causing the legs of his chair to scrape and bounce. He's nearly jumping off the floor.

"You're right," I tell Sealy. "But allowing the bomb to detonate while we leave fifteen men behind — fifteen men *we* tied up — as opposed to simply letting the bomb detonate in an abandoned section of railyard we've had our people clear out — it's not the same thing."

Sealy takes a step in my direction. He doesn't raise his rifle, but he may as well have. "I'm not going to let you cut them free," he says. "They deserve this fate. It is our duty — "

"It is not our duty to commit murder," I say.

The eyes of Anatoly are frantic, following Sealy's and my conversation like a tennis match. He continues all but hopping in his chair.

"Bullshit," Sealy says. "They cornered you. Us. Into doing what had to be done to rescue their victims. Let them live and they could restart what we've now stopped. Leaving them here to die is preventive medicine."

"Sounds very similar to the study group's logic behind starting a war with South America."

A gunshot sounds out downstairs, then three more. Sealy motions with the gun as though it's simply an extension of his hand. I've got all fifteen commissioners' legs free and begin on the wrist bindings.

"If we let them go," he says, "they won't leave you alone. They'll come after you. Me. Us."

I look at him. "I'm willing to take that chance," I say.

Sealy stares me down — then shakes his head in disgust. "Goddamn you," he says. "Goddamn you, Mr. President."

I realize, not for the first time, that I'm not sure it's the right thing to have won him over. It may be, as before, that *he's* the one who's right.

Anatoly has pulled himself three-quarters out of the chair, so that he is standing, hunched, arms still strapped behind the back of his chair. I approach him, cut the duct tape from his wrists, then rip off the piece covering his face.

He stands, speaks, and heaves in air all at once — an explosion of noise.

"*Chort voz'mi!*" he says. "What time is it?"

Sealy has the gun at him. "Time for you to crawl under a rock," he says.

I check my cell. "6:48," I say. *T-minus 17 minutes.*

"*Govno*," Anatoly says. He slumps. "Surely too late." I feel a sinking sensation in my gut. It sends me back to commissioner number twelve and his line terrorist *acts* —

Plural.

"What are you talking about?" I say. "Tell me what you're talking about, there's no time!"

"What do you *think*, Mr. *President*? You know the old Russian saying as well as I do, eh? Trust, yet verify! You expect us to trust one amateur terrorist cell with an initiative of this importance?"

"Trust, yet — "

"There is a second device! It will detonate at the same time!"

It hits me in that way when you know you should have gotten it all along.

Of course there is.

I turn, snatch the gun from Sealy's hands, grab Anatoly with my left hand, and jam the barrel of the assault weapon deep into his throat with my right. I break his skin with the rifle, jamming it so hard into his throat that blood spurts from around the barrel end. I follow with a claw-like grasp with my left hand around his throat, all but choking him out.

"Where?" I say. "Where is it! Give me everything you know and I'll consider letting you live!"

"*Govno! Chert voz'mi!* That's what I've been trying to tell you," he spits out between gargles, the barrel tip against his larynx. "It is a bakery, a god-damned warehouse on W street. Thirteen hundred — "

"*Fuck —* "

This exclamation has come from Sealy, not out of rage but pain. I turn and see the residual contrail from the gunshot that has struck him, a flailing mist of red raining to the floor following its exit arc from his right shoulder. Barely an instant later, overlapping Sealy's curse, the *crack* of a high-powered rifle blast echoes through the blown-out window ledge and across the cavern of train tracks.

A sniper has just picked him off from the windows across the interior tracks, some fifty yards distant. He has spun halfway around from the impact and trips, stumbling, then falls to a knee. But it's here that he steadies his fall, holding himself firm, before grasping the open wound on his right shoulder with his left hand.

"I'm good," he says, which may be a lie.

I feel Anatoly go suddenly stiff and heavy in my hands as another *crack* rings in my ears. Anatoly too is now drenched in red. In the confusion I have no way of knowing whether I've pulled the trigger — whether it's my own bullet or the sniper who has taken Anatoly down.

I release my grip and he drops to the floor. My left arm is suddenly killing me, and I realize that some of the blood appears to be coming from me, a gash torn through the outside of my upper arm. Maybe by a brush from the same bullet. It stings like hell now that my adrenaline has relented and I see the wound.

"Go!" Sealy says, jutting his chin at my wound. "You'll be fine with that — keep pressure on it if you can. Take the gun and go."

I look around at the half-untied commissioners, some wounded. None are fully free of their binds.

"Fuck them!" Sealy says. "Just for once, listen to me. Let me have my way one fucking time, sir!"

I consider this for a single instant.

"What about you?"

"I told you I'm good," he says. "Collarbone's probably shot, but it's only a shoulder hit. Through-and-through. It's time to get the hell out, sir."

I move behind him, reach under his good side with mine, help him to his feet, set a hand on his good shoulder, and eye him from close range.

"Fine," I say, "you win. Fuck them."

He nods, his reaction slow with the direct hit he's taken. "I'll find my way out of here," he says. "Go!"

I strap the assault rifle around my right shoulder and cross the platform, Sealy not far behind, moving at a snail's pace. The cacophony of screaming pleas from the abandoned commissioners echoes around us.

I shuffle down the stairwell as quickly as my old knees allow.

-92-

SWAT TEAMS BURST INTO THE building through a cross-hatched web of windowpanes off to my left, so I turn the other direction at the base of the stairs. This takes me into one of the empty loading bays, where a steel door is built into the far wall beside the standard roll-door. The searing pain in my arm is starting to overwhelm my senses but I try to ignore it, keeping some pressure on the wound with my good hand when I can.

The steel door has a push-bar in the middle. I heave my right shoulder into it and stumble out onto concrete platform at the back corner of the storage yard. Our TV truck is to the left, but the batch of decrepit old vehicles and machinery and railroad ties and lengths of track block some of the view between me and the swirl of lights and personnel that surround it. It's loud — voices, yells, scuffling, running, and helicopter rotors beating at the air in the sky above.

I leap awkwardly from the platform and turn away from the cacophony, cutting around the corner of the building where I lean my back against the wall and find that I'm alone with six sets of tracks, most empty, some holding stationary Amtrak cars.

Focus.

I pull the iPhone from my pocket and check the time: 6:50 p.m.

T-minus 15 minutes.

As I do this, the screen's notification bar announces that I've got 14 missed calls — with the data indicating a number, the borrowed phone not identifying the contact. Then I see the number has a Carmel area code: 831.

Billie.

I return the call and she answers instantly.

"There you are," she says.

"Where are you?"

"Across the main tracks. Behind the newer building. Can you get here?"

I survey the vast expanse of tracks and orient myself. The sleek new maintenance facility is all the way across the six sets of tracks — a long route to traverse under helicopter surveillance, but it's possible I might remain hidden from the ground troops with the older building as my shield.

"There are snipers," Billie says, "and police or army personnel with shields and helmets on the street side," Billie says. "It's a war zone. Some of our team got away. Some were arrested. Some may have been shot. Rachel is in custody — she waited as long as she could to keep your signal working. If you can get over here, I've got a way out for us."

"What way is that?" I say.

"My preferred mode of transportation. I found a bike."

"Good," I say. "Because I'm going to need a chauffeur again. We've got to get to the second location."

"Second location?" she says. "If you learned something at the end of the broadcast, I missed it. Had to leave the truck earlier than planned to make it out."

"There's a second device."

"A second bomb?"

"Yes."

"And you want to ride *toward* it?"

"That's the general plan," I say. "Here I come."

I shove the phone in my pocket, swivel my head to see if any commandos are following and, finding none, start across the expanse of tracks as quickly as I can move. Which isn't very quickly.

A blaring noise blasts my eardrums and the rush of heavy power disrupts the air around me. I stumble as the Acela passenger train that has just missed me by a foot continues on the track I've just crossed. The locomotive and its eight cars clack past behind me. I regain my breath, gather my footing on the gravel, and keep moving, this time checking for trains as I do it.

I pull out the iPhone on the way — it's 6:52. I tap the Apple Maps icon and input the address Anatoly gave me in his last words. I only need to enter 1300 W before the app offers a nearby auto-fill address:

```
1300 W Street Northeast, Washington, DC
```

I select it and the directions materialize with a red pin marking the destination, north of where I am by two very long-looking city blocks. The app appears confused, jigging back and forth, since I'm not starting out on a city road. It looks like we're going to have to loop around the railyard, going the long way around in order to get there without crossing the tracks or the police zone.

I find Billie on the service road behind the newer building, straddling a rusty old bike. We grasp each other in a frantic hug, from which I quickly withdraw in total agony.

"Shit, sorry," she says. "You're bleeding like hell."

"I believe Sealy would call it through-and-through," I say. "I can take the bike and go solo. You should get out — run south, away from the yards, and don't turn back."

"Get on the handlebars," she says.

Between Sealy and Billie, the degree of stubborn insistence is untenable.

I shake my head and climb on. She gets us rolling.

"You know where we're going?" she says.

The voice of Siri cuts through the cacophony of industrial and police noise with her frustrated plea.

"Proceed to the route."

"Yes, sort of," I say, and I direct her with a gesture while trying to avoid falling from the front of the bike.

We turn into a large parking lot dotted with more active maintenance, construction, and government vehicles. It's a rough ride but we're on the move and Siri settles into the blue-lined recommended route on the iPhone's screen. We turn right out of the lot.

"Care to explain why we're riding toward the other ground zero?" Billie calls out over my shoulder.

I crane my neck. The helicopters and wind noise from our ride require us to yell. "Remember the American scientist on the interrogation tape?"

"Yes!"

"He talked about fire. How 'the Pest' doesn't survive fire?"

"Yes!" she says, pedaling at her usual impressive pace. At Siri's direction we make a right, heading north, onto Ninth Street, a wider arterial. The app indicates we'll be at our destination in two minutes, and though this might represent the pace of a motor vehicle, Billie isn't much slower.

The screen tells me it's 6:54.

T-minus 11 minutes.

"The device," I call back to her, "is designed to detonate at a low-grade temperature that blasts the spinners into the air but doesn't kill the Pest. We need to raise the temperature. It's the only way to kill it off!"

We've turned another corner and are now headed what I believe is east. We're one long block north of the service roads swamped with law enforcement personnel, our route on Ninth Street having taken us back over the tracks on an overpass. Given the presence of the helicopters, I doubt our solace will last, but the egress points for the old building are at the other side of the yard.

"So you want to start a fire?"

"That's the idea!"

"How?"

I shake my head and offer my standard response.

"I'll have to come back to you on that!"

379

-93-

THE BUILDING WITH THE FADING numerals 1300 painted above one of its roll-doors is a massive box of a warehouse at the end of a cul-de-sac of industrial buildings comprising the eastern stub of W Street. A city bus roars by in a cloud of exhaust and swings through its turnaround in the cul-de-sac as we approach the front of the building.

What little routine activity that typically takes place here appears to be proceeding as usual despite the overhead thrum of helicopters and nearby wail of sirens. Billie pulls to the curb and I stumble to the sidewalk.

"Assuming Anatoly didn't bullshit me in his last breath," I say, "this is it."

The building is as big as a concert hall and resembles a rotting country barn. Maybe fifty years old, its windows are mostly missing, paint faded, exterior beams sagging. Its wood construction didn't hold up the way the steel did in the Amtrak building of similar age. An illegibly-washed-out brand name and the word bakery are almost invisible on the rotting exterior skin, where a faded for lease sign with an unreadable phone number has been hung. There are no cars parked on the street in front of the building nor in its lot, where the demarcations of parking spots have long since faded.

We cross the asphalt and I try the pair of doors that appear once to have functioned as the entrance. Locked. Reversing the assault rifle, I smack one of the doors near its dead bolt to no effect, but the doors, made of wood like the rest of the decrepit warehouse, look to be in pretty feeble condition. I turn to Billie.

"Probably not the greatest idea," I say, step back, and plow my healthy shoulder through the middle of the doors. Shards of wood scrape my face, neck, and arms, and the concrete floor hurts as I land on the other side.

But I'm in.

Rising as Billie steps through the scraps of broken door, I check my surroundings: huge, cavernous, dim, empty, silent. Roll-doors and loading docks in the rear. Occasional bulbs are lit inconsistently in long ceiling banks of otherwise blown-out fluorescents. There are decrepit dividers, an occasional bench and stool, wires protruding from sockets, dangling beams broken and unrepaired. Shadowy markings in uniform rows on the old concrete floor, dotted at regular intervals by electrical outlets and capped gas lines, bely the former locations of the ovens and other baked-goods appliances.

In one corner stands a rectangle of unpainted walls, reaching less than half the height of the ceiling. It looks like managerial office space, or the former company kitchen, or restroom, or possibly all three. Paraphernalia of all sorts is strewn along the rim of the building — crates, scrap metal, extension cords, paint cans, collapsed cardboard boxes — and finally — partially obscured by the interior walls of the kitchen-office —

A forty-foot steel intermodal shipping container.

Stored against the rear exterior wall, the container appears to be exactly the same shape, size, and design as the one that held the weapon aboard the *Sandoval.*

Wordlessly we approach the container, seeing as we near it that its doors are splayed open. A wooden crate like the one that housed the weapon aboard the *Sandoval* is tilted halfway out the doors, askew and unbalanced, as though its transporters tried but failed to drag it all the way out.

"We've got to open that crate," I say.

Billie pushes past me and together we rip apart the crate's wooden planks. We get one side of it dismantled in seconds, revealing a squat, oblong canister standing on four legs, about the size of an industrial freezer laid on its side but with smooth and rounded gray metal skin.

A black cube protrudes from the top of one side of the orb, on which a tiny screen with an LED readout displays red numbers. Leaning close enough to read them, I can make out the numbers as they drop from 4:57 to 4:56 to 4:55.

"Five minutes," I say. "Shit."

I check the iPhone and confirm that it's 7:00 sharp. As Anatoly indicated, this timer is on the same countdown as the bomb in the Ivy City Yards. Only difference being, this device hasn't had the benefit of Gomez's dismantling efforts. And even if my three weeks of on-the-job training with her in Colombia had provided me explosives-defusing skills — which, as water-carrier for the team, it did not — we certainly don't have forty minutes to work on extracting spinners.

How to start a fire —

Some of the lights are on.

The building has power.

The walls are made of old wood.

Fuel.

We need an accelerant . . .

I look around the sides of the building — *Old scraps of metal and wood. Paint cans. Cardboard boxes.* It isn't much, but with the cardboard, paint, and wood —

"Everything into a pile," I say, starting into it, and between the two of us we get the full complement of broken-down cardboard pieces and wood scraps mounded against the crate.

"Kindling," Billie says.

"Yes. Now the paint."

We carry four cans at a time. A rifle-butt smack succeeds in opening the cans, and enough of them still contain liquid to serve their purpose. Maybe.

What can the building do for us? If the power is on —

I go to the walled-in room. It's bigger than it looked from across the floor, containing an office, bathroom, and the employee kitchen as suspected. Sketchily assembled cabinets, Formica countertops, refrigerator, microwave, toaster —

And stove.

I twist one of the knobs and get that familiar clicking sound.

"Come on!"

It clicks and clicks, until finally there comes a puff of flame.

"Yes!" Billie says. "But let's do it a better way. Help me pull it back."

She turns off the burner and grasps the side of the range, pulling it back from the wall. I take the other side, feeling stabs of pain in my arm as my stronger counterpart handles far more than her share, and we get the stove clear of the countertop. A pair of rodents flee as Billie finds the tube that feeds the gas to the stove and rips it from the back of the range. It comes neither violently nor visibly, but gas shoots from the hose in much greater volume than from the individual burners.

"Now we need a match," I say. "A lighter we can operate without standing in the middle of the flames."

"How about the rifle?" Billie says. "Will a bullet from the doorway be enough to ignite it?"

"I doubt it."

I look around again — and then *hear* something. The sound registers in an odd way. It's a familiar noise, coming from outside — a noise I remember from our arrival in the cul-de-sac. A noise I remember hearing often, all the way back to my childhood.

A typical background sound in any city.

"Where are you going?"

There's no time to answer Billie as I hurry outside through the busted door. The source of the sound I've just heard — a city bus — is busy engaging in a turnaround loop in the cul-de-sac before it resumes the westbound portion of its route on W Street.

I move as quickly as my knees can take me and get there ahead of the bus while it works through the loop.

Then I stop and stand in its path.

When this doesn't seem to inspire the driver to react, I lower the barrel of the assault rifle, pull the trigger and fire once into the asphalt, then take aim at the windshield.

"Stop!" I yell, trying for that law-enforcement baritone. "Stop the bus! *Now!*"

In panicky jerks and fits, the driver slows, turns, bumps the curb, and finally the bus shudders to a stop. I run to the side door, keeping my gun trained in the vicinity of the driver so nobody gets any ideas now that I'm no longer standing in the way.

"Open the doors!"

The accordion doors *hiss* open, and I see that the driver I've been screaming at is a fiftysomething woman. In the seats behind her are three passengers — one woman and two men. One of the men stands up.

"You a terrorist? I'll kick your ass," he says.

The driver, captain of her ship to the end, says, "The hell you want?"

"I want your bus. Everybody out. Run. Leave." I wave the gun toward the west. "Go in that direction. There's a bomb in this building about to go off, so do it fast."

The would-be ass-kicking hero makes some noise but complies, and the others don't hesitate in following my directive.

I check the iPhone — 7:03 — and climb into the driver's seat. The four strangers move away up ahead, jogging together, necks craned to see if I'm giving chase, or maybe checking whether they can spot the bomb. I've almost figured out how to get the brake off and the bus in gear when Billie ascends the stairs to the fare box.

"How is this going to work?" she says.

I shake my head. "Time has run out," I say. "Get off the bus, get on your bike, and follow those people. Get as far away as you can. We're out of time," I say, knowing I'm repeating myself.

"What are you talking about?"

I rev the engine. Seize the gearshift. Jam it into Drive. The bus jerks forward. I stab my foot onto the brake pedal. Billie stumbles but doesn't fall, seizing one of the poles the signs recommend she grasp.

"This bus is your *match*?"

"That's right," I say, feeling the strong need for Billie to leave. "Now get out while you goddamn well can!"

I know I won't be able to push her out this time and can't wait any longer. I release the brake and mash the gas pedal. The bus lurches forward, weaving until I get a handle on the steering. I drive almost all the way back to Ninth Street, passing the driver and her three former passengers on my route west. They do not appear to have slowed their jogs. Before reaching Ninth, I start in on a wide U-turn. As I get the bus straightened out, I decide to take one more shot at coaxing Billie to save herself and turn to start in on my pitch — but I don't see her. The articulated front door remains open, yet she's not on board.

Good.

Staring out the front windshield at the decaying building, I take in what will be the last six hundred yards of my life. It appears that the conclusion of this gigantic mess — all started with a single note hidden in the spare-tire kit of my mountain bike — will mark my demise. But it's a demise that may yet have some purpose.

Maybe.

What *is* certain — unless I manage to discover a cruise-control feature on this vehicle — is that I'm about to go down in flames. What's less certain is whether the flames will burn hot enough to kill the pathogen loaded into the three dozen spinners set to be blasted from inside the wooden crate.

Maybe this is the way all suicide bombers come to feel — at peace. It isn't just the right decision — there *is* no other decision. I convinced everyone around me to risk their own lives in hopes of revealing the secret of the study group to the world on national television, and some of them died as we did just that.

Now my time has come.

I stomp on the gas pedal, keeping my left foot on the brake. The RPMs churn like a jet engine building steam at the foot of the runway.

I release the brake. The bus surges forward —

And my death run is on.

Fifty yards in, the speedometer needle crossing 30, a loud banging distracts me. I turn to my left — where Billie has just whacked on the window from outside the bus.

"Use your gun!"

She's on her bike — pedaling at the same speed. The speedometer crosses 40 as Billie gets hold of the rear-view mirror, using the bus to tow her now.

"Let go!" I say. "Get the hell away while you still can!"

She doesn't.

"Mr. President, use your gun! Jam it against the gas pedal!"

45 — almost to 50 miles per hour. Two hundred yards of asphalt ahead.

"Keep the bus going with the gun and jump on! You're still my favorite president! I love you and I'll miss you and I'll never forget you — but if you take the next five seconds of your life to lock that gas pedal down, you can keep your life and live it with me!"

She bangs the window with her fist. The window cracks.

"*Now, goddammit!*"

Snapping out of my peaceful stasis far too late, I snatch the assault rifle from the floor and stick its barrel beside my foot on the gas pedal. I try to jam the stock against the seat beside my thigh. It doesn't reach. I see a black lunchbox on the floor. Grab it. Hold it against the seat with my elbow. Push the butt of the gun against it. Jam the end of the barrel onto the pedal. Lift my foot as carefully as possible.

It holds.

"*Get out!*"

I look up to see the massive building looming over me, blotting out the sky behind it. Scrambling up on the seat, I pull the window open, step onto its ledge, wonder perversely whether it's too small for me to fit, push, squeeze, duck, and then, free of the window frame, I plunge out and down, caught in freefall until the hard handlebars of the bike interrupt my descent.

We're going sixty miles an hour as I feel one of Billie's arms wrap around me, and she gets our arc pointed away from the structure, but the arrival of my weight and the release of her hold on the mirror cause the bike to rove into a terminal weave. The iron whine of old bicycle brakes screeches as Billie tries to slow the inevitable, but our wobble has stolen all control. The front wheel hits a curb in the adjoining property's parking lot so hard I feel it in my groin. In fact, I feel it in my shredded arm, in my ribs, pelvis, spine, neck, and head, and then I'm flailing through the air and bouncing and rolling on the pavement.

I fight to stay conscious and lift my head. I might have broken half a dozen bones in the fall, but I know we need to run. I find Billie splayed on the sidewalk beside me, the bike crumpled beneath her. She's rising from the wreckage, and I grab her forearm and help her to her feet. She's up and we're pulling at each other and limping away, not nearly fast enough.

As I turn to steal my last look at the bus, the vehicle literally disappears, crushing through the façade of the old wooden warehouse as if its walls were made of rice paper. It occurs to me that if my aim was off and the bus misses the container, it will simply crash out the back of the building the way it entered the front —

But then there's a *thud,* the gut-smacking, satisfying feel of a metal-on-metal collision. After the briefest delay, a louder, more enveloping rush of noise explodes from inside the building, and then, its momentum gathering power within the confines of the old structure, fire becomes visible, first in licks and pops of yellow, then soon, more explosively, in roiling balls of orange-black flames. Painfully slowly, almost as though it's catching one board at a time, the tendrils of fire begin to spread.

Knowing that the fire must get fully involved in order to be hot enough make any difference, I scream, "Burn, you son of a bitch!" but feel useless against the march of time as we drag ourselves up the street.

"Burn, dammit!" Billie echoes, and we continue to yell at the building while we limp away, moving slowly and painfully back and away from the inevitable detonation.

Flames break through the roof, charcoal billows of smoke unfurling skyward as we nearly make it to the cross-street of the next block.

Then it ends.

The sheer, profound violence of the concussive impact of a large conventional bomb is impossible to fathom without experiencing the effect, something few who feel it survive to tell. It is visceral; it is massive; it is all-encompassing. You are frail, and all is frail around you, including the air. There is the impression of everything around you instantaneously disintegrating, down to the particles of humidity in the atmosphere. You are pushed on all sides, including from the inside, and thrown, the direction random, the vector of the toss one of the factors on which your survival hinges.

A second concussion, similar but less severe, hits at us like a distant echo, and in my semiconscious state I know that it is the de-fanged Ivy City Yards detonation, emanating from blocks away but still of brutal substance. Feeling the second impact gives me the vague sense that I may have survived the first, and I wonder all at once whether our fire might have accomplished its purpose; whether the team responsible for the second device might have run out of time in failing to pull the crate entirely from the shipping container; whether the spinners succeeded in clearing the confines of the container; and finally whether the *Y. pestis* is now airborne, misting onto this street, into my lungs, across the skies of Washington — or dead on arrival against the heat of our flames, trapped by the steel barrier of the container.

When I look up, I don't see an explosive cloud of spinners. I see windows blasted out in every building, and I see the rising ball of black and orange that is the burning warehouse and its detonation plume. I see another cloud of black smoke rising into the sky from the railyards.

I see Billie beside me, eyes open but unmoving. I think that she must be dead, but then her chest moves, and so do her eyes. They take in the billowing clouds of smoke and flame as I have.

Then her eyes find mine.

"Did we do it?" she says. I can barely hear her after the damage to my head from the blast, but the words are simple enough to allow me to read her lips.

"I don't know."

"I think we did," she says. "I think you just saved a lot of lives."

"You just saved mine," I say. "Again."

"A habit I seem unable to shake."

Billie blinks and reaches with her hand to cover her eyes. There's a gust of wind, dusty and constant, blowing against us. I look up, searching for the source of the unnatural wind, and see the underside of a helicopter hovering fifty feet above. Thinking the authorities have finally descended on me for good this time, I look more closely at the chopper and see something different.

Bright blue characters are painted against white on the landing skids, the three letters of a local TV station occupying a circle, its channel number incorporated into the design. It's the traffic helicopter from one of Washington's network affiliates, in fact the station I remember as having the most aggressive news department in town. The pilot pulls up against a gust of wind and I see their news camera protruding from the open doors of the chopper.

I strain to see and believe I detect the pinpoint of red light on the beak of the camera, just above the lens.

We're on live.

Another chopper approaches, this one arriving from the direction of the railyard. It features no markings, only a flat black paint job generally reserved for government aircraft belonging to three-letter agencies or their military equivalent. On the street beneath the helicopter, multiple black-and-whites rip around the corner. As is becoming a common occurrence in my life, a cadre of flak-jacketed authorities burst from the cars, shouting, pointing, taking aim with their guns.

Probably because it's amplified — sourced, by my guess, from a megaphone aboard the law enforcement chopper — my damaged eardrums can actually detect the words blasting at us from yet another voice of authority.

"Raise your hands!"

"Keep them where we can see them!"

But this time the voices of authority sound hollow. With the news helicopter keeping us squarely in the sights of its camera, we're being watched by every viewer in the greater Washington area. In fact, I'd say it's likely that the images from the camera fifty feet above our heads are currently being picked up by every news organization in the world. All this following the lead-in of a half-hour interview special that told the story we're now completing — prone, broken, and bruised in the middle of W Street.

"Face-down! Hands out! Now!"

I roll onto my stomach, catching Billie's eyes as I extend my arms. Her eyes shine back at me the way I remember first noticing them behind the counter of the smoothie shop and, before that, in that yoga class where we first met. They appear to me now as they did then: crystal-clear and bright blue, full of empathy and promise.

"Stay down! Arms behind your back!"

We're smiling as we do our best to follow their orders with our damaged bodies, heads turned and facing each other, cheeks laid flat against the warm, muggy asphalt.